Beth
IS DEAD

Author photo © Mae Haines

Katie Bernet lives in Dallas, Texas. As one of three sisters, she's a die-hard fan of *Little Women*. *Beth Is Dead* is her debut novel.

Visit Katie online at
katiebernet.com
or on
Instagram @katiebernet.

Beth IS DEAD

Katie Bernet

📖 SCHOLASTIC

Published in the UK by Scholastic, 2026
Scholastic, Bosworth Avenue, Warwick, CV34 6UQ
Scholastic Ireland, 89E Lagan Road, Dublin Industrial Estate, Glasnevin, Dublin, D11 HP5F

SCHOLASTIC and associated logos are trademarks and/or
registered trademarks of Scholastic Inc.

First published in the US by Sarah Barley Books, an imprint of Simon & Schuster Children's
Publishng Devision, 2026

Text © Katherine Elizabeth Bernet, 2026
Cover illustration © Ben Fearnley, 2026
Author photograph © Mae Haines, 2026
Cover design by Lizzy Bromly
Inside design by Hilary Zarycky

The moral rights of the author, illustrator and photographer have been asserted by them.

ISBN 978 0702 34344 5

A CIP catalogue record for this book is available from the British Library.

All rights reserved.
This book is sold subject to the condition that it shall not, by way of trade or otherwise, be lent, hired out or otherwise circulated in any form of binding or cover other than that in which it is published. No part of this publication may be reproduced, stored in a retrieval system, or transmitted in any form or by any other means (electronic, mechanical, photocopying, recording or otherwise), or used to train any artificial intelligence technologies without prior written permission of Scholastic Limited. Subject to EU law, Scholastic Limited expressly reserves this work from the text and data-mining exception.

Printed in the UK.
Paper made from wood grown in sustainable forests and other controlled sources.

10 9 8 7 6 5 4 3 2

This is a work of fiction. Any resemblance to actual people, events or locales is
entirely coincidental.

Scholastic does not have any control over and does not assume any
responsibility for any third-party websites or other platforms, or their content.

www.scholastic.co.uk

For safety or quality concerns:
UK: www.scholastic.co.uk/productinformation
EU: www.scholastic.ie/productinformation

For my sisters

Beth
IS DEAD

CHAPTER ONE

(NOW)

On the first morning of a new year, Beth is not in her bed.

From the hallway, I peer into her room, and my heart moves to my throat. Sunlight falls on her pillow, dust suspended in the air. Beth should be here, tucked under her quilt, chest rising and falling, but there's only a dent in her mattress.

I stand on tiptoe and sigh a little breath of relief. Amy's not here either, the top bunk unmade, blankets in a heap. She's younger than Beth by about two years and ten thousand brain cells, but I feel better knowing they're together. This isn't the first time Amy's spent the entire night at Sallie Gardiner's annual New Year's Eve party.

Last year she passed out in Sallie's claw-foot tub—wouldn't it be nice to have a claw-foot tub?—until Mom showed up the next morning and dragged her to the car. Embarrassing, to say the least.

It's hard to believe she'd do it again after the way Mom worried, but that's Amy.

I text her, and her alone, because I know this isn't Beth's fault.

Where are you???

Three dots appear, but after a second of rippling, they stop.

I swear, if Mom wakes up to these empty bunks, I'll wrestle Amy to the ground. Mom doesn't deserve that kind of stress, especially not after a New Year's Eve night shift at the hospital—stomachs pumped, fingers blown off by misfired fireworks.

I text Amy again.

If you're not home before Mom's up . . .

I leave it at that, an open threat, and return to my room to keep working on my manuscript. I meant to stay up all night, but I've been crashing lately, snoring on my desk when I can't keep my eyes open any longer. I don't believe in writer's block—my creativity is a constant, unstoppable force—but right now my thoughts are moving like wet concrete.

I open my notebook to the page that acted as my pillow last night. It's smudged, but I can still make out the last of my scribbles.

I need a better idea. Something good enough to convince my editor that she didn't make a mistake by offering me a book deal. I rev myself up to start working again, when the back staircase creaks.

At once I jump up from my desk, a rush of relief. "Okay, next time you two want to pull an all-nighter, maybe you can shoot me a—"

Amy stares back at me, hunched and alone. At fifteen,

she's still flat-chested and skinny, with blond hair cut to her shoulders and streaked pink.

"Keep it down," she whispers.

"Where's—"

"Seriously, shut up. Mom's door is wide open." She eases up the final step and sheds her coat, revealing the skintight dress she wore last night. As she enters the bunk room, she furrows her brow. "Where's Beth?"

I cross the hallway, a bite in my voice. "You tell me."

Amy looks stunned, slow to process. "She's not home?"

"Does it look like she's home?"

"Shit," she exhales. "Mom's going to kill me."

I picture our doe-eyed sister alone at Sallie's party, passed out on one of the Gardiners' leather couches, too drunk to drive—or even walk—home. "You're worried about Mom? What about Beth?"

Amy whips out her phone to call our sister, but it goes straight to voicemail. "I'll try Sallie. She was with Beth when I left last night."

"Last night? You left last *night?*"

Amy grips her phone between her shoulder and her ear so she can search a pile of clothes that has gathered on the floor.

I duck to interrupt. "Where the hell did you go?"

"I stayed with . . ." She pauses, and I can't tell if she's listening to Sallie's voicemail message or searching for an answer. "Florence. Yeah, I stayed with Florence."

I look at her sideways.

Amy and our cousin, Florence, are a matching set. Both

of them blond, attached at the hip, but if they'd left the party together, they would've crashed here. Florence lives in a house with rules. Not the kind of rules that Mom enforces—be thoughtful, clean up after yourself—but the tightfisted kind that make you want to break things. Strict curfew, no makeup, no dating until college. "You went to Aunt Mary's after midnight?"

"We snuck in," says Amy, but her cheeks flush pink.

"And you left Beth alone?"

She finds a hoodie, tugs it over her head. "She's my big sister. I'm not her babysitter."

"She doesn't party like you do."

"What's that supposed to mean?"

Amy knows good and well what it means. Beth doesn't take stupid risks the way she does. Doesn't ruin things the way she does. Beth wouldn't stay out all night unless something happened—especially now. In just a few short days, she leaves for boarding school, and she has a million things to do before we send her off.

"Come on," I say. "Let's go find her."

"No." Amy beats me to my keys, holds them behind her back. "We'll wake Mom."

She's not wrong. My army-green Jeep has an old, grimy engine that sometimes takes three, four rattling tries to get going. "You expect me to walk?" I ask.

"The Gardiners' house isn't that far."

I glance back at my writing, a mess of half-baked ideas. This excursion will waste twenty minutes at the very least, but I'm the oldest sister now. That's what Meg said when she went to college. Distractions come with the territory.

"Fine," I huff. "But we're taking the shortcut."

Amy hates taking the shortcut from our neighborhood to Sallie's, up a steep bridge and through the park. I think it reminds her of Dad, who's been away for six months and thirteen days (not that anyone's counting). When we were little, he'd take us to the park to stargaze, and I'll admit, it hurts to remember those moments—but the park's our quickest shortcut by at least a mile.

Amy storms ahead of me, leads me into the cold. When the wind blows, she tightens her arms across her chest, but her teeth chatter like her body's too exhausted to keep warm. Like she didn't rest at all last night.

As we trudge toward the end of the block, Laurie's house looms overhead. He's the only kid in town who lives in a modern home instead of an old colonial, the result of his grandmother having just enough money and influence to sway the historical society into allowing her to build new.

His room looks dark, and I figure he must be sleeping. He and I have forgone Sallie's party since we met there freshman year, because both of us hate that sort of thing, but he usually stays up well past midnight toasting the New Year with his grandmother. "She's the best company," he always says.

Out of nowhere, Amy stops and we collide.

My voice comes out on a forced exhale. "What're you—"

"Jo." She gazes into the distance, squatting for a better view up the street. "What is that?"

I shove past her, less than amused. "I know you hate the shortcut, but this is getting a little—"

"Jo, wait." She tugs my coat hard and stares at the hill next to Laurie's house, a steep luge of rocks and tree roots. "I thought I saw . . ." Without warning, she charges ahead, tearing through brush and snow.

"Amy!" I yell.

But she keeps going, forging up the hill beside the bridge.

"Amy, stop!"

She ventures into the trees, takes an uncharted path up the steepest rocks.

"You're going to fall," I say.

She stops at the base of an old gnarly tree, and her phone slips from her hand, her knees bending ever so slightly, as if the earth is shifting beneath her.

I draw a shaky breath. "Come down from there."

But just then she lets out a sound that I'll never forget as long as I live. Her voice breaks from her chest, brittle and crumbling. "Beth?"

That single syllable echoes down the street, and all other sound falls away. Snow clings to the air for a moment, unmoving.

Amy screams. "Jo!" She grips her knees, shuddering. "Jo!"

Without a thought, I run, and unlike Amy, I don't stop, only slow. The sight at the base of the tree is so unimaginable that I'm pulled toward it.

At first it's like a poem that doesn't make sense until you've read it a few times.

Beth is lying in the snow. And the snow is red. And the red isn't just pooled around her but seeping from her. And her eyes are open, but behind them, she's gone.

CHAPTER TWO

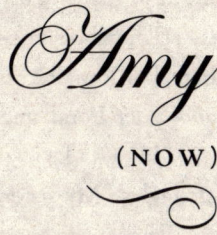

(NOW)

I lunge toward Beth, a cry scraping the bottom of my lungs.

"No." Jo fights me back. "No, we have to call the police."

I struggle against her grip, tears streaming down my face, my breath coming in gasps like I've been underwater for too long. I shove Jo off and fall to my knees in the snow, my dress so tight it hurts to bend. A pulse. I have to find a pulse. But when I hold my fingers to Beth's neck, the skin depresses.

I let out a shuddering scream, and suddenly, Jo's around me, shushing. "It's okay. It's okay."

But it's not okay.

This is not okay.

I stare at the ground, because I can't bear to look at Beth's face, a deep gash on her forehead, her skin bruised. She's covered in dirt from careening down the hill. And blood, so much blood. In all my years of painting, I've never seen a color so red. A shock of crimson splattered and pooling on the stark white snow.

"What happened?" I ask, but I'm not sure the words make it out of my throat.

"I'm calling nine-one-one." Jo dials, and I recognize the tones—high, low, low. She called a few years ago when I fell through the ice at Walden Pond, under for so long, I stopped being cold.

"Hi, I'd like to report— Um, I need to report— Um—" Jo struggles. "My sister," she tries again. "I think she's dead."

The words hit me like a punch to the gut.

Dead.

I think she's dead.

Screw Jo for saying it like that. As if it's already decided. But it is, isn't it? I force myself to look into Beth's hazel eyes, but for the first time ever, they're not glittering and full of life. They're dull and empty, blood drying on her lashes. Slowly, gently, I reach for her hand. Her fingers feel like ice, stiff against mine.

"No," I sputter. "No, no, no."

Jo listens to the 911 operator, his voice calm and muffled. At his instruction, she holds two fingers to Beth's neck, but it's no use. "Nothing," she says into the phone.

The operator asks another question, but down the way, a door opens, and I lose focus.

Laurie rushes out of his house and up the snowy hill. He tugs at his coat, his dark brown skin a contrast to the blinding white snow. "Jo? Amy? Is that you?"

Jo's voice breaks for the first time. "Laurie, thank god you're here."

He climbs toward us, twigs cracking under his boots. "What's going on? I heard screaming."

"Don't look." Jo holds him back, but he sees Beth over her shoulder, and his jaw drops.

"Oh my god."

Sirens swell in the distance. I can't count the number of times I've heard them in the background of the town, tourists hurt, attics catching fire, but they sound so different now. Like they're wailing just for us.

Jo wipes her nose on the back of her hand. "I need to get Mom."

Mom.

We have to tell Mom.

Mom has to see this.

Jo runs, and when she's halfway down the road, Laurie staggers toward me, voice trembling. "Is she . . ."

I nod, Beth's frozen fingers still resting in my palm.

"You should get out of the snow," he says.

I've never been this cold in all my life, but I don't want to leave Beth's side. Laurie doesn't give me a choice. He slides his strong arms under my shoulders and hoists me off the ground, my bare knees wet and raw.

I wish I could stand on my own, but I'm too weak, too sick. I'm forced to lean against Laurie, my forehead on his shoulder, his steadying hands on my back. In a flash, I remember last night, the two of us groping for each other in the dark. I swallow a lump of embarrassment.

"How did she get here?" he asks, dark eyes growing darker.

I think of the party. Sallie Gardiner's bathroom. Beth crying on the edge of the claw-foot tub. "I don't . . ."

"How did she get here? How did this happen?" Laurie drags a hand over his tight fade, repeating himself like his mind's skipping.

My memory's hazy from downing champagne, but I can still hear the low thud of rap music, the laughter downstairs clashing with the sound of Beth yelling at me.

"It's my fault." My voice comes out so quiet, it's almost nonexistent.

Laurie grips me tighter. "Don't go there."

"I said horrible things."

He gives me a knowing glance. "You were drunk."

Shame blends with terrible grief. I wasn't just drunk, I was wasted, and I know my sisters to their very bones, which means that when Beth and I fought, I knew exactly how to make it hurt. "I left her. I broke her down, and I left her."

Laurie steadies my shoulders, and I think of last night. He wasn't planning to go to the party, but he came to see me right toward the end, and it's hard to believe what happened next. First, Laurie wrestling me away from Beth, urging me into his car, whispering, "Chill. Please. Everyone's watching." Then, drive-through tacos, laughing in a parking lot, a ridiculous attempt to sober me up. Then, the warm glow of his room, his bed like a cocoon, my lips against his, our clothes on the floor, reaching, pressing, and out of nowhere, "Ames, we can't do this."

I squirm out of his grip just as footsteps pound up the hill behind us.

Jo returns with Mom, who's running the way she does at the hospital when someone's coding. She must've been so tired last night that she fell asleep in her scrubs, her messy hair pulled back in a clip. Maybe that's why she's able to stay standing at first. Because her hospital badge is still pinned to her pocket. Because she can be a nurse instead of a mom if only for a moment.

She stops halfway up the hill to look at Beth, eyes darting from one horrifying detail to the next. "Elizabeth." The name escapes her like a prayer. And then she dives.

"Mom, no!" Jo cries.

But Mom doesn't hear. Or maybe she doesn't care. She lifts Beth out of the snow and clutches her tight, but Beth's head lolls back, neck sickly limp, hair matted with blood.

I vomit, every ounce of me coming out, and for the first time in my life, I'm sure that bodies and souls are two different things. That isn't my sister. Not anymore.

Mom buries her head in a stiff and empty chest, not quite crying but moaning like a part of her heart has been clawed out.

I have no idea what to do, and for once it seems like Jo and Laurie don't either. We stand in silence while the sirens swell and the first responders arrive as swiftly as the snow.

CHAPTER THREE

Meg

(NOW)

My phone rings, and the high-pitched trilling incites a headache for the ages.

I grope for the noise, hoping it doesn't wake Annie, but the two of us share a room, her twin bed shoved so close to mine that she's already rustling. "Sorry," I groan.

She buries her head under a pillow. "Who could possibly be awake right now?"

The sun's up, sharp rays breaking through the windows, but it feels much earlier. Annie and I didn't get home until well past midnight, the very last of the stragglers celebrating New Year's Eve at the piano bar just off campus. I never stay out late, and I never guzzle gin and tonics like it's my job, but last night John Brooke headlined the bar, and when he plays the piano, all my sense melts away.

My phone rings again, and Annie lets out a deep, protesting growl.

Whoever's calling deserves to be ignored. Don't they know

that even the slightest chirp would make my head explode? But they called twice, so I answer. "Hello?"

"Meg? Are you up?" Jo's voice comes through heavy and thick, her tone so out of character that I sit up, instantly sobered.

"What's wrong?" I croak, my mouth dry.

"I don't . . ." She draws a shallow breath. "I don't know how to say this."

The room spins, but I'm awake now, heart charging. "What's going on? Is Amy okay? Did she stay out again?"

"Amy's fine," says Jo.

"Then, what—"

"It's Beth."

I get up, cold floors stinging my feet. "What happened? Sallie's party?" I fight to keep my voice low, but it comes out hot and urgent.

I knew Beth should've stayed home, but I kept my mouth shut when she called me last night. Annie and I don't even go to Sallie's parties anymore, and she's our third roommate, our best friend. It's like she can't grow up, can't stop throwing these ridiculous high school ragers.

Jo breaks into tears, which scares me more than anything. She's usually so stoic. "She's gone, Meg. She's gone."

I turn to stone, the apartment coming into sharp focus. I notice things I haven't noticed before: a hole in the ceiling, a drip from the faucet, dust collecting in the corners of the room. "What do you mean? You can't find her?"

"We found her by the bridge."

My stomach lurches, and I dive to the ground, grasping for a trash can, the ghost of a half dozen G&Ts burning my nose. My eyes water, which gives way to tears.

"Hey." Annie peels back her covers, a gentle question. "What's going on?"

I can't answer, can't speak. I can only listen to Jo, who explains through shuddering breaths that the paramedics declared Beth dead on arrival, and now the entire Concord Police Department's swarming our block, including a medical examiner who will take her away.

"Take her where?" I ask.

Jo sips the air, struggling to calm down. "I don't know."

The thought of Beth being taken anywhere alone makes me sick again. I wipe my mouth and fight to catch my breath. "Where's Mom?"

"With a detective."

"A detective?"

"Come home," says Jo.

I shut my eyes hard, hot tears rolling down my cheeks. I'm so tired, so grossly hungover, but I have to get off this floor.

Jo must be wrong. Beth can't be gone. I'll figure this out. I'll find out what happened.

Annie's at my back, holding my hair.

"I need to get home," I say.

She wipes her hands, digs for her phone. By the look on her face, I know she overheard enough to understand what's happening. Her voice comes out breathy, urgent. "I don't think I can drive, but I'll call you an Uber."

In a daze, I let her pack for me. A change of clothes, pajamas, a coat. I have just enough forethought to realize that it may be a while before I'm back on campus.

I trudge into the cold and my vision blurs, tears forming against the bitterness of the wind. Harvard rests, not a single footstep disrupting the snow. Most people are still home for the holidays.

I should've been home.

It's my job to watch out for my sisters, and I wasn't there. Annie and I wanted to stick it to Sallie, prove that we have better things to do than relive high school at a party she should've stopped throwing years ago. It all seems so petty now.

A beige car pulls up, a Maine license plate. "Concord, ayuh?"

"Yes." I slide into the back.

"Lotta news about Concord lately. Those March sisters live there, don't they?"

I draw my backpack close, unearth a Red Sox cap that I've been carrying since the first time a stranger recognized me. I smoosh my curls, pull it low over my forehead. "Oh yeah." I try not to swallow. "I've met them once or twice."

CHAPTER FOUR

Meg

(THEN)

It's the first tender night of summer break, warm and balmy. I just came home from Harvard, ready to sink into a bubble bath and watch mindless TV, but Jo hasn't stopped nagging me since I walked in the door. "Meg, please. We can't miss the launch party."

"Mom said no," I remind her for the umpteenth time.

"Mom's working a double," says Jo. "What she doesn't know won't hurt her."

I'm not above lying to Mom. She works so much as a trauma nurse at Concord General that it's not exactly hard to slip one past her, but I can't think of anything more infuriating than showing up to support Dad.

"He lied to us," I say.

"He didn't lie. He withheld the truth."

"For years. He withheld the truth for years."

Jo rolls her eyes like I'm being difficult, but Dad has been writing a book about my sisters and me since I started high school, and he managed to conceal it all that time.

"It was a side project," says Jo. "He never thought he'd publish it."

That's what he told us. A defensive story about the pressure from his publisher, his lack of ideas, this manuscript that should've been a secret, ready to send. But when his publisher announced the book and he couldn't keep it hidden any longer, his eyes shone. He's proud of his work, happy to see it out in the world.

"I'm with Mom," I say. "If we show up, we'll be the center of attention, which could be dangerous. Uncomfortable, at the least."

"Dangerous?" Jo mocks.

"I don't know. This book's getting a lot of attention."

Jo unleashes a grin, her green eyes flashing. "All the more reason to be there."

A sick feeling clings to my stomach, but I don't have the energy to argue with Jo. Her ability to dig her heels in surpasses mine on my very best days, and honestly, I'm curious. Dad usually fills the house with advance reader's copies of his novels, but he's kept this one under lock and key. Even Jo hasn't gotten her hands on it.

"Fine. We'll go. But if anything's weird—"

"We're out of there," she promises.

As we buckle into Jo's Jeep, Beth and Amy seem neutral about the book launch, not exactly dreading it like me but not buzzing like Jo.

"It's a little fucked up," says Amy.

"Language," I snap, a habit I picked up from Mom. Hypocritical, considering I curse under my breath every time I so much as stub a toe.

She shrugs, a hand shoved through her pink-streaked hair. "Dad's been writing this book for, what, five years? And he never told us about it, not even once."

"He wanted to surprise us," says Beth.

"Nice surprise," says Amy.

Jo cranes to look at the backseat before pulling out of the driveway, her messy braid swinging. "Aren't you desperate to read it?"

I answer before Amy or Beth has a chance. "I'm worried."

"You're always worried," says Jo.

"Don't you wonder how Dad portrayed us?"

We idle at the end of the block, a stop before a wide left. I expect a snappy retort from Jo, but she gives me an earnest glance. "It's all I can think about."

We all love Dad, but Jo treats him like he created the heavens and the earth. He's everything she wants to be: intellectual, accomplished, and lean-in fascinating. Plus, he's published more than ten award-winning novels, a bragging right for which Jo would kill. She must be desperate to see how she fares in his eyes.

"I just hope he was honest," I say.

Amy balks. "I hope he wasn't. Do you really want all your screwups immortalized and sitting on a shelf?"

"Some of us aren't screwups," says Jo.

Amy kicks the back of her seat, and the Jeep veers.

"Careful," I say.

When the ride smooths out, Beth leans over to Amy, her voice like a balm. "Dad loves us. He wouldn't write anything too bad."

Amy doesn't argue, but as she slumps down in her seat, we share a knowing glance. I appreciate Beth's eternal optimism, but in this case, she sounds a little naive. I've read some of the prelaunch chatter surrounding Dad's book. Early reviewers have called it "unputdownable." One said, "I devoured it like a handful of bittersweet chocolate."

You don't get that kind of praise without a little drama.

The bookstore's in Boston, a half hour outside Concord, which proves that this novel is already bigger than the rest of Dad's backlist combined. Most of his launch parties have happened in our neighborhood bookshop, attended only by family and a handful of Dad's author friends.

A few blocks from the bookstore, traffic congests the streets.

Jo leans over the steering wheel. "No way."

Even Amy sits at attention. "This isn't for the launch, is it?"

"It can't be," says Beth.

My gut says otherwise.

Dad's spent his entire career trying to break out of critical success and into the mainstream. "I appreciate the accolades," he's said more than once, "but accolades don't pay the bills."

It seems like he's finally done it, and sadly, we're his secret weapon.

Jo parks the Jeep as fast as she can, hardly able to stay in her seat. Her enthusiasm rubs off on Beth, and the two of them leap from the car, ready to run across the street.

"Wait," I say. "We need to stay together."

People crowd the block, a line forming outside the bookstore, a palpable energy in the air. It strikes me as odd that most of these fans are women. In the past, Dad's readership has been decidedly male. But we keep walking, pressing closer to the excitement, until I notice the signs.

"What is everyone holding?" asks Amy.

Beth stands on tiptoe. "I can't see."

Jo charges forward, but when my gaze settles on one of the signs, I yank her back. "They're protesting," I say.

She wriggles out of my grip. "Protesting what?"

The air tightens. Two women brush past us, their voices bitter. "I heard he's poised to make millions," says one.

"It's not about the money," says the other. "It's the principle. He's a man writing about women."

My stomach hardens. I've been angry with Dad for putting our lives on paper without permission, but I haven't even thought of this. In the evening light, the bookstore glows, a stack of novels visible through the windows. Dad told us the title, but it hits me sideways now.

Little Women.

Jo plows through the crowd.

"Jo!" Without thinking, I yell her name. Then I wince, hoping not to be recognized. "Come back here," I half whisper.

She doesn't so much as glance over her shoulder. With a quick maneuver, she cuts the line, marches right up to the door, and faces a bookseller like she's ready for a fight.

I hurry through the crowd, desperate to stop her from making a scene.

The bookseller guards the door, eyes wide like she had no idea what she was getting herself into tonight. "We're not letting anyone else in."

Jo snaps back, "We know the author."

The woman lets out an uncomfortable laugh. "You and all the rest of these people."

"We're his daughters."

The woman stills, her bewildered gaze shifting from Jo to the rest of us. "You're his . . . You're the girls in . . ."

"I'm Jo."

The woman takes a moment to reply, and when she does, she sounds mournful. "I'm so sorry."

At first I think she's apologizing because she's not going to let us inside. But when she opens the door, I understand with a pang. She pities us.

I clutch Jo's shoulder, my breath hot in her ear. "We're leaving. You promised."

With a flare in her eyes, she steps inside. Beth and Amy follow like moths drawn to light, and as the crowd swells behind me, I'm pushed over the threshold. The bookstore's more packed and chaotic than the street, hordes of people facing a podium, all of them clutching signs.

GIRLHOOD BELONGS TO GIRLS!

WOMEN WRITE WOMEN RIGHT!

MARCH AGAINST MARCH!

Jo scans the room, shoulders growing heavy. "They hate him," she says.

"They're so pissed," Amy laughs.

I pull my sisters into a huddle. "We need to get out of here. This isn't—"

Just then Dad staggers up to the podium. He's a different man than he was this morning, face shadowed, hair disheveled like he's been wringing it for answers. He taps the mic, draws a breath, and stares at the audience like he's facing a firing squad.

"I'm—" He only gets out a single word before a chant rises through the crowd.

"March against March! March against March!"

The protestors on the street join in, their voices muffled by the windows.

Dad leans into the mic, sweat shining on his brow. "Thank you all for coming. This isn't the release day any of us expected, but I'd like to address—"

"March against March! March against March!"

"I'm aware of the situation on social—"

"March against March! March against March!"

"If I could just—"

Jo opens her phone, and we close in around her to look. Just yesterday, the hype surrounding Dad's book was mostly positive, but now the hashtag #MarchAgainstMarch brings up thousands of posts.

"Why is everyone so angry?" asks Beth.

I read over Jo's shoulder, absorb everything I can. "They're saying Dad exploited us, used our stories in service of his own career."

"Hear! Hear!" says Amy.

"That's bullshit," says Jo.

She looks to me for support, but with every new post that

loads on her screen, I feel more and more validated. These people are saying exactly what I've been feeling. "I think they're right. I didn't ask to be a character in a novel."

A voice with a journalistic weight comes up through the crowd. "Rob, early reviews have called *Little Women* a stunning portrayal of girlhood. What makes you think you're the right person to tell that story?"

"He's our dad," says Jo.

I nudge her in the ribs, a silent plea to keep quiet, but she's never been good at keeping quiet. She grabs a chair, plants her foot on the seat.

"Jo, please. Come on." My stomach dips.

Despite my begging, she stands on the chair. "Stop it! Stop it right now!"

She shouts loud enough that the chanting slows and heads turn. Beth shuffles behind me, and Amy picks her nail polish like she always does when she's uncomfortable. I try my best to stand tall.

"This is wrong!" Jo shouts. "You're all wrong! He raised four daughters. Our story belongs to him as much as it belongs to us."

A ripple of awareness moves through the audience as people make the connection between the tomboy drawn on their book covers and Jo, clad in boots and baggy jeans, fresh-faced and freckled.

My cheeks burn. I speak without moving my mouth. "We really need to go."

The mic squeals. "Girls?" Dad loosens his tie, wipes sweat

from his brow. "Girls, I didn't think you were coming." He looks nervous, overwhelmed, like the crowd is an ocean and we're about to drown.

A voice, the journalist. "Tell us the truth, Jo. Did your dad get permission to write about you?"

Jo shrugs in defiance. "He didn't need it."

My stomach plunges. It's the wrong answer, and criticism fills the room. Snippets of conversation snap like firewood above the chatter.

"Betrayal of trust."

"Just kids."

"Right to privacy."

I grab a novel off the stack, flip through it as fast as I can. I'm so heated, so shaky, that I can't process much, but a few personal details leap off the page: my first period, my first kiss, the time I cried on the bathroom floor about my breakup with John Brooke.

My blood boils. This is my life—my life—poured out on the page. My friends will read this book. My professors will read this book. Strangers will read this book.

"I'm leaving," I say as I pivot toward the door.

Amy's right behind me, but Beth waits for Jo, who takes ages to climb down from the chair like she can't stand to admit defeat. I burst into the street, head straight for the car.

"Meg!" Jo storms after me. "We can't just leave. We have to do something."

I whirl around. "Want to do something? Hand me a sign."

"You can't agree with these people."

I shove the book into her hands. "Dad wrote about everything. All our most private experiences."

"He's an author," she says, like that's any excuse.

"He used us." I let my words land, then I leave her in the street.

When I've gained some distance, she holds up the book. "Did you steal this?"

I don't indulge her with an answer, just shut myself in the car. Yes, I stole the book, but I swallow my guilt. It's my story. I simply stole it back.

CHAPTER FIVE

Meg

(NOW)

As we turn into the neighborhood, time comes to a drawn-out pause. Squad cars crowd the block, an ambulance silently flashing. From here, I count enough first responders to save an army, and yet none of them rushes.

My driver slows to a stop, adjusts the rearview mirror so he can see me. "What is all this?"

News vans are parked in front of our house, reporters clutching microphones. I crack a window just enough to hear their overlapping voices.

"... at the home of bestselling author Rob March ..."

"... sixteen-year-old daughter ..."

"... dead in the snow ..."

No. No. This isn't happening. It can't be true.

My driver gives me a steadying look. "I'll drive yuh 'round back."

"Don't bother." I brace for the cold and throw open my door, but as soon as I stand, my knees buckle.

At the end of the block, Laurie's house punctuates the landscape, a steep hill just beside it. There, in a mess of stones, a circle of officers stand straight-backed against a gray sky, and beyond them, a sparkle in the snow.

Beth's dress.

We picked it out on FaceTime last night before she left for the party, a sequined boatneck borrowed from Jo.

I hang on to the car door and pull a breath through my nose, trying not to be sick again.

"Is that one of the sisters? Is that Meg?" Cameras pop off in every direction. I tug the brim of my cap lower and force myself to stand.

Up ahead, a dark-haired woman strides out of our house and down the porch steps. She carries herself like she's in charge, which makes me trust her almost immediately. "Meg," she says. "Come inside."

Jo stands behind her, shoulders thrown back, a look of defiance. "Leave us alone!" she yells to the press, but it only incites another click-click-click of the cameras.

Oh, how the world loves Jo.

The dark-haired woman lays a firm hand on my back, flashes a badge pinned to the hip of her pantsuit. "I'm Freya Kirke. Detective with the Concord Police Department."

I follow her up the walkway, but when we reach the porch, I look back at the woods, the police tape. "I want to see my sister."

Detective Kirke angles her brow, a grave warning. "I don't think that's a good idea."

I draw a breath to argue. I want to see Beth. I need to see

Beth. But Jo reaches for my hands, eyes red from crying. "She's right. It's awful."

I've seen death. I saw my grandfather's body on the cold morning after he passed away, I saw my uncle in a casket wearing a tie he would've hated, and on my first day shadowing the nurses at Concord Gen, I saw a stillborn baby, tiny and purple. I should be able to look at a body, but this is Beth.

Detective Kirke stops me before I enter the house. "Prepare yourself. We have quite a few people inside."

I nod like I can handle it, but I'm not ready. The house doesn't smell right. Cheap cologne and the chemical stench of polyester uniforms.

Amy runs into my arms, trembling. I grip her shoulders, her head, her solid form. "Where's Mom?"

Detective Kirke ties her curls into a bun, revealing the sharp edges of her face, her nose, her jaw. "Your mother made contact with your sister's body. She's in the kitchen with a forensic—"

I run to the kitchen, but once there, I pause. Mom sits at the table with a vacant expression. She's covered in blood, palms upturned in her lap, and the truth hits me slowly. This isn't just any blood. It's Beth's blood.

I can't breathe, but I force out dry words. "What happened?"

Detective Kirke blocks my view of Mom. "We can't say definitively. Beth might've fallen down the hill, but it's unlikely. Her injuries were severe. Right now we can't rule out homicide."

My stomach lurches. "Homicide? Mom's not a suspect—"

"No," says Kirke. "She's not. But she touched the body. We have to follow procedure."

Jo's voice shoots across the room. "Don't you dare call Beth a body."

I sidestep Detective Kirke to kneel in front of Mom while a man in uniform circles her with a camera. The flash snaps, but she stares unblinking.

I bury my face in my hands, pressure building behind my eyes. I knew this would happen. I haven't felt safe since the moment Dad's book hit the shelves. One of us was bound to get hurt. "It's all his fault," I say.

Jo storms into the kitchen. "Don't even start."

"He wrote that book, and we turned into spectacles. Most of all Beth."

"That's not the reason—"

"Why else would someone kill her?"

Jo looks like I just slapped her in the face. Unlike the rest of us, she's never acknowledged the dark side of *Little Women*. She basks in the attention, replies to every DM, posts reel after reel with quotes from the novel.

I stand to face her, tears falling. "It could've been a protester."

Jo shakes her head. "It was Sallie's New Year's Eve party."

"Someone trying to make a point."

"All those rich kids who think they're invincible."

"Those rich kids are my friends!"

"Sallie Gardiner isn't really your—"

"What if she jumped off the bridge?" Amy's voice stops

our argument, though it comes out quiet and broken, her arms gathered around her waist.

"Oh, Ames." I pull her into a hug. "Beth would never jump. Ever."

Amy sobs. "What if she did?"

"She didn't," I promise, but at the fingertips of my mind, I wonder. Beth questioned so much of her own personality after she read the way Dad portrayed her in *Little Women*. She felt pressured to do more, to be more—as if she wasn't enough.

I shake off the thought, refocus on Detective Kirke. "It was the book. Dad got canceled for writing it. We've had protesters, someone vandalized our garage, and in July—"

Jo groans. "Do we really have to talk about what happened in July?"

"—someone broke into our home, planted a recording device under Beth's piano."

Detective Kirke carries a steno pad, pages full of notes. "Meg, you said something intriguing. Something I haven't heard yet." She pauses, furrows her brow. "Why was Beth a bigger spectacle than the rest of you?"

I rub Amy's back as her crying subsides. "I guess you haven't read *Little Women*."

Kirke shakes her head. "I missed the craze."

"Then you haven't heard what happens?"

"Enlighten me."

I steady myself, the irony almost too much to handle. "Beth dies at the end."

CHAPTER SIX

(THEN)

I'm alive.

It's terrible that I have to remind myself, but thanks to Dad's book, I've been questioning my own vitality for days.

Jo sits at her desk, phone illuminating her face. "This is getting out of hand."

I plop onto her bed, which usually brings me instant comfort, but ever since *Little Women* hit the shelves, I can't shake the feeling that I'm being watched and judged.

I hug my knees. "What is it now?"

"More of the same," says Jo. "Everyone's pushing Dad's publisher to stop printing the book."

"Do you think they'll give in?"

I'm hoping the book will quietly disappear from shelves, but Jo raises an eyebrow, and I understand. This morning *Little Women* hit number one on the *New York Times* bestseller list. Dad's publisher wouldn't dream of pulling it now.

"You've gotta be kidding me!" Amy shouts from the next

room, and her footsteps land hard down the hallway. "Have you seen this?"

Jo's glued to her phone. "BuzzFeed?"

"You read it?" asks Amy.

"Skimmed it," says Jo.

Amy jabs her phone in my face, and a headline comes into focus. TWENTY REASONS WE LOVE TO HATE AMY MARCH.

Amy's cheeks turn pink to match the streaks in her hair. "Everyone thinks I'm a villain."

"At least they *love* to hate you," says Jo.

Amy throws her phone on the floor and falls to her back beside it. "Oh, shut up. You're just happy because you're the favorite. Everyone's dying to be Jo March."

I rest my chin on my knees, a bottomless pit in my stomach. I shouldn't be jealous of Amy. No one wants to be hated. But what happened to me feels so much worse. "At least you survived the car crash."

Jo looks up from her phone, eyes full of sympathy, which only makes me want to burrow farther into the covers. "It's just a story," she says. "Dad had to fictionalize a few things in order to make it interesting."

I nod, but I can't swallow the lump in the back of my throat. Dad didn't fictionalize a few things. He fictionalized one thing. My last breath. Which, by the way, shouldn't be considered interesting.

Even the car accident happened in real life.

Two years ago, my sisters and I were driving into Boston to tour Harvard with Meg when a van swerved into our lane and forced us into oncoming traffic. Meg's Subaru had to be towed straight to a junkyard, and I spent a night in the hospital. I'll never forget the way Mom and Dad raced to meet me, rode in the back of the ambulance, held me in the emergency department. It was such a miracle that my injuries weren't any worse. My survival would've made a great ending to a novel.

Jo tilts her phone in my direction. "If it makes you feel any better, everyone's devastated by your death. Seriously, no one's written a review that doesn't mention full-throttle sobbing."

I sink into Jo's pillow, my voice flat. "Yeah, thanks. I feel way better."

Meg comes in from the shower, a towel around her hair. "I have two hundred and fifty-three DMs."

"Ten thousand," says Jo.

Meg gawps, but I'm not surprised. Jo had a healthy following long before *Little Women* stirred up our lives. She's not the kind of influencer who pushes skincare products or assumes we care about her #OutfitOfTheDay, but she has a knack for romanticizing her everyday life and posting one-liners that make it impossible not to click through and read her personal essays.

Meg joins Amy on the rug, sits crisscross as she wrings out her hair. "I don't know how you put up with the attention."

"I love it," says Jo.

Meg screws up her face like she just ate a lemon. "Your messages must not be as . . . flirtatious as mine."

Jo shrugs. "You're the pretty one."

"It's gross. And demeaning."

I grab another pillow, squash it against my chest. "At least everyone knows you're alive."

The room stills. Since the day the book launched, I've been tagged in dozens of memorial posts made by people who know me well enough to care but not well enough to know that I'm not really dead.

Meg crawls onto the bed, snuggles me tight. "I don't think I'll ever forgive Dad for doing this to us, especially to you, but it'll pass. I promise it will."

I want to believe her, but I can't imagine this confusion will ever leave me. It's tangled around my muscles, my nerves. All four of us were in the car that day, but Dad didn't kill all four of us. He killed me. Just me. I've tried to ask him why, but I can't find the words. I guess I'm afraid to hear his answer. Afraid he'll say that I'm flat and lifeless, that he couldn't envision a future for me.

Without warning, Jo leans into her phone. "Holy shit."

"What is it?" I ask.

Amy stays on her back like nothing would surprise her at this point. "Don't tell me. Oprah's read the book, and she absolutely *loves* to hate Amy March."

Jo ignores her sarcasm. "*Teen Vogue* wants an interview."

Meg hasn't let go of me yet, her arms like anchors. "*Teen Vogue?*" she asks. "Does anyone actually read that?"

Jo balks. "They have millions of social media followers. I've pitched them a handful of stories."

"I'm not talking to anyone," says Amy.

Jo jumps onto the bed, squishes between Meg and me. "Look at this."

Her DMs give me anxiety, so many unread I can hardly

keep from groaning, but the message from *Teen Vogue* holds my attention.

@TeenVogue: Hey, Jo! Fascinated by Little Women *and the surrounding controversy. Would love to talk with you and your sisters.*

You and your sisters.

Sisters.

Plural.

I sit up slowly, Jo's quilt sliding off. "They want to talk with all of us?"

Jo glances back, a sparkle in her eye. "Why wouldn't they?"

"We're not doing it," says Meg.

But a light flickers on inside me. A hope that I haven't felt since the book launch. "I think we should."

Meg looks shocked. "You actually want to?"

The pit in my stomach lifts a little. In all the chaos surrounding Dad's book, no one's been interested in hearing from me. "Yeah," I say. "I think I do."

Meg looks impressed, a smile edging into her cheek. "Okay. If Beth's in, then I'm in."

"Amy?" asks Jo.

"Whatever," says Amy.

Jo responds quickly, her thumbs racing across the screen.

@JoMarchWrites: All four of us are in.

They respond immediately.

@TeenVogue: All four of you?

@JoMarchWrites: Yep.

Three dots appear, and they ripple for a while before another message comes through.

@TeenVogue: I'm so sorry, but we thought Beth died.

The pit returns, deeper and darker than it's ever been before. I bury myself under the covers.

"This is crazy," I moan, but "crazy" doesn't begin to cover the emotion. I know I don't have main-character energy like Jo, but I've never felt so insignificant.

"What's wrong?" asks Amy.

Jo stalls. "They, um . . . they think Beth is dead."

"Fuck 'em." Amy shoves a middle finger in the air.

Jo's voice pitches up. "Chill. It's fine. I'll fix it."

I peek out of the quilt to watch her respond.

@JoMarchWrites: Beth is very much alive.

Four messages blip through in quick succession.

@TeenVogue: Wow.

@TeenVogue: Wild.

@TeenVogue: We want to talk to Beth.

@TeenVogue: Just Beth.

My heart suspends. I get off Jo's bed, suddenly too hot for the covers.

Jo moves to her knees, her gaze dripping with drama. "You have to do it."

"Alone?"

She leans in close. "Come on, Beth. This is your chance. You want to prove that you're alive? Do this interview."

My throat tightens. I've never wanted to be a front-page story, and I don't need an inbox full of DMs, but Jo's right. I need to prove that I'm more than the girl who dies at the end of the book.

CHAPTER SEVEN

(NOW)

"I'm not sure I understand." Detective Kirke takes a wide stance in the kitchen, pen poised on her steno pad.

"I know it's hard to stomach," says Meg, "but Beth dies at the end of the novel."

I need to interject, but I can hardly breathe. The house doesn't look right, like someone moved everything around, and I can't shake the image of Beth covered in blood.

Meg trains her focus on the detective, a fire in her deep brown eyes. She's wearing a Harvard sweatshirt, which always earns her immediate respect—unfairly, if you ask me. "The book destroyed Beth's psyche. She's gotten so much unwanted attention."

I let out a bitter breath. "You just want to blame Dad."

Meg snaps her gaze back to me. "You're the only one who doesn't."

I lean against the counter, struggling to stand. It's eerie—downright sick—the way real life is mirroring Dad's novel, but

I won't apologize for defending him. He didn't mean to hurt anyone.

I let out a stale breath. "Beth didn't get any attention until she did the *Teen Vogue* interview, and that wasn't Dad's fault, that was mine."

Detective Kirke looks up from her notes. "*Teen Vogue?*"

I really thought the article would be good for Beth. A chance to tell everyone she was alive, like a magician coming out to bow after being sawed in half. "I pushed her into it, and the whole thing went sideways."

Meg shudders. "She was honest with the interviewer. Told her how much it hurt to be written off, presumed dead."

"They twisted her words," I say.

"Dad had critics before that, but after, he got death threats."

I move between Meg and Kirke to wrangle the conversation. "Dad's not the first author to get death threats for killing off a character."

"We're not characters!" Meg shouts.

"You haven't even read the book."

"I refuse to read a story in which my sister dies."

Her words hit me harder than usual. I've always considered the girls in *Little Women* to be characters, inspired by us—not our persons through and through. But now . . . "It's just a story," I say weakly.

"Does it feel like a story, Josephine?" Meg flushes, gestures to the room, the forensics team, the cops stationed at the front door.

Anger leaps to my throat, and it's a familiar drug. It grounds

BETH IS DEAD

me in the room. "Dad could never have known that this would happen."

"That book was bad enough before—"

"Dad's only mistake was choosing Beth. If he'd killed me off, you wouldn't care at all."

"Enough!" Mom yells from the kitchen sink. She's scrubbing her forearms with a bar of soap, and the sight of Beth's blood takes the air right out of my chest. It doesn't matter what we think of Dad's fiction. This is reality. Beth died today. She actually died today.

Detective Kirke gives us a moment to breathe before she continues. "We'll look into the book. If your father received threats of any kind, it's possible someone acted on them."

Meg sucks back her tears like she's satisfied with that plan, but I saw Beth's body, the gaping wound on her forehead, the blood staining her delicate face. That wasn't some stranger. That was personal. "You should be looking into the Gardiner party."

"Of course," says Kirke. "My partner's heading down to the bridge to take statements. Quite a crowd."

My stomach turns at the thought of our friends and classmates edging out of their homes, standing on tiptoe for a glimpse at the crime scene.

I focus on what I know. "Amy said she last saw Beth with Sallie Gardiner."

"Sallie Gardiner's my best friend," says Meg.

I draw a hot breath, revving up, but Mom flinches like she can't stand another argument, so I empty my lungs, let my heart rate recede. "I'm just stating facts."

Mom dries her hands on a kitchen towel, sets her attention on Kirke. "We need to tell my husband what's happening."

The woman nods. "I'll get in contact with him. Where is he now?"

I share a glance with Meg, wondering which of us will break the news of Dad's whereabouts. No matter how much Meg disapproves of what he wrote, neither of us wanted him to leave home.

"He's in Canada," I say.

Meg nods. "Vancouver, we think."

"You think?" asks Kirke.

My chest aches from missing Dad, but I step forward to explain. "He's camping in the Canadian Rockies."

"Hiding," says Meg.

"He's not hiding. He left to protect us."

"Protect his ego, more like."

Kirke stops taking notes, a hint of frustration in her brow. I'm sure it's hard to keep up when Meg and I bicker. "Mrs. March?"

Mom doesn't like talking about Dad—not since his book launched—but after a heavy sigh, she says, "Rob's a dual citizen. He grew up in Vancouver, so he drives out there every now and then. When the protests escalated, he packed his car, and we haven't heard from him since."

I remember that evening like a film in my mind, the word "killer" dripping down the front of the garage, Dad packing his duffel, telling his publicist to make it known that he'd be fleeing the country. "Draw the attention away from the house," he said on the phone.

"When do you expect him back?" asks Kirke.

Mom shakes her head like she doesn't know, and this time I don't have the energy to interject. I thought Dad would be gone for a few weeks and nothing more.

Kirke keeps her focus on Mom. "How long has it been since you've heard from him?"

Mom twists her wedding ring, her finger turning red. "He left in mid-June."

"And you haven't had any contact?"

"He does this," says Meg. "He shuts people out."

Meg always makes it sound bad when Dad goes off the grid—like he's ignoring us, abandoning us—but it's not about us. He thrives in nature, where he can hear himself think for a change.

When we were kids, he loved taking us to our family cabin in Mount Washington, where there's no electricity or running water. Without cell service or Wi-Fi, we spent time together chopping firewood, catching frogs in our palms, identifying constellations. I understood why he craved a life in the wilderness.

"He's always been a fan of Thoreau," I say. "You know, 'Resign yourself to the influence of the earth.'"

Kirke furrows her brow. "He hasn't checked in?"

"He's camping," I remind her.

But Kirke doesn't want to hear from me. Once again she's waiting for Mom.

Mom takes a long time to answer, and when she does, she sounds hollow and sad. "He needed space. We all did."

Kirke lets out a low "mm-hmm" like she finally understands the dynamic of our family, but she's getting the wrong idea. Mom didn't want space. She begged Dad to stay.

"He was scared," I say. "After the garage. After that idiot found our address."

Kirke nods. "Did the police investigate the vandalism?"

"No," Mom laughs, bitter. "They told us it was a low priority."

"And the recording device? Did anyone look into that?"

The question raises the hair on the back of my neck. I picture the detective who investigated the incident, the grooves of his face forged by decades of judgment. I thought it would be obvious that a protestor must've placed the device—open and shut—but my family endured weeks of the detective's questioning. "You're an attention seeker, Jo," he said in the end.

Mom straightens up, quietly seething. "Ask your department about the recording device. Maybe they can explain why their lead investigator blamed my daughter for staging a break-in instead of finding the criminal who invaded our home."

Kirke looks stunned. "Lead investigator?"

"Detective Davis." Mom says his name like it's a bad word.

My stomach churns at the way she defends me. She doesn't know the whole truth, and I shudder to think that one day she might look at me the way Detective Davis did. Thankfully, we'll never have to see that man again. He retired the week after he closed our case, the whole department clapping him on the back for understanding my motives. But he got it wrong. I promise he did.

Kirke stiffens, professional. "I'm new to the department. I

don't know the details of what happened in July, but I feel I should warn you—"

Whatever she's about to say, Mom doesn't let her finish. "I feel like I should warn *you*, Detective Kirke, that your department has lost my trust. If Detective Davis had solved our case in July, then my girl"—her voice breaks—"my Beth might still be—"

"I understand," says Kirke, but she looks suddenly worried, uncomfortable. She checks her watch, her phone, her walkie-talkie. "Excuse me for a moment. And please—don't go anywhere."

She leaves through the front door, and a moment turns into a long stretch of time. An hour, maybe more. In that pause, the four of us do nothing but sit by the fire while officers move through the house like slow blurs.

Amy cries intermittently, and we take turns holding her, the rest of us numb.

I begin to wonder if we'll stay like this forever. If time has lost meaning without Beth. And then—the front door crashes open.

Mom startles.

I jump too, nerves firing.

A man enters the foyer. "Sorry. There's a storm coming."

I know that voice like a chill down my spine. Boots land in the entryway of our house, and my whole body recognizes the cadence of his footsteps, a slow drag of his left, the planting of his right.

Detective Davis enters the kitchen, gray hair and gray eyes, his face rough and red from the cold. "Mrs. March." He folds his hands, hangs his head. "My deepest condolences."

"What are you doing here?" Mom stands up slowly like she's preparing to defend her territory.

Davis does his best to sound warm and reassuring, but underneath, he's a wolf. "I need to take statements from everyone in the family. The sooner the better."

"Absolutely not." Mom shakes her head. "I don't want you in my house."

"Mrs. March . . ." Detective Davis uses a warning tone, then clears his throat and says nothing else. He's comfortable in silence, choosing not to fill it so that others will spill whatever they're holding inside.

"Out," says Mom.

Detective Kirke scrambles in behind him, flushed and apologetic. At once I understand why she was gone so long. She must've been trying—and failing—to get someone else on the case. "Mrs. March, I know this is difficult, but we can't lose any time."

"Then get him out of my house and solve the case yourself."

Kirke winces, an apology in her shoulders. "I just made detective. I can't lead—"

"Then find someone else."

"There is no one else." Detective Davis silences the room, his voice like a deep growl. "Do you know how many homicides we've seen in Concord, Massachusetts, in the past couple of decades?" He doesn't wait for an answer. "None. Not a single one. The department isn't trained for it, but I am. I did a stint in

Chicago and one in Detroit before moving to Boston, and I've solved so many homicides that I can't remember all the faces anymore." He pauses for a heavy breath. "As a nurse, you should know what that means."

"You're heartless," says Mom.

"I'm old. And I didn't raise my hand for this. I left my crossword and my bathrobe at home because the chief needed the best. I'm the best, and I'll bring your daughter's killer to justice."

Mom remains cold, arms crossed tightly over her chest. At first I think she's angry, then I notice tears pooling in the corners of her eyes and realize she's trying not to cry. "Fine," she says tightly. "But you'll treat my daughters with respect."

Detective Davis doesn't give her a chance to change her mind. He says to Kirke directly, "There's a study at the front of the house. It's private enough."

A fist tightens inside my chest, squeezing, squeezing. I don't want to be interrogated by a man who doesn't understand me, who can't possibly understand Beth. I step forward, brazen. "I'm sure you have questions for me."

The detectives hardly open their mouths before I continue—

"Well, guess what? I'm not cooperating."

Detective Davis sets his jaw. "You're not interested in helping your sister?"

"Not if you're in charge."

My skin tingles. I expect to be grabbed, handcuffed, forced into the study. Instead, Detective Davis offers one decisive nod. "That'll be fine. I'm more interested in talking to Amy."

CHAPTER EIGHT

Amy

(NOW)

My heart stops beating, just the hollow whoosh of blood in my ears. Of course Detective Davis wants to interrogate me. I'm the one with the most to hide.

"Amy's in shock," says Jo.

A light appears in the detective's eyes like he just heard an important detail. "And you're not?"

Jo stutters. "I didn't mean . . . That's not the point. Mom, you can't let him do this. Don't we need a lawyer?"

Mom's barely standing, leaning against the counter. "Jo, please."

The whooshing gets faster, so fast I have to bend my knees to keep from fainting.

So that's it. Mom wants us to cooperate.

Detective Kirke speaks up, kinder than her boss. "Amy, do you mind? We'll make it quick."

For a moment I consider refusing like Jo, but I'm the one who left Beth alone at the party. If I don't talk, I'll look suspicious as fuck. I get up from my seat, and Mom follows. "I'm coming with you."

"No." The protest leaps from my chest before I can measure it. Mom can't be in the room. She can't know what happened between Beth and me. Or worse, what happened between Laurie and me. "No," I repeat, more gently this time. "I'm okay. You should rest."

She hesitates, but purple shadows have formed under her eyes and she's trembling like she's desperate to sit down. "Okay," she says finally. "But if you start to feel uncomfortable—"

"I'll be fine," I say, but dread fills my body from head to toe.

Detective Kirke waits for me, a hand outstretched, but Davis plows ahead to the study, where he arranges chairs, two facing one.

"Have a seat," he says.

I'm afraid he'll hear my heart thudding, so I sit as far back on the chair as possible, wooden dowels digging into my spine.

Kirke opens her steno pad, but Davis doesn't take notes. He doesn't do anything that would break eye contact. "I'd like to know more about the party," he says.

My muscles tighten, my throat so dry, I can't speak.

Kirke adds to the prompt as if it'll make this easier. "Let's start at the beginning. Who threw the party?"

My voice shakes, but I swallow hard enough to smooth it out. "Sallie Gardiner throws a New Year's Eve party every year. Her parents are always in Paris around this time, but they don't care. It's not a secret."

Davis leans in. "What's your relationship to Sallie Gardiner?"

"She's Meg's best friend."

"How well do you know her?"

I shrug, relieved that they want to talk about Sallie instead of me. She's been friends with Meg since the days when they played dress-up and hosted tea parties with teddy bears, but I don't know her that well, considering. "Sallie's older than me, but I hang out with her little brother, Ned, every now and then. He's kind of an asshole, though."

Davis looks amused, but he hides it quickly. "Sallie goes to Harvard with Meg, is that right?"

"Yup."

A memory of Meg's senior year, the picture that went viral. Three girls from one graduating class, all accepted to Harvard: Meg, Sallie Gardiner, and Annie Moffat.

"The Harvard Three," says Davis.

I let out a wry laugh. "Yeah. Some people called them that."

Detective Davis looks me right in the eye. "If Sallie and Meg are friends, is it fair to say that Sallie and Beth were friends?"

"Oh." I pause. "No."

The detectives wait for me to keep going, but it's hard to explain Beth's feelings toward Sallie. She never much liked the girl, which was weird because Beth could see the good in everyone. Weirder because everyone loves Sallie Gardiner. She's gorgeous and popular and almost as smart as Meg. Smarter, depending on whom you ask.

Davis doesn't move, but somehow it feels like he's right in my face. "Sallie made it sound like she and Beth were close. Like Beth was a little sister to her."

"That's funny," I say flatly.

"Why is that funny?"

"Beth doesn't like Sallie Gardiner." A bolt in my chest. "Didn't, I guess."

Davis adjusts his footing, chair creaking beneath him. "Then why did a whole group of kids report watching Beth sob into Sallie's shoulder toward the end of the party?"

I stiffen, my face suddenly hot. "I don't know anything about that."

"You don't have any reason to believe that Beth was upset last night?"

I panic, the urge to lie filling my chest. "I'm ... I don't know."

Davis glances back at Detective Kirke, like he's granting her an opportunity. She eases forward, an earnest expression. "Amy, we have reports of a fight in the upstairs bathroom. A fight between you and Beth."

The humid bathroom. The claw-foot tub. Beth sobbing, mascara smeared under her eyes.

Suddenly, I feel dizzy, tricked, like the detectives had a map for this conversation, and I can't find north.

"It wasn't a fight," I say.

"Sallie Gardiner described running upstairs to find Beth in tears."

I'm going to be sick. I forgot the details of that moment, but they're lurking in my memory. Sallie Gardiner barging into the bathroom and holding Beth like she needed protection.

I can't stop my voice from shaking now. "We had an argument, but it was nothing."

Davis sits back. "Sure. Sisters fight."

"Not us. Not Beth and me."

"But you did last night."

"What does this have to do with anything?"

"You tell me," he says.

Now I understand how Jo must've felt in July, the narrative turned on her like a spotlight. Pressure gathers in my throat, behind my eyes. Everything's getting twisted, and I can still hear Beth crying, and it's possible, truly, that leaving her in that state is what caused her death.

Davis dips to find my eye, as if we're in this together. "I know it's hard, but honesty's very important here. What did you and Beth fight about?"

Sweat gathers on my brow. I get close to the truth without being totally honest. "Beth was enrolled at Plumfield, and she was supposed to be leaving soon. I didn't want her to go."

"Plumfield's a boarding school?" asks Kirke.

Davis waves her off like that's not important. "Amy, you need to tell the truth."

"I am." It's not the whole story, not even close, but I don't let it show.

Davis stares at me like he's desperate to uncover the details. "Let's talk about this morning."

A flash of our frigid street, the hill beside Laurie's house, Beth's freezing hand in mine.

"You woke up at home?" asks Davis.

Laurie's bed, his comforter thick and warm.

"I came home around eight."

"Eight a.m.?"

"Yeah."

"You often stay out all night?"

He's judging me, and I can't stand it. I've endured enough judgment from the people who read *Little Women*, who called me the party girl, the mess. Oh, Amy? That one's a wreck.

"Amy?" Detective Kirke softens the question. "Where did you spend the night?"

Tears blur my vision. I blink to stay focused. This morning I lied to Jo about where I spent the night, and I have to stick with that story. If she finds out that I slept in Laurie's bed, that we kissed and almost went further, then she'll never speak to me again. I can't lose another sister.

"I stayed with our cousin. Florence Carrol."

Davis levels his tone. "Florence Carrol, as in the Carrol Museum—"

"Yes." I answer without flinching. Florence will cover for me, no problem. She'd do anything for me.

"I didn't know you two were related," says Davis.

It's an insult, I'm sure. Aunt Mary and Uncle Carlos own one of the country's largest collections of Catholic art, so I'm used to the look of surprise when I tell people I'm Florence Carrol's cousin. She's my best friend, my partner in crime, but she's everything I'm not: rich, sheltered, and respected.

Detective Kirke keeps her pen poised. "So you left the party and went to the Carrols' house?"

"Yes."

She writes it down like it's the truth.

Then Davis leans closer. "Amy, you know it's a crime to lie to the police."

It's a statement, not a question.

My heart thuds in my chest, my whole body going hot. "I know."

He nods. "Then how about we try that again? Where were you after midnight?"

He doesn't know. He can't possibly know. "I told you. I stayed with my cousin."

Davis slides a steno out of his back pocket, opens to a page of slanted cursive. "I heard a different story from Theodore Laurence."

My stomach plunges, fear rising like water. I struggle to breathe.

"He said you left the party together, spent the night together."

I glance over my shoulder to make sure Mom's not standing outside the door.

"Would you rather we talk at the station?" asks Davis.

I shake my head.

"Did Beth know about you and Laurie?"

My vision tunnels. For a moment I can only see Davis, his gnarly face, like he's dangling me over the edge of a cliff.

"I don't . . ."

"I see a story here, Amy. You're a sophomore dating a senior, Jo's best friend."

"We're not dating," I say.

"Hooking up, then."

A flash of heat in my cheeks. "We're not even—"

"You and Laurie wanted to keep your relationship private, and then Beth found out. You had a fight."

"That's not—"

"Beth died on the hill beside Laurie's house."

"We were drunk. We barely kissed. We fell asleep."

The detective's eyes shine like he's caught me in a trap. "Do you realize how close you were to the crime scene?"

I can't speak. I feel like I've been knocked to the ground, my head hot and spinning. I knew I was responsible for leaving Beth at the party, distraught and alone, but I didn't think about our proximity to the crime scene. Whatever happened to my sister happened right outside Laurie's window.

"What time did she die?" I ask.

Detective Davis sits back. "What time did you leave the party?"

A lump forms in my throat. I feel cornered, trapped, and smaller than ever. This man thinks I killed my sister over a boy?

I look at Detective Kirke for rescue, but she believes it too. I can see it in her eyes. "You're wrong. Beth didn't know about Laurie and me. There wasn't anything to know until last night."

"Then what did you fight about?" asks Davis.

Nausea creeps through me. I can't tell these detectives about the real fight, the anger I've been bottling up for months. If they know, I'll be pinned with my own sister's murder. "I think I should get my mom."

Davis stands up, gestures to the door. "That's okay. We have everything we need."

CHAPTER NINE

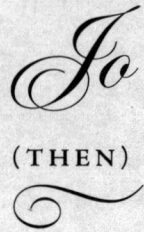

(THEN)

"You know that's not getting any better, right?" Amy stands at the end of the driveway, a stain of disapproval on her face.

"Thanks a lot." I plunge my rag into a bucket and slop it against the garage door. My arms ache from scrubbing, but I won't stop until I've worked away every last stroke of red paint.

Amy moves closer, scowling. "I can still see the *K*."

Sweat drips down the back of my neck, my breath coming fast and hard. I've moved on to the end of the heinous word that someone so heartlessly sprayed on our garage, but when I look back at my progress, my anger flares. The letters *K-I-L-L* still cling to the door.

I whirl around to face Amy. "Are you going to help, or what?"

"What's the point?" She leans against the garage, the pink streaks in her hair looking faded and orange. "Dad's leaving whether you clean it or—"

"Mom will change his mind," I say.

Meg's shadow stretches up the driveway, her gentle voice

more aggravating than ever. "Jo, he's almost done packing. You should put that down and come say goodbye."

I dip my rag in the soapy water, elbow aching, hair sticking to my face. "I'm not saying goodbye, because he's not leaving."

"It's just for a while," says Meg. "Just until the protests die down."

I grit my teeth and lean into my work, wearing down the *E* and the *R*.

It's not fair. Dad's been getting a lot of hate, but most of it's happening online. So one person managed to track down our address? So what? Why should this one person scare Dad enough to leave?

"I can't put the girls in danger," he said to Mom this morning while she tried to reason him out of the road trip.

Personally, I think his logic's flawed. If he really believes we're in danger, he should stay here to protect us. Instead, he wants to draw the danger elsewhere. ROB MARCH GOING ABROAD IN SEARCH OF SOLACE. That's the headline he pitched to his publicist.

Meg eases up to the garage, tries to slip the rag from my hand. "Jo, please."

I yank it back so fast that we're both splattered with dirty suds.

Meg looks disgusted, makes a show of wiping her face. "Fine. Do whatever you want. But Dad's leaving in a few minutes, and if you don't come inside—"

"I'll come in when I'm done."

Meg backs off while I attack the *R*, scrubbing so hard that veins pop out of my neck. Amy follows her into the house, and for a while I'm alone under a blaring sunset, the pressure of tears behind my eyes.

I fight the urge to cry until the door clicks open and voices spill out of the house. "Don't forget your Red Sox cap," says Meg.

Dad's voice comes out lower and more gravelly than usual, like he's carrying the world. "You should keep it. At least until I get back."

I squeeze my eyes shut, wrestling with my tears. I can't stop scrubbing. I need to keep working. Working so that Dad never has to see this paint again. Never has to stand slack-jawed on the driveway staring at the word "killer" with a darkness in his eyes like he's starting to believe the people who think he's evil for exploiting us. For ending Beth's story.

His footsteps come up behind me, and I know he's wearing his hiking boots. The sound takes me straight to the trails in Mount Washington, Dad letting me lead, his bear-like frame always close behind, there to catch me if I fall.

"Jo," he says gently, and my tears spill over.

The rag slides out of my hand and down the garage door. "I tried so hard. I tried so hard, but this paint is—"

"I love you," he says.

I want to be stubborn, but I can't help turning around and burrowing into his chest like I did when I was little. "Please don't go."

He holds me tight, whispers, "Jo, it's just a chapter."

He's always loved this metaphor. That life is a novel and

hardships are only chapters. It's helpful to think of pain this way—to know that someday we'll turn the page—but it doesn't ease the lump in my throat.

"You're a writer. Edit this chapter out."

He lets me go, laughs the way he does when he's reading Vonnegut. "I would if I could."

Dad's car sits by the curb, loaded with camping gear. The old white Cherokee brings back memories of eighties rock, lungs burning from singing along, laughing through the lyrics.

"How long will you be gone?" I ask as we make our way to the trunk.

My sisters come up beside us, all three of them eager to hear his answer, and I wish the protesters could see this moment. Meg's been so angry about *Little Women*—storming through the house yelling, "You ruined my life!"—and even she doesn't want Dad to go.

She blinks back tears. "Just a few weeks, right?"

Dad glances at the house, where Mom's inside refusing to come out. I have half a mind to drag her out here because I know she'll regret not saying goodbye, but our parents have been fighting lately. Yelling in a way I've never heard. "Rob, you used their names!" Mom cried last week. And last night? They fought after midnight about Dad's questionable decision to donate the first sizable advance he's ever made to an organization for the empowerment of women.

I could've told him it would backfire, that his haters would see right through the gesture.

Dad nudges his glasses up his nose, lets out a heavy sigh.

"I'm not sure when I'm coming back, but I'm hoping this'll be one of those really short chapters—"

"Like Stephen King. 'Nothing much happened for the next two weeks,'" I say, quoting an entire chapter from Stephen King's *It*, one that Dad and I have always admired.

"It's genius," he told me once. "Giving a single sentence the weight of a chapter."

He looks at me now, a glimmer in his eye. "Just like that." He wraps the four of us into a breathless hug. "Exactly like that."

CHAPTER TEN

Jo

(THEN)

A lot of stuff happens without Dad.

CHAPTER ELEVEN

(NOW)

While Amy's in the study with the detectives, I shut myself in my room.

I can't believe this is happening. Nothing feels real. Even my own hands look like they belong to someone else.

Beth died today. She actually died today.

I sit on my bed, the springs squeaking in a way I've never noticed.

Beth died, and Detective Davis, of all people, will be determining the narrative. I think I'm going to be sick, but only a hiccup comes out.

I haven't eaten. When was the last time I drank water?

I need to do something.

Like a bad habit, I consider opening my phone, going live to tell my followers what's happening, but that would be absurd—cruel. I need to respect my family's privacy. Beth's privacy.

But I'm itching. Squirming. Dying to put this experience into words. I dig under my pillow until I find my notebook, crack it open to a blank page, and let the story drain out.

I write about this morning, finding Beth in the snow, her empty eyes reflecting the sky, the gash in her forehead so deep, I worried that her memories and thoughts had escaped with the blood, the screaming of the sirens, the quiet footsteps of the first responders, Detective Kirke's firm handshake, calling Meg to deliver the news, and Davis—his arrival, the knot in my stomach, the fear of what's coming.

My hand cramps, and I realize that for the first time in weeks, maybe months, I'm writing without questioning every word, my internal editor silenced by the weight of my grief and panic.

So this is how it feels to write what you know.

In a fleeting thought, I picture my editor, Nan Dashwood, a brash woman with curly red hair and a literary eye that even Reese Witherspoon would envy. When she DM'ed me last summer, I thought my account had glitched, but it was real. She liked the essays I'd been posting, wanted me—Jo March—to write a response to *Little Women*. "We'll call it Jo's Version," she joked on the phone. "Tip our hat to Taylor Swift."

I loved the idea, loved it so much I couldn't breathe for days. But when I turned in my first draft, Nan ripped it to shreds. Her editorial letter contained five pages of single-spaced criticism, but when boiled down in the brain, they reduced to a single word: "boring." I reacted to *Little Women*, and Nan fell asleep on her Kindle. Yes, she actually said that.

She wanted more. More drama. More intrigue. More of a reason for the reader to snatch my book off a shelf. "Think

Jennette McCurdy, *I'm Glad My Mom Died*. That title alone does the trick."

A slippery thought worms through my mind, but it disgusts me. I snap my notebook shut, slide it under my legs. I must be sick. Deranged. I can't believe what I'm thinking. But my current reality would make an incredible book. A murder. An investigation.

I throw my notebook against the wall, hating myself for even prodding the idea with a ten-foot pole. I must be in shock. I must be broken. I must be damaged, because a title floats into my mind . . . *Beth Is Dead*.

I dive for my notebook and write it down, hands trembling, guilt wrecking my stomach.

Then a knock at the door sends my pen across the room.

Meg's gentle voice comes through a crack. "Jo? You okay?"

I sit straight-backed on the floor, my notebook smacked against my chest. "I'm fine."

She comes in. "I just want to apologize for— What're you doing?"

"Nothing." I shove my notebook under my pillow and stand to face her.

"You seem—"

"I'm fine. I'm just . . . taking notes."

"Notes?"

I think on my feet. Find a lie that's close to the truth but not nearly as sickening. "I don't trust Detective Davis to find out what really happened, so I'm taking notes on the investigation. Anything that might be important."

"About that." Meg sits on the edge of my bed, a truce in her posture. "I'm sorry for blaming Dad. I don't really think it's his fault." She wipes her eyes. "It's just easier to imagine a protester who did this—someone faceless."

It's hard for me to agree. I'm afraid to imagine Beth's killer as a stranger, because then it could've been anyone. And then this whole thing could be pinned on Dad for putting words on a page. Something I, myself, can't seem to control.

"Want to make some tea?" I ask.

Meg nods, eyes closed in relief. Tea is one of our rituals as a family, boiling the water, steeping the leaves, stirring in honey. It's something we do together, and it means that even if we're not on the same page, we're okay.

I stand to follow her to the kitchen—but just then, a sound comes up the street. The growling of a truck that's barely running. Meg's face falls, and my stomach plummets just the same. I know that sound.

"Henry," I say, and I take off down the stairs.

Guilt overrides every other emotion.

I can't believe we forgot him.

I throw the door open, a gust of snow, just as Henry jumps from his grandfather's truck. "Jo!"

"I'm so sorry," I try to say, but my throat's too dry.

Henry's out of breath, his cheeks stained with tears. "Tell me it isn't true," he says. "Tell me they're wrong."

He holds out his phone showing texts from kids at school.

Haven't you heard?

I thought you should know . . .

Beth March is dead.

I don't want to tell him. I already had to tell Mom and Meg. I can't bear to shatter another person. "Henry—"

The tremor in my voice must be enough. Enough for him to sprint toward the porch and into the house. He bounds up the stairs and stops at the bunk room. "Where is she?" he screams.

The detectives emerge from the study with Amy, all of them stunned.

Davis takes charge, plants a few heavy footsteps on the staircase and stops halfway up. "Who are you?" When Henry doesn't answer, he looks to us. "Who is this?"

"I'm Henry Hummel." He struggles for breath, clutching his knees. "I'm Beth's boyfriend."

CHAPTER TWELVE

Beth

(THEN)

The first week of my junior year has been the worst of my entire life. Everyone, and I mean everyone, is talking about me.

Friday night my sisters and I drive up to a student-council fundraiser, and people stare through the foggy windows of the pizzeria. I can imagine what they're saying, because I've been hearing it all week at school.

Yeah, that's Beth.

Have you read it?

I thought she was dead.

I bury my face, exhausted from the whispers, the pointing, the memes that've been sent back and forth. "Maybe I should go home."

Amy hops out of the car. "Are you kidding? People are finally noticing you. Enjoy it."

My heart lurches. I've never wanted to be noticed, at least not in this way. I thought my interview with *Teen Vogue* would stop the rumors, but they've only changed in tone. I was quoted saying, "My story ends in the book, but wait and see what I do next."

Now everyone's doing just that. Waiting. Eager for my next move as if I really have one.

Jo offers a hand to get me out of the car. "Don't worry. Just hold your head high."

Easy for her to say.

She loves being one of the little women, and everyone loves her. As we enter the pizzeria, Amy dashes to meet her friends in the corner, and people flock to Jo. She glows as she answers every wide-eyed question. "Are you in love with Laurie?" "Did Amy really fall through the ice on Walden Pond?" "Is it true that you hesitated before fishing her out?"

I'm not hungry, but I order from the counter for something to do, cheese pizza and a Cherry Coke. Food in hand, I settle into a corner booth, away from the crowd, but as soon as I'm comfortable, a boy slides in across from me.

He eases down, a knowing grin. "That's a large pizza."

I recognize him right away. Thick dark hair and a worn-out bomber jacket. "You're the new kid."

He fights a smirk. "Is it that obvious?"

I blush, surprised that a guy like this would sit down with me in a room full of options. He's broody and cute, and I know more about him than I should. "You're Henry, right?"

"Henry Hummel. How'd you know?"

This is my third year serving as the school office aide, a position I hold near and dear, and the staff gossips more than I'd like to admit. According to them, Henry didn't want to move here from Rhode Island, but his mom passed away a few months ago and he had to come live with his grandpa. Maybe he could use a friend.

"Email," I say, a half-truth.

"Email?" he asks.

"The monthly update from school. You were mentioned at the bottom. You and a girl from Connecticut."

He nods slowly, shifts his focus back to my pizza. "You ordered a large. Must be hungry."

I shake my head, a little shrug. "I just wanted to be supportive."

"How is a cheese pizza supportive?"

"It's a fundraiser." I gesture to the signage.

"So, you're not going to eat it?"

I nudge it toward him. "Have all you want."

I expect him to dig in, but he sits back, grins. "What's in it for me?"

"Excuse me?" I laugh.

"If I eat this pizza to help you support the school, then what do I get in return?"

"Dinner," I say flatly.

Henry leans on his elbows, his blue-gray eyes like the sky in winter. "How about this? If I eat your pizza, you'll tell me your name."

A smile edges into my cheeks. I forgot how it feels to meet someone without any preconceived notions of who I am. "You don't know my name?"

"Why would I?" he asks.

"Everyone does."

For a moment Henry stares wide-eyed like I'm the most arrogant girl in the world, and I think maybe I'm not the talk of Rhode Island, too. Then a light comes on behind his eyes. "You must be a March sister."

Rain's been falling for a few minutes, gaining intensity, droplets like a heartbeat.

"I haven't read the book," says Henry. "I'm not a big reader, but I know about your dad. I know he got canceled."

"You know why?"

He shakes his head. "I heard the book was sexist or something."

I let out a bitter laugh. "I wish it were that simple."

Henry stares at me, but his attention feels different than the attention from the kids who've been shooting glances across the room. Like he's interested in the truth, like he cares. "What's the real reason?"

I shouldn't tell him. I should bask in the glory of being with someone who doesn't picture me in a casket. But something about Henry makes me want to unload. "I die at the end."

He coughs, practically choking on his pizza. "What?"

"Car crash. Last chapter. And I don't even fight to stay alive. My last words are, 'Isn't it a beautiful night?' And it's not even a statement. It's a question. Like I can't make up my own mind."

"That's messed up."

"Tell me about it."

Henry reaches for my Coke, takes a sip without asking. I'd usually be annoyed and a little grossed out sharing a straw, but he makes me feel like we've known each other for a long time. "Your dad sounds like a psychopath."

"He's a writer," I say. "And I guess I can't blame him. I haven't given him much to write about."

Henry wipes his mouth on a greasy napkin. "What do you mean?"

"My life isn't much of a story."

"I highly doubt that."

"It's true. I haven't done anything interesting." My honesty surprises me, but I feel comfortable across from Henry. "I've never had big goals like my sisters. I've never fallen in love. But I'm trying to be different from the girl in my dad's book."

Henry takes a bite of pizza, a gulp of Coke. "What's she like?"

The answer comes to me slowly, a dozen descriptions rising and falling: sensitive, sweet, shy, angelic. "She's perfect."

Henry considers for a moment. "That doesn't sound too bad."

On the surface, it's not. I'm grateful that Dad didn't make me seem selfish and melodramatic like he did Amy or status-seeking and vain like he did Meg—but I don't want to be the Beth in his book. "Perfect isn't always a good thing. He wrote me as someone who never pushes back, never speaks up, never wants anything, I mean really *wants* anything, for herself."

Henry finishes a slice, holds my gaze. "Is that true about you?"

At first I'm taken aback, but he's not accusing me of anything. It's a genuine question, and it takes me a while to answer. "I don't know."

Henry thinks for a beat, and I like the way we can sit in silence. "Look," he says finally, "I've only known you for, what? Ten minutes? And I can already see that you're anything but perfect."

I scoff, pretending to be wounded.

"You're drinking a Cherry Coke, which is an insult to the original. And you're passing up a damn good cheese pizza. That's a major red flag."

Laughter warms my chest.

"Plus, you still haven't told me your name."

I tuck a smile into my shoulder, extend a hand across the table. "I'm Beth."

Henry takes my hand, and an unfamiliar electricity fills my whole body. I hate that he lost his mom, that he was uprooted without a choice, but selfishly, I think he showed up just in time.

CHAPTER THIRTEEN

Meg

(NOW)

Henry sits on the staircase with his head in his hands. "I should've been there," he sobs.

The poor thing found out about Beth in a text message. I hate myself for not even thinking to call him, the first boy who ever made Beth so happy, she couldn't hide it, drawing hearts on her notebook. "He just gets me," I remember her saying.

I ease a hand onto his shoulder. He's not wearing a coat. Must've rushed out of the house and forgotten to grab one. "Come to the living room. It's warmer by the fire."

He shakes his head like he can't imagine moving, his chest heaving.

Detective Kirke sits beside him on the steps. I wonder if she always goes in first for questioning, if it's a tactic they use to make people more comfortable. It doesn't make me feel any better. "Henry, we're trying to piece together what happened last night," she says.

He wipes his eyes, his nose. "I should've gone to the party."

"Why didn't you go?"

"I had to work. Well, I chose to work. Lotty's pays time and a half on holidays."

"Lotty's?" asks Kirke.

"The diner on—"

"LeBlanc. I know the place." Detective Davis moves in, leans against the staircase. "Mind if we call your manager to corroborate?"

Henry pauses, awareness settling into his muscles. "Am I—"

"You're not in any trouble," says Kirke. "We're just trying to establish a timeline."

Henry seems reassured, but I don't trust Detective Davis. Not after what he did in July, accusing Jo of faking a break-in and planting a recording device under Beth's piano. Jo can be crafty and devious, but she'd never do anything like that.

He leans closer to Henry. "What time did you leave the diner?"

Henry thinks. "My shift ended at midnight, but it took me a half hour, maybe more, to lock up and get home."

"Anyone else in the house?"

"Just my grandpa."

"Name?"

"Max Hummel, but he's not always . . . He has dementia."

Davis firms his lips like he understands. "I'll keep that in mind."

I've met Max Hummel a few times. He's a kind and gentle man, but he often wanders to the mailbox in his underwear and sometimes ends up in shops saying, "How did I get here?" I have a friend who works in a salon where, more than once, they've found Mr. Hummel sitting under the hair dryers singing to himself. Henry's an angel for taking care of him.

Detective Davis offers a glance to his partner, and she closes her steno pad. "We may have more questions later," she says.

Henry nods, bleary-eyed. "I'll do anything to help."

Then, as if they have plenty to go on, the detectives gather their coats.

"Wait." The word leaps out. I'm not exactly eager to be interviewed, but I'm confused. They said they needed statements from everyone in the family, but they've only spoken to Amy. "Aren't you interested in talking to the rest of us?"

Detective Davis shakes his head, and a strange, thick worry settles into my stomach. Amy's young enough to implicate herself without realizing. What did she tell them?

"We'll be back," says Detective Kirke. "And, Mrs. March?"

Mom's standing in the kitchen doorframe.

"Please let us know if you're able to reach your husband. We'll make some calls on our end as well, but these things are much easier coming from family."

Mom doesn't answer, just closes her eyes, as if she can't even muster the energy to nod. I feel the same way when I think of Dad, a heavy combination of missing him and blaming him for being gone so long.

The detectives are just about to shut the door when Davis turns back. "Henry?"

The boy glances up, and I can see why Beth was so drawn

to him. He's tough, but he has a humility that's rare in Concord, a humble work ethic. There are things about him that you can't see until you're close enough: a sadness in his eyes, a softness to his skin, a scar above his eyebrow.

"How about we follow you home?" Davis isn't asking. There's a command in his voice. "We can talk to your grandpa together."

Henry looks at me like he doesn't want to leave. He just got here. He must have questions for us, and I'm sure he doesn't want to be alone. But the detective stays in the doorway, boots firm on the mat, until Henry reluctantly hoists himself off the staircase, hangs his head, and follows.

"We'll call you," says Jo, squeezing his hand on his way out.

And with a click of the door, it's quiet.

We stand in the foyer for a while, longer than we should, as if we've lost a cog and our gears are jammed.

Then Mom says, "Let's make some tea," and the dam breaks, all of us rushing to help, anything to keep our minds off the ache.

"I'll boil the water," says Jo.

"I'll get the honey," I add.

Amy's distracted. She stares at her phone, held low at her side. "I think I need a shower."

"Of course," says Mom.

"You okay?" I ask, an eye on the phone. I worry about Amy more than my other sisters. Jo's always been so public on social media, sharing DMs and texts, but Amy's phone holds a world I'll never see.

She tucks it quickly into the pocket of her hoodie, straightens. "I'm fine," she says as she turns and trudges up the stairs.

The water's hardly boiling, the kettle just beginning to whistle, when the doorbell rings.

All of us still, eyes darting to the foyer.

"What now?" asks Jo.

"I'll get it," says Mom.

"Hold on." Through the decorative glass on the front door, I spot a figure. Tall, dusty-haired, and so familiar, I can't help but run.

I hoist the door open, and John Brooke stands before me like a lighthouse cutting through fog.

He wipes his boots on the mat, carries take-out bags in his hands, thank-yous printed urgently down the sides. "I came as soon as I heard."

I bite my tongue, nearly crying at the sight of him. I would've called him eventually, but I'm sure he heard the news from his parents, who live a block over, and I'm glad he did.

I didn't know how much I needed him.

He sets the takeout on the porch and pulls me into his coat like he can't bring me close enough.

I breathe in his scent, wood and lacquer, like a well-loved piano.

"I'm so sorry," he says.

I bury my face in his chest. "I'm so glad you're here."

I pull him out of the cold, dust the snow from his old brown coat.

And then, "Oh my god. Your car."

The front bumper's dented, but he waves it off. "Doesn't matter. Just a fender bender."

John's been driving the same cherry-red Ford since high school, a hand-me-down from his dad, barely running. He can't afford to fix it. Can't afford much of anything on what he brings in teaching piano lessons.

"When did it happen?" I ask.

He's not listening. He transfers the takeout to the table, and in seconds Mom's beside him. "It's good to see you, hon."

She's always loved John, ever since he was the lanky little boy who lived down the street. His hardworking parents, his good manners. He's been teaching Beth to play the piano since he hit middle school, his first real job, and when we broke up after high school, Mom might've been more devastated than me.

"I brought chicken noodle, tomato bisque."

As he spreads out the food, he gives me an urgent look. I know him well enough to know that we need to talk.

"What's wrong?" I whisper.

Mom has gone into the kitchen to fish spoons from a drawer. Amy's upstairs. Jo's by the fire.

He angles toward me, his voice low. "I wanted to call you the second I heard, but I didn't feel right telling you over the phone." He holds himself up, knuckles white against the table. "I saw Beth last night."

CHAPTER FOURTEEN

Jo

(NOW)

I wasn't supposed to hear it—the secret whispered only to Meg—but I'm always listening.

"I saw Beth last night."

The room falls painfully still, the crackle of the fire the only sound.

Meg keeps her back to me, her voice so quiet that her words come out broken. "What do you mean?"

I strain to hear John's answer, desperate to judge even his intake of breath.

He checks over his shoulder. "Can we go outside?"

"It's snowing," says Meg.

"Your room, then."

Meg shifts like she's ready to lead him upstairs, but I can't let them go. I'm desperate for information, like a desert waiting for rain. "I want to know." My voice echoes off the walls, the hardwood floors. "I deserve to know."

"Know what?" Mom returns, spoons in a fist.

John looks nervous, but I'm not afraid to put him on the spot. I've never much liked him, because everyone loves him—gentle, handsome, talented musician. There's something eerie about people who can hide their flaws so well. "He saw Beth last night."

John eyes Meg like he'd do anything to explain himself in private, but it's too late. He's cornered, so he nods. "It's true. It was late. After midnight."

Meg leans in. "After we left—" She stops herself, and I realize that they must've been together last night. Meg swore she'd never date John again, determined to focus on her new life—and the new boys—at Harvard, but she's been happier than usual, and she told me she spent New Year's Eve at a piano bar. No one loves the piano more than John Brooke.

Fear stains his voice, the muscles in his neck drawn too tight. "She called me from a party. She was . . ." His gaze flickers to Mom like he's apologizing for what he's about to say. "She'd been drinking. She was really upset, and she needed a ride home."

Meg's face pinches. "What? You should've called me."

John rubs his forehead so hard, it turns red. "Beth asked me not to tell you, any of you. She made me promise, and I thought I was doing the right thing, keeping her trust, but now—" His breath hitches, and he can't continue.

"It's okay." Meg nestles herself in John's arms, rests her head on his chest. "It's okay."

A thousand questions fight for the right to come out of my mouth, but for a moment I can't think about anything other than the way Meg's hugging John. It's too raw, too charged. They're seeing each other again. I'm sure of it. And they haven't told a soul.

At first I'm suspicious, angry with Meg for keeping me in the dark, but watching them together, I feel suddenly cold, like I've stepped outside without a coat. They look safe, sheltered, and I can hardly imagine what that feels like. I've never let anyone hold me that way—not even Laurie.

Mom sits at the table, eager for the rest of the story. "John, did you drive Beth home?"

He eases his grip on Meg, a solemn nod. "I picked her up at the Gardiners' house and brought her here. She wouldn't let me help her to the door, but I waited in the car until she made it inside. I promise, Mrs. March, I waited until she made it inside."

"She came inside?" The question escapes my chest like a rabbit from a trap, fragile, timid.

John nods.

"No," I say. "That's not possible."

I rack my memory of last night, mining for a detail I didn't notice in the moment—the door clicking open, Beth scuffing her boots on the mat, cold wind whipping through the foyer. I can't remember anything other than the sound of my own mind whirring, computer keys clacking. But of course, I fell asleep.

John lowers into a chair. "It would've been one, one thirty, maybe."

"Are you sure?" I ask. "I should've heard the door. Woken up. It's not a big house."

John shrugs like he doesn't know what else to say—but there's something in his eyes, something he's not telling us.

I lean in. "If you brought her home, I would've known. Would've seen her one last . . ."

My voice pinches, and Meg tries to comfort me, a gentle hand on my shoulder. "You must've been exhausted."

I picture myself passing out on my notebook, missing my last chance to see my sister, and it hurts like a knife to the stomach. I lash out. "Why should we believe him?"

Mom shoots me a look of disapproval. "Jo, I know this is hard, but—"

"What if he didn't bring her home?"

Meg turns fiery red. "Do you realize what you're saying?"

"He lost his job as her teacher."

Mom quickly discounts me. "No, he didn't." She turns to face him with reassurance. "You didn't. We only hired someone to help with her audition. Only for a while."

Meg clucks. "Yes. John agreed that was the right thing to do."

He tries to sound calm. "She chose a very difficult piece."

Maybe. Maybe that's true. "But he yelled at her," I say, unable to stop myself. "A few weeks ago, during one of her lessons. I don't know what he was shouting about, but when I walked into the room, Beth was crying, and she told me later that John totally lost his—"

"That was—" John stands up, full of steam, fists clenched.

"It was a mistake," says Meg, an air of diplomacy. "John lost his temper for half a second, and he apologized."

John steels his shoulders, but he's angry, fuming.

I've almost got him. "Apology or not, I didn't hear the door last night."

Meg looks at me like I'm a monster, and I get it. John Brooke has spent so much time with our family, I should consider him a brother, but he's not perfect, and I refuse to believe that Beth came home last night. If she did, then I could've saved her.

John reclaims his seat, rings of exhaustion under his eyes. "I know how it looks."

I can't stop myself. "It looks like you're lying. If Beth needed a ride, she would've called me. I was home. I have a car."

"She didn't want to talk to you," says John.

"Oh, really? Why not?" I try to sound caustic, but my questions come out with a tremor.

He hangs his head, backtracks. "I mean, it's not about you. Not *just* you. She wanted to talk to someone outside of the family."

My heart thuds in my ears. "Why?"

"I don't know the whole story, and I really don't want to cause more trouble, but something happened between Beth and Amy."

The moment settles like a stone.

I think of Amy coming home this morning, the empty staircase behind her. "I knew it."

Mom stands up like she can sense a tidal wave coming. "Now, Jo—"

"Amy left the party without Beth. I knew something was wrong."

"We can't do this," says Mom. "We can't start blaming each other."

I don't want to blame my sister, but Amy's been acting strange all day—feral, cornered. "She's hiding something."

"That's enough," says Mom, like a lid closing tight. "Sit down. We haven't eaten all day, and John's been kind enough to bring—"

Before she can finish, I'm halfway up the stairs, bounding two at a time.

"Jo!" Mom shouts.

I tear down the hallway toward the sound of the shower, water spitting. "Amy!"

We have an agreement in our house: the bathroom door stays unlocked. Too many girls, not enough sinks, toilets. Amy brushes her teeth while I'm in the shower. Meg pees while Amy curls her hair.

I throw the door open and yank back the shower curtain. Steam clouds the air, water splattering an empty tub.

Amy's gone.

CHAPTER FIFTEEN

Amy

(NOW)

I seal myself in the bathroom, back against the door, and text Laurie again.

We need to talk.

My head throbs, flashes of memories.

I'm in Laurie's room. The scent of his cologne, mint and eucalyptus, his lips pressed against mine, his hands on my sides, my whole body lighting up. Then, my dress on the floor, our hips fitting together, and right when I reach for his boxers, a T-shirt appears. "Amy, please. Just put it on."

In the moment I couldn't see past my embarrassment, the shame of rejection. I thought of nothing beyond burying myself in Laurie's sheets, pretending to sleep.

But his bedroom overlooks the hill. If I'd been paying attention to the outside world instead of sulking, then maybe I would've seen Beth. Maybe I could've saved her.

I clutch the shower curtain and double over, but nothing comes out, just bile in the back of my throat.

I was there.

I was right there.

The shower steams. I'm desperate to strip my clothes, climb inside, and scrub the past twenty-four hours off my skin, but Laurie answers.

Laurie: Where?

Me: Meet me at the swings.

Ten minutes later, I've climbed through my bedroom window, down a trellis strangled with dead vines, and walked the long way to the park, avoiding the crime scene and the cops who remain.

Laurie takes longer to show up, and when he does, he's so nervous that he can't stop clutching his coat and looking over his shoulder. "Why'd you pick the park?"

This is our spot, the place where Laurie and I always ramble endlessly while Jo lies in the grass to work on her writing, but that's not why I chose it. From here, I can almost see the police tape through a thicket of trees. "Nobody will be brave enough to come through here right now."

A flash of understanding, then a somber nod. Laurie takes a seat in the swing next to me, his sneakers grazing the snowy gravel. "Are you okay?" he asks first.

I shake my head.

"Yeah," he sighs.

We both stare at our feet for a moment like we don't know where to begin, and then like vomit, Laurie's words come out. "I had to tell the police."

He looks sick, nauseated, like he's been agonizing over it. "A detective came to the house, and I wanted to keep quiet, but my grandma told me to answer their questions."

Laurie's grandma is one of the smartest women in Concord. An ex-politician who now leads a nonprofit to help people of color who've been wrongly accused. If she tells him to answer, he'll answer.

"I couldn't lie," he says. "I needed an alibi."

Regret pins me to the swing, the old rubber cutting into the backs of my thighs. "I wish I'd known. I told them a different story."

Laurie's been swaying on his swing, but now he stops. "What?"

"I told the detectives I stayed with Florence, but . . ." I trail off, shaking my head. "They think we're suspects, Laurie."

His breath comes fast, hot. "What're you talking about?"

"They think we've been hiding our relationship. That Beth found out about us."

He stands up to pace, kicking up snow. "Us? What us? There's no us."

"Wow." I let out a bitter laugh, sobered by his honesty.

Laurie swoops in close. "I didn't mean—"

"I know what you mean."

"I just mean that we don't have some long-standing secret romance. And even if we did, we wouldn't hurt Beth over it. Over anything."

I stare at the ground. "I know."

Laurie squats in front of my swing, a hand on my knee. All the heat in my body gathers there, and for a second I want to kiss him, to forget everything.

"Let me be clear," he says. "I don't regret what happened last night. Not even a little."

When I look at him, I feel all the years I spent in Jo's shadow, running after Laurie, wishing he would see me. Last night he looked at me like I was the only person in the world. "Why did you stop?"

"We were drunk," he says.

"I was fine."

"Ames." He stares like he can see right through me. God, he can. "I didn't want it to happen like that. And if you're honest, you didn't either."

A lump forms in my throat. I want to believe him, but I'm afraid he's just painting over the truth. He still loves Jo, and that's why he can't love me.

Laurie comes back to his swing, sways gently. "I need to know something."

My focus ticks up.

"What did you and Beth fight about?"

I shake my head, my chest full of sludge.

"If the cops are coming after us, I need to know." He pauses. "I deserve to know."

He's right. He deserves to know, but I can't tell him. Everyone sees me as the bad guy. Everyone but Laurie. I wouldn't survive if he changed his mind. "It was nothing."

"Amy."

"It was just a sister thing."

"She was bawling. And you were so angry. I practically dragged you into my car. That wasn't just a sister thing."

My heart beats in my temples. It's so hard to focus. "I don't know how to explain it."

Laurie stills, lets out a long, heavy sigh. "Ames, I think we need to stay away from each other for a while."

My chest goes hollow. "Are you kidding me?"

"We're dangerous together."

I can't believe what I'm hearing. I've been waiting years for Laurie to see me, *really see me*, and last night he finally did. He showed up to the party to be with me, and though he cut our night short, we were finally making progress. "Please don't say that."

"Then tell me about the fight."

I can't speak without crying. My words sound broken. "It was stupid."

Laurie looks pained, dark eyes glistening, but his voice remains steady. "We look guilty. Hiding from Jo. Lying to the police."

"So this is my fault?"

"We spent the night beside the crime scene. We almost hooked up. You're a sophomore, I'm a senior."

"That's ridiculous. I've known you forever, and you're young for your grade. We're only two years apart until you turn eighteen."

"The police aren't going to care about any of that."

"So that's it?" I ask.

"For now," he says. "For a while."

I can't bear to look at him. Jo's always claimed Laurie as her best friend, but in reality, he's mine. When she fought with him,

I was there. When she didn't have time for him, I was there. When she refused to see the way he loved her, I was there.

"I need you," I say.

"I'm so sorry." He stands up, and as he walks away, I'm desperate to tell him the truth. Beth and I fought about Plumfield. We fought because I'm selfish and greedy and everything else they call me online, but I can't get it out.

I'd rather lose Laurie than let him see who I really am.

CHAPTER SIXTEEN

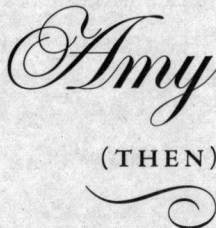

(THEN)

July, azure and cloudless, Beth sits at the piano playing Beethoven's Sonata no. 29 for the hundredth time. I don't know anything about sonatas, but I know I hate this one. Beth's sheet music calls it *Hammerklavier*, which seems fitting for a forty-minute hammer to the head.

I collapse into an armchair, groaning, "Beth, I'm begging. You've gotta stop. Or at the very least, play something else."

She doesn't hear me. When Beth plays, she enters another world, so concentrated that it's like we're in different rooms or even on different planets. I can almost relate, but when I paint, I draw inspiration from the world around me. Beth seems to draw inspiration from within, as if she was born with an enormous well of creativity inside.

It's disgusting.

And honestly, amazing.

She sways on the piano bench, fingers flying up and down the keys. She's lost in the music, and for a moment I try to enjoy it. I don't blame her for practicing nonstop, burying herself in music. It's been a couple of days since her tell-all with *Teen Vogue* hit the internet, the hot-pink pull quote shared by everyone we've ever known.

"Wait and see what I do next."—Beth March

In a matter of hours, Beth became her worst nightmare: a social media sensation that rivals Jo. She's been turned into memes, candid photos overlaid with bold type. And girls everywhere have spoken up, proud to be like Beth—a poem written by a fan was shared thousands of times: *To all the introverts, the homebodies, the music lovers, the beauty seekers, the quiet ones, the girls whose dreams are still embers only smoldering for now.*

Beth leans into the piano, the music angry and panicked all at once. I'm about to jam my headphones over my ears when Jo comes through the front door, backpack sliding off her shoulder. "Again?" she asks.

Nobody loves Beth's music more than Jo, and even she can recognize that this has gone too far. She squats beside me, whispers, "How many times has she played this today?"

Beth's practice sessions have blended one into the next, but she's been playing since I woke up. "Literally nonstop," I say.

"Her fingers are going to fall off."

"Beth!" I yell. "Jo's home. Why don't you take a break?"

Beth loves Jo a hundred times more than she loves the rest of us, but even this doesn't interrupt her focus. Not for a second. She's determined to finish this run.

With no other choice, we settle in to endure the crescendo. Beth grits her teeth, sweat shining on her forehead as she brings the piece toward its complicated end, and when at long last she reaches the final note, it hums through the whole house.

"Beautiful," says Jo.

"Finally," I mutter.

Beth hardly pauses. She stretches her fingers and returns them straight to the keys. "I'm still botching the adagio. I need to play it again."

"No." I shoot up. "You need a break. *We* need a break."

She looks at me like I told her to drop acid, wide-eyed and red-faced. "It's not perfect."

"Who cares?"

Jo cuts in front of me. "It'll never be perfect if you wear yourself out. You need to rest."

Beth tucks her hair behind her ears. "I *need* to get it right."

I don't understand why. Beth doesn't play for real audiences, doesn't play for anyone other than the family and John. "What does it matter?" I ask.

"It matters," she says.

"Why?"

"I need to prepare." Her admission comes out hot and fast, her hands balling into fists.

Jo and I share a glance, both of us confused. Beth has never had a recital or anything like it. Nothing that requires preparation. I lean against the piano, eyebrows rising. "The heck are you talking about?"

Beth hesitates, a tremor in her voice. "I didn't know how to tell you."

"Tell us what?" asks Jo.

"Aunt March called."

At the mention of Aunt March, my shoulders knot. Every time that woman calls, I end up feeling like gum on the bottom of a size-eight stiletto. She's the kind of person I'd consider a role model if not for the fact that she hates me. Forty-something with a badass job at a record label and an apartment that overlooks Central Park.

"When?" asks Jo.

"Why?" I add.

Beth stares at her hands like she knows how much this news will hurt. "She got me an audition at Plumfield."

I let out an involuntary "Seriously?"

"I know it sounds crazy." Beth stands up, paces the way Jo usually does. "I can hardly believe it myself, and I have no idea if it's the right thing to do, but she saw the *Teen Vogue* article, and she thought I sounded different, ready for something, so she pulled some strings."

My chest feels empty, not a single retort to dig up and spit out. I'd do anything to attend Aunt March's alma matter, Plumfield School for the Arts. "I don't believe this," I mutter under my breath.

Jo looks inspired. "How do you feel? Are you ready for something like that?"

Beth works her fingers into her hair. "I don't know. I think I might be."

"This is bullshit." I can't help myself. Aunt March wanted children but never had them, and though she always brags about supporting her nieces, she only supports Beth.

Beth rushes to my side. "Oh, Ames, I'm so sorry. I know you'd love to go too. You should ask Aunt March."

Jo lets out a flat laugh. "Plumfield's the most prestigious boarding school in New England. Amy would never make it there."

"Nice," I say, stung.

"Come on. It's true. You've been suspended, what, three times? And your grades suck."

"Plumfield's an art school," I say. "They'd care more about my portfolio."

Jo shakes her head like she knows better, and anger crackles through me.

"Whatever. I don't need to leave Concord High. I actually have friends."

Beth looks hurt, but she hides it with a self-deprecating smile. "There's still a good chance I won't get in. And either way, I can't attend until spring semester. That was the deal. So there's plenty of time to think."

"You'll get in," says Jo without a shred of doubt.

I don't know how she can be so supportive. In just a few short months, Jo will apply to college, and she's already panicking about how to pay for it. She's smart but not book smart like Meg, who got a full ride to Harvard. She could use Aunt March's money too.

Beth keeps going. "John thinks they can't refuse me if I play Sonata no. 29."

"You told John?" Jo sounds betrayed.

Beth scrambles to answer. "Just this morning. I was planning to tell you, I swear. I've just been weighing it all."

I want to pretend that I don't care, but my anger leaps so high, I can't contain it. "Weighing it?"

"It's a big decision," says Beth.

"You don't even want to go, do you?"

Beth's voice rises, her cheeks red. "I don't know what I want, but I'm trying to figure it out."

My stomach churns. Beth doesn't deserve this opportunity. She's afraid of Plumfield. I can see it in her eyes. As much as I hate to admit it, Dad pegged her in his book. Shy, timid, and lacking ambition.

"I'd go in a heartbeat," I say.

Beth sputters like she's searching for a retort, but before she can find one, Jo crouches beside me and peers into the darkness under the baby grand. "Hold on a minute. Do you see that?"

At first I think she's just trying to distract us from fighting. "Get up," I say.

But she sounds worried. "I'm serious. Look at this."

With a dramatic sigh, I get to my knees and follow her line of sight. Something blinks beneath the piano. A dim red light. A boxy object taped to the wood. Jo crawls toward the black plastic . . . What is it? A phone? She moves deeper, disturbing dust, and with a groan, reaches up to grab the thing.

Beth leans over. "What are you doing?"

The red light blinks in Jo's hand, and a chill passes through every inch of my body. "What the hell?"

Jo moves into the light, a rectangular device in her palm. "Someone's recording us."

"What?" Beth sounds horrified.

Jo squints at the device and drops it like it's dangerous, like it could bite. "Look at the time stamp. It's been running for seventy-six hours."

Beth hovers, studying it with fear in her eyes. "I'm calling Mom."

"She's at work," I say.

"I'm calling her," Beth repeats.

"We should call Dad," says Jo.

I balk. "When's the last time you heard from Dad?"

Jo's voice rises. "He thought leaving would make us safer, but look at this. We're still being targeted. It doesn't make any difference that he's gone. He should just come home."

I reach for a sneaker. "Cover your eyes."

Jo snatches the device out of harm's way. "We can't smash it. We need to show Dad."

Beth gets Mom's voicemail, hangs up with a huff. "We need to show the police."

Jo stops the device, and the red light blinks off. "I'm sending Dad a picture."

Beth sits on the piano bench, brings her knees to her chest. "I can't believe this is happening."

"See?" I whisper to Beth. "Wouldn't you love to get out of here?"

She pales, swallows, and I can't stand her indecision. I leave the room with a low belly groan.

Aunt March handed an opportunity to the wrong sister. Beth hides from life. I'm ready to reach out and take it by the throat.

CHAPTER SEVENTEEN

(NOW)

Amy's only missing for twenty minutes, but it's enough to send the family—and the news reporters—into hysterics. Mom stays home in case of her return, and John races the rest of us through the neighborhood in his battered car, whipping around corners, tires screeching.

When we finally spot her trudging back from the park, Meg leaps from the moving vehicle and runs until Amy's in her arms. "What were you thinking?" she asks as cameras snap.

"What the hell?" I follow, completely out of breath.

"I needed some air," Amy grumbles, to which I reply flatly, "Open a window next time."

At home in the living room, Mom echoes our fear, clutching Amy like she could turn to dust. "We don't know who did this or where they might be. You have to stay safe."

I'm relieved to have Amy back in our sight, but I can't shake the feeling that I need to rip her open, sink my teeth into her lies, and refuse to let up until the truth comes out. "You need to tell us what happened last night."

Mom shoots me a glance. "Not now, Jo."

I ignore the warning, desperate for answers. "You're the only reason Beth went to that party, and you left her behind. Why?"

Meg moves between us. "We're all emotional. This isn't the time—"

I sidestep her to stay in Amy's face. "What did you do?"

Amy hardens. "It's not my fault."

My stomach roils, sick and thrilled at the same time. I'm winning, stripping Amy down. "Beth called John after you abandoned her. She told him you had a fight."

Amy mines her fingers into her hair, the box-pink streaks reminding me that she's still immature and unpredictable. "Beth started it."

My breath comes out hot. "I'm sure that's not true."

"Right, because she's so perfect."

"She wouldn't start a fight with you."

Amy pulls her arms across her chest, a sad attempt at looking bitter. Behind the act, I can see that she's scared. She has a story to tell, and I won't rest until I force it out of her. I move in closer, and she starts to talk. "I just wanted to have a good time, but Beth wouldn't stop talking about Plumfield. She kept reminding me that she'd be leaving soon."

Meg softens. "You were going to miss her."

But that's not it. Amy didn't start a fight over the thought of an empty bunk, a lonely room. "You were jealous," I say.

She glares, defiant. "Beth was rubbing it in my face."

I'm right. I'm right, and it feels so good. Like I've been striking flint, and at long last the fire's burning. "What did you say to her?"

Mom tries to stop us, but she's so grief-stricken, she doesn't have the energy. "Girls, if we could just—"

"What did you say to her?" I shout.

Amy sets her jaw, stills her quivering lip. "I told her she didn't deserve it."

I can't believe what I'm hearing. I look at the others, mouth agape.

Amy continues like a spool unraveling. "She didn't even want to go. She was so scared, so back and forth."

"That doesn't mean she didn't deserve—"

"I would've done anything for that opportunity."

I lean into Amy, growling, "You're the least deserving person in the world."

"That's enough," says Mom.

Amy's crying now, tears streaming down her face. She struggles for air, gaze pinned on me. "I'm not going to lie. I said something awful to Beth, but I thought she'd be okay. It was just a fight. Like you and me."

I shake my head. "She's not like you and me."

"I know, but—"

"She's sensitive."

Amy's face turns red, squished. "What if she jumped? What if she jumped because of what I said?"

All at once my breath leaves my lungs. For a second I'm floating, suspended. "Ames . . . no."

BETH IS DEAD

"She could've jumped," Amy repeats. "Or fallen."

"No," says Mom, more emphatically than I thought possible in her state. "I'm a nurse. I saw the wound. Someone hit her. Or shoved her hard enough to crack her skull."

The image shocks us all into stillness.

"I hurt her." Amy echoes my accusation, and I feel like a monster.

Mom sandwiches Amy's face between her hands, for a moment unflappable. "You didn't cause this; do you hear me?"

Amy only closes her eyes.

"Do you hear me?"

Amy nods.

"I'm sorry," I mutter, wrecked, numb. "I'm so sorry."

Mom turns to me, hands on my shoulders instead of my face like she's grounding me, holding me down, and though she sounds clear, tears stain her eyes. "I know you need answers, but this stops now."

I nod.

"We can't let this family fall apart."

I nod again.

"Sit down," she says, and I obey.

I can't feel the chair. Can't feel anything. Beth came home. She came home last night, but I didn't see her, and she went back out to die, and it's not Amy's fault, I know it's not, but it can't be mine. I need someone to blame.

I'll find someone to blame.

CHAPTER EIGHTEEN

Amy

(THEN)

Florence pays for an Uber to Boston, and we squeal the whole way there. Nothing this interesting has ever—ever—happened in Massachusetts, and we're not going to miss it.

I tumble out of the car, excitement like soda fizzing through my veins. An art gallery beckons at the end of the block, sophisticated people drifting through the doors. We run toward it, tripping over our feet, then I stop us both. "Wait. Cool. We have to be cool."

Florence tightens her ponytail, hikes up the crop top I let her borrow. "How's my makeup?"

She put it on in the Uber, so her eyeliner's a little rough, but it's not bad. "Your parents would kill you if they saw you like this."

She cracks a devilish smile. "Good."

"And me?" I give her a little spin, show off my leather skirt and band tee.

She pops her thumb. "I think we're ready."

We're not ready. We could never be fully prepared to meet Fred Vaughn, the British art god himself, but we're doing our best. "Slow and confident," I remind her.

My heart beats hard as we glide up the street, and I hope like hell that we're giving "icons in the making" instead of "fifteen-year-olds from Concord High."

When we enter the gallery, I step carefully, expecting pin-drop quiet, but EDM plays over the speakers, and my muscles unravel. This is why Fred Vaughn is my favorite artist. He's not pretentious. He makes art about real life, messy and thrilling, and his music choice proves it.

With hungry senses, I take it all in. The sweet scent of acrylic and canvas. The people who aren't just artists but art themselves.

A man walks by with a tray of red wine, and I swipe a glass without being questioned. The bitterness curls my lips, and I whisper to Florence, "I think this might be the best night of my life."

The gallery holds at least fourteen of Vaughn's original works, all of them vibrant acrylic shapes arranged to look like portraits, triangles and hexagons that somehow feel human and emotive.

I've been obsessed with his work since sixth grade, when Jo gave me a book of contemporary artists for Christmas, and I found a portrait of a girl made only of pink circles, none of which closed. I can't explain why exactly, but I felt like she was me.

We stop at the first painting, and I lose myself in the colors.

It's a portrait of a kid, I think, a massive square for a face. I get the feeling it's about clumsy dreams, not realizing that your head's too big for your body.

"This one's depressing," I say.

Florence isn't paying attention. She scans the room. "I don't see him. Do you?"

I drag my focus away from the painting to search for Fred Vaughn, but the gallery's so crowded, everyone shoulder to shoulder. And then I see it: a pattern of movement, people swirling toward the back of the room.

"There," I say.

"Where?"

I can't see him, but I know he must be tucked in the corner, an epicenter. I take Flo's hand, and we weave through the crowd like we're doing a lap at one of Sallie Gardiner's parties. Sure enough, at the coziest edge of the room, where the music's louder and the lighting's lower, Fred Vaughn greets his guests.

Florence pulls up behind me, her breath warm in my ear. "Is it just me or is he cuter in real life?"

Vaughn looks different in person, younger and, dare I say, hotter. He's wearing baggy jeans cuffed over Converse and a green jacket that looks like a thrift-store find. His hair's chestnut brown, his glasses match, and his five-o'clock shadow makes the final touch.

I turn around immediately. "We can't go over there."

Florence catches my shoulder. "Yes, we can."

"Do you want me to faint?"

She pins her gaze on Vaughn, confident because she knows

she won't have to do the talking. I always take the lead. "Comes on, Ames. We're just as cool as him."

We're not. At all. Fred Vaughn has traveled the world. His paintings have been shown in England, Rome, and Spain. If I'm a free glass of art-gallery red, then Fred Vaughn is an Italian vineyard.

Florence shoves me forward, and I trip into Vaughn's orbit. He catches my elbow, and my wine sloshes, garnet splattering his clean white Converse. "Oh my god." I find my footing. "Oh my god, your shoes. I'm so sorry. I can't believe—"

Vaughn looks at his feet, and I'm sure we'll be thrown out, revealed for the kids that we are. I swear, I can already feel the bouncer's hands beneath my armpits. But Vaughn offers a playful smirk. "Don't think twice. They look better this way. Like a Jackson Pollock."

Florence snorts, but my chest's still caving in. "I'm seriously so sorry."

"I'm Fred Vaughn." He offers his hand like he needs an introduction, like his paintings aren't the screen savers on my laptop.

"We know," Florence giggles.

She reaches around me to shake his hand, but even while she's saying her name, he's staring at me. "You look really familiar," he says. "Have we met?"

I'm speechless for a second, mouth open. Fred Vaughn is looking at me. Talking to me in his buttery British accent. And he doesn't seem to care that I ruined his shoes.

Florence jabs me in the back, and my voice flies out. "No.

Sorry. We haven't met. I wish. I'm a huge fan of your work, especially the girl made of pink circles, I think about her almost every day, and I think your art is something totally new and unexpected, like Rothko and Vermeer had a baby."

Vaughn's smirk sharpens, and I kick myself somewhere deep inside. This is the one quality that Jo and I share, a complete and total inability to shut up.

I start to apologize, but Vaughn cuts me off. "Rothko and Vermeer? Cute couple."

My chest warms, my shoulders easing just a little. "Too bad they're centuries apart."

"You must be an artist," he says.

"Aspiring." I step aside, gesture to Florence. "We both are."

Vaughn flags down the waiter, takes a glass of wine, and sips thoughtfully. "None of that bullshit. If you make art, you're an artist."

Warmth spreads through me, stronger than the wine. I feel dizzy, like I've just been told I won the lottery. "I'm Amy March."

He inhales so sharply he chokes on his drink. "You're Amy March?"

I nod slowly.

"You're one of the little women." It's not a question. He doesn't squint like he's trying to place me. He's read Dad's book. He knows.

Heat rises to my cheeks. I drain what's left of my wine, and though I'm deeply embarrassed, I work hard to hide it. "Guilty as charged."

BETH IS DEAD

Vaughn raises his glass, a throaty laugh. "That's exactly what Amy March would say."

I'm used to this. People talking about me like I'm someone else. I usually hate it, but this time I'm thrilled.

Vaughn throws an arm around my shoulders. "Amy March. Amy March." He tries out my name like it's a new language. "I didn't know I'd be meeting a celebrity tonight."

God, I'm blushing. My cheeks must be straight-up primary red. I shuffle out of his hug. "I'm not a celeb—"

"You're my favorite of all the sisters."

My heart comes to a full stop. I've never heard this, never read it on the internet. People love Jo, love Beth, and some even love Meg, but nobody ever chooses me.

"You know why?" asks Vaughn.

I shake my head, dumbfounded.

"You're unashamed. You are who you are, and I love you for that."

I think of the people who've dragged me online with words like "selfish," "immature," "spiteful," and "whiny."

Unashamed.

That's a new feeling. Something I can carry with pride.

Vaughn swirls his wine and sips. "You know . . ." He peers over the rim. "I'm accepting applications to my summer program."

The whole room seems to fall silent, heat building in my temples. Florence swallows a squeal, and I step in front of her, trying to stay cool. "Summer program?" I ask, as if I've never heard of it before, as if I haven't considered applying a dozen times.

Vaughn nods. "It's brilliant. All summer, nothing but art. We start in London, hop over to Copenhagen, Madrid, Vienna, and so on. We live like a family, one big house, with shared meals. It's a retreat, but it's work. The hardest work you'll ever do."

My veins pulse, my whole body thrumming. I can't imagine anything more magical than apprenticing with Fred Vaughn in the European sunshine, but in the past I've counted myself out. I thought I was too young, too inexperienced as an artist.

Now Vaughn eyes me. "Amy March, one of the little women, in *my* summer cohort. I like the sound of that."

"I'd kill to go," I say.

Vaughn licks his lips. "I get hundreds of applications every year, but it helps that we've met in person. I like your vibe."

I feel warm, spotlighted. I try to act casual, but when I pull a hand through my hair, my fingers get stuck on a tangle. I awkwardly tug them out. "We'll apply."

Vaughn finishes his wine, hands it off. "You damn well better. And you know what? You should stop by my studio. I'm living in Boston for the next few months."

I gape, my words hardly coming out. "That would be amazing."

Vaughn takes my phone from my hand, adds his number, and passes it back. "I should probably circulate, but don't hesitate to text me, love."

Love.

He called me love.

I back up, taking Florence with me, both of us near collapsing. We scurry to the edge of the gallery, where we breathe against the windows.

I grip my forehead, sweaty and crazed. "We have to apply."

Florence whips out her phone, starts googling. "Applications are due in a couple of months. Deposits are due in January."

"Deposits?" I ask.

She keeps scrolling, but my mind has snagged on the mention of money. I can only imagine how much the program might cost. Plane tickets, lodging, meals, tuition.

"How much?" I ask.

She looks at me sideways. "Don't worry about that right now."

"How much?" I insist.

She tilts her phone, and a figure comes into view. It's more than some people spend on a year of college.

"Twenty grand?" The number sounds even higher when I say it out loud.

Florence waves me off. "We'll figure it out."

Easy for her to say. Her parents have money for vacations and fancy cars. My family's living on a nurse's salary, Dad's latest book check donated to some women's charity.

"I'll never be able to go."

Florence laces her arm through mine and leads me around the gallery. "Don't worry about it. We'll come up with a plan. Didn't you say Aunt March was going to pay for Beth's school?"

"Yeah."

"Who's to say she wouldn't pay for this?"

An idea. A prickle of electricity. Aunt March didn't give me the opportunity to audition for Plumfield. But maybe she'd give me this. Maybe I just need to ask.

CHAPTER NINETEEN

Meg

(NOW)

Later, the house is quiet, all of us heavy. We eat the soup that John brought, a few bites swallowed with great effort, and I walk him to the door.

When we're outside, away from the others, I thread my arms under his, listen to his heartbeat. "Don't leave," I say.

He kisses the top of my head. "I don't want to leave."

The news cameras have gone, the street so quiet, I can hear the snow whispering through the trees. It would be beautiful if not for the terror of the day. "Stay with me tonight."

"I can't stay. What about your mom? Your sisters?" He brings me closer, and I think of his apartment, crowded and safe, hardly big enough for the two of us and his piano.

"Take me with you."

"I can't do that," he says.

"Why not?"

He looks at me like I should know the answer. "It's not what you really want."

I hear the ache in his voice, pull back so I can see him. I've been so cruel to John lately, desperate for his company but noncommittal. When we broke up after high school, he said, "You shouldn't let anyone hold you back," and it shattered my heart, but I couldn't argue. I was going to Harvard, and he was going to keep teaching piano lessons. Our futures looked so different.

"I can't be alone," I say.

"I'll come back in the morning."

I clutch him tighter, breathe him in. "I miss you."

"I'm right here."

"I miss you even when you're right here."

He rubs my back with his wide, patient hands. Hands that teach. Hands that make music.

I lean back so I can cup his face in my palms. "Thank you for taking care of Beth. I believe you. I know you brought her home safe."

John's shoulders tighten, a flash of worry through his honey-brown eyes. With a pang of guilt, I realize my mistake. By saying that I believe him, I've implied that someone else might not.

I scramble to reassure him. "Beth needed help last night, and she chose to call you."

He draws a steadying breath. "What if I was the last person to see her?"

A chill reaches the back of my neck. "Talk to the detectives. Tell them everything. It'll be easier that way."

John nods and turns to go, but after a few steps, he looks back. "Meg?"

"Hm?"

"She wanted to back out of Plumfield."

"What?"

"Plumfield."

My heart drops, my stomach along with it. Weeks ago, when John lost his temper, it all started with Plumfield. Beth told him her concerns, and he called her a spoiled brat for even thinking about wasting an opportunity so golden. It was a mistake, and he's told me how deeply he regrets shouting, but if she tried to back out last night, it could've set him off again. At least, that's what the detectives will think.

"Are you sure?" I ask.

He nods. "That's why she called me."

I draw a breath through my nose and imagine the way the cops will view this information. John's a talented musician, but he taught himself to play on YouTube. He never had a teacher, never had a shot at a fancy prep school for artists. And it's true that when Beth neared her audition, Mom hired a more prestigious instructor for a few weeks. Temporary or not, it may look like a slap in the face. "Did you snap again?"

"Meg. No. I swear."

I look him right in the eye. "Really?"

"Really."

"Okay, then. Talk to the detectives. Tell them everything. But her backing out is not important."

He nods, and I hope with all my might that he really understands. No matter what he does, he can't tell the detectives that he and Beth discussed Plumfield just hours, maybe minutes, before she died.

If he does, he'll have a motive.

* * *

When John's gone, I get ready for bed with a pit in my stomach. Annie packed my pajamas, but they're the ones I never wear, itchy and too short.

I drift down the hallway toward the bedroom I share with Jo but stop at the bunk room, where Amy's tucked under a blanket. She gulps every now and then like she's sobbing and trying her best to hide it.

I don't feel like talking, but I can't let her suffer alone, so I climb to the top bunk and snuggle her into my arms.

It's not long before Jo appears in the doorframe, head hanging low. "It's too quiet in our room."

Amy stiffens like she's afraid of Jo, afraid of being blamed again, and this isn't my bed. As much as I want to invite Jo up the ladder, it's not my place.

In the silence, Jo sighs, kicks the carpet. "Look, I know I went too far, and you don't have to forgive me, but I'm so sorry, Amy, and I'm scared, and I'm heartbroken, and I really just need—"

"Come on," Amy concedes, and she open the covers.

Jo doesn't waste a second. She climbs the ladder and wedges herself into the bunk, holding us both. "I'm so, so sorry."

"Me too," says Amy, and the three of us breathe.

After a long time has passed, long enough that I'm able to forget everything outside the bunk, Amy nudges me. "Hey, Meg? Are you and John Brooke, like, together again?"

I almost chuckle. It's so weird to feel a second of joy amid all this grief, but here it is: a tentative flutter in my chest.

Jo sits up, the bunk swaying. "I saw it too."

"While we were eating," says Amy, "I thought you both seemed a little . . ." She trails off, but Jo's never at a loss for words.

"Tangled up," she says.

"We're not together," I say.

"But you're seeing him?"

"We're not together."

"I knew it." Jo smirks like she's oh so clever.

I comb my fingers through my hair, feeling suddenly messy. "We've been talking. Hanging out."

"You're dating," says Jo.

"Not dating."

I don't know how to explain what John and I have been doing. We're friends. Best friends. And in high school, he was my first kiss, first everything. But we're not official. Not in the slightest.

Amy's smile splits in two. "You're totally in love with him."

The statement lights a spark that warms me through. But I say, "I am not."

Jo nods. "Of course you're not. John's just familiar, comfortable."

"He and I are just—"

"Hooking up?" asks Amy.

I swat her arm.

"You're blushing," she presses.

I bury my face in a pillow, hiding from the dim light.

Amy snuggles me, but Jo stays upright. "You can't, Meg. You can't fall in love with John. He's not as smart as you. He's not even going to college."

"That doesn't mean he's not smart." I defend him quickly, a bite in my voice, but deep down, I've thought all the same things. John's a piano instructor taking gigs on the weekends, with no plans for his future, holes in his sweaters. I'm trying to build a life, and he's just living.

Amy leans in. "Is he still a good kisser?"

"Shut up." Jo gags, squirms to the edge of the bunk.

I wrestle her back and exaggerate because she hates getting mushy-gushy. "Honestly, I could kiss him for days."

Amy and I laugh, and soon Jo's laughing too. Laughing until tears run down her cheeks. Until it sounds less like joy and more like pain escaping her body.

"Beth would be happy for you," Amy whispers, a crack in her voice.

Jo wipes her tears, gives a determined nod. "She'd be happy that you're happy."

An image of Beth comes to me, her smile so radiant, it steals my breath, forces a question out of my lungs. "How are we supposed to do this?"

"Do what?" asks Jo.

I should be strong for my sisters, but I need to get this out. It comes quietly, gently, like I'm afraid of putting it into words. "I don't think I can live without her."

Amy lets out a sob, and for the first time all day, the three of us break. It happens slowly at first, Jo sucking in air like she's holding a paper bag over her mouth. Then she gasps into her hands and covers her eyes. I cry so hard that my nose runs and my chest burns.

It hurts.

It hurts so much that I feel like I'm changing, losing sight of the person I was yesterday.

I clutch Jo and Amy, grip them tight, and for just a moment I can almost convince myself that Beth's here in the tangle of arms, and as long as I pretend, I can breathe.

CHAPTER TWENTY

Jo

(NOW)

The day after she's taken from us, a vigil is organized for Beth at the end of our block. We hear about it through the grapevine, all of us from different people, texts pinging in, and it feels like we've been invited to some vulgar party.

Candlelight vigil at eight p.m.
Apple cider and music.
Hope you can make it.

Amy calls bullshit on the affair, stays home with our cousin, Florence, and Mom stays with Aunt Mary, who helps with the awful organization of death—notify Plumfield, call distant family, locate Beth's car, which has been seized as evidence, and find a funeral home that's willing to assist when the investigation is over.

After sundown Meg and I walk through the snow alone.

I'm expecting a small gathering, friends of our family, but candlelight glows from the end of the block, a halo forming over a crowd.

Meg smiles like the turnout's a gift. "This is amazing. All these people here to support us."

For her, it's true. All her old friends are here, droves of college kids who are still home for winter break.

We migrate toward her closest friends, Annie Moffat and some others.

"Who did all of this?" she asks them, basking in the effort.

A framed picture of Beth, flowers laid beneath, Belle Moffat playing violin, the aroma of cinnamon warming the air.

Annie swivels toward us like she has the latest gossip. "Sallie put it together."

Meg folds her hands in gratitude. "That's really thoughtful."

I nearly gag. Of course Sallie Gardiner put this together. She's the hostess with the mostest—graceful, loaded, and known for throwing parties that people talk about for years. I wonder how long people will talk about this.

Annie pulls Meg in close. "How are you feeling? I haven't eaten since you got the call."

Consensus spreads through the group, all the girls nodding, hands over hearts.

Sickness curls through me. All around us, people are crying, arms draped over shoulders, heads bowed in prayer. It feels like a performance, just like what the people who have been posting about Beth on social media are doing. All these distant acquaintances claiming grief.

"This is gross," I say, but Meg isn't listening.

I weave through the crowd clocking everyone who's here—and everyone who's not.

Henry didn't make it. Laurie hasn't come out of his house. And John Brooke is nowhere to be found. It seems like the people who care most about our family couldn't bring themselves to show.

I love them all the more for that.

My stomach turns at the sight of every stranger—people who are only here for the drama. Some dude's even watching from his car, idling up the road like we won't notice him gawking at our misery.

"Take a picture!" I begin to yell at him, but before I can finish the cliché, a hand meets my shoulder.

I jump, whirl around. "Laurie. I thought you weren't here."

His eyes look rounder than usual, full of sorrow. "Sorry. Didn't mean to scare you."

I hug him, but it's clunky, a strange tension remaining between us.

Last summer Laurie admitted what I've always known: he loves me. At the time, I couldn't reciprocate, but I'm trying to get there. Laurie's the greatest pal I've ever known. We push each other to dream bigger, startle each other with the most pointed and honest advice, and take opposite sides of a debate just to have it out. He's witty and whip-smart, and I think the world of him. Maybe love is just that—admiration.

"I'm glad you're here," I say.

"Sorry I'm late. I kept walking to the front door, but I couldn't force myself to come outside."

"I get it."

He looks around, grips the back of his neck. "Is it just me, or is this vigil a little fucked up?"

This.

This is why Theodore Laurence will always be my number one. In a world full of shams, he's real.

"Yeah," I say. "This vigil's a lot fucked up."

We stand for a minute, shoulder to shoulder, the cloying sweetness of violin music drifting over us. Then he turns to face me. "Hey, Jo?"

I'm half listening.

"I need to tell you something." It comes out quickly, roughly, and at the wrong moment, like he's been working up the courage.

I give him my attention, but before he can say another word, Sallie Gardiner taps a mic at the front of the crowd.

She faces us, snow-white skin glowing in the candlelight. She's pretty in the way of people who pay for their looks: expensive clothes, expert makeup, a glossy manicure. "Thank you so much for coming," she starts.

In another life, I might've been friends with Sallie. She's majoring in English literature at Harvard, and she's obsessed with Jane Austen. We might've gotten along if she weren't a Gardiner, worried about galas and charity dinners, her sorority at Harvard.

She draws a sad breath. "Tonight we gather to remember our dearest Beth March."

I look at Laurie, stomach twisting.

Sallie hardly knew Beth, only through Meg, but she

talks like they were terribly close and starts to share stories that don't ring true. Through tears, she remembers a time when Beth asked her for advice about boys. A time when she borrowed a dress. "And, oh, wasn't it cute when she performed in the Christmas pageant? I was the angel once. I taught her the dance."

I could vomit, retch, lose my insides right on my boots. Sallie Gardiner's giving a eulogy. A eulogy! This should've been my job. I'm Beth's sister—and a writer for god's sake.

"I can't watch this," I say, and shove through shoulders. A phone's knocked from someone's hand, apple cider spilling on the sidewalk.

"Jo, wait!" Laurie follows me, the crowd parting.

And then Meg, her footsteps light and quick. "Jo, what's wrong? Are you okay?"

I turn on my heel. "Of course I'm not okay. Nothing about this is okay."

Meg softens. "I know it's hard, but—"

"Don't you think it's weird? She's acting like she knew Beth—really *knew* her."

"Who? Sallie?"

Meg can be so dense. All those years spent in Sallie Gardiner's clique. Even Beth, who could see the best in everyone, saw Sallie for the mean girl she's always been. Lording over Meg and the others. Using her money to stay on top.

I lower my voice, seething now. "Beth hated Sallie. And Beth was always an excellent judge of character."

"That's not fair," says Meg.

"Look around. This vigil isn't about our sister. Sallie's doing it for herself."

"How can you say that?"

Meg acts like grief isn't a badge of honor, but I swear, it is. I've written loads of personal essays in my life, some light, some dark, and the ones that get compliments, real traction, are the ones about pain, strife. In July I wrote one about being watched, the recording device taped in our house, and it went viral.

Like it or not, suffering makes a person interesting.

"Amy was right," I shout. "This is bullshit."

Laurie shoves his hands in the pockets of his puffer, voice tight in my ear. "Maybe we should go."

Heads turn, murmurs through the crowd.

Sallie glides toward us. She's done with her speech, and she looks worried—worried that I'm ruining her perfect party. "What's going on?" she asks.

"Nothing," says Meg.

I get right in Sallie's face, gesture to the crowd. "Why did you do this?"

She looks around, an innocent blue-eyed blink. "What do you mean? I thought you'd appreciate it."

"You and Beth were never close."

Sallie draws a sharp breath, like I punched her in the ribs, but she quickly regains her composure. "I understand why you're upset. I'd lose my mind if I lost my sister."

"You don't have a sister!"

She swallows hard, sleek black hair falling from its bun. "No. You're right. I'm not lucky enough to have a sister, but Meg

BETH IS DEAD

and I have been friends since kindergarten. I can't remember a time before I knew Beth. We may not have been family, but I loved her, and she died after my party. This is the least I can do."

Tears roll down Sallie's porcelain cheeks, and I'm so angry, I could slap them off.

Then it hits me—a shock all the way down my spine.

She died after my party.

At once I'm sure. Sallie didn't host this vigil for attention. She's trying not to look guilty.

CHAPTER TWENTY-ONE

Meg

(NOW)

When we get home from the vigil, Jo's livid and unbearable.

I boil water for tea, trying hard to stay calm, but I had to practically drag her away from the crowd, my gaping friends.

She circles the kitchen island, right on my heels. "Meg, I know you're mad, but Sallie Gardiner—"

"Is one of my best friends."

"She's acting suspicious. Overcompensating."

I stop, steel my shoulders. "I'm so tired of making excuses for you."

"Excuses?"

"You embarrassed me."

Jo levels her gaze, anger sharpening. "Well, I'm sorry you're embarrassed, but Beth is dead."

I flinch, her words like a slap.

"Sallie knows something," says Jo. "I can feel it."

The kettle begins to whistle, a gentle whine. I talk over it. "Sallie would never hurt Beth."

"Maybe not, but if something happened at her party, she might cover it up."

I stiffen, considering the pressure Sallie's been under since we were kids. Once, when we were side by side at a sleepover, she told me, "I wish I didn't have to be a Gardiner." Her parents met at Harvard, and now her dad's a big-shot corporate lawyer, and her mom's a respected professor of English literature. They have a house on Nantucket, an apartment in Paris, and they expect Sallie and her brother, Ned, to maintain their reputation for excellence.

"No." I shake my head. "If Sallie knows anything, she'll tell the police."

Jo doesn't seem convinced. "What if she's afraid? What if there was some kind of accident? A fight? What if she's a witness?"

My heart beats hard against my sternum, but I keep shaking my head. "Beth didn't die at the party. John drove her home."

"Even if that's true, she didn't stay home. She went back out, back toward the Gardiners.'"

My throat tightens. "You didn't find her at the Gardiners'. You found her on the hill by Laurie's house."

"Think, Meg!" Jo slaps the counter. "Any number of things could've happened. Someone could've moved her."

The kettle screams. I'm stunned for a second before I snatch it off the stove, weighed down by the image of someone dragging Beth's limp body. "How can you think about that?"

"We have to think about every angle," says Jo.

I pour the tea, hands trembling. "I don't want to talk about this anymore."

"We need to find out what Sallie knows."

"I won't interrogate my friends."

Jo slumps against the refrigerator, arms crossed. "Fine. But if you don't, I will."

"You can't."

She thinks for a moment, a brief respite. "Do you remember when Beth came to see you at school?"

The memory comes back with so much beautiful force that my eyes burn. Beth driving up to Harvard, staying the night in my apartment, convincing me to watch reality TV instead of studying, a break I desperately needed.

Jo paces. "I never told you about this, but she came home really upset."

"What?" My breath catches.

"She was worried about you. Said you hadn't been sleeping. Said it had something to do with Sallie."

"That's ridiculous." I grip my mug and stare into my tea.

"Beth thought Sallie wasn't a good friend. Thought she was taking advantage of you."

"She's not."

"You scrub the toilets, don't you?"

I shrug, my cheeks going hot. "I clean the apartment because I pay less rent. It's only fair."

Jo looks disgusted. "Sallie uses people."

It's not true. Sallie doesn't use people, people use Sallie. For her money, her influence. Once, she looked at me with tears in her eyes and said, "I'm not sure I have any true friends."

I turn to leave the kitchen, sick of talking.

Jo follows. "What if Beth confronted Sallie about your unbalanced friendship?"

I set my mug down with so much force that the tea sloshes out. "Drop it, Jo."

"Aren't you desperate to know what happened?"

"Of course I am. But I'm not going to turn against my best friend, and I'd appreciate it if my own sister didn't turn against me."

Jo softens for a second, and I grab my coat off the back of the couch.

"What're you doing?" she asks.

"I need to pick up my car, swing by my apartment."

"Now?"

"I only packed for a couple of days."

It's a thin excuse. I haven't been home for long, but really, I need to be alone. To get away until I feel like myself again.

Jo presses. "You can borrow whatever—"

"I want my own clothes, Jo, and I need a minute, just a minute, to myself. Is that so hard to understand?"

Jo looks wounded, defeated, and for a brief moment I feel guilty. She's managing her pain by churning out theories, but I can't take it. Especially not when her theories involve my mistakes.

CHAPTER TWENTY-TWO

Meg

(THEN)

I can't wait to get out of the apartment.

It's like this every weekend lately, a mad dash from my room to my car, a gnawing desire to leave Harvard in my rearview. I thought college would be the best years of my life, but I've never been so tired, my eyes constantly burning, my mind reduced to sludge.

And there's nothing worse than living with Sallie, the constant reminder that she pays substantially more for the apartment we share, that Annie and I owe her. Especially me.

"Sallie's looking for you," says Annie as I run out the door.

My heart skips a beat, but I pretend not to hear. Sallie's looking for me because I promised her something important, but I can't handle it tonight. I have somewhere to be.

John's apartment sits three stories up in the cozy heart of Allston-Brighton. It's a college neighborhood—mostly Boston University and Northeastern students—where he moved to get better gigs. And to get out of his parents' house.

When he opens the door, I hug him fast, inhaling his familiar scent. He's wearing a T-shirt that's been washed too many times, glasses with tape around the bridge.

He chuckles, staggers back. "Someone had a rough week."

"Do I ever have a good week?"

"You need rest. Maybe you should change your major—"

I cut him off with a sharp shake of my head. I'd never change my major, not when the world needs me more than ever. Who better to become a women's health professional than the daughter of a nurse, the oldest of four sisters? And anyway, my major isn't my problem.

I peer up at John, swipe the glasses off his nose. "You need to get these fixed."

"Too bad you're not Hermione."

He doesn't have the money to fix anything. His glasses, his weathered shoes, his laptop that glitches every time we watch a movie.

"I brought pizza coupons." I unearth them from my bag.

"Papa Gino's?"

"I wouldn't suggest anything else."

Just the thought of Papa Gino's brings me back to high school, late nights after football games, John and I crammed into a booth, greasy fingers and full hearts.

As long as I've known him, he's been my escape, a respite from the pressure of being friends with Annie Moffat and Sallie Gardiner, from clawing toward the world of platinum credit cards and trust funds.

"Finish your ethics paper?"

I'm staring out the window, a dreamy view of the neighborhood, my thoughts loosening. "God, I wish. I'm still working on Shakespeare."

John stops at the fridge, two sodas in hand. "Shakespeare?"

The street narrows, and a dog barks down below. I turn around slowly, heat rising to my cheeks. "Oh, um..."

"I didn't know you were taking Shakespeare."

I tuck my chin, working hard to hide my panic. "I didn't tell you?" My voice comes out an octave too high.

He shakes his head.

"I've been taking it all semester. Don't you remember? I had to perform a scene from *Romeo and Juliet*? I was freaking out for weeks."

John fixes me with a look of bewilderment. "I don't remember that."

It never happened, of course, but he pinches his brow like he's trying to recall.

Guilt swirls through my stomach.

"You want pepperoni?" I open his laptop and pull up Papa Gino's website, desperate to change the subject. "We can even get olives," I add. "Just this once."

A smile tugs at the corner of his mouth. "Green olives?"

To me, green olives are worse than anchovies. They'll ruin the pizza, but if they'll stop him from prying, I'll eat them on every bite. "Green olives it is."

John cracks his soda, and I jump at the sound.

"Sorry," I laugh, but it sounds manic. "I'm so tired."

He chuckles along with me, but as it peters out, his concern comes back. "Hey, Meg?"

I pretend to be focused, finishing the order, but our confirmation sits on the screen. "Thanks, from your Papa Gino's family!" I can't look at John, can't let him see me.

He reaches for my hands, eases them off the laptop. "Are you okay?"

I flash a smile, widening my eyes to look awake. "Of course."

"If something was wrong, you'd tell me, right?"

"Nothing's wrong," I say, but pressure gathers behind my eyes. "I'm just tired. My course load's insane this semester."

My phone buzzes next to us.

Sallie.

I can't read the whole text, but I see enough to feel sick.

Meg, wtf?

John squints, his broken glasses sitting sideways on his nose. "I wish you didn't hang out with her so much."

I snatch my phone so he can't read the message. "She's my roommate."

"I've never liked those girls."

He's talking about Sallie, Annie, their whole crew. In high school, I would've done anything to be one of them. I still want what they have, vacations in faraway places, enough money to stop worrying—but their friendship gets harder every day.

"Forget about Sallie," I say.

She texts me again, the buzzing impossibly loud.

"She's always bugging you."

I get up from the table, slide my phone into my pocket.

"She's not bugging me. She's just making plans. There's a frat party—"

"Fun." John rolls his eyes.

A part of me loves the way he rejects all things college. He's a reminder that none of it matters as much as it seems.

"I think you'd like frat parties." I grab my soda off the table, crack it, and sip. "We practically have one right here."

John makes a show of glancing around his apartment. "Really? I don't see a single rich assho—"

"Rich assholes are optional. In actuality, frat parties only require three components: drinks"—I lift my soda can—"music"—I gesture to John's piano, which takes up most of his cramped apartment.

"And the third?" he asks.

I tease him with a smile. "You'll have to wait. Every fraternity has customs that only the inner circle can learn."

He moves closer, a sly smile. "How do I join the inner circle?"

The evening sun warms the space between us. I kiss his cheek, gentle and quick. "Play me something."

John moves to the piano, the leather bench worn in the middle from the hours he's spent practicing. "Anything in particular?"

I look at him like he should know.

"Again?" he asks.

I shrug, because no matter how many times he plays my favorite piece, it'll always be my favorite.

He lets the first note of "Clair de Lune" ring out, and I'm

transported to high school, John teaching Beth in our living room. I thought about him constantly back then, coming up with reasons to pass by the piano: carrying laundry, opening windows, walking outside to check the mail.

I had such a terrible crush that I couldn't exhale until we finally started dating. Even now, we relax when we're together, like otters holding hands while they sleep.

He plays, and I imagine his fingers on my lips, my cheek, the crest of my hip. He glances up at me, his hands so practiced, he doesn't need to look at the piano. "You okay?"

"Just thinking." I sit beside him, set my phone on the coffee table.

"About?"

"The third element of frat parties."

John's fingers slow on the keys, the piece lagging. "Have I earned the answer?"

I lean toward him, my heartbeat drawing out. "I think so."

"Meg." He says my name, half longing, half questioning, like he's not sure what I want. We've been hanging out for weeks, but we haven't kissed. Not since our senior year of high school.

Our lips meet slowly at first, and then urgently, like we're making up for lost time.

"What are we doing?" he asks.

"I don't know." I can hardly speak, my whole body alight.

Eyes closed, I picture us behind the football stadium, outside the science lab, in the back of his cherry-red Ford. We're different now, older, more complicated, and somehow that makes the moment even better.

He moves me toward him, his hands on my hips. We kiss on the piano bench until we can't get close enough, then we stumble toward the couch.

My phone lights up on the table, and as we lower down, I catch a glimpse of Sallie's latest texts.

We're out of time.

Literally. Where the fuck are you?

I grope for my phone and turn it over.

John cradles my head. "Sallie again?"

"Don't worry about it."

"Give me your phone. I'll call her. Tell her you're busy."

He's joking, but a lightning bolt cracks through my chest. John can't get involved, can't find out what Sallie and I are doing.

He holds me tighter, and I try to come back to him. We kiss again, his hands in my hair, and he lets out a joyful laugh. "I've missed you so much."

"I've missed you too," I say, but it sounds flat.

He pulls back. "Are you okay?"

I nod, but I feel like I'm going to cry. "Yeah. Sorry. I'm just—"

He sits up. "We can stop."

"I just need to answer that text."

"Are you serious?"

"I'm sorry."

I reach past him and find a new barrage of messages.

I swear, Meg.

If you embarrass me.

I'm gonna fucking kill you.

I respond.

I'm at the library.

I'll get it done.

She comes back too quickly, like she's been staring at her phone.

I'm coming.

Oh god, why did I mention the library? Why did I have to lie? I stand up, heat rushing through me. Heart racing, I scramble across John's apartment, find my bag, my jacket.

"Where are you going?" he asks.

I can hardly catch my breath. "I'm sorry, I'm so sorry, but I have to go to the library."

"Why? Is it Sallie?"

"I have to finish something."

He stays on the couch, confused, wounded.

"I'm sorry," I say again while I'm halfway out the door. "Next weekend?"

He nods, but it's not a yes. He's processing, realizing he's not my priority. "Next weekend," he says, and it breaks my heart in two, because next weekend won't be any different. Sallie will still have me in a choke hold.

CHAPTER TWENTY-THREE

Amy

(NOW)

While the others go to the vigil, Florence keeps me company. She hauls a bag of candy up to my room, gummy for me, chocolate for her, and we shut the door like we can shut out reality.

At first I can't settle down. I keep glancing at my shoes like I'm going to shove them on and run down the street, but my stomach aches at the thought of memorializing Beth, and I can't imagine seeing people from school, seeing Laurie.

I lie on the rug, bite the head off a gummy frog, and stare at the ceiling. "I'm glad we're not going."

Florence peels open a Snickers bar, agrees through a full mouth. "Beth would've hated it."

"Totally," I say, but I'm not so sure.

Beth loved apple cider, and she would've loved to hear Belle Moffat playing the violin. I can picture her shutting her eyes, and exhaling. "Wow, this is beautiful." But she would have hated being the center of attention. At least that much is true.

I chew for a while, unsure of what to say. Earlier today Florence showed up with Aunt Mary and a cheesy-rice casserole, and we all cried in the formal living room, saying things like, "She's in a better place," and, "God doesn't give us more than we can handle," but Florence and I haven't talked for real. That's always harder.

"Hey, Flo?"

She turns to look at me, yellow hair splayed out on the rug. Since she's not allowed to wear makeup, she's always fully herself in a way that's both comforting and startling.

"How much did you hear?" I ask.

"Of what?"

"The fight. Beth and me."

Florence fidgets with her candy wrapper. "I was downstairs at first. I didn't hear that much."

I sit up, clutch a pillow in my lap. "I'm really scared."

"Why?" She props up on her elbows, a look of sympathy on her clean face.

My voice gets quiet and thick. "I think I might've caused it. Caused her death."

Florence moves across the rug, shaking her head. "Amy, what are you talking about?"

"We had never fought like that before. Beth was so upset. Mom said it looked like someone hit her, like it was murder, but she could've jumped off the bridge. It's a long way down from the top."

Florence grabs my hands. "Amy, come on. She didn't jump."

"Maybe not. But even then, Beth was drunk, and after our fight, she probably had more. She could've stumbled."

"Amy—"

"A bunch of the guys were talking about an after-party when I left. What if they went to the park? What if Beth went to hang out with them because I told her she'd never done anything exciting? And what if—"

"Amy, breathe."

My voice breaks. "I'll never be able to tell her I'm sorry."

Florence wraps me in her arms, and I cry into her shoulder. My mascara stains her shirt, but I can't get a grip.

"It's okay," she says. "It's okay."

I cry until my eyes hurt and my nose runs, and when I can finally slow down my breathing, I lean against the bunk. "Everyone's right about me. I'm a horrible person."

Florence chews her lip like she's holding something back.

"What?" I ask.

"Nothing. It would be wrong to admit."

"Tell me."

She weighs her words. "Okay. What happened to Beth is a horrible tragedy, and hindsight is obviously twenty-twenty, but I think you said what needed to be said."

A momentary burst of relief, vindication. I swallow hard to keep it down. "No—"

"I'm sorry, but it's true. Beth was never ambitious, but you and I have real dreams."

A stone lands in the pit of my stomach. Europe. Fred Vaughn's summer program. When Florence and I got our acceptance emails, I felt like I'd stepped into the light. We were planning to see London, Madrid, Vienna, and more. To soak up Fred Vaughn's brilliance and make art that would launch our careers.

My chest feels hollow. "None of those dreams matter anymore."

"Are you kidding?" Florence rises to her feet, voice swelling with urgency. "They matter more than ever."

I glance at the door, afraid Mom and Aunt Mary will hear downstairs. I haven't told my family about Europe, not yet. I figured I'd have time to get the money, figured it would all work out in the end.

"Florence," I whisper, exhausted. "My sister died."

Her stark face turns pink, frustration spreading. "I know that. You think I don't know that?"

"We're not going to Europe."

"Beth would've wanted you to live your life."

"You have no idea what she would've wanted."

"She was my cousin."

"It's not the same." As soon as the words leave my mouth, I wish I could take them back. Florence doesn't have siblings. She lives alone with Aunt Mary and Uncle Carlos, and she's told me time and time again that she wishes she could be one of us. The fifth March sister. "Flo, I'm sorry."

She looks hurt, her straw-colored hair curtaining her face. "It's fine. I get it. You're grieving."

"That's no excuse."

She crosses her arms, tears spilling from the corners of her eyes. "I was really excited about Europe. You and me together."

A lump forms in my throat. Excited doesn't begin to cover

how I felt about Europe. The promise of that trip turned me into a different person. An artist. Someone confident enough to spend time with Fred Vaughn. He's been telling me about his former protégé, Kitty Bryant, a girl from London with hooded eyes and sharp black bangs. She completed his summer program years ago, and now she's selling paintings to multimillionaires. "I think you might be the next Kitty," he said to me once.

Florence moves back to the floor, finds my eyeline. "Promise me you'll think about it."

My throat's too tight to answer.

"Fred will be devastated if we back out now."

I look at my cousin sideways. "Since when do you call him Fred?"

She shrugs like it's no big deal, but I don't even call him by his first name, and I've spent a lot more time with him.

Florence reaches for the candy, takes a gummy frog, and twists the leg off. "We've worked too hard to give up now."

She has a point, but my insides feel scrambled. Beth would want me to live my life, but it feels sick to live the dream that might've led her to death.

CHAPTER TWENTY-FOUR

(NOW)

Sunday morning, bright and early, I wake up with a plan. I need to investigate Sallie Gardiner, and with any luck, she and her brother, Ned, will be at church. They're not the kind of people who actually follow the rules of their savior—be kind, help others—but they post pictures of mission trips, and every Sunday they go to services.

While Mom and my sisters are still waking up, I sneak out of our house, through the park, and up the road to hide behind the Gardiners' massive hedges. A mansion like this should really have cameras, but that's the thing about Concord—the richest families tend to be the most complacent.

Sallie's room glows at the front of the house. As far as I can tell, she's not home. Her car's gone, Ned's too, and though their parents' cars are parked in the garage, I'm almost certain they're still in Paris.

I crouch low and think through my memory of the house. I've only visited once on New Year's Eve, but I remember a back door with a broken lock.

I circle the mansion and jiggle the handle, but of course, it's been fixed. And so I lift doormats and tip stone animals in search of a key.

Then I see it.

A window open on the second floor.

With a little boost, I could climb. Just a few careful footholds would get me to a pergola, where I could shimmy sideways through the window. With my grace, I'm bound to fall, but I can't think about that right now. I have to get inside.

Heart in my throat, I move a chair, grip the pergola, and hoist myself up. My arms tremble, but I manage to wrench myself to the top, lie flat on my belly, and wriggle over to the window, legs dangling.

There, I look down, and it's a big mistake. I feel weak, queasy, but I pull hard, swing my legs, and fall across the windowsill with a heavy thud.

The house feels empty, but I brace for a moment until I'm sure, and then I creep down the hallway. The rooms feel so different when they're not packed with partiers. Each of them is decorated like a room in a catalog, lovely and lonely.

I have no idea what I'm looking for, but when I make it to Sallie's room, a chill works down my spine. The place looks perfect in every way. Bed made, off-season clothes hanging neatly at the back of her closet, dressage ribbons gracing the walls.

I scan the decor and stop at a picture of Meg, a news article about the Harvard Three. ". . . and leading the pack, Sallie Gardiner has been selected as the winner of Harvard's admissions essay contest. The dean of admissions said, 'Her perspective on Jane Austen's body of work offers a fresh angle on feminism and success in the modern world.'"

I forgot about this.

I find the essay framed on Sallie's wall and read it top to bottom. I wish it were terrible, but it's so moving, I'm nearly in tears when I reach the final sentence. Sallie's a dud in person, but I must admit, she's a damn good writer.

I search the rest of her room, a desk and a small library, and just when I'm about to move to her dresser, it hits me. Something's missing.

I scan her library again, a finger traveling the spines. Sallie owns a paltry collection, mostly books we're assigned at school, and she doesn't own any Jane Austen. I glance back at her essay, and my stomach does a somersault.

But no. I need to calm down. I'm jumping to conclusions. Seeing what I want to see. Sallie could've taken her Jane Austen novels to Harvard. That's it. She must keep them in her apartment.

But what if she doesn't?

What if she's never read a word of *Pride and Prejudice*? I think of news stories about admissions scandals, services that help rich kids get into college. Fudging transcripts, altering athletic records, ghostwriting award-winning essays.

My heart thumps hard in my throat, a swelling feeling.

That would give her something to hide.

I head for the door, ready to leave, when a stray detail catches my eye. A letterman jacket sits beneath Sallie's bed, a torn sleeve that I recognize all too well, the fabric gaping like a smile.

My heart falls as I sink to my knees and reel the thing in. It smells familiar, like mint and eucalyptus. A lump forms in my throat, pressure behind my eyes. Just when I thought I had answers, the questions have changed.

Footsteps in the hallway followed by a voice. "Sallie?"

It's Ned, Sallie's brother, his voice tight and sharp.

"Sallie, is that you?"

I run from the room and down the back steps, Ned plodding close behind. "Sallie, wait. Please. We need to talk."

I tear into the snow and dart to a thicket of trees. My lungs burn, but I don't stop, the jacket tucked under my arm. There must be an explanation, but I can't imagine it now. I know who owns this jacket—and on the night of the party, he promised he was staying home.

CHAPTER TWENTY-FIVE

(THEN)

I'm a freshman in high school, and if you ask Meg, that matters for one reason and one reason only—I'm finally invited to Sallie Gardiner's New Year's Eve party.

Meg stands in front of the mirror, her fourth outfit change. "Would you call this fairycore?"

"Fairy what?"

"Sallie told us to dress fairycore. Am I doing it?" Meg shoves her phone in my face, an inspiration board complete with shimmery dresses, long braids, and flower crowns.

I tip my head and squint briefly at her sequined dress and butterfly clips. "Yeah, yeah, you're doing it."

She groans. "Jo, be serious."

"Because fairycore is so serious."

Meg races around our room, tossing clothes onto her bed.

I slump onto my own bed in jeans, a brown crop top, and an oversized blazer. "If we don't leave soon, I'm changing too. Into my pajamas."

"Oh, shut up." Amy appears in the doorframe. She sinks wistfully to the floor, a strand of blond hair twined around her finger. "You're so lucky you're invited."

Meg swaps her dress for a tighter one, compares herself to the inspiration board. "You'll be invited too, in a couple of years."

Amy whines, "Ned's my age, and he gets to go."

"Ned lives there," I say flatly. "He doesn't have a choice."

Meg seems satisfied with her outfit but returns to the closet. This time she holds a handful of dresses up in my direction. "Jo, can't you at least try to be on theme?"

I glance down at my neutral outfit. "I am on theme. I'm dressed like a mushroom."

Meg huffs and drops the dresses at my feet. "If you're not going to change, then you can't be seen with me."

"What makes you think I'd want to be seen with you?" I sound brash and confident, but deep down, I'm afraid of showing up at this party unless I'm tucked behind Meg. I've been going to Concord schools since kindergarten, and I thought I had friends, but somewhere along the way, people started hanging out on the weekends, not just during class, and I missed the memo.

Meg shoots me a dull, flat look. "Are you ready?"

"Oh, Meg, you look so pretty." Beth sighs, rests her head on the door, her hair more strawberry than blond in the evening light. "And, Jo, you look so cool." She says it without an ounce of irony, which is why I've always loved her best.

"Remember everything so you can come home and tell us."

BETH IS DEAD

To my surprise, Beth sounds almost as jealous as Amy.

I'm jealous of *them*. They're both wearing silly paper crowns with the new year printed on top, beads draped around their necks. Mom's not working this year, and Dad turned in a manuscript last week, so they'll be counting down to midnight together.

I hop off the bed and plod to the top of the stairs. "Let's leave before I change my mind."

Meg slings an arm around my shoulder and squeals, and for just a moment as we run down the stairs, I almost share her rush of excitement. Maybe this night will change things for me, maybe I'll make some friends.

Mom tells us to be careful, forces me to put on a coat. Dad's in front of *Dick Clark's New Year's Rockin' Eve*, Ryan Seacrest interviewing a crowd about the year to come, but he's not watching. Instead, he's scribbling in a notebook.

"Dad, I thought you turned in your manuscript."

"Mm-hmm," he says.

"What're you working on?"

He struggles to pull his focus off the page. "Nothing. Just a new idea. Had to get it down."

Mom bristles, and I think of an argument they've had more than once lately. Mom feeling underappreciated, unimportant, and Dad saying, "I'm sorry. It's my job."

It's not untrue. His editor's always pressuring him for his next manuscript.

I slide a silly paper crown onto his head before we file out the door. With any luck, it'll remind him to stay in the moment.

Snow blankets the neighborhood, so Meg and I take the shortcut up the bridge behind Laurie's house and through the park. The Gardiner mansion thuds from afar, music playing so loudly, the whole neighborhood could dance. When we reach the circle drive, a group of girls spills from the front door, swallows Meg up, and carries her inside like a mutant wave.

"Have fun," I say under my breath. "Oh, you too," I say back to myself in a high-pitched imitation of Meg. "And Happy New Year."

"Who are you talking to?"

A voice meets my ear, gentle but self-assured.

I wheel around to face Theodore Laurence, dark skin and dark eyes, a smile almost as sideways as mine. I've seen him around the neighborhood since he moved here at the beginning of freshman year. Heard his parents are diplomats stationed overseas, and they insisted that he complete high school here in the States. But we've never actually talked. He and his grandmother mostly keep to themselves.

"It's rude to eavesdrop," I say.

He smirks. "On the conversation you were having with yourself?"

"There's no one else to talk to."

"It's a party."

"Exactly."

He looks amused. "You're Josephine March, aren't you?"

I bristle at the sound of my full name, suitable only for future book covers and—according to Mom—wedding invitations. "I'm Jo. Only Jo. And you're Theodore, aren't you?"

He nods. "Most people call me Laurie. Only Laurie."

"Laurie?"

"Sports nickname." He adjusts his letterman jacket, the shoulders still stiff and brand-new.

I angle myself away from him, weighing whether or not to walk away. "Tell me you're not one of those jerks on the lacrosse team."

Laurie turns his nose up. "You think I'd hang out with those guys?"

"I don't know you well enough to—"

"I row crew."

It's still a pretentious sport, but I picture the river, cool and gleaming in the early morning sun, and the image seems to suit Laurie, his thoughtful composure.

He tips his head toward the front door. "You want to grab a soda or something?"

I take a step forward but can't quite put weight on my foot. There are so many people inside, and all of them seem to know exactly what to do at a party. The girls all followed the fairycore theme, ridiculous sparkles and wings, and they sip from red Solo cups while they dance in tight clumps.

"Okay, here's the thing."

Laurie glances back, expectant.

"I'm a terrible dancer. Really bad. Maybe the worst."

"Who said anything about dancing?"

"Well, that's the natural progression of things, isn't it? We grab a soda, and then we start dancing?"

Laurie has a light behind his eyes that seems to switch on every time I speak.

"You think I'm funny," I say.

"I think you're . . ." He considers for a moment. "A breath of fresh air."

The metaphor catches me off guard. It's clichéd for sure—not poetry or anything close—but I never expected to hear it from a guy at a party, especially not one as shy as Theodore Laurence, who speaks only when teachers call on him.

He offers a hand, and I take it to weave through the living room. We pour sodas and stand at the edge of a rug that's somehow been designated as a dance floor.

Laurie leans toward me. "Okay, here's the thing. . . ."

It's not lost on me, the way he repeats what I said on the front porch. Laurie's clever, and it's not often you meet someone clever in Concord.

". . . These parties are the best place to dance, because nobody's paying attention to anybody else. We could do cartwheels in the middle of the room, and they wouldn't even see us."

I laugh at the thought, a cartwheel through all this bumping and grinding. "Prove it," I say.

"What?" Laurie laughs.

"Prove it. Do a cartwheel right through the middle of the rug. If you're successful, I'll dance with you." I rest against the wall, certain I'll never have to move a muscle.

But Laurie hands me his drink.

He observes the group for a moment as if to identify

safe passage through the tangle of arms and legs. The music escalates, some sort of EDM that Amy would love and I can't stand, and as it gets higher and faster, the dancing gets larger and more erratic.

I move to make Laurie call off the cartwheel, but before I can tap his shoulder, he dives. His hands meet the rug, his legs catapult upward, and just as he crests, his feet peeking up above a sea of heads, he crumples.

"Laurie!" I bust through the crowd, wondering if I should laugh or call an ambulance.

When I see his face, I know for sure.

He crouches on the rug, wearing a smug expression like he deserves a gold medal. "Did you see that?" he asks.

I let out a laugh so loud, you can almost hear it over the music. Laurie's cheeks are flushed, and his letterman jacket's ripped. I point to the sleeve. "Um . . ."

He holds it up, and the fabric gapes like a smile. "I like it better this way."

"You're ridiculous," I say.

"What?"

"You're ridiculous," I say louder.

He taps his ear like he still can't hear me. And so, on the floor in the midst of a dancing crowd, I decide to lean in and say something else. "You're a breath of fresh air."

CHAPTER TWENTY-SIX

(NOW)

Back home, I stand motionless in the hallway with Laurie's letterman jacket in my arms. I don't understand why he would lie about going to the party. We don't lie to each other about anything. Once, we sat on the rug in his room and expelled all our secrets, big and small. I told him that I'm afraid I'm not as clever as people think, and he told me that his parents broke his heart. That he wishes they wanted to live as a family no matter how much better his schooling is here. We share our deepest shames and insecurities, but a party? He lied about a party?

"I just want to celebrate with my grandmother." That's what he said to me on New Year's Eve, and I never doubted him, not for a second.

But he was at the party.

In Sallie's bedroom.

His letterman jacket forgotten on the floor.

Amy stalks out of her room but stops when she sees me. "What are you doing?"

I should be doing something, but I'm stuck in the hallway, my thoughts like a story half erased. I thought I knew Laurie down to his bones, but he's been lying about the night Beth died. The most life-altering night in all my eighteen years.

"Nothing," I say to Amy. "What are *you* doing?"

She shrugs, head tipped toward the bathroom. "Have to pee."

"Go ahead," I say.

Amy crosses the hall and sits on the toilet. Our bathroom's not big, and though Amy's mostly concealed, I can still see her face. "Is that Laurie's jacket?" she asks.

I nod.

"Why do you have it?"

My mind moves slowly, every thought a new ache. "Was Laurie at the party?"

Amy leans out of view, rustles the toilet paper. "Laurie?"

"I found his jacket at the Gardiners' house."

Amy moves quickly to zip her jeans. "Why were you at the Gardiners' house?"

"He told me he didn't go to the party."

Amy flushes and washes her hands, palms rubbing hard like she's trying to get a spark. "What were you doing at the Gardiners' house?"

"Looking for evidence."

Amy winces. "Tell me you didn't break in."

"Back to Laurie."

"You can't just break into people's houses."

"But Laurie—"

"Hangs out with Ned every now and then." Amy practically shouts. "They row crew together."

The jacket feels lighter in my grip but only for second. "I found it under Sallie's bed."

Amy towels her hands, huffy. "You and Laurie haven't talked lately."

I stiffen, a tightening in my gut. "What's that supposed to mean?"

Amy shoves past me. "It means what it means. You and Laurie haven't been hanging out as much. You don't know what's going on in his life."

I hold Laurie's jacket a little tighter, and my heart sinks like silt falling to the bottom of a lake. Amy's nasty, but she's right. I'd do anything to rekindle the friendship that Laurie and I once had—the truth telling, the roughhousing, the raucous, life-giving laughter—but when he told me he loved me, I ruined it all. "I guess that's true," I say.

Amy stops short of the bunk room, and we're both quiet for a moment. In the next room, Meg's binge-watching Beth's favorite show, a laugh track haunting the hallway.

Amy looks worried. "Has she been watching that all night?"

I shrug, but I'm worried too. "It's not the worst thing she could be doing."

Amy watches Meg's door for a beat, then returns her focus to me. "Jo, why did you go to the Gardiners' house?"

Thoughts of Laurie still surround me like water, slow me down. I think of us skating on Walden Pond, performing uproarious two-person plays in the attic for no audience at all, and slipping jokes into each other's lockers to see who could get the bigger laugh.

But I can't let the memories take hold.

I force myself back to what felt like a lead. "You remember Sallie's Harvard admissions essay?"

Amy lets out a flat laugh. "How could I forget? They made the whole school annotate it. Jane Austen, right?"

"Sallie didn't have a single Jane Austen novel in her room."

Amy cocks her head. "Maybe she keeps them in—"

"Her apartment—I thought of that—but it's bothering me. What if Sallie didn't write that essay?"

Amy pauses, a quick tip of her head. "Okay, sure. But what does that have to do with Beth?"

I lean against the wall, stringing my thoughts together. "I've been thinking about that weekend when Beth went to visit Meg at school."

"I remember," says Amy.

"She came home hating Sallie, acting like she didn't deserve to go to Harvard. I don't know." I pause. "Beth was an observer, a listener. What if she overheard something that ended up getting her in trouble?"

Amy absorbs my statements, then reaches for her shoes. "I have an idea."

My blood pumps hard, fortified by Amy's partnership. For the first time, I don't worry that I'm getting carried away. At least I'm not the only one.

"We need to hack Sallie's computer," says Amy.

The idea thrills me. I follow her down the stairs. "Where are we going?"

"You know where," she says.

"I do?"

"Think."

The answer comes slowly. A bomber jacket. A dimpled smile. Thick hair, often crowned with a video game headset.

We only know one person who wouldn't blink at the challenge of hacking Sallie's files.

"Mom!" Amy shouts through the house. "We're going to see Henry Hummel."

Mom replies from the kitchen. "Take him some breakfast, will you?"

Henry's house smells closed-up and musty, like he and his grandpa haven't been getting out much. I don't blame him. He loved Beth.

Amy and I both hug Mr. Hummel, even though he's not sure who we are, a fog floating through his eyes.

"They're Beth's sisters," Henry explains.

The old man warms up, accepts our gift of blueberry muffins—from a package, of course. "Oh, Beth. She's a good one. Treat her right, Henry, you hear me?"

Henry looks exhausted, eyes shadowed, and for a moment he stalls out like he's not sure if he should explain that Beth is gone or go along with his grandfather's reality. I've seen him make this kind of decision on a smaller scale. Tell Grandpa that Walter Cronkite's no longer on the news or just hand him the remote?

In the end, he sighs. "I'll do my best."

When we make it to Henry's bedroom, he shuts the door and breathes deeply, like he's trying to hold it together. "Sorry about that. I'll tell him again tomorrow. It's just hard for me to repeat—"

"We understand," I say.

"Totally," says Amy.

Henry takes a seat in front of three different monitors, and I remember snippets of what Beth told me about his dreams for the future. "He's going to study video game design," she said once. "I think he has a shot at MIT. He's one of the smartest people I've ever met."

I'm not sure where to sit, mostly because Beth has been in this room, and it hurts to imagine. She loved coming to Henry's house. They'd spend hours tackling quests, beating levels, talking about their future. "We could make games together," Beth said once. "He'll do the coding, and I'll do the music."

Henry looks as ragged as I feel, but eager to help. "All right." He taps his computer keys like he's been waiting for a purpose. "Whose privacy are we invading?"

"Sallie Gardiner's," I say.

His eyes widen like we've suggested hacking the queen, but he opens a browser. "What are we looking for exactly? I can probably get into her email, her Google Drive."

"We're looking for an essay. Or the absence of an essay."

Henry nods, and a thrill chases through me. Beth told me all about his talent, how he'd crack open video games to see the code, like dismantling a car and putting it back together.

Amy hovers over Henry's shoulder, every bit as invested as me. "She would've written it a couple of years ago. When she was applying for college."

He types faster, windows opening and closing. "It might take me a second to— Okay, I'm in."

I lean in so close, I'm practically hugging Henry. And he deserves it. Sallie Gardiner's Google Drive unfurls on his center monitor, chock-full of papers she's written for school.

I squint to scan the files. "We're looking for something about Jane Austen."

Henry scrolls and fresh titles populate. College papers, sorority budgets, drafts of important emails. "Do you see it?" he asks.

"Keep scrolling."

We reach her high school papers—AP Art History, AP Latin—and for one glorious second, I think we're not going to find it. I picture us moving on to search her email, digging up an exchange with a ghostwriter, turning Sallie over to the Honor Council at Harvard.

Then I see it. The very title that hung on Sallie's wall: "Becoming Jane: Growing Up with an English Lit Professor."

I'm ridiculous. Delusional. Searching for scandals that don't exist.

Henry takes his mouse and clicks around, but the effort gets under my skin. It's no use. The essay's right here in Sallie's drafts. She wrote it. I was wrong, and Meg was right—I just wanted someone to blame.

"Hey, guys." Henry moves closer to his monitor. "Look at this."

Amy and I flank him to stare at the drive. With a few quick keystrokes, Henry uncovers the history of Sallie's essay. Time stamps show exactly when she wrote every word, made notes and revisions—and there's something else. Something that turns my stomach upside down.

"There's a second author," says Henry.

Amy looks stunned, and I feel the same bolt of adrenaline. The second author shows up as an email address, one that I recognize all too well.

CHAPTER TWENTY-SEVEN

Meg

(THEN)

"Be honest," says Sallie.

I sit on the floor of Sallie's bedroom under a row of dressage ribbons, laptop heating my thighs. I've read her college admissions essay a dozen times, desperate to find something we can work with, but with every pass, it's gotten worse. "Okay, it's not a big deal, but—"

"You hate it."

"I don't hate it, but—"

"Oh, you really hate it." Sallie's eyes widen, a gentle shade of blue that so easily lends itself to tears.

I set my laptop aside, wave my hands. "No, no, no, it's okay. It's not bad, it's just a little generic. I think you might need to write about something else, something more personal."

"You think I need to start over?" Sallie lowers to the edge of her bed, breath coming faster and faster. "This one took me a month, maybe more. I don't have time to start over."

"Don't panic."

BETH IS DEAD

"Meg." She drops her hands, eyes welling. "I have to get into Harvard."

Sallie's room seems to echo her words. A Harvard sweatshirt thrown over the back of a chair, a Harvard pennant beside her bed. She's had these things since we were kids, since she was old enough to know that her parents met in undergrad after midnight in the Harvard Library.

"You'll get in," I say, and I believe it. Sallie might not have the highest IQ of all our peers, but she's a dedicated student, in the top 10 percent of our class, and she's racked up more extracurriculars and volunteer hours than anyone I know. "You're going to Harvard," I repeat. "But we have to fix this essay."

Sallie wipes her eyes, nods like she's working herself up for a battle. "Okay, okay, how do we do that?"

The prompt for the year asks Harvard hopefuls to write about something we learned from an influential figure. "Why did you write about Hillary Clinton?" I ask.

Sallie stares at me like the answer's obvious. "You said you were writing about Ruth Bader Ginsburg."

I swallow a smile. "Yes, but I'm applying to study premed, going into women's health. For me, it makes sense to choose someone who stood up for reproductive rights."

Sallie paces, fingers mining into her shiny black hair. "What am I supposed to do?"

"You need to write about something that matters to you, something that comes from the heart."

"I don't know what matters to me."

"Yes, you do." I shouldn't laugh, but I can't help it. In public, Sallie's always so confident and graceful; it's nice to see her unravel. Reminds me that she's human. "Sit down." I pat the rug. "We'll figure it out."

She drops onto the ground with a great harrumph and hangs her head. "Here's the problem. There's only one thing that's ever mattered to me."

I'm waiting for the answer when it comes to me. "Harvard," I say.

She swallows, her voice gluey. "But I can't write an essay *about* Harvard *for* Harvard. That would be embarrassing."

I rest against the wall, gears turning in my mind. "Sallie . . ." An idea rises through my chest. "Why do you care so much about Harvard? Why have you *always* cared about Harvard?"

She draws her shoulders up to her ears. "I don't know."

"Think about it."

"My parents, I guess."

"Your parents. Your mom in particular." I grab my laptop, open a Google Doc so I can take notes. "You're planning to study English lit. Why?"

Sallie slants her gaze, a wry joke. "Because it sounds easy."

"No."

She gives in to a shrug. "My mom studied English lit."

"That's personal." I sound convinced, because I share her motivation. I'm studying to become a doctor because my own mom always dreamed of achieving that milestone, but she only had the time and money to become a nurse.

Sallie leans against her bed, drags her hands down the length of her face. "Okay, but doesn't that make me sound stupid? Choosing my major just to copy my mom?"

"Not if we spin it right." My fingers fly across the keys of my laptop, ideas flowing. "We'll talk about feminism, your mom's success in a historically male-dominated field, and we'll tie it into a novel. Something from Margaret Atwood or the Brontë sisters or— Oh my god."

Sallie peeks out of her hands. "What?"

"Your mom's name is Jane."

"Uh . . . yeah?"

My voice glimmers. "We'll write about Jane Austen. Tie the themes of her novels into the themes of growing up with an English PhD for a mom. Call it something like, 'Growing Up with Jane' or 'Living Like Jane,' I don't know. We can workshop it."

Sallie's face drains of color, and she lets out a heavy sigh.

"Sorry." I stop typing, pull my hands off the keys. "I'm getting carried away."

"How do you do it?" she asks, exasperated.

"I'm sorry. I'm a nerd. I love English lit."

It's true. English literature brings me a rush of joy that's hard to explain, but I'd never let myself pursue it. I'd hate to end up like Dad, more concerned with fiction than reality.

Sallie shakes her head, eyes wide. "I don't know anything about English lit."

I want to tell her that she's overreacting, but honestly, I've never seen Sallie pick up a book that wasn't assigned at school. "You could choose a different major."

She wheezes. "I don't know anything about *anything*."

"That's not true."

"I'm not witty enough to be a lawyer, I'm too squeamish to

be a doctor, business would bore me to death, and I promised my mom I'd follow in her footsteps."

"Okay." I reach for Sallie's hands, squeeze them until I have her focus. "We just need to write this essay."

Sallie fights tears. "I don't know how."

"I'll help you."

Her eyes shine. "You will?"

I sit back, settle in. "I'll help you with an outline, but you should read some Jane Austen. Start with *Pride and Prejudice*."

Sallie nods, but she doesn't seem to be processing what I'm saying. She's melting toward me like she's indebted. "Meg." She waits until I look up from my laptop. "I don't know what I'd do without you."

"You'd figure it out," I chuckle, but it's nice to think that she wouldn't. I've always pictured Sallie on a high shelf, one that I can't quite reach, but maybe we simply have different advantages.

Sallie calms her breathing, fixes her hair. "I owe you."

I shake my head. "This is what friends are—"

"I'm serious, Meg. You're saving my life. I would literally pay you for this."

I look up, a twinge in my chest. Surely, it's just an expression. Sallie wouldn't pay me to do her work. That would be unethical. "I take Venmo," I laugh.

But she holds my gaze, an unspoken agreement forming between us.

"We couldn't," I say.

"Of course not," says Sallie.

But we haven't broken eye contact, not even for a second.

CHAPTER TWENTY-EIGHT

Meg

(NOW)

All day, I rot in bed with the blinds shut tight and an oversized sweatshirt pulled up to my chin. Episodes of *Friends* blend one into the next until Ross and Rachel's off-and-on relationship almost makes me feel better about the tenuous relationships in my own life.

Sallie Gardiner's not taking advantage of me. Jo needs to get that straight. Last night my sister suggested that I'm some kind of victim, and that Beth might've gotten hurt trying to defend me. As Amy would say, that's bullshit. I know exactly what I'm doing with Sallie, and Beth promised she'd never tell.

Ross and Rachel are on a break when Jo cracks open the door. "Meg?"

A beam of light cuts into the room, and I sink deeper into my pillows. "Go away."

"We need to talk."

"I don't want to talk to you."

She eases in, Amy close behind. Both of them tread lightly, as if they're afraid they might upset me.

They must know. It was only a matter of time before they figured out what I'm doing. Jo has her ways.

"Good episode." Amy curls up next to me on the bed.

"Can you pause it?" asks Jo.

I shake my head, and the two of them share a glance like they're not sure how to start this little intervention. I'm not going to make it easy. As the oldest, I don't have to put up with advice from my little sisters. It's my job to dish it.

Jo fidgets with her braid, strands of hair fraying out. "We know about the essay."

I remain calm, my gaze flat. "Which one?"

Jo blinks like she's missing a piece of the puzzle.

"What? You thought it was a onetime thing?" I laugh into my pillow. "Come on. I've been doing Sallie's coursework for almost two years, so which essay were you able to dig up? There's one about *Beowulf*, one about themes in Renaissance literature, two about Shakespeare—"

"Oh, Meg." Jo softens toward me like I'm breaking, but I'm not.

I sit up, tighten my topknot. "Don't look at me like that. I'm not pathetic. I'm smart enough to do four course loads. Five! Six!"

Amy takes a moment to catch up, gears turning behind her eyes. "Holy fucking shit."

"Language," I snap.

"You're doing all Sallie's work. Like, all of it."

I almost pity Amy. She thinks she's so mature and experienced, but deep down, she's still a kid. "It's not a big deal."

"Beth was right," says Jo. "Sallie's taking advantage of you."

I shove my comforter and get out of bed. "No one's taking advantage of me. Sallie pays me more than she should. You should see my Venmo history."

Amy drops her jaw. "Sallie's paying you?"

Heat rushes to my cheeks, but I shoot her a knowing glance. "You think I'd write her papers for free?"

"Meg, that's super illegal," says Jo.

Amy scrounges for her phone. "Can you go to jail for that?"

"Don't Google it." Jo knocks the phone from her grip.

I shove my hands into the pocket of my sweatshirt, but I shouldn't have to hide. My arrangement with Sallie may be immoral, but it's not illegal. It's just a job, a side gig, a profitable business. "College is expensive," I say. "Even with my scholarship, I have to pay for housing, textbooks, food."

"Don't you have a work study?" asks Amy.

"That only helps with tuition," says Jo.

They're judging me, but they don't understand. I'm not just trying to keep myself afloat, I'm trying to keep up with Sallie and Annie. "You think it's hard going to Concord High? Try Harvard. My friends have five-course sushi dinners and split the check at the end. And next semester, they're all going to Cabo for spring break."

Jo gapes. "Do you hear yourself? You're committing academic fraud in exchange for spring break?"

"That's not—"

"Meg," she sighs. "This isn't you."

My chest aches, but I'm used to ignoring it. Jo and Amy don't understand the responsibility of being the oldest. Mom doesn't confide in them the way she confides in me. They don't know how hard it's been to stay in our house since Dad donated his advance, to replace the broken furnace and cut down the old oak that was threatening to fall on the roof. They don't know how worrisome life can be without money and how weightless it feels to watch your bank account climb. "I'm doing what I need to do."

Jo can hardly look at me. "How much did Beth know?"

With a rush of shame, I remember the time she came to visit me at school. I thought she was out grabbing coffee, but the shop had been closed, and she'd come back too quickly. She overheard a fight between Sallie and me, a paper I hadn't finished yet. I thought she'd be angry, disgusted, but she was only worried. A hushed plea. "If this gets out, Sallie's family will protect her. They have lawyers, money, but you'll be in trouble."

I sit up straight. "Jo. I know you need answers, but you're looking in the wrong place."

Jo paces, working herself up, shoulders tightening. "We've all been worried about you."

"Worried?"

"You're exhausted," she says, a gentle sigh. "We all see it."

Amy nods, and I feel exposed. I thought I was hiding my exhaustion, carrying it well, but even Amy's noticed. "I'm fine." I try to sound certain, but my voice trembles.

Jo stops, softens her tone enough that it hurts. "We don't

blame you, not even a little, but what if Beth thought she was helping? Protecting you by confronting Sallie?"

Amy chews her lip so hard, it bleeds. "She had a lot of champagne at the party, and after we got into it, she was really upset. She might've been feeling brave."

"And Sallie might've panicked," says Jo.

My heart thuds at the base of my skull. I don't want to believe that Sallie could've snapped, but she's been anxious lately, insisting that I never work on her papers at the library or the coffee shop across from our apartment. "Only at home," she said. "Only in private."

Jo moves closer, imploring. "We have to tell the detectives."

"We're not telling anyone." I clench my fists and steel my jaw, unwilling to let go.

Jo looks calm, her unhinged energy leveling out. She's not theorizing anymore. She believes that she's right, and it scares me.

"Sallie wouldn't," I say, but my voice comes out weak, breathless. I've seen Sallie lash out. Once, Annie flirted with a guy that Sallie had claimed to like, and Sallie yelled so much that our neighbors called in a noise complaint. And once, just once, I missed a deadline for one of Sallie's essays, and for half a second, she drew her hand back like she was going to slap me.

"Okay." I empty my lungs. "I'll talk to her."

"What if she's dangerous?" asks Jo.

"I'm not afraid of my best friend—"

"You should be careful," Amy interjects.

"—and I'm not going to blow up her life, *my life*, unless I know for sure." I search for my shoes and shove them on.

"You can't go alone," says Jo.

"Then come with me."

We're at Sallie's house in minutes, the three of us loading out of Jo's Jeep. We stride up the driveway, but short of the house, we stop.

A police car is parked behind a massive hedge, the front door of the Gardiners' house wide open, light pouring out. Ned Gardiner speaks with an officer, his eyes red with exhaustion.

We stand in silence for a moment, and my heart stills in my chest. I don't know what's going on, but my mind jumps straight to a second death, another murder, and I can't handle it.

The cops turn and Ned charges out of the house.

"Ned!" I call out.

He blows past me. "Not now."

"Ned, please. What's going on?"

He stops at his car, a gleaming Land Rover. "Sallie's missing."

My sisters and I don't waste any time at the Gardiners' mansion.

With Jo behind the wheel, we screech to a stop in front of the Concord Police Department and sprint through the parking lot. I'm winded by the time we reach the information desk, my heart beating in my throat. "We need to see Detective Davis."

A young officer sits behind the front desk with a half-eaten protein bar and muscles that tell me he spends way too much time taking gym selfies. "Is this an emergency?" he asks without looking away from his computer screen.

Jo shoves in front of me. "Do you think we'd be here in person if it wasn't?"

The officer shifts his gaze but not his posture. "Detective Davis isn't here right now."

Jo leans through the window. "Can you find him?"

The man looks annoyed, so I move in front of Jo. I admire her intensity, but sometimes it gets us absolutely nowhere. Sometimes you have to act like a damsel to get what you want.

"Officer," I sniffle, "we're the March sisters."

He pauses, protein bar between his teeth.

I flutter my eyelashes, hedging to sound unsure, in need of guidance. "What about Detective Kirke? I believe she came to our house. I think she might be helping with our sister's case."

The officer flexes, uniform stretching. "Detective Davis and Detective Kirke are both out in the field."

"Do you know when they'll be back?" I ask.

"What's got you girls so eager?"

Jo groans, and I sense a schooling on the tip of her tongue. "If we were men," she wants to say. I hold up a hand, silently begging her to stay quiet. If we were men, this officer would take us seriously, but we're not men, so we have to get creative.

I wipe my eyes again. "Sallie Gardiner, a local girl—she's missing."

"Our guys are on it."

"Sir." I wait for his gaze. "Sallie's one of my best friends, and she's been involved in something . . . nefarious. It's very important for us to find her—"

Jo shoves in front of me. "We have reason to believe she's responsible for our sister's—"

"She's a murderer," Amy pipes up from behind us.

The officer reaches for a notepad. "You want to report something in particular?"

My throat tightens. In the car on the way to the station, Jo accused Sallie of fleeing, but we have no idea where she's gone. She could be hurt. She could be the next victim. "If you could just call Detective—"

"I told you, girls. The detectives aren't available right now."

Amy shouts, and the rest of us flinch. "Are you listening? We have information about a potential murderer! What else could the detectives be doing that's so fucking important?"

The officer stands up slowly, inflates his chest. "Listen, girls—"

"Stop calling us girls," says Jo.

He shakes his head, a frustrated smile. "Aren't you girls?"

"It's not *what* you're saying, it's *how* you're saying it, but I don't expect a thick-headed *boy* like you to under—"

The word "boy" hits the officer the wrong way. A vein throbs in his neck. "*Ladies.*" He draws it out. "I'm sure you have important information, but our detectives are out in the field, and I'm not allowed to disclose . . ." He trails off as a squad car pulls up in front of the station, headlights flooding the lobby.

We all squint, time slowing as we turn around.

It's late by now, dark outside. Snow falls under streetlamps, obscuring our view, but I can make out two people.

Jo rushes to the windows. "That's Detective Kirke."

I recognize her hair, curly and whipping as she rounds the car.

"And Davis," says Amy.

The old man climbs out of the driver's seat with a grim expression, coat braced against the cold. Detective Kirke opens the back door, and when a passenger emerges, my knees buckle.

He's backlit by the headlights, but I know his figure, his gait. The detectives flank him like he needs to be watched, and as they come inside, light spilling on a face I know so well, my vision blurs.

"John?"

He pauses, eyes widening like he never imagined he'd see me here. "Meg?"

The detectives didn't expect to see us either. They share a determined glance, and Davis lays a firm hand on John's back. "Through that door."

John's forced to walk on, but his focus trails behind. "I didn't do this, Meg. I didn't do this. I swear on my life."

As he defends himself, I realize what my body already knows. John, my John, is under arrest.

This can't be happening.

Detective Kirke places us in a cold, fluorescent room, and I feel the same way I did when I found out about Beth, sweating and shivering at the same time. "Detective Kirke, please. He didn't do this. It's not possible."

I think of all the times I've snuck away from school to meet John, his apartment filled with laughter and piano music, his gentle voice saying, "I've missed you so much, Meg March."

"We have enough evidence to charge him," says Kirke.

Behind her, the station rests. It's late enough that we're mostly alone, chairs empty, computers dark. It shouldn't be this way while John's under arrest. The whole department should be lit with panic, poking holes in this theory, looking for alternatives.

"It's my fault," I say. "I encouraged him to reach out and give a statement."

Kirke looks eager to get back to her duties, but she stops, a hand in her curls. "What do you mean?"

"John told us what happened the night Beth died, and he was afraid it would look bad, but I told him to be honest. I promised you'd understand."

"Meg—"

"John volunteered his story. That should count for something."

"John never spoke to us."

Behind me, Amy mutters, "Oh my god," and Jo draws a hand to her mouth like this confirms a deeply held suspicion.

But this isn't a nail in John's coffin. It's great news. I sigh in relief, my shoulders loosening. If John never gave a statement, the detectives haven't heard his side of the story. "That's good. This is good. Give him a chance to explain. It'll all make sense."

Detective Kirke nods, but it feels like she's nodding to a child, agreeing to check under a bed for monsters. "Stay here. I'll be back soon."

She closes the door, and I feel trapped, my heart pounding like it's trying to break free of my rib cage. I look at my sisters. "They have it wrong."

I need indignation from Jo and Amy, an energy that matches mine, but they both blink until Jo starts gently, "Meg . . ."

"No," I shout. "Don't you dare act like he might've done this."

Jo talks like she's onto something, voice rising, and I'm disgusted by how quickly she can switch gears, Sallie to John.

"It was a little strange," she says. "John showed up at our house right after the detectives left. It's almost like—"

"He was waiting," says Amy.

Chills run down my arms, but I rub them away. John didn't get the news about Beth in a timely manner. He had to find out through his parents. It's my fault that he showed up late.

"This is absurd," I say. "John loved Beth like a sister."

I close my eyes, and I'm in his apartment, familiar and warm, his Concord High sweatshirt slung over the back of his couch. He doesn't have much, but he has a piano, and when he plays, I sometimes feel like I'm looking at my future, the person I'm supposed to be with forever. I've ignored that feeling for too long.

"He would never hurt her," I say, and the words taste like salt. I realize that I'm crying.

Jo edges closer, a hand that's meant to be comforting.

I shove her away. "John was the last person to see Beth alive because he helped her. Now we have to help him."

Jo and Amy exchange a look as if they're trying to decide where their loyalty lies.

My voice strains. "You don't really think he did this."

Jo stands to match my height. "I love John. We all do. But I can see why they brought him in. He spent a lot of time with Beth alone, he called her a spoiled brat a few weeks before she died, and that night—he says he brought her home, but I didn't hear the door."

"You fell asleep," I say.

Jo speaks matter-of-factly, rationalizing. "Why would she go back out? If he brought her home, she would've stayed home."

Amy sits down on a couch, pulls her legs up to her chest. "It's freaky, Meg."

They don't realize what they're doing. Accusing John is like accusing me, because I chose him. I chose him long before I let myself believe it. "You're both horrible," I say.

Before my sisters can respond, a voice carries through the station. The meathead cop from the front desk. "Yeah, we found her."

I press myself against the glass door, desperate for every scrap of information.

"Boston Logan," says the cop. "Bought a ticket to Paris."

They're talking about Sallie Gardiner. Little snake bought a ticket to Paris. Jo was right. She was trying to flee the country.

"Did you hear that? Sallie was trying to get away. She's the answer. She killed Beth, and she was running. This has nothing to do with John."

Jo looks blank-faced, like she doesn't know what's right anymore. "Sallie's parents are in Paris. Maybe she was going to see them."

"Don't defend her now. She's been manipulating me for years, and I thought I had control, but I don't. I don't. She killed our sister." Without thinking, I throw the door open and charge through the station. It's small and organized, a bullpen surrounded by heavy doors.

I pound on each one, determined to find the detectives. "I need to tell you something! I need to tell you something now!" I yell so loudly, my lungs burn.

The meathead cop watches me from the edge of the room like he's trying to decide if he should detain me.

Detective Kirke cracks a door, careful to conceal what's inside. But I know. I can picture the room. A metal table, a bright light, two against one. They're interrogating the love of my life, accusing him of my sister's murder. But they're on the wrong track, because they don't know what I did. What I've been doing for years.

"You have the wrong person," I say.

Kirke raises a hand like I need to calm down.

"Sallie Gardiner had a motive."

Kirke joins me in the bullpen, easing the door shut behind her back.

I can't stand still. My heart's racing, erratic. "Sallie and I have been cheating. We've been cheating for years, and Beth knew about it."

I don't care about keeping my secret anymore. I don't care if people see me as a sellout, if I'm expelled. John can't go down for a murder that's my fault.

"Why don't you take a seat?" Kirke gestures to a desk chair.

I can't even look at it. "Sallie's been paying me to do her schoolwork since twelfth grade. We're breaking the law, deceiving Harvard. Harvard!"

I'm flying, lifting off the floor. I've been carrying this weight, and I'm shedding it now.

"Meg, please take a seat."

"Sallie has a dark side. Her parents expect her to be perfect, and she would die if they found out what we've been doing."

"Meg, Sallie was picked up by one of our officers at Boston Logan airport just a few—"

I get right in Kirke's face, yelling. "I heard. She bought a ticket to Paris. She was fleeing the country. Why isn't that suspicious? Why isn't she under arrest?"

I've never seen Kirke lose her composure, but she does now, curls jumping as she shouts. "Meg, sit down! Now."

"But—"

"If you don't, I'll let Officer Nelson put you in handcuffs."

The meathead cop lays a hand on his cuffs like he's ready, like he'd be glad to wrestle me down. If I were Jo, I'd stand my ground, let him force me into a chair, but I'm too afraid of getting hurt. I sit slowly, straight-backed and tight-lipped. "Detective Kirke. This is my fault."

She sits across from me, looks me in the eye.

"It's my fault," I repeat, tears falling. "Sallie killed Beth because of me, and I won't let John go down for it." The truth pours out, unstoppable. "I love him. I love him so much. He wouldn't do this."

Kirke rests her elbows on her knees, lowers her voice. "Sallie Gardiner's innocent. We pressed her brother for information, and he produced cell phone footage of the two of them dancing in the living room around the time of Beth's death."

My breath heaves. "She could've slipped out and gone back."

"Beth was killed on the hill in front of the park, and Sallie didn't leave the Gardiner house all night."

I feel like I'm falling, grasping. "Then why was she trying to flee the country?"

Kirke glances back like she's telling me a secret, something she's not supposed to spill. "Sallie shared some very helpful information in her statement. I have reason to believe she might've been scared."

I'm stunned, my mouth so dry, I can hardly speak. "What information?"

Detective Kirke exhales. "Meg, there are things I can't tell you, but I need you to understand that we've placed John at the crime scene without a shred of doubt. Whatever story he gave you, it's not entirely true."

My whole body goes numb. I know, in the strongest muscles of my heart, that John didn't kill my sister, but I can't find the words to defend him.

"Meg." Detective Kirke looks me right in the eye. "Sallie Gardiner isn't a suspect. This is not your fault."

A fist unclenches inside my chest, and though I need to protect John, all the fight has drained out of me. It's not my fault. I needed to hear that.

Suddenly, a door opens, and Mom bursts into the room, winded. "Girls? Where are you? What happened? Are you okay?"

I'm too ashamed and devastated to look at her, and though I try to move, I can't. Then a familiar hand squeezes my shoulder.

I'm still mad at Jo, but she anchors me.

"Let's go home," she says.

I don't want to leave John in this cold station, but I don't have a choice, and my sisters are hoisting me out of my chair. I stumble, but they hold me up, and we leave arm in arm.

"We'll prove them wrong," says Jo. "I promise we will."

CHAPTER TWENTY-NINE

(NOW)

The next morning a knock on the front door draws me out of bed. I know right away that it's Detective Kirke, her rapping delicate but decisive.

Mom answers the door in sweatpants and a Concord Gen sweatshirt she's owned since she started working at the hospital. I honestly can't believe it's still hanging together. "It's early," she says to Kirke.

The woman nods. "I was hoping to catch you before your daughters got up."

At this, I freeze, tuck myself against the wall.

Mom lets the detective in with an understanding sigh, and I lower to my knees at the top of the stairs, crouching so they won't be able to see me.

"Coffee?" asks Mom.

Kirke rubs her eyes, and I wonder if she slept at all. It was already late when we left the station, and she must've spent hours dealing with John—and the paperwork. On TV, there's always paperwork.

"I'd love a cup," she says. "But only if it's easy."

Mom nods. "I could drink a whole pot myself."

As they move through the house, I creep to the back staircase, which feeds down to the kitchen. From there, I can only see a sliver of the breakfast table, but Kirke takes a seat in my line of sight, and her voice echoes up to the second floor. "I wanted to talk to you about your husband."

I hold my breath and stay in the shadows, desperate to know if the detectives have been able to reach Dad. I've tried a couple of times, but his phone goes straight to voicemail, like it always does when he's pitched his tent in the middle of nowhere.

Mom hands the detective a cup of coffee, sits just out of view. "I'm sorry we couldn't talk about him the other day. My girls are just—"

"You don't have to explain," says Kirke.

I wish I could see Mom's expression. Her voice sounds rougher without us around, like she's not quite holding herself together. "They miss their dad."

"You don't?"

The question seems unfair, caustic. Mom takes a long time to answer—but I know what she's going to say. Of course she misses Dad. She must. When he decided to leave, she tried so hard to talk him out of it, rationalizing at first, and then simply begging.

"It's complicated," she says finally, and I think of the day Dad drove off, Mom stubbornly shut inside the house. When she couldn't change his mind, she turned cold.

Kirke softens her tone. "Pardon my asking, but did you and your husband consider his leaving some kind of—"

"Separation?" Mom chuckles, bitter. "Not exactly."

I ease down to the top step, a risk I'm willing to take for a view of Mom's face.

To my surprise, she's crying, clearing a tear with her thumb. "I didn't want my husband to leave, but he was drowning in negativity. His career, his very person, had been under fire for weeks."

Kirke consults her steno pad. "He told the press he was fleeing to protect his daughters."

Mom's voice goes flat and dry. "He's a very good storyteller."

All at once I want to launch myself down the stairs—but I resist the urge, because I've never heard this unfiltered version of Mom. This grit in the back of her throat.

Kirke continues her questioning. "Is he really in Canada?"

Mom leans back, and I can't see her anymore, but surely she's nodding.

"Honestly," she says, "he could be anywhere, but I have no reason to think he's not in Vancouver."

Detective Kirke sips her coffee, steam shrouding her eyes. "Forgive me, Mrs. March, but it's hard to believe he's been camping for six—"

"I know," says Mom. "He hasn't been in touch, and it's hurting the girls, especially Jo. It's easier for her to believe that he hasn't had cell service."

My head swims, my pulse pounding behind my eyes. I'm impossibly hot, a rush of anger—or is it embarrassment?—

and yet I refuse to believe what Mom's saying. Dad wouldn't willingly ignore me. Maybe my sisters. Definitely Mom. But not me.

"What're you doing?" Meg's voice startles me, a shock of adrenaline that turns my sweat cold.

I press a finger to my lips, and she crouches beside me. Most of the time she wouldn't be so compliant, but she tossed and turned all night, wept over John's arrest. She must be too tired to fight.

Kirke clears her throat. "Have you tried calling your husband since—"

Mom leans forward, coming back into view, her head in her hands. "I keep getting his voicemail."

"Do you find that strange?"

Mom drags her hands over the length of her face. "Detective Kirke, are you married?"

The woman shakes her head.

"I love my husband, but our life hasn't always been easy. He's consumed by his work, self-centered at times, and when he chose to leave—to walk out on his family—I couldn't . . . I snapped. I told him that if he drove away, he could never come back."

Everything stops.

I feel like the staircase has disappeared, like I'm suspended in midair.

"Did you mean that?" asks Kirke.

"In the moment?" Mom doesn't say anything else, but the answer's clear.

This, of course, is why Dad has been gone so much longer than we anticipated. I can hardly believe it, and yet it makes perfect, terrible sense.

Something shifts inside me. Underneath it all, I've been angry with Dad for staying away, and now this blame lands squarely on Mom.

I try to rise, but Meg holds me down. "Jo, don't."

"How could she?" I ask through gritted teeth.

The detective glances at the stairs, but it's so dark in the narrow passage that she doesn't see us. With a watchful eye, she leans toward Mom. "Mrs. March, your husband hasn't responded to any of our messages."

Mom starts, "Well—"

"It's not normal for someone to ignore the police. Not unless—"

"He may not be charging his phone," says Mom. "He was getting twenty, thirty calls a day from protesters before he left."

"Don't you think he's seen the news?"

Mom goes cold, lets a long silence pass. It takes every muscle in my body to keep from flying down the stairs, yelling, "Of course he hasn't seen the news!"

This shouldn't be a question. If Dad knew that Beth had been killed, he'd be here.

"What are you insinuating?" Mom asks at last.

Kirke isn't ruffled. "I'm simply suggesting that—"

"Rob's never been gone this long, but this isn't the first time he's chosen to shut out the world. When he's writing, he doesn't check his phone, doesn't watch TV, doesn't care about anything beyond the page. Want to know why I snapped the day he left? There's your answer."

Kirke nods, but there's something sharp in her gaze. Like she thinks Mom's holding something back. "We'll try his email. And if you have any contacts—old friends, relatives—please send them our way."

Mom gets to her feet, chair scraping the floor. "My girls will be up soon."

"Right." Kirke folds her notebook. "I'll get out of your hair."

Mom doesn't bother showing the woman out. She stays in the kitchen, where she waits to make a call.

On the phone, her voice stays low. "Rob, it's Maggie. I'm starting to worry. And the police are starting to think . . ." She trails off. "I know I said some terrible things, but this is about our girls. You have to come home."

Just then Amy's door opens behind us, and she staggers out bleary-eyed. Though she's heading for the bathroom, she stops when she sees Meg and me crouched at the stairs. "The fuck are you both doing on the—"

"Shh," we hiss.

And just like that, Mom's gaze snaps toward us.

"Please come down," Mom says for the third time.

Meg nudges me, but I shake my head, block my sisters from descending.

"All right, then." Mom sets her shoulders and climbs.

A fire builds inside me, and I welcome the heat.

My anger.

The one thing on which I can always rely.

Mom joins us on the steps, and I move up, so I can tower over her.

She doesn't even try to match me. Just folds her hands. "How long have you been listening?"

"Long enough," I say.

Amy's still standing above us. Despite the cold, she's wearing cutoff shorts and a tank, her feet bare. "What's going on?"

"Mom kicked Dad out of the house," I tell her.

Suddenly, Amy's awake. Eyes growing wide. "Sorry, what?"

Mom speaks calmly as if our family isn't falling apart. "No one said anything about—"

"You told Detective Kirke—"

"I made a mistake," says Mom. "I said something I didn't mean."

I need to move, but Meg's above me, Mom below, and the walls feel like they're closing in. "No wonder he's ignoring us."

A new picture of Dad forms in my mind. Instead of camping, he's renting a one-bedroom apartment in Vancouver, writing under bad light with a fridge full of single-serve meals.

But no.

It can't be.

He must be out in nature, dreaming up stories under snowy pines.

"You had every right to be angry," Meg says to Mom.

Mom rests her head against the wall, exhaustion forming circles under her eyes. All my life, she and Dad have been a unified front. Sure, they've snipped at each other, but at the end of the day, they've always been a pair. Now I wonder how much she's been holding back. "I couldn't stand the thought of him leaving," she says.

Amy looks just as disillusioned as I feel. "I thought you agreed that he was—"

"Protecting you? I know." Mom sighs. "That's what we said, but it never felt that way to me. It felt like defiance, a screw-you to his naysayers."

I'm shocked at first. Not only by the revelation but also by Mom saying "screw you."

Meg nods—big and repetitive like she couldn't agree more.

And I guess if I'm honest, Mom's words resonate with me, too. I never thought it made sense for Dad to protect us by driving away. His decision to flee seemed just as performative as his decision to donate his advance.

But still, I miss him.

My voice cracks. "Can you imagine how lonely he must feel?"

"I have a pretty good idea." Mom's voice comes out fast, pinched, and it culminates in tears. She cups her mouth like she's shocked to be crying. "I'm sorry."

"Don't apologize." Meg shoves past me to thread an arm around Mom's shoulders.

Mom lets out a few sobs, then collects herself. "I love your father, and I understood long ago that I'd always be second to his writing, but sometimes it hurts. He should've put his daughters first."

There's a wrinkle in her thought process. She doesn't realize that by taking second place, she accepted the same for us.

I've never expected more from Dad—but I won't say that. Not now.

"What if he doesn't come home?" I ask.

"He will," says Mom.

But I'm not so certain. Detective Kirke thinks that Dad must've seen the news, and I wonder if she's right. Even if he's camping, he must've hit a Laundromat, a diner, a convenience store. He must've seen the near-twenty-four-seven coverage of the investigation. And if that's true—if he's still not coming home—then he must blame himself.

"Detective Kirke thinks he's a suspect," I say.

"You're kidding," Amy laughs. "They think Dad killed Beth?"

"No," says Mom, but they do. And moments ago she supplied them with a motive.

Dad lost his career.

His family.

And it all started with Beth.

Beth, who made him a villain when she told *Teen Vogue* that his book stole her light.

"We have to find him," I say.

"How?" asks Amy, like the task would be impossible.

"Don't worry." I storm off down the hallway. "I'll figure it out."

CHAPTER THIRTY

Beth

(THEN)

Henry parks his grandpa's truck under a red maple, and I feel like we're the only people in the world.

We climb into the backseat, both of us giggling, his head bumping the roof, and when we get comfortable, hips pressing, lips meeting, I feel like a character in one of Dad's better books, one that pops off the page.

Henry and I have been dating for one month and eighteen days, and I haven't stopped smiling for a second. We talk about our future all the time, the two of us moving to California to make video games, epic worlds of our own design. Meg would tell me to slow down if she knew, but it's impossible to slow down when your heart's always fluttering.

Henry slides his fingers under the hem of my shirt, and my breath catches in my throat. He's the first boy I've ever kissed, and until now, that's all we've done, but I want more.

I ease my shirt over my head, and the chill of October draws goose bumps to the surface of my skin. Henry slides a gentle hand under my back and pulls me closer. He's so calm, so confident. I'm sure that means I'm not his first, but I push the thought from my mind. "You're perfect," he's told me.

That word has taken on new meaning since I met Henry. He hasn't read *Little Women*. I made him promise he'd never open it, so when he calls me perfect, I don't think of the sheltered, quiet girl in Dad's book. I think of something else entirely.

His fingers find the clasp of my bra. "Is this okay?"

I nod, breathless, and the elastic loosens from my ribs.

Henry kisses me deeper, slips the straps from my shoulders. My heart quivers, a dizzying mixture of nerves and excitement. What would my sisters think if they knew what I was doing? Meg would be motherly. She'd encourage me to be smart. Amy would smirk, impressed, but what about Jo? Would she judge me for falling in love?

"You want to stop?" asks Henry.

I shake my head and tug at his shirt. With a laugh, he tosses it on the floor and pulls me so close I can hardly breathe. "You're amazing," he whispers in my ear.

I lose myself in his blue-gray eyes, stunned by his choice of words. I've been called responsible and thoughtful, but never amazing. I pull his lips to mine, every kiss like diving underwater.

Then his phone rings.

He reaches into his back pocket to decline the call.

"Who is it?" I ask.

"Who cares." He runs his fingers down my shoulder, across my chest.

I'm floating, then his phone rings again.

"You should get it," I say.

He sits up and answers gruffly, "What is it?" His face falls. "Oh. Hannah. Sorry."

I find my clothes and sit up, suddenly worried. This isn't the first time Henry's gotten a call from his grandpa's nurse. When he does, it's never good.

"Is he okay?" asks Henry.

I can't hear the answer, but Henry relaxes just enough for me to know that his grandpa's at least alive.

"Which hospital?" he asks. "Okay, I'm on my way."

Henry scrambles for his shirt and drives as fast as he can, explaining that his grandpa had a heart attack and he's going into surgery. "He's all I have," he tells me, his eyes never leaving the road.

"You have me now." I squeeze his shoulder, heartbroken and infatuated. Henry takes such good care of his grandpa, spends time with him when other kids our age are staring at their phones or out partying.

At the hospital we speak with a nurse, who explains that Mr. Hummel's surgery could take hours. "You can wait here," she says, and we settle down in the cold blue waiting room.

I text Mom to tell her we're here, but the emergency department's never slow, so I doubt she'll be able to break away.

Henry keeps his head down, a hand on the back of his neck.

"It'll be okay," I say.

He nods.

"He'll be home before you know it."

He nods again, and I get comfortable in the silence. If Jo were here, she'd do everything in her power to fill it, but I can relate to

BETH IS DEAD

Henry. Sometimes he needs a moment inside his own head. When he's ready, he looks at me. "My mom died in a hospital like this."

I stay quiet, giving him space to open up. He hasn't told me much about his mom, only that he misses her every day.

"We were supposed to move out here together. That was the plan when my grandpa started getting sick. She seemed excited. We both were. But when we started packing, she freaked out, decided she didn't want to leave Rhode Island. We had a really bad fight, and then the next day she overdosed."

I try not to look shocked, but the news strikes me so hard. "I had no idea."

"She struggled with addiction for a long time. Always up and down. She'd be good for a while and then bad again."

"I'm so sorry."

He stares at the tile floor. "Sometimes I think she overdosed on purpose. Like she thought I'd be better off without her, but I'm not."

Across the hall, lights flash, the sound of cartoons through a half-open door. I take Henry's hands and pull him up. "Come with me."

"Where?"

"Just come."

The kids' waiting room isn't much better than the main one except for the TV that plays *Tom and Jerry* instead of CNN and sits on a cabinet full of video games.

Henry cracks a little smile. "What're we doing?"

I lead him to the cabinet and unearth one of the best creations this planet has ever seen: a vintage Nintendo 64.

Henry rummages through the drawer, pulling out ancient editions of *Mario Party* and *Diddy Kong Racing*. "How did you know about this?" he laughs.

"I know everything," I say ominously. "And my mom's a nurse here, remember?"

Without a kid in sight, we settle in to play, each of us claiming a saggy beanbag chair, and for a couple of hours, we don't talk about anything other than Yoshi versus Luigi, the obvious cuteness of Koopa Troopas, and the understated cuteness of Bowser.

I think about what Henry said, that his mom might've overdosed on purpose, and how it feels when someone leaves, like Dad, who's currently off in the Canadian Rockies. "She loved you," I say out of the blue.

Henry's thumbs move rapidly on his controller. "What?"

"I know your mom loved you."

"How do you know?"

"It would be impossible not to love you."

In the middle of a mini game, Henry sets his controller in his lap and moves his beanbag closer to mine. On screen, the computer-controlled characters win the game, Wario and Princess Peach. "Peach has got it!"

Henry's dimples appear, a haughty grin. "Are you saying what I think you're saying?"

"What if I am?" The words come quickly, confidently. I almost sound like Jo.

Henry tucks his chin like he's trying to hide the intensity of his smile. "What if I'm saying it back?"

Meg has been in love, and she's told me how it feels. "Like

your heart's lifting off."

But this is different. It's like all my life I've been hovering above the earth, not really living but watching other people do it, and now I'm coming down to land.

"I do love you, Henry."

He touches my shoulder, and warmth spreads through my whole body like I'm standing in the sun. "I love you too, Beth March."

I lean in for a kiss, and for a moment I'm lost, melting into Henry, shifting from my beanbag to his.

Then, a knock at the door. A throat cleared. "Henry Hummel?"

I shoot back, remembering where we are. Fluorescent lights. A sterile smell. The beeping of monitors across the hall. I blink at the nurse who's standing in the doorframe, and my cheeks burn. She's young and blond, and I've met her a dozen times when I've come to visit Mom.

She remains professional. "Your grandfather's out of surgery. You can see him now."

Henry scrambles to his feet, straightening his clothes. "Right. Yes. Sorry."

The young nurse purses her lips like she's judging us, but when Henry rounds the corner, she winks at me. "He's a cutie."

I blanch. "Are you going to tell my mom—"

"Not my story." She mimes zipping her lips.

I exhale, and when she's gone, a smile returns to my face.

She said, *Not my story.*

As if I, Beth March, have a story.

CHAPTER THIRTY-ONE

(NOW)

Two nights after John's arrest, I've called every campground near Vancouver looking for Dad. I'll work my way through Calgary next, Edmonton after that, and if I'm still coming up dry, I'll go through the Maple Ridge High School yearbook to track down all his old friends.

I won't give up until I find him. Until he's home.

Around sunset the Gardiner family sends us a spaghetti dinner from the best restaurant in town to express their condolences, and despite my enduring suspicions about Sallie, I sit down to enjoy. The smell of garlic fills the house, and my mouth waters. I haven't eaten a real meal in days, sickened by the idea of food, my own needs and desires, but for the first time since our lives turned upside down, I give in.

Amy rips a hunk from a buttery roll. "Damn, this is good."

I agree with a groan. "Too bad a murderer covered the check."

I'm not sure I actually believe Sallie Gardiner's a murderer,

BETH IS DEAD

but I need to blame someone, and I can't blame John—not in front of Meg. She hasn't spoken all day except to complain about the conditions at the Massachusetts Correctional Institute: rock-hard mattresses, a lack of privacy, food that tastes like cardboard. "He doesn't deserve it," she keeps repeating, and maybe she's right. Maybe John's really innocent, but the judge who charged him with murder clearly didn't think so.

"Mom." Amy talks through a full mouth. "Are you really going to make us go back to school tomorrow?"

I stare at my plate, but my ears perk up. Mom's been adamant that we return to school and routine, despite everything going on. "We need to stay busy," she's been saying. But I can't imagine staying busy on anything other than the investigation.

Mom moves her salad around her plate. "School will be good for you. We need a routine. We need to keep living."

I don't think Mom wants to keep living. I think she'd rather lie in bed all day crying into a pillow, but she's always been the kind who heals by following order. It's the trauma nurse in her—control the bleeding, clear the airways, stabilize the patient.

"We could skip a semester," says Amy.

I almost chime in to agree, but Mom shoots Amy a look so sharp, I'd rather not get involved. "We're not talking about this anymore. You're going tomorrow."

Amy scowls for the rest of dinner, and I want to scowl along with her, but I focus on the silver lining of returning to Concord High. Most of the school went to Sallie Gardiner's party, so I'll be surrounded by people who might know what happened to Beth—and if they do, I'll find out.

Mom's unboxing dessert when she gets a call from Detective Davis. "Hello?" She pauses. "Um . . . I'm not sure that's appropriate." She scrunches her face, a look of concern, but after a moment of listening, concedes by offering me her phone. "He wants to speak with you."

"Me?"

She shrugs. "He promised it'll only take a minute."

I take her phone, and it's heavy in my hand, cold against my ear. I worried this was coming. Detective Davis hasn't yet forced me into giving a statement, but I knew someday he'd turn me over carefully like a rock in a dark place.

I answer with a bite to hide my fear. "What do you want?"

He sounds like he's been run over, flattened out. "Jo . . ." He leaves a long breath of air between us like he's weighing a big decision. "I'm calling to apologize."

My eyes widen, and I draw a hand to my mouth.

"What is it?" asks Meg.

"Put it on speaker," says Amy.

I give them both my shoulder, listening hard. "Forensics have come back on John Brooke's fingerprints, and they match a set we have on file." He pauses again, like he's struggling to admit a mistake, but I already know what he's going to say.

"Jo, they match the second set of fingerprints from the recording device you found in July."

I sip the air, afraid I might be sick. In July, Detective Davis found two sets of fingerprints on the recording device that was taped under Beth's piano—one that he couldn't identify and one that belonged to me.

At the time, he didn't care about the unidentified set. Thought it must've been a store associate, a delivery driver, someone insignificant.

"I was wrong," says Davis.

I should be relieved, elated. At long last, I've been exonerated, and Davis—ruthless, awful Detective Davis—is coming to me with his tail between his legs.

But I can't believe what I've done.

"It wasn't John," I say.

Detective Davis tries to be gentle, but the roughness returns to his voice. "I know John's close to the family. This must be hard to believe."

It's not just hard to believe. It's dead wrong.

I breathe through my nose, mind whirring. I can't tell the truth. I've been denying it for so long, and my family's been defending me. I never imagined that my little crime would get wrapped up in a bigger one. "Maybe there was someone else. Another set of prints that you never found."

Detective Davis sounds so certain. "John Brooke had a key to the house. I should've looked more carefully at him in July."

I can't let this happen. They can't use this evidence against John. I know how it feels to sit in a cold room while your story's getting twisted. "Detective Davis—"

"I was wrong, Jo. And I'm sorry."

I realize what this means, the narrative that's falling into place. Detective Davis thinks that John killed Beth, and now he believes it was premeditated, planned as early as summer, when John started listening to Beth's private life from afar.

"It's not true," I say. "John wouldn't spy on my sister. He doesn't have a motive."

At this, Meg grabs for the phone. "What's going on? What is he saying?"

I stand up to dodge her as Davis continues, "Jo, I didn't call to argue—"

"You were wrong about me. Who's to say you're not wrong again?"

"I just wanted you to know that I'm sorry."

When the detectives brought John into the station, I believed—for a second—that he might've killed Beth. He's tall and stealthy, hands so wide, he could palm her head, but he's gentle, too. And the evidence they have against him doesn't hold up. I should know. "What else do you have on John?"

"I can't share the details of an ongoing—"

"Tell me."

A long silence. Then, "Jo, I have to go. I just wanted you to know that I'm going to do better."

Without waiting for a response, he hangs up, and when I finally lower Mom's phone, everyone's waiting for an explanation. I'm hollow and squirming, but I tell them. "I'm off the hook for the recording device."

Meg sucks in a breath like she knows what's coming before I say it.

"John's prints match the second set," I finish, heart thudding.

Fresh tears roll down Meg's cheeks. She leaves her plate of spaghetti untouched at the table and heads upstairs.

"I'll go." Mom follows, but Meg can't be comforted. She's

been crying so often since we left the police station without John.

I don't know what to do, what to say. If I tell Detective Davis that I'm responsible for faking a break-in, he'll think he had it right all along. But he'd thought I did it for the attention of my followers—as if all girls crave attention.

Amy takes another heaping spoonful of spaghetti. "Shit."

"What?" I ask.

"I guess John really did it."

"We don't know—"

"I mean, what kind of creep tapes a recording device under a piano?"

"John's not a creep." I feel suddenly defensive.

Amy reaches for the dessert, takes a slice of tiramisu. "It's kind of crazy when you think about it. Davis should've looked at John the first time. He makes a lot more sense than you."

"Davis doesn't know anything," I say.

Amy shrugs, but I'm serious. Davis has faulty evidence, and if it's all he's got against John, then John needs my help.

I know just the person to help him.

Laurie's room smells like his cologne, mint and eucalyptus. The scent reminds me of all the times we've spent lying head-to-head telling stories and asking, "Does this make me a bad person?" "Am I terrible for thinking this?" I can tell Laurie things that I'd never tell other people. Things I'm sometimes afraid to tell myself. If anyone can understand me now, it'll be him.

"Sit down a second," I say.

He stands awkwardly in the center of his room.

If things hadn't gotten bent up between us, he'd flop onto his bed with his chin on his fists, but now he looks nervous, unsure of himself.

I sit on the bed so he can take the desk chair. I've never met a boy as organized as Laurie—even his sneakers are clean and placed on shelves. I used to find it endlessly charming, but today it makes me uneasy. I need clutter, a mess in which to hide.

"Laurie, I don't know what to do." I get it out on a tight breath.

He shifts toward me on the chair. "What's wrong?"

"I don't know how to tell you."

"Pillow?"

A little laugh floats through my chest. Laurie and I have a tradition of holding pillows in front of our faces when something's too hard to admit. He did it when he told me he felt lonely at Concord High, and I did it when I told him I wasn't sure yet if I liked boys or girls, or anyone for that matter.

I shake my head. "I need to do this without a pillow."

He swallows, nods. "Take your time."

I pick my cuticles, focus on the sting. "I messed up. I messed up really bad."

Laurie moves to the edge of the bed. He knows me too well, recognizes the anguish in my voice. "What's going on?" he asks.

I can barely form the words, my voice just an exhale. "John Brooke's in jail because of me, and I was wondering, I guess I was hoping, that your grandma's nonprofit might help him get out."

Laurie shakes his head like he can't catch up. "What are you talking about?"

"You remember what happened in July?"

He shifts, muscles tightening, a flash of anger. "Yeah, I remember. Some creep was listening—"

"It wasn't some creep."

Laurie stills, gaze falling gently on the side of my face. "Jo." He sounds desperate and disappointed at the same time. "Please tell me you're not saying—"

"I did it."

Laurie scoots back like he needs to see me from a different angle. "You didn't."

"I did."

"You've been so adamant, fighting that detective. You're saying he had it right?"

"He didn't have it right." I stand up, straighten my arms in defiance.

"But you faked the break-in?"

I storm around the room. "Detective Davis thought I did it for social media followers, and that's just—it's insulting."

Laurie stares like he's trying to figure me out. "You posted that essay."

From the outside, my motive looks pretty straightforward. I planted the recording device so that I could write an essay about finding it, about the terrible fear of being watched, but I never imagined it would go viral. "It wasn't about the likes," I say. "I just wanted him to read it."

Laurie furrows his brow. "Who?"

I don't answer, but Laurie's expression settles like the truth's falling into place. "Your dad," he says.

I sink to the edge of the bed, drained and ashamed. "I thought I could change his mind."

It sounds so ridiculous now, a sad attempt from a little kid. "He told me he was leaving to keep us safe, so I thought . . ." I trail off, afraid Laurie's going to judge me, but he lays a strong, supportive hand on my back.

"I get it. You thought he'd realize you were in danger, with or without him here. You thought he'd come home."

The words alone bring a knot to my throat. I try to speak, but I don't want to cry.

Laurie moves closer, his arm wrapped firmly around my shoulders. "You gotta tell the police."

Tears roll down my cheeks. I imagine telling Detective Davis that I stole a recording device from the back of John's car, that I'd seen him using the damn thing in sessions with Beth, playing back her rehearsals, and I'd had an idea. "I can't."

"I don't think you have a choice. You can't let John get in trouble for something you did, and my grandma's nonprofit won't help with this. It's on you, Jo. But I'll go with you down to the station if you want."

I look into Laurie's deep brown eyes, and I respect his bluntness, his offer. I don't know what I did to deserve a friend like him. He fears the police, but he'd go with me. I know he would.

"You don't have to do that," I say.

It would be too selfless—and I have a better idea. I don't

have to trudge over to the station. I have a platform. With the tap of a button, I can get the truth off my chest, share it widely, without ever facing Detective Davis.

I stand up to go when Laurie stops me. "Jo?" He sounds nervous. "I need to tell you something too."

I nod. "Pillow?"

He shakes his head, rubs his brow like this news has been weighing on him. "It's about the party."

I think of his letterman jacket peeking out from under Sallie Gardiner's bed. "You were there, weren't you?"

He lets out a heavy sigh. "I should've told you sooner, but everything's been so—"

"You said you hated those parties."

Laurie's eyes grow wide and sad. "I know I said that, but—"

"You said you'd never go back after freshman year."

"I don't hate those parties, Jo. I just liked hating them with you."

A fault line forms down the middle of my heart. I love nothing more than hating things with Laurie, but when I told him that I didn't share his feelings, I rejected "us against the world."

"I've missed you," I say.

"Yeah." He stares at his hands.

If only I were different. If only I were Meg, who can love so quickly and fully. To me, the concept of love is like an ill-fitting sweater. It should be comfortable but it's itchy and overly warm, and it takes a long, long time to break it in.

"There's something else," says Laurie.

I nod, waiting.

"I didn't just go to the party. I went to the party to see Amy."

The room seems to warp like we've entered a different reality, but no, this isn't a big deal. Laurie and Amy have always been close, because Laurie and I are closer than close. "Okay . . ."

"We kissed," he says. "After the party. I thought you should hear it from me."

A wave of heat, my stomach suddenly weak. I convinced myself that this would never happen, but I can picture them laughing together, sharing glances. "You kissed my sister?"

"That's all we did. I promise."

I look at him sideways, shocked that he feels the need to qualify, as if they might've gone further. "I don't understand."

"It just happened," he says.

"Do you love her?"

He drags a hand over his head. "I don't—I don't know."

"Because you said you loved me. Just this summer." My voice breaks, and I wish it wouldn't. I turned Laurie down. I'm not allowed to be hurt.

He looks up, eyes full of confusion. "I don't know what to say."

In a flash I think of all the time we've spent as a trio—Laurie, Amy, and me. I should've been better. I should've focused on Laurie instead of focusing so much on my writing.

Of course he fell in love with Amy.

Of course he kissed Amy.

Of course I'm the one who ends up alone.

Laurie moves closer. "You're upset."

"I'm not upset." I shrug him off. "But she's my sister. My sister, Laurie."

"I know."

"You told me you loved me."

Laurie keeps his head down, his voice small. "You broke my heart, Jo. And Amy's always been there for me."

Every word feels like a knife to my chest. "I'm happy for you," I say, but I sound sarcastic. "I'm happy for both of you."

"Don't be like that."

"I have to go." I turn to leave, and for a few long strides, I'm certain Laurie will stop me on the stairs. He'll order me to come back, and we'll have it out like we always do.

I slow down, give him the chance, but he doesn't say a word.

This time, he lets me go.

CHAPTER THIRTY-TWO

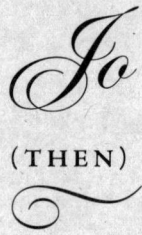

(THEN)

There's never been a Concord summer I didn't love, but this one in particular glistens with possibility. I lounge on the dock at Walden Pond over a manuscript that's been pouring out of me. The title? Just as Nan Dashwood suggested—*Little Women: Jo's Version*.

I press my nose to my notebook, mind thrumming with ideas, when Laurie splashes me from the pond below. "Come on," he says. "The water's perfect."

I snag my pages out of harm's way. "I'm working."

"Race me to the other side. I dare you."

I love a challenge, and he almost has me, my toes tingling at the thought of the cool water. But I don't have time for silly games, not anymore. My editor—my real, live editor—is waiting for this manuscript. "One more chapter," I say.

Laurie throws himself back in the water, shining and dramatic. He's objectively handsome, the kind of boy who belongs in a story, dark skin and taut muscles, eyes that sparkle with insight. "You know what, Jo?"

I reply tersely. "What, Laurie?"

"I think you might be the most boring girl I've ever known."

He's goading me, but I can't help looking over the brim of my notebook, my pen holding still. "I'm fascinating, and you know it."

"Not today. Not lately."

"Hush," I say, but I'm bothered, and Laurie's not wrong. He and I used to spend all day outside, marching through the woods while we talked about . . . everything.

He sinks low enough to blow loud, frustrated bubbles in the pond. "Come on. You're going to waste your summer working."

I wave him off. "Working is never a waste."

"That doesn't sound like you."

He's right. It doesn't. I've always preferred adventure to work, but writing is an adventure of its own.

I look at Laurie, try a different tack. "I'm not going to race you when I know I can't win."

Laurie's a great swimmer, his body strong from rowing crew.

He treads water, a smirk on his lips. "What if you happen to beat me? Just this once? Just today? Then you'd really have something to write about."

I can imagine the feeling, heat in my lungs, legs sore from kicking, the elation of gaining on Laurie, reaching the far end of the pond a split second before him.

It's that image that propels me into the water. That, or the sound of Amy sitting somewhere on the bank offering, "Laurie, I'll race you."

He's my best friend—not hers.

I plunge into the water, come up for air. "On three. And don't you dare let me win."

We're off. Laurie kicking cleanly, my gawky legs stirring up dirt and weeds. He pulls ahead before I can even find a rhythm, beats me to the other side, and gloats at the top of his lungs.

I suck in a mouthful of water and spit it toward him in a disapproving arc. "If you think about it, you should've beat me by a mile, which means that I actually won."

"You wish." He smirks.

I splash him, and he splashes me back, and after a round of laughter, we settle, both of us relaxing against the shore. It's quiet here, far from Amy, and my arm rests so close to Laurie's that a prickle of electricity builds between us. I brush it off. "We should swim back."

"Jo?" He squints at me, into the sunlight. "There's something I want to tell you."

I sit up, nervous for what he's about to say. Over the past few months, something's been growing between us, a tension like the wings of a hummingbird, fast and frail. "We should swim back," I say again.

"Just wait a minute." He fidgets. "Please."

I slip into the water, sink to my chin. I've been avoiding this conversation for a while, but I've known it was coming. Laurie's been looking at me differently, more intensely. "I need to get back to my book—"

"I like you, Jo. I like you a lot, and I always have." He spits out the words like he's been carrying them for too long.

My heart stoppers my throat. I wish I had a pillow to hold in front of my face. "I like you, too. You're my best friend."

He shakes his head like I don't get it. "That's the thing. I want to be more than friends."

"Laurie, I—"

"Don't answer right now. Just think about it."

I stand in the water, and my feet sink into a patch of slimy moss. I shiver, nervous. "I don't have to think about it."

Laurie moves toward me. "I know this kind of thing makes you uncomfortable—"

"I'm not uncomfortable."

"—but I need you to know how much I like you." He pauses. "I love you."

I can't help but laugh. "You don't love me."

"I do. I have for a long time." He looks so sincere, so determined, his brow holding sunlight.

My heart aches. I love Laurie more than life itself, but not in the way he wants, and the disparity makes me angry. I step away, feet squelching. "Take it back."

"Why?" he asks.

"You can't love me. You shouldn't love me."

He lets out the most tender laugh, a laugh that admires me despite my faults. "I do anyway. Even more when you tell me not to."

In a book, a girl would melt over this sort of thing, but I won't stand for it. "I want to be *friends*. Jo and Laurie. Just like always."

Laurie sighs. "One date. Give me one date, and if we don't have a good time, I'll back off."

"We'll have a great time," I say. "You know we will."

"Then what's the problem?"

I don't know exactly how to explain it, but the idea of loving someone—I mean, really loving them—feels like a bottomless pond, fathoms of deep dark water below, and I prefer to have my feet planted firmly in the muck. "I'm not sure I'll ever have a boyfriend. Or a girlfriend. Or anything like it."

"Why not?" asks Laurie.

I don't know how to answer this without undoing myself. Most people want love, and for some reason, I can't be bothered with it. Maybe I'm defective. Afraid. Or maybe I'm truly ambitious, and I can't stand the idea of someone weighing me down. I really don't know which one is true. "I have better things to do," I say at last.

Laurie lets out a short, bitter laugh. "Right. Got it."

Regret washes over me, and I wish I could take back what I said. "I didn't mean it like that."

He's hurt, but he's trying to hide it. "It's fine. I understand. I'm not as important as your writing."

It stings to hear him say this. I've thought it myself about my relationship with Dad. I'll never be as important to him as his work, and it sucks. I sound like Amy, but yeah, it sucks.

"That's not true," I manage to say.

Laurie shakes his head. "You don't have time for me."

A dagger through my heart. "Laurie—"

"I should swim back."

"Laurie, wait."

Before he kicks off, he turns, expectant.

"It wasn't supposed to happen like this. You weren't supposed to get hurt."

"Excuse me?"

My heart struggles to beat. I'm saying it all wrong, and I can't lose my friendship with Laurie. He's the only person I know who loves my flaws as much as my strengths. "I knew you had feelings for me, it's been obvious, but I thought we could get past it."

Laurie rubs his neck, head hanging low, and he chews on his words like he's trying not to be angry. "You knew? You knew all along? Jo, I've been agonizing over this. It's not something I can *get past*. I have real feelings for you."

The lake goes still, my whole body frozen. I need to tell Laurie that love terrifies me, that I'm afraid I'd have to lose a part of myself to gain him, but that's real—too real—so I splash him. "Stop being so serious."

This isn't us. We don't hurt in each other's company. Even when we fight, it's all for fun, for the thrill of opposition.

Laurie wipes his face in one swift motion, nods like he understands me now, and swims away.

"Laurie, come on," I say, but he can't hear me. He's halfway across the pond.

CHAPTER THIRTY-THREE

Meg

(NOW)

Four days and fourteen hours after John's arrest, his charges are dropped and he's released from prison. I wait in the shadow of a cold cement building until a uniformed man walks him through a barbed-wire fence.

John's ragged, already thinner than he should be. The sight of him weakens my knees, but I stand strong against the bitter wind, refusing to let the guard see how close I am to breaking. I accept a bag of John's belongings—his wallet and keys, and nothing more.

"I'm sorry," he mutters, but he doesn't need to apologize. It's not his fault that he was wrongly accused, and I don't mind picking him up in the snow. I'd pick him up anywhere.

I reach for his hand, warm and gentle, and clutch it until the guard disappears. Then I pull John into my arms. He rests his head on my shoulder like he's a child, and he gets heavy, heavier, until I'm afraid we'll both end up on the ground.

I help him to the car and crank up the heater, John crouched and shivering. "I can't believe they let me out."

"You're innocent," I say, and it's indisputably true.

Though I haven't been allowed to see it, the police found footage from a video doorbell that corroborates John's story: he drove Beth home, and she walked safely inside.

Plus, Jo admitted to planting the recording device, so the theory that John had been plotting Beth's murder for months thankfully disintegrated.

"Jo confessed to it on social media," I tell him, unable to hide my disapproval.

I share the video, but he can hardly watch. When my sister admits to her followers that John used the device for his music lessons, that she nabbed it from his car, he pushes my phone away.

"I'm so sorry." I apologize on Jo's behalf, but I know it's not enough.

At the end of her video, my sister explains her actions, and I understand that she felt desperate to draw Dad back home, but she hurt John in the process. And that much is unforgivable.

"You're okay now," I say.

John doesn't seem to believe it. He slumps like he doesn't have the energy to buckle his seat belt. "There are some things you need to know."

I take the wheel, determined to get him home. "You don't have to explain anything to me."

He reaches for my hands. "Meg—"

"I'm sure you want a shower, a hot meal."

"Meg." He pries my hands from the wheel, holds them until I meet his gaze. "The police had a whole narrative against me, and I don't want you hearing it from anyone else."

"I trust you," I say.

"I lied about my car. It wasn't a fender bender. I hit a tree by the woods, because Beth got sick."

"You've been cleared. You don't have to—"

"Forensics found a scrap of my jacket at the crime scene." He lets me process, then he raises his sleeve to reveal a pink scratch on his arm. It's shallow, nearly healed, but it holds my attention. "They also found my DNA under Beth's fingernails."

My heart stops, but only for a moment. "John, I don't need to hear any of this."

He looks determined, despite the bags under his eyes. "Beth didn't want to go home that night, but she was wasted, and I didn't think she'd be safe at that party, so I managed to get her in the car. Some of the kids said it looked like a struggle."

"You did the right thing."

"She rode with me for a few blocks, but then she got sick, and we hit a tree. After that, she jumped out of the car, and I had to chase her up the bridge beside the Laurence house."

My heart pounds, moves up my throat. I struggle to form a full sentence. "This is not— They can't blame you for—"

"She was talking about the park. Said your dad used to take you there, and you'd all lie on the ground to look at the stars."

"That's true," I say.

He softens his tone. "Beth told me you'd all make wishes, and that she never knew what to wish for, not once."

I nod, unable to speak.

"She got really worked up about that, really frustrated with herself for not knowing what she wanted out of life. She was upset, pacing, and that hill is dangerous."

"Stop."

"It was dark, and Beth tripped, and—"

"John, stop it!" I yell, and in a fleeting thought, I imagine the guards rushing over to investigate the disturbance. I lower my voice. "John Brooke, don't you dare tell me you actually had something to do with this."

He pulls in a shaky breath, levels his shoulders. "I didn't, but, Meg, they really thought I did, and I'd understand if you think so too."

I close my eyes because I can't bear to look at him. "I won't survive if you hurt her."

John comes closer, his voice softer. "She slipped, and I caught her. She ripped my jacket, scratched my arm, and after that, she calmed down. The shock of it all. She got in the car, and I drove her home."

I keep my eyes shut. "I want to believe you."

"Believe me," he urges.

I still can't look at him, but I feel him pleading, head bowed, and when I finally open my eyes, all my doubt washes away. John's not completely unassuming, but he's thin and tender and deeply humble. Just now, he's surely hungry and tired, and still he looks at me with nothing but love.

"Believe me," he says again, like he's aching for it.

"I believe you," I say, and when the words leave me, a new weight takes their place. The rest of the world won't be so quick to accept John's story, his jacket torn, the scratch on his arm still fresh. They'll think he got off easy. They'll think the video footage isn't enough.

I start the car, a sudden urge to get him away from the prison, but he keeps talking. "You said something at the station the other day."

I glance at him sideways, imagining all the things he might've overheard. "I lost control of myself."

"You said you love me." His voice sounds gentle but sure. "Is that true?"

I know my answer, but I need a deep breath.

John can't seem to wait. "I hope it's true," he says, "because I love you, Meg. I love you so much."

"I love you too." I turn slowly, strain against my seat belt to look him in the eye. "I really do."

He smiles, wide and bashful, and for a brief moment we kiss in front of a prison. Then my phone rings.

"Who is it?" he asks.

It's Mom. She's supposed to be at work, and she texted three times before calling. I answer in a panic. "Mom? What's wrong?"

She lets out a sigh that sounds more disappointed than despairing. "I need your help."

"Anything."

"Amy's been suspended. Again."

"What happened?"

Mom huffs. "Something about a hard lemonade."

"A what?"

"A hard lemonade. Alcohol. At school. Can you pick her up?"

I look out at the prison, and the contrast is so ridiculous that I can't help but laugh, Amy's suspension against John's arrest. "I'll be there soon."

"What is it?" asks John.

I should be upset, frustrated with Amy for causing trouble, but picking Amy up from the principal's office feels so normal, so typical high school compared to the horror we've all lived through, that it warms me. I laugh so hard, I snort. "We're going to Concord High."

John looks at me like I've lost my mind. "To do what?"

"To pick up another hardened criminal."

I can't stop laughing, which makes John laugh too, and as we drive away, I think maybe, just maybe, we'll be okay.

CHAPTER THIRTY-FOUR

Amy

(NOW)

I pour a glass of wine from Mom's stash and laugh at the irony in every sip. Concord High suspended me for drinking a hard lemonade behind the art studios, and now I have all day to drown my sorrows at home.

I don't even like the taste of wine, but it's the only way to cope with the investigation, our lives turned inside out.

Laurie told Jo a watered-down version of what happened between us on the night of the party, and she hates me for it. If only she knew about our clothes on the floor, the way my fingers slipped beneath the waistband of his boxers. Then she'd really have a reason to be mad.

I'm partway through a bottle, finally losing track of my pain, when the doorbell rings and panic shoots through me. Mom's at work, Jo's at school, and Meg's with John, so I'm home alone.

I shrink down on the couch, worrying over who could be here. If it's one of the detectives, I can't answer the door, not with a bottle of wine in my hand. Could it be someone from school? A guidance counselor checking up on me? That would be better but still pretty bad.

I consider running upstairs or retreating into Mom's bedroom, but the visitor knocks, a muffled shout. "Open up, for god's sake! It's me!"

"Holy shit," I whisper under my breath. I know that voice, and it's the last person I want to see.

I grab the wine bottle, shove the cork in its mouth, and hide it in the kitchen. "Shit, shit, shit," I mutter, glancing at the back door, wondering if I can escape through the yard.

"Amy, I see you! Open up!"

"Shit," I say again, but I don't have a choice.

I straighten my posture and answer the door. "Aunt March?"

She carries an expensive duffel bag, sunglasses perched on her head. "Shouldn't you be at school?"

I stumble aside to let her in, and she bursts into the house, her broad shoulders and brash personality filling the entryway. "Why are you in your pajamas? And what have you been drinking? Merlot?"

I wipe my mouth, and a red stain shines on my hand. I swallow my embarrassment. "I didn't know you were coming."

"I didn't call." She steps out of her boots, makes herself comfortable. It's been a few months since I saw her last, and she hasn't changed. She's bleached blond and corporate, wearing a sharp blazer and a neat button-down. "I'm guessing your mom's at work. So, what? Are you ditching?"

"Suspended," I mumble.

"Again?" She looks shocked, but she doesn't have the right to judge. She may be a badass executive now, but Dad's told us too many stories about Aunt March in high school, smoking in the bathroom, setting off fire alarms.

"I'm glad you're home," she says. "We need to talk."

The entry hall goes quiet, and I try not to swallow. I knew Aunt March would show up eventually, and I knew she'd want to interrogate me. I do my best to distract her. "It's weird having you here. I don't remember the last time you came to Concord."

"Christmas," she says. "Seven years ago."

It comes back to me slowly, a memory of my aunt bawling over a cup of cocoa. She'd been engaged in her thirties, and when her girlfriend broke it off, she came to spend the holiday with us.

She drops her bag by the staircase, moves to the kitchen. "I guess my brother's still out in the woods."

I shrug. Jo's been searching for Dad, but she hasn't found him yet, and the police haven't heard from him either.

Aunt March leans against the counter. "Goddamn mountain man. Loves going off the grid, just like our dad and his dad before that. I hate to think of what'll happen when he finally gets Wi-Fi."

I picture Dad being flooded with messages from the past seven months, the latest information that will bring him to his knees.

"So, where's that wine?" asks Aunt March.

"What?"

"The wine you've been drinking in the middle of a school day."

My cheeks fill with heat, but I point to the toaster, a bottle of merlot sticking up behind it. Aunt March swoops over. "Thank god. LaGuardia's a nightmare on Mondays."

Aunt March hardly ever travels in from Manhattan, but when she does, she always complains. She's been living there since she turned eighteen, and I don't know why. She never has anything nice to say about the city. Then again, she never has anything nice to say at all.

She pours herself a glass, and to my surprise, pours one for me. I hesitate. "You're not going to tell my mom?"

She nudges the glass toward me, a little laugh. "Underage drinking's the least of our problems, don't you think?"

I take a careful sip. "What do you mean?"

"I have some questions, Amy." She peers over the wine, gaze boring into me. "I need to know if I killed Beth."

CHAPTER THIRTY-FIVE

Amy

(THEN)

The bus to Manhattan reeks of tuna fish and pickles, and it's obvious Florence would rather be anywhere else in the world. She hugs her knees to her chest, nose pinched in the window seat. "We could've taken an Uber."

I look straight ahead, determined to make the most of this trip. "A four-hour Uber? Even *your* parents would notice that charge."

Florence groans because she knows I'm right. Her parents may be rich, but they don't spend their money willy-nilly. They're careful. And if they spotted our little adventure on Flo's credit card bill, we'd never hear the end of it.

Today they think we're visiting Meg at Harvard, a lie that made my aunt Mary and uncle Carlos swell with pride. Florence and I will never get into Harvard, neither of us has the grades, but we can let them dream.

We tumble off the bus somewhere in Manhattan, sucking in air that seems fresh compared to the confines of the Greyhound.

"Never again," says Florence, smoothing her dress.

"Again in a few hours," I say as I orient to the grid of the city streets.

People pass by, all of them in a hurry, and my heart soars. I can't wait to live in a big city. In cities, people never lack purpose. They always have somewhere to go, something important to do.

Florence looks uncomfortable. "Where—"

"Upper East Side," I say with a point.

Ask me for directions in Concord, I'm useless. Though I've lived there my whole life, I've never really cared to know where I'm going or how to get anywhere. Here, I'm prepared.

I study the street signs, numbers growing in one direction, and we head toward Central Park. We walk for at least an hour, blisters forming on my heels. I hardly notice the pain, enthralled by the shops, the loud-honking cabs, and the wildly interesting people who knock into our shoulders.

I lose myself in the commotion, so much so that when we reach Aunt March's apartment building, and Florence says, "You ready?" I almost ask, "For what?"

But as I stare up at the high-rise, a doorman waiting just inside, my task comes back to me like a rock in my stomach. I catch my breath against a tree. "I'm not so sure about this."

Florence tightens her ponytail. "You can do it."

"What if she says no?"

"What if she says yes?"

I'm not sure I can ask her. In fact, I know that I can't. I don't even like Aunt March, Dad's younger sister. She has all his ego and none of his talent. "It's too much money. It's too much to ask."

"Amy." Florence waits for me to look her in the eye. "Think of Kitty Bryant."

Google searches. Articles. A website studded with prestigious awards. We've been stalking Kitty Bryant since we met Fred Vaughn. She attended his summer program two years ago, and then she blew up. Last week one of her paintings sold to a Dutch heiress for a sum just shy of a million.

"Okay," I breathe. "You're right."

Florence doesn't relent. She clutches my shoulder. "This program could change our lives. And I'm not talking, like, 'I won tickets to a Beyoncé concert' kind of life changing. I'm talking goodbye old life, hello new, bibbidi-bobbidi-freaking-boo."

I look up, a smirk cutting into my cheek. "You're so weird."

She curtsies like it's a compliment.

Maybe it is, because she's right. Traveling Europe with Fred Vaughn wouldn't just be a vacation of picnicking on the Seine and lounging in a Greek Airbnb, it would be an open door to a new future. I wouldn't have to stress about getting into college. I wouldn't have to bury myself in mountains of debt just to earn some stupid degree. I'd go straight to being an artist, my paintings in the homes of the rich and famous.

I collect my posture and march up the steps, reminding myself that A) This apartment is on the Upper East Side, which certainly isn't slumming it, and B) My European education will cost only a fraction of Beth's Plumfield tuition. In context, I'm not asking for much.

Thanks to Florence, the doorman lets us up without question. She has those eyelashes, too long for her own good, fluttered along with a lie. "It's her aunt's birthday. We want to surprise her."

Outside Aunt March's door, I knock with confidence and listen for her footsteps, decisive and striking. She answers in a blazer, her phone in her hand. "Amy? What the hell are you doing here?"

My nerves tangle right back up. Partly because, no matter how you rationalize it, I'm asking for twenty grand. And partly because Aunt March is so unflinchingly cool. As much as I despise her, she has the life I want more than anything. An apartment of her own in a big city, a gorgeous leather couch, half-eaten takeout on the coffee table.

"Hey." I fidget. "Um . . . sorry I didn't text you first."

She raises an eyebrow. "You in some kind of trouble?"

I harden, arms drawn across my chest. Why is that her first assumption? She must talk to Dad too much, stories filtered through his judgmental eyes. I decide not to justify her question with a response. "You remember my cousin, Florence."

Aunt March leans against the doorframe. She's met Florence at family gatherings, but they're not directly related to each other, and I think Aunt March is glad she doesn't share blood with the Carrols. "Yeah, I remember. How's Mary?" she asks with a hint of sarcasm.

"She's great," says Florence. "Opening a new gallery."

"Catholic art, right?" Aunt March turns, walks deep into her apartment with the door wide open. "Fascinating."

She catches my gaze from across the room, a brief eye roll that reminds me she's always considered religion to be oppressive. I ease inside without being invited, gesture for Florence to follow.

Aunt March puts a kettle on the stove. "Tea?"

It's a funny thing the way habits bleed through families. She seems like a whiskey-drinking woman, but her kitchen smells like peppermint, Dad's favorite kind of tea.

Neither Florence nor I answer, but Aunt March pulls three mugs from her cabinet. "Your mom know you're here?"

I sit at her cramped kitchen table. "No, and I'd appreciate it if you could keep this between—"

"I'm not going to rat you out." She cracks a window, lets in the sound of the city, and looks at me like she's waiting for an explanation.

Florence nudges me under the table.

"I need to ask you something," I spit out.

Aunt March chuckles. "I'd be surprised if you came all the way to New York without anything to ask me."

"Florence and I— You see, we've been accepted— There's a summer program—"

"She needs money," says Florence.

Aunt March nods with a mixture of smugness and disappointment, like she knew money would be the only reason I'd come see her. "How much?"

"My favorite artist in the entire world is teaching a workshop in—"

"How much?" She cuts me off like she doesn't care what the money's for, like it'll make no difference.

I wince as I answer. "Twenty grand."

Her eyes widen as she stirs her tea, the spoon clinking. "You know, Beth calls me once a week. Asks me about my job, my girlfriend. We broke up, by the way."

"Holly?" I ask.

"Hollis. But it's fine. You're busy. I get it."

I swallow my guilt, wishing I could be as thoughtful as Beth. I'm a jerk for coming out here, visiting Aunt March only when I need something. But then it strikes me. Aunt March is an adult. "It's not like you ever call me, either."

Her focus ticks up.

"You could ask about school. My friends. I got suspended, by the way. Dress code protest."

Aunt March stares for a second, and I think she's offended, but then she smiles. "You're right. I could call. So, this summer program?"

I take a cup of tea and tell her about Fred Vaughn, the way he shepherds his students to all the right places and all the right people, the studios, galleries, the wild success of the cohorts who came before us.

"I've heard of Kitty Bryant," she says when I'm finished. "She was in *Vanity Fair*."

I'm winded now, too excited to hide it. "I could be the next Kitty Bryant."

Aunt March inhales the steam from her tea. "It sounds like a dream, but there's only one problem: I don't have twenty grand."

"Your apartment says otherwise," Florence mutters under her breath.

I'm shocked she has the gall to say something like that, but then again, it's easier to be bold when you're doing it on behalf of someone else.

Aunt March laughs. "Florence, I'm surprised your parents are paying your way."

Florence stares into her mug. "They, uh—"

"I'm guessing you glossed over the details. Left out the part about sharing an Airbnb with a grown man."

Florence shrugs, red as a stoplight. "They know enough."

Aunt March eyes my cousin, a slow warning nod that says her parents will know everything if we're not careful. "Look, I promised Beth I'd pay for Plumfield, and Plumfield's not cheap. My apartment looks fancy, but it's rent stabilized, and I've got money tied up in investments. I don't have anything else to offer right now." She pauses, sips. "However . . . Beth isn't sure about Plumfield. We've had some back-and-forth about it."

I look up, hope inflating my chest.

"If she decides not to go, I'd be willing to pay for this program."

"Are you serious?" I ask.

Aunt March sizes me up. "I think so. But you have to promise you won't tell Beth, won't try to sway her in any way."

"I promise."

"Really, Amy."

"I won't breathe a word, I swear."

Aunt March peers over the rim of her mug. "All right, we have a deal."

My heart soars. To Aunt March, this deal is just a what-if, but in my mind, I'm already packing my bags. There's no way Beth's going to Plumfield. She'll never have the guts.

CHAPTER THIRTY-SIX

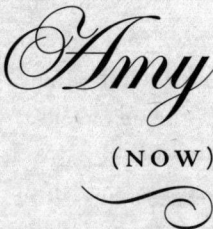

(NOW)

Aunt March drains her wine and stares me down. "Be honest. Is it my fault?"

I take a slow, calculated step away from my aunt. I'll admit, I'm a little tipsy, but I'm not too drunk to pick up on her sick accusation. "You think I killed my sister."

"Did you?" she asks, her tone so blunt that I almost laugh.

"You think I'd trade Beth for twenty grand?"

Aunt March pours herself another glass and gulps it down like she needs the sedative. "I don't know, Amy, I can't sleep. Can't eat. Can't stop wondering if I caused her death by promising you that money if she didn't use it."

I can't believe what I'm hearing. I've been blaming myself for yelling at Beth and leaving her alone, but it's ridiculous to think I could've killed her with my own two hands. "You have no idea what you're talking about."

"Then tell me. What happened to Beth?"

"I don't know."

"I read in the news there was some kind of party."

I draw my arms tight across my chest. I'm not going through this again. I already told the detectives my story. "You know it's been ten days since Beth died? Ten days, and you haven't even bothered to call."

Aunt March winces. As much as she claims to want a relationship with each of her nieces, she doesn't make much of an effort. "You were at the party, weren't you? You and Florence?"

I turn my back on Aunt March and rush to the bathroom, where I clutch the sink and splash cool water on my face. She follows me, her wineglass full and sloshing again. "Beth was killed a few days before she was supposed to leave for Plumfield. Tell me that's just a coincidence."

I drag a towel over my face. "What do you want me to say?"

"I want the truth."

My smile cracks open. "You know what? Fine. You're right, Aunt March. You killed Beth. It's your fault."

She sets her wineglass on the counter like she can't be trusted to hold it. "Explain."

"I told Beth about our deal. Told her she didn't deserve your money and begged her to give it up. I left her sobbing at that party, and a couple of hours later, she was dead. Everyone's calling it homicide, but I don't believe it. We found her right by the bridge. Why don't they realize she could've jumped? I destroyed her. It's my fault. *Your* fault for giving me that power. And we'll have to live with that for the rest of our lives."

My voice echoes through the bathroom until it fades, and we settle.

Aunt March opens a window, fishes a cigarette from her pocket and doesn't speak until it's lit, until she's taken a couple of calming drags. "Your dad was right. You really are arrogant."

"Excuse me?" I look up, stunned.

"You think Beth threw herself off a bridge because you said something mean? That's a little self-important, don't you think?"

I feel like she slapped me, and at the same time, the tension in my chest lets up.

Aunt March sits on the bath mat, stretches her legs out, and smokes. "You need to give your sister more credit. She was way too strong to let a little fight send her over the edge."

I'm trembling, but her words begin to steady me. I join her on the floor. "You really think so?"

Aunt March takes a drag, laughs it out. "This may come as a surprise, but I'm not that great with people. Beth reached out. She got to know me even though I make it hard. If that's not strength, I don't know what is."

My chest burns like something's been wrenched out of it. I always thought strength could be measured by the space we make for ourselves, like elbowing through a crowd, but Beth did something harder than that. She made space for others.

"I wish we'd had more time," I whisper.

Aunt March gets up, and just when I think she's about to leave me alone on the bathroom floor, she extends a hand.

CHAPTER THIRTY-SEVEN

Beth

(THEN)

"You ready?" asks Jo.

It's a simple question, but as we stand at the gates of Plumfield, I can't find the answer.

I'm ready for my audition. I've practiced so many times that I could perform my excerpt from the *Hammerklavier* backward and blindfolded, but the drive to New Hampshire felt so long—more than an hour without stopping.

Jo tugs my arm, desperate to stoke my enthusiasm. "This place is literally gorgeous."

Crisp red leaves surround a building draped with ivy. It's so much prettier than Concord High, it's a wonder they're both called schools. Students mosey up from their dorms clutching coffee, carrying not just backpacks but also instruments and sketchbooks.

"You would fit right in," I say.

Jo surveys the campus, a glimmer in her eye. "You'll fit in better."

The campus glistens, so energizing and creative that I can't help but think of Amy. She's desperate to get out of Concord, misunderstood at school, and she would instantly mesh with these students, her splatter-paint personality and pink-streaked hair. A whisper escapes me. "Amy should've had a chance to—"

"Amy will find her own way," says Jo. "This is yours."

I steady my breathing the way my new piano instructor has taught me to do. She's not as kind or fun as John Brooke, but she's been preparing me for the audition, and she knows techniques that I can't wait to share with him. Today, however, her breathing exercises fall short. "Thank you for driving me," I tell Jo, my heart still racing.

She gave up an entire day to drive me here and wait in the auditorium, and she hasn't complained once. "I wouldn't miss it," she says. "I wanted to see your future home."

Those words tighten my heartstrings. This school is beautiful, but it can't be home. Nothing can be home without my family, without Henry.

I stop on the path to the auditorium. "I'm not so sure about this."

Students pass us on both sides, all of them confident and independent, chasing their dreams.

Jo pulls me into the grass. "You're just nervous."

"What if I don't belong here?"

"You'll make a place for yourself."

"I belong at home. With the people I love."

Jo grips my shoulders, looks me in the eye. "You can love us without living right on top of us."

"It won't be the same."

"No, but—"

"It's not just you. I don't want to leave Henry."

"Henry?" Jo screws up her face. "You've only known him for a couple of months."

It's true, but the months I've known Henry have been some of the best of my life. "I love him, Jo."

"It'll pass," she says.

I don't want it to pass. I want to hold on to Henry forever.

Jo eyes me carefully, like she's worried I'm about to make a mistake. "You're a great musician, a natural talent, and John's a good enough teacher, but imagine what you could do with real training."

I picture a future that's all about music. I could teach at a music school. I could play in an orchestra. And if I get really brave, I could be a recording artist, have a Grammy in my living room.

Jo brings her voice to a smolder. "You told *Teen Vogue* to wait and see what you do next." She gestures to the auditorium. "This is it. This is the most exciting chapter in your story."

A tingle rises from my toes, and I focus on the possibilities. I could be a brilliant musician. I have the passion, the drive, and with this school, I'd have a springboard. "Maybe there's a way to have both. Henry and I can handle a long-distance relationship."

"Maybe so," says Jo, though she clearly doesn't care.

I think of the park back home, the way Dad used to lie with us in the grass and ask about our goals. Jo would always shout first, "I want to be a writer!" "An artist," Amy would chime in. Meg would dream of a rich husband, a house on Nantucket, and after a long silence, I'd admit that I didn't know what I wanted.

"You ready?" Jo asks again.

"Will you stand in the wings?"

"Of course," she says, and though I still don't know what I really want, it's time to find out.

CHAPTER THIRTY-EIGHT

(NOW)

I wake up to a tapping at the window.

At first the sound goes in one ear and out the other, my thoughts sluggish from all the wine. But there it is again, a quick and quiet tap-tap-tap.

Laurie.

Could it be?

Last time we talked, he wanted to keep his distance, but he's the only person who's ever climbed the lattice on the side of the house and tumbled through my window.

Granted, he's never done it for me. He's always passed through my room to go hang out with Jo, but today his knuckles hit the glass with a quiet urgency. An urgency that belongs to us.

I open the window, and he comes in on a gust of cold wind. As soon as he's in my room, I realize how much I've missed him. The scent of his cologne, his presence, calm and wise.

Today he sits on the windowsill, warms his hands between

his knees, and though he looks worried, he's still solid and strong. "Sorry to show up like this. I know it's early."

I wipe my eyes. "I'm sleeping like shit anyway. Last night sucked."

Aunt March didn't even stay the night, but she couldn't leave without telling my whole family about Fred Vaughn's summer program and how I'd arranged to get the money. "You're disgusting." That's all Jo said to me, and that's exactly how I feel. Disgusting.

Laurie doesn't move for a while, just stares at the carpet like he's going to be sick. "Something happened, Ames."

I stay a few feet away, unsure of where we stand with each other. I don't know if I'm allowed to touch him, but he's scared, shoulders set hard, and I can't bear to leave him alone like that. I lock my bedroom door before wrapping an arm around his shoulder. "What's wrong?"

He shakes his head.

"You can tell me," I whisper.

"Detective Kirke came by with a warrant."

"To search your house?"

"They tore it apart."

My throat tightens. Now that John's charges have been dropped, the detectives seem to be doubling down, interrogating everyone who came within ten feet of the Gardiners' party. But I haven't heard of anyone else being served with a warrant. "What reason do they have?"

"We lied, Ames."

He means that I lied.

"And my house is right by the crime scene." Laurie rubs his forehead so hard, it turns red. "They found something."

My heart stills in my chest, but it doesn't matter what bogus evidence the detectives think they found. Laurie's the last person who would ever hurt Beth. "Don't worry. We were together all night. If they think you did something, they'll have to assume we did it together."

Laurie swallows hard. "Okay, but the thing is . . ." He pulls a breath through his nose. "We weren't together all night."

"Yes, we were." I laugh, remembering the way we slept back-to-back.

He shakes his head. "The detectives checked my house alarm. It keeps a record of when we come and go."

"But you didn't go anywhere."

"There's something I haven't told you."

I let go of his hands, scoot back on the bed so I can see him clearly. "What are you talking about?"

"That night, after you passed out, I got a call from Ned Gardiner. Your cousin needed a ride home and she tried him first, but he was too drunk to drive her, so he asked me for help."

"Florence?"

Just the thought of my cousin sends a whisper of anxiety down my spine. She's been acting weird since she found out about Beth, not depressed and grieving like everyone else but determined to keep living.

Laurie stands up to pace like this story's been rattling around inside him for days. "It seemed like an emergency, and I was sober, so I told Ned I'd help."

My breath comes quickly, but I don't know why. The Gardiners' house is only three minutes away from Laurie's. If he drove Florence home from the party, he couldn't have been gone for long. "So what? So, you were out for a few minutes?"

Laurie stops pacing. "I was out for an hour, maybe more."

The room goes cold, and I realize the window's still cracked. I shut it hard while Laurie continues.

"Florence wasn't at the party. She was at a hotel. In Boston."

I still. "What the . . ."

"Some guys were talking about an after-party. I figured she went with them."

"To Boston?"

He rubs his forehead, eyes full of regret, like he wishes he'd asked more questions in the moment. "I didn't really think. I just drove."

I can hardly breathe, but I stay calm for Laurie. "It's okay. If you picked up Florence, you have an alibi. She can tell the police—"

"She denied it, Ames."

My mind snags, heart thudding.

"The cops believed her," he adds. "They don't trust me because I didn't say anything about Boston during my first interview."

"Why didn't you?"

He lets out a heavy sigh, sits back on the bed. "I guess I thought it looked bad."

"Why would Florence deny it?"

"I don't know, but I think something happened at the after-party. When I picked her up, she was quiet, and, Ames, I could be wrong, but it seemed like she'd been crying."

My mind skips, trying to keep up. Florence and I have talked about the night of the party, and she hasn't told me anything about going to Boston. I don't understand why she'd keep it from me.

Laurie wrings his hands. "I'm really sorry about this."

"You didn't do anything wrong. You were helping a friend."

"No, I mean this . . ." He gestures to the air between us. "I never should've said we couldn't see each other."

My voice cracks. "You were just—"

"I was scared, but I know you're scared too, and now I'm coming to you with all my problems."

I take his hands, steady them between mine. "I'm glad you're here. Problems and all."

He looks so relieved, and so tired. "I don't know what to do."

For days I've been depressed, flailing, but I can surface for Laurie. I breathe, rise, and move to my closet.

"What're you doing?" he asks.

"We're going to Boston."

He pinches his brow. "I have school."

I rifle through a pile until I find my coat, shove my arms in the sleeves. "You're not going to school."

Laurie looks depleted, like he didn't sleep all night. "I don't want to cause any more trouble."

I head for the door, leave him standing in the middle of the room. "Hotels have security cameras. If Florence went to an after-party, we can prove it, find out who else was there. Now, do you want to get your alibi?" I pause. "Or would you rather I go alone?"

* * *

The hotel's a Marriott, the fanciest one I've ever seen. Tall, ornate, and right on the harbor. Laurie parks across the street in an apartment lot, like he's trying to be discreet. I don't have the heart to remind him that, at this point, we have nothing to lose.

I open my door, but Laurie catches my elbow, nervous sweat on his brow. "We can't just walk in."

"Why not?"

"We need a plan."

I've never been one for making plans. That was Beth's thing. Last year she bought a calendar for our room, hung it on the wall, and begged me to use it so we could keep up with each other's lives. She even bought a pink gel pen just for me, but I never touched it. To this day, the calendar only has purple events on its pages. All her plans.

"We shouldn't have come here," says Laurie.

"It's fine," I say. "We'll just talk to the front desk."

"And ask them what?"

"We'll see if they recognize her. If they know why she was here."

"They're not going to tell us—"

I hold up a hand to stop the logic. I'm not stupid. I know the hotel probably won't remember Florence, and even if they do, they won't give out personal information. But I don't have any other ideas.

"Laurie, please." I turn to face him. "We have to try."

He softens like he's giving in, but his shoulders don't relax. "Okay, we'll ask, but if they don't want to answer—"

"I won't cause a scene." I give him a reassuring look, but as I step out of the car, I'm not sure I can keep that promise. I'm not leaving the hotel until I know what Florence was doing there.

Laurie stays behind me as we enter the lobby, taking careful, measured strides. I think it's an attempt to blend in, but it's only making him look shady.

"Chill," I whisper.

He tries to shake it off. "You'll do the talking, right?"

It's not like him. He's usually so confident and comfortable talking to adults.

"You're going to be okay," I say.

He nods curtly. "Just be polite. Don't make them angry."

I stride forward like I know exactly what I'm doing, but my heart pounds while we wait in line. A couple stands in front of us, checking out of their room, a giggly man tucked up against his partner. Their happiness sits with me, because it feels so out of place. I forgot that there's a life outside this investigation.

"Excuse me? Can I help you?" A manager stands behind the desk looking expectant, like he's already asked me once.

"Sorry. Yes." I hurry forward, fishing my phone out of my back pocket.

"Checking out?"

I should've prepared a preamble, but I'm so nervous, I just shove the phone in his face. "I'm wondering if you remember this girl."

The manager tips his head.

"She would've been here on New Year's Eve." I turn up the brightness, push the phone closer.

The manager squints. "I don't think so. There were a lot of people here on New Year's Eve."

"We think she came for a party. A bunch of high school kids."

"I don't remember."

"Do you have security cameras? Could we look and see if she walked in?"

The man straightens, returns to his computer. "I'm afraid I can't help you. Now, if you don't mind, I have guests." He gestures to the line behind me, and a woman moves forward.

"We're not done," I say.

Laurie shifts uncomfortably. "We should go."

"Listen," I say to the manager, "this is really important. We're in the middle of a murder investigation. I'm sure you've heard of Beth March—"

"Should I get security?" asks the manager.

Laurie's breath comes hot in my ear. "Ames, let's go."

I shake him off, keep my focus on the man behind the desk. "This girl's my cousin, and she won't admit to being here on New Year's Eve, but we know—"

Laurie takes off, and my focus slips.

"Laurie, where—"

He charges through the lobby, rushes through a revolving door. At first I think he's freaked because I'm pushing too hard, but out of the corner of my eye, I watch him take a few long strides up the block and carefully approach a maid who's drinking a Red Bull while leaning against the building.

I smile at the manager. "If you'll excuse me . . ."

I hurry after Laurie, find him outside with the maid, a thirty-something woman with bright blue hair.

"What's going on?" I ask.

Laurie waves me over. "Amy, this is June. She was here on New Year's Eve. I remember because of—"

"My hair," says June, a quick flip and giggle.

Laurie stays calm, but I can tell his energy's rising. He thinks he's onto something. "She remembers Florence," he says.

June takes a long sip from her can. "Yeah, I remember your friend, and I'm only telling you because I think something might've happened to her."

"Like what?" I ask.

She purses her lips like she has a theory but isn't willing to share. "She was crying, and she came to the hotel to wait for a ride."

Laurie nods. "Did you talk to her?"

"Didn't seem like she wanted to talk, but I kept an eye on her. This isn't the safest area at night."

Laurie and June keep discussing, but my thoughts snag. "Hold on a second. You said she came to the hotel for a ride."

June takes a sip of her drink. "That's what I said."

"So, she didn't come out of the hotel?"

June shakes her head, points across the street. "She came out of those apartments, booked it over here like she couldn't get away fast enough."

It's the apartment building where we parked Laurie's car, a gorgeous high-rise with a doorman perched inside the lobby.

"She was running?" I ask.

"Stumbling, more like."

I shift my focus to Laurie. "What the hell?"

He stays calm, voice measured like there must be an explanation. "The after-party could've been there. The Gardiners have an apartment in Paris. Maybe they have one in Boston, too."

June leans against the building. "Sorry I don't know more."

"That's all right," says Laurie. "You've helped enough."

Before we go, he gets June's number. She's willing to confirm his story with the police, and she's almost certain she can get security footage from the hotel. It's enough to bring the life back to Laurie's eyes, but I feel heavier than I did when we arrived.

Laurie slips an arm around my shoulder and leads me down the block, but I drag my feet. "It doesn't make sense. Why would the Gardiners throw an after-party for their own party?"

He shrugs. "Maybe it was Ned. New Year's Eve has always been his sister's thing."

"Ned was home. The cops told Meg. They have proof."

Laurie holds open the car door, and when we're both safe inside, he buckles his seat belt like he's ready to drive back to Concord.

I grab the steering wheel and hold it still. "We're not leaving."

Laurie sighs. "I'm not going into those apartments if that's what you're thinking."

"Something's off." I pull out my phone and Google the complex, desperate to understand why my cousin ended up here.

Laurie takes a gentle breath. "Let's do some research at

home. We're not going to find anything helpful while we're sitting—" He stops midsentence, strains against his seat belt. "Hold on a second. Do you recognize that guy?"

I look up, and for a second that feels like a year, I stare at my mentor. "Hide."

"What is it?" asks Laurie.

I duck for cover, pull him down with me.

"Amy?" A muffled voice from outside the car. Louder and closer. "Is that you?"

"Drive," I say to Laurie. "Drive now."

Laurie obeys, and as we speed out of the parking lot, I lock eyes with a man I thought I knew. Chestnut-brown hair, five-o'clock shadow, and an army-green jacket. "That's Fred Vaughn."

Laurie's breath comes fast. "The artist?"

A loud ringing fills my head, and a memory of Sallie's party surfaces. My phone vibrating in my back pocket, Fred Vaughn texting me again and again. I ignored him that night, preoccupied with Beth, but I vaguely remember letting Florence borrow my phone.

"Ames, what is it?" asks Laurie.

I open my messages, but my thread with Vaughn is missing. Heart pounding, I navigate to my recently deleted texts, and there it is.

HNY, love!
Having a little get-together.
Wanna join?
I never responded, but someone did.
Yay! Come pick me up.

CHAPTER THIRTY-NINE

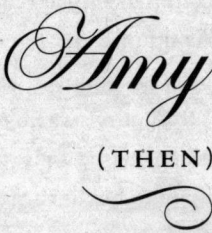

Amy

(THEN)

I'm never happier than I am in Fred Vaughn's studio, sunlight spilling over concrete floors, a brush in my hand, the sweet scent of acrylic paint.

EDM plays over the speakers. It's not as loud as it was on the night of the gallery opening, but it's loud enough that Vaughn has to shout when he comes up behind me.

"That's brilliant," he says, his British accent laid on thick.

I toss a grimace over my shoulder. "You really think so?"

He chuckles, turns the volume down. "Kitty used to be self-deprecating like you."

I blush, but I love it when Vaughn compares me to Kitty Bryant as if I'm his new protégé.

"I think my proportions are off." I step back and tilt my head so I can see my canvas from a different angle. I usually paint my sisters, but Vaughn convinced me to try a self-portrait.

"You deserve to be in a gallery," he said.

Vaughn grips my arms from behind, his chin practically

resting on my shoulder. "Your proportions are fine. It's your confidence that needs work." He turns me to face him, a smile rising into his five-o'clock shadow. "You're special, Amy. You just don't know it yet."

A fire warms me from the inside out. I'm almost embarrassed by Fred's confidence in me, afraid I'll never live up to it, but at the same time, I believe him. He has the greatest eye of any artist I know. Who am I to question what he sees in me?

He steals the brush from my hands, sidles up to my painting and adds a stroke. "Kitty came out of her shell in Italy. Something about the villa, the vineyards. I have a feeling you'll do the same."

He winks, and I wonder if I should wink back. I'm not sure how to act around Vaughn. I want him to think I'm cool and casual, but I've never been so swept up by another person.

"I really hope so," I say.

He looks back, a twinge of worry on his brow. "You haven't got the money yet, have you?"

"I'll get it. I promise."

"I know it's a pain, but I have to start paying deposits next month. These villas book up so fast—"

"It's not a big deal. My sister has a couple more weeks to decide if she's going to boarding school, but she won't. I'll get the money. You don't have to worry."

Vaughn nods. "I can't imagine running the program without you."

"I'll be there," I say, concealing my smile.

Vaughn comes closer, lowers his voice. "Look, if you can't get the money—"

"I will."

"But if you can't, we can work something out."

I look up, heart fluttering. "What do you mean?"

He shrugs, cheek to shoulder. "Ah, nothing. I'm just saying we can figure it out together." He pauses, reaches for my hand. "I'd take you anywhere, Amy."

For a moment I feel like I'm floating, anchored only by the feeling of Fred's rough palm against mine. I've always known I'm a good painter. My teachers at school have said things like, "You'd be really successful if you didn't get into so much trouble." But for the first time in my life, I feel like an artist.

I picture myself traveling with Vaughn, meeting his friends and colleagues, showing my work with his endorsement. I search for the right words to thank him for believing in me, but before I can find them, he leans in.

At first I don't know what's happening.

But a real, dense heat builds between us.

He moves his hands to the small of my back, and slowly, deliberately, closes his eyes. Is he actually trying to kiss me? Surely not.

He steps closer, then a little cough echoes through the gallery.

"Hey, um . . . you ready to go?" Beth stands at the edge of the room, voice squeaky, gaze averted like she's uncomfortable.

I spring away from Vaughn. "God, Beth. Can't you wait outside? You're like ten minutes early."

Her cheeks flush. "I have a piano lesson."

She saw.

She saw what nearly happened. Vaughn's face just a few inches from mine.

But then again, I'm an idiot to think that this man wanted to kiss me. Me! More likely, he was leaning in to share some words of wisdom.

I swallow my embarrassment, say to Vaughn, "Sorry about her."

He shrugs and lets out a little laugh like we share something Beth will never understand.

"See you next week?" I ask, desperate to hear that this isn't over, that Beth hasn't ruined my private lessons.

He nods. "We'll talk about tuition then."

Outside, Beth unlocks the car, but she doesn't get in. I can tell she has something to say, and the look on her face puts a fist around my heart.

I do my best to sound irritated instead of nervous. "How long were you standing there?"

Beth looks worried. "Not long, but, Ames . . ."

I toss my backpack into the passenger seat, wishing I had the freedom to live without her oversight. If only I had a license instead of a learner's permit. If only we didn't have to share her shitty hatchback.

"Did I walk in on something?" she asks finally.

I force a laugh. "What are you talking about?"

She struggles to look me in the eye. "You and Fred. It felt like he was . . . it just seemed a little . . . intimate."

"Intimate?" I mock.

"It looked like he was going to kiss you."

"How long were you spying?"

"I wasn't spying—"

"Were you eavesdropping, too? How much did you hear?"

"I didn't hear anything. I just saw the way he was looking at you."

I shove past her to get in the car. "You're so naive."

Beth keeps her voice low but urgent. "He's an older man, and you're a beautiful young woman."

I gag. "Gah. Gross, Beth."

"You are."

"It's not like that. He's proud of my work. He thinks I'm the next Kitty Bryant." But I feel the ghost of his hands on my back. His breath on my face.

Beth ducks to look me in the eye. "I'm sure that's true. I just think you need to be careful."

I feel a ripple somewhere deep in my stomach. Maybe it's a warning, but I choose to ignore it. "He's British. If he was trying to kiss me—and that's a big 'if'—it wasn't a real kiss. He's just casual like that."

Beth struggles to keep her voice down. "Kissing your thirty-something teacher isn't casual."

"Is everything okay out here?"

Vaughn's question shocks us both. We jump, then I clutch my chest and push out a laugh.

"Oh my god, you scared me," I say.

He eyes us like he's trying to suss out a betrayal. "I thought I heard an argument."

I step in front of Beth and silently beg her stay quiet, but she always finds her voice at the worst possible times. "We're not arguing," she says. "I'm just looking out for my little sister."

Vaughn stiffens, a forced smile. "She's a special one, isn't she?"

Beth glares at him, but I glare at her harder. "Aren't you in a hurry?" I ask her.

She looks like she doesn't want to leave. Like she's ready to stand here until Vaughn admits to something he hasn't done, but at long last, she gives in. "Yeah. Yeah, I am."

CHAPTER FORTY

Meg

(NOW)

On the third full day of her suspension, Amy doesn't get out of bed. I pace back and forth past her door, trying to decide if I should wake her up or leave her alone. During one of my longest hesitations, a hand on her doorknob, my phone buzzes.

Sallie Gardiner: Come outside.

I stiffen, a glance over my shoulder, the creeping feeling of being watched. Earlier this week, I used every bit of air in my lungs to accuse Sallie of killing my sister.

Does she know?

Or is she simply here about a preterm paper? Another thing she needs from me?

My pulse climbs higher, higher, but I pin my shoulders back and march into the bitter wind. "Sallie?" My voice echoes up the street. "Sallie, where—"

She appears from behind a snowy shrub, where she must've been crouching.

I lurch, my breath catching. "God." I settle. "Why are you hiding?"

Sallie's hair isn't as shiny as usual, roughed into a messy bun, and she's checking the street like she's afraid of being overheard. "We need to talk," she whispers.

I cross my arms against the cold, gesture to the door. "Do you want to come in—"

"No," she snaps.

"I'm freezing—"

"Meg, it's over."

I turn to face her, and she scurries right up to me, blue eyes wide with worry.

"The detectives know what we've been doing. My admissions essay, my coursework, all of it."

I swallow, trying not to betray that this isn't news to me. "Are you sure?"

"Sure? Of course I'm sure. That disrespectful, unforgiving— Detective Davis, is it? He came to my house, questioned me for hours. He thinks I killed Beth because she found out I've been cheating, which is just . . ." She trails off, seething, like there's not a word to explain how awful it feels to be demonized.

I don't know what to say, how to stand. I'm thrilled, relieved, at least, that the detectives are taking my accusations seriously. And at the same time, I'm sick with guilt for putting Sallie under a microscope.

"I have a lawyer," she says. "Best one in the state, but, Meg, there's no way around it. We're going after John."

The wind seems to stop. If only for a moment.

Then it's back again, lashing.

I harden against it. "What do you mean?"

Sallie purses her lips. "Look, I'm sorry. I wish there were another way, but my lawyer did some digging. Apparently, the detectives found out about our cheating on the night of John's arrest. He must've ratted."

Slowly, deliberately, I widen my eyes. "Sallie—"

"I'm not a complete idiot. I know you've been hooking up with him—god knows why—and I know you must've told him about your little side gig."

Rage. Deep and overwhelming. "*My* side gig?"

"We're suing him for defamation. I just thought you should know."

I feel like Jo, anger charging through my body in a way that I can't handle. "I have proof, Sallie. All the papers I've written. The texts you've sent me."

I pull out my phone, but Sallie shoves my hand back down to my side.

"We'll slam John with legal fees. That, or he can tell the detectives he was lying."

Beth warned me about this. Sallie's family has enough power to dig themselves out of any hole, and they don't care who they bury in the process. "John can't afford a lawyer, you know that."

Sallie simply shrugs, and with that one flippant gesture, she loses me. For years I've endured the frustrations and humiliations of her friendship, because I wanted to be like her. To be her. But now I can't imagine living in her selfish skin.

"I'm the one who told the detectives." My voice comes out clear and crisp against the cold. "I told them about everything. The coursework, the money."

Sallie shakes her head like she can't believe I'd be so bold. "You're just trying to protect—"

"I told them you could have hurt Beth. And, Sallie, I believe it. You don't care about other people. Only yourself."

She eyes me. At first with caution. And then with a smugness that flickers through her eyes. "It's wild, the things people will do for money. I hate to say it"—she sniffles, putting on a performance—"but I think Meg March would've been willing to bury her own—"

"I was in Boston the night Beth died."

"Really? All night? Because the doorman at our apartment saw you leaving—"

"Oh, come on." She's lying. Reaching. Spinning stories that no one would believe. Unless . . .

Her family could bribe the doorman. Bribe kids from the party. The Gardiners could destroy me without losing any sleep.

I tremble, but I fight to stay strong. "You can't hurt me, Sallie. My sister's dead. There's nothing worse."

She stares at me for a moment, the two of us solemn, and when it seems like she's ready to speak again, I speak first. "I'm turning myself in to the school. I've already set an appointment with the Honor Council, so fair warning. We'll probably be expelled."

Sallie doesn't break her stare, but behind her eyes, there's a hint of panic. She knows that everything's falling apart.

Just then the door opens. "Meg? You good?"

It's Amy, hair mussed, pajamas wrinkled. She looks ridiculous in shorts and a tank, and yet, I'm so happy to see her.

I don't need Sallie. I never have.

I glare at the girl who used to be my friend. "I'm good. Sallie was just leaving."

Inside, I don't want to talk, and to my great relief, Amy doesn't either.

We sit in the living room, both of us despondent, until my stomach growls and I realize that Amy must be hungry too.

"You want some breakfast?" I finally ask.

She stares at her phone. "I don't feel like eating."

"You sure? I'll make pancakes."

"Bleh."

"I think I saw some chocolate chips in the—"

"Chocolate chips? Oh, that changes everything."

Her sarcasm stings, but I refuse to let it bother me. "I'm just trying to help."

At once she gets a string of text messages, her phone buzzing again and again and again. As they come in, she flinches.

"Who is that?" I ask.

"No one," she says, but her voice comes out too loud, frayed.

"Ames, what's wrong?"

"Nothing. God. Can you leave me alone?"

I'm so tired, so wrung out from my confrontation with Sallie, that at first I actually obey. I get up and head for the kitchen, but Amy's phone buzzes so many times, I can't help coming back. "Okay, seriously. Who is that?"

She crams the phone under a pillow. "None of your business."

Another text.

Another.

Amy groans. "It's nothing. It's a friend. It's—"

Text. Text. Text.

"Is someone harassing you?" I reach for the phone.

She stops me, a hand closed tight around my wrist. "It's Henry, okay? Just Henry."

I'm skeptical. "Henry's texting you nonstop?"

Amy grips her forehead like she can't keep up. "Yeah, it's only Henry, and it's not a big deal. It's just . . . his grandfather's in the hospital."

I have a hard time believing Henry would text Amy this many rapid-fire messages. With Beth, he was always so polite, but if his grandfather's really in the hospital again, he must be panicking. "Was it another heart attack?"

Amy shrugs. "He says he's fine, but I don't think he should be alone. I should go sit with him, Beth would want me to do that, but I can't leave the house. I really—" Her voice cracks. "I just can't deal."

My heart aches. Amy's lumped on the couch, and I know she doesn't want to be touched, comforted, but I sit beside her and stroke her hair. She flinches at first, like she's about to push me away, but she doesn't.

"It's going to be okay," I say. "Maybe not today, but eventually."

It's clear that she knows what I'm talking about. She

absorbs it, but she doesn't want to discuss Beth now. Her words come out staggered, like she's trying not to cry. "Can you go to the hospital? Just to check on him?"

I can't stand the thought of leaving Amy alone in this state, but Mom will be home from work soon, and Henry shouldn't be at the hospital without support.

"I'll go," I say.

She's crying now, her voice barely there. "Thank you."

I search for my keys, and as I leave the house, she gets another text, another, another.

This may be an unpopular opinion, but I've always loved hospitals. I don't want anyone to be sick or hurt, but that's life, and if we didn't have hospitals, we wouldn't have any hope of getting better. Typical premed opinion, I'm sure, but I'd rather have hope than nothing at all.

Concord General seems particularly hopeful in the winter, industrial heaters pumping much-needed warmth into every nook and cranny.

Some of the hospital staff know me well enough to wave. "Want me to page Maggie?" one of them asks.

It'd be nice to see Mom. She's been working more than ever to keep her mind off the investigation and keep up with the bills, but I politely decline. "I'm here to see a friend."

I find Henry in the cardiac ICU, head down.

"Hey," I venture.

He startles. "Meg. Wow. I didn't know you were coming."

I approach the way I approach patients in clinicals, not an

ounce of pity, only confidence and understanding. "Amy told me you were here. How's your grandpa doing?"

Henry shoves his phone into the pocket of his hoodie. "It wasn't a heart attack this time, but they're doing some tests."

"I'll wait with you."

Henry looks uncomfortable, a little nervous, and I'm sure it's my fault. I've been in college since Beth started dating Henry. He and I don't know each other very well. I search for something to say. "Have you eaten today? I can go grab you something to—"

Just then a doctor walks in. "Henry Hummel?"

He shoots up, worry tightening his shoulders, but I know it's good news. The doctor has her hands in her pockets, her chin in the air. She wouldn't look so cool and casual if they'd made a terrible diagnosis.

"Just a little angina," she says. "You can go see him now."

Henry glances back, as if to apologize for leaving me so soon.

"Go ahead. I'll hang out for a while."

He nods, but as he turns his back to follow the doctor, I pull out a copy of *Little Women*, and he freezes.

"Why do you have that?" he asks.

I turn it over in my hands. "Honestly—"

"Beth hated that book."

I don't think he's entirely right. Beth always seemed to see both sides of every argument, even the ones we had over Dad's book. But I realize that Henry must've seen a different version of my sister, a version who wasn't trying to please me or Jo.

BETH IS DEAD

"I've been blaming this book," I say. "For everything that's happened. And the truth is, I've never even read it."

Henry shakes his head. "You're better off."

"You've read it?"

"Once or twice."

"What did you think?"

Henry walks off, his answer tossed over his shoulder. "Your dad deserved to be canceled."

CHAPTER FORTY-ONE

Beth

(THEN)

We slouch shoulder to shoulder on Henry's bed, playing a video game that's always been one of his favorites. It's a little slow, but it's beautiful, a color-filled garden for our characters to tend. The problem with this game is that it never offers a stopping point, and there's something I need to get off my chest.

I've been waiting for the right moment to interject, but every time I draw a breath, something happens to our garden—a thunderstorm, a theft, a giant whose footprints destroy our crops.

Henry plants a packet of seeds, and before he has time to water them, I blurt out the truth. "I need to tell you something."

He finds a watering can, carries it carefully, and pours its contents over the freshly mounded earth. "After we plant the sunflowers?"

I rest my controller on a pillow and turn to face him. "It's about Plumfield."

At that, he shifts his focus without pausing the game. "Oh yeah?"

My whole body hums with nervous excitement. Three weeks ago I received a call from Plumfield's headmaster. I'd been accepted "enthusiastically" and given until the end of the month to make a decision.

"It's been really hard," I say, "but I know what I want to do."

On-screen, rain falls. Henry's character points to the sky, and a speech bubble appears: "I need an umbrella." Henry doesn't bother to open one, his attention fixed on me.

I clasp my hands, draw a breath. "I've decided to go."

Henry falls completely still, and at first he says nothing.

I ramble to fill the silence. "I've been debating it every minute of every day. I talked to John, and it didn't go very well. He was mad that I'd ever consider turning Plumfield down, and you know what? I think he's right. It's a great opportunity, and while I'm absolutely terrified, I can't pass it up. If I do, I'll always wonder how my life might've turned out."

"I don't believe it," says Henry.

At first I think he's amazed, and it fills me with joy. "I wasn't sure I could take the leap, but—"

"How can you do this to me?" His voice darkens the whole room.

I tip my head, taken aback. "What do you mean?"

"You're leaving me," he says flatly.

"No. Henry. We talked about this. We can stay together. I know long-distance isn't easy, but I found a nonstop bus route from here to New Hampshire. It's not a bad ride. I'll visit on the weekends, and you can come stay in my dorm whenever—"

He stands up, a harsh interruption. "I can't believe you're actually going."

"You're mad," I say, stunned, deflated.

He wheels around. "How am I supposed to feel?"

"I told you this was a possibility."

"I didn't think you'd actually do it."

For a moment I'm frozen, stung. When I finally speak, my voice cracks. "I thought you'd be proud of me."

Henry stares at me like he's offended, enraged, then he blinks like he's realizing his mistake. He regains his usual kindness. "I am. I am. I'm so proud of you. I'm just shocked. I thought you were on the fence."

"I was."

"I thought you didn't want to go."

"Well, I do."

He swallows hard. "You're sure?"

Pressure builds behind my eyes, in the back of my throat. If I speak, I'll cry, so I simply nod.

"I'm sorry," says Henry. "I'm sorry I freaked out."

I fight tears, but I can't blame him for panicking. I've been wishy-washy about Plumfield. I didn't prepare him for this. "I'm sorry too. I shouldn't have sprung this on you."

Henry shakes his head. "I'm glad you told me. I'm just . . . I'm going to miss you so much."

At this, my tears fall in warm streaks. Since the night Henry and I met, we haven't gone a single day without seeing each other. At this point, I'm forgetting where he ends and I begin. "We'll still be together."

He eases down beside me, hands tucked in his lap. "I'll take the bus."

"It's really not so bad."

"I'll come stay in your dorm if it's allowed. And if it's not—"

"We'll sneak around," I say.

He laughs, and when his laughter subsides, he repeats my promise with an edge of fear. "We'll still be together."

CHAPTER FORTY-TWO

Meg

(NOW)

I finish reading *Little Women* in one sitting, so absorbed in the story that I forget I'm occupying an uncomfortable plastic chair in the cardiac ICU.

When I reach the back cover, I'm the only person in the cold blue waiting room, so I ask a nurse to tell the Hummels I'll be heading home for the night. In minutes I'm bounding through our front door and up the stairs to find Jo.

Our room's been shut tight, and when I barge in, Jo shrieks. She's splayed out on her bed, nose in a notebook, surrounded by pages that she's ripped out and crumpled. "What's your problem? Can't you knock?"

An apology leaps to my throat, but I swallow it down. "This is my room too."

She snaps her notebook shut, gathers the loose pages, and tucks them in her lap. "I'm not used to sharing anymore."

I think of the apartment I share with Sallie and Annie just a few blocks away from Harvard's sprawling campus. Aside from Sallie's financial shaming, I felt so independent in my own space, free to do and think whatever I wanted. Jo must've had a taste of that freedom with her own room, and now I'm invading her privacy, unable to bear the thought of leaving home. "I'm sorry," I say. "I know this isn't ideal."

She tries to smooth her hair, but it's so frazzled that her fingers aren't enough to tame it. "You startled me. That's all."

I sit on the edge of the bed, and Jo scoots back, rakes her pages closer.

"What're you working on?" I ask.

"Nothing."

"Your manuscript?"

"It's not a manuscript—not yet. It's just . . ." She lifts the pages and watches them fall. "Trash."

I think of the feedback she got from her editor, a mile-long letter without the slightest bit of sugarcoating. Nan Dashwood told her to scrap what she'd written and try again with more emotion. "Open your veins on the page," she'd said.

"Jo," I start, "I know you don't want to hear this, but I think you need a break."

She shakes her head, wide-eyed and worried. "I'm running out of time."

"You're grieving."

"I'll lose the book deal."

"So what?"

Jo looks at me like I'm suggesting cutting off all her hair. "Beth wouldn't want me to give up."

I think of Beth, her heart-shaped face and strawberry-blond waves. She was always Jo's biggest fan. She read every one of Jo's personal essays, even the early ones that dragged along and didn't make sense, and when she was done, she'd say, "You're a genius. Write me another."

I reach for Jo's discards. "Let me see what you've written. There's gotta be something—"

"No." She bats my hand away.

"Come on. I may not be a writer, but I'm a good sounding board."

Jo rushes off the bed, whips up her notebook, and shoves it in the trash. "I thought I had an idea, but it's not right, it's not me, and I don't want to talk about it, okay?"

I wish I could comfort my sister, help her regain her creative spark, but in this moment I think the best thing I can do is change the subject. "Okay," I say. "Then sit down and listen, because I read *Little Women*."

Jo pauses with her foot in the trash can. "Are you serious?"

"Do I look serious?"

"You read the whole thing?"

"Whole thing. One sitting."

Jo yanks her foot from the can to swoop in beside me. "And?"

I struggle to admit the truth. "I'm sorry I didn't read it sooner."

Jo settles. "You loved it."

"I thought it was interesting."

She squeals. "I knew you'd love it."

I move to my knees to be taller than my sister. Her

energy's rising, and I have to stay in control. "I don't love it. It's problematic. I still think Dad exploited us to tell a great story, but you were right. It's a great story."

Jo smirks, and I swat her arm. "Don't look so satisfied."

She wipes the smugness right off her face, and that's how I know she's genuinely interested in hearing my opinion.

I grab a pillow, relax a little. "I think people are missing the point of the book."

"Yes, yes, tell me more."

"Take my character, for example. Everyone calls her vain, mocks her for being materialistic, but she's a lot more than that."

Jo gives me one big nod like I'm voicing a point she's been holding all along.

"I thought Dad made me a stereotype, but the fans did that."

Jo looks like she could cheer and cry at the same time.

"Yes," I continue, "Dad made me a little vain. He wrote about my unbalanced friendship with Sallie Gardiner and accused me of treating John Brooke like a back-pocket boyfriend."

"That's good writing," says Jo.

"It's painful writing, but it's not untrue, and it's not the only side to my character. Dad also made me clever." As the words come off my lips, a lump forms in my throat. "He made me caring, too. And wise."

"Because you are," says Jo.

I swallow, nod. "I didn't expect that."

Jo moves closer, voice filled with passion. "You're right about the readers. They latched on to the most basic and stereotypical parts of us. People remember me for being brave and ambitious, but they ignore the fact that I'm also quick-tempered and painfully lonely. And Amy? They call her a brat, a screwup, but she'll probably be more successful than the rest of us combined."

I chuckle, but I don't disagree.

"Beth, too." Jo's voice catches in her throat. "Critics have called her a flat character, but she's more complicated on the page than everyone likes to believe."

I let out a little laugh that rolls into tears. "I think the most complicated thing a person can be is kind."

Jo nods, and it's hearty, true. "I asked Dad about the ending once. I asked him why she had to die."

My chest tightens. "What did he say?"

"You're not going to like it."

"Tell me."

Jo takes a moment to get the words out as if they're boulders in her chest. "He said that Beth was the best of us. And that her loss would stay with his readers forever."

I stew in that answer. It seems selfish and shortsighted to care more about the success of a story than a real person's feelings, and I'd like to think that Beth's life alone would be just as memorable as her death, but underneath my rage, I understand what Dad meant.

None of us will ever forget losing Beth March.

CHAPTER FORTY-THREE

Amy

(NOW)

After my three-day suspension, school sucks even more than it did on my first day back from winter break. All my friends act like I'm some kind of hero for getting suspended, like it's the old days, and I got sent down to the principal's office for violating the dress code or hiding profanity in one of my paintings.

They don't understand that this suspension was different. They don't understand that I'm drowning.

By the end of first period, I have eleven texts from Fred Vaughn, some apologetic, some threatening to show up at school. He's been bombarding me for two days straight, message after message after message, trying to parse out what I know.

I'm not sure what I know, but my gut says it's not good. I'd bet money that Fred Vaughn picked Florence up from Sallie Gardiner's party, brought her to his own party, and after that, I can only guess.

I find her in the hallway between classes. She stands at her locker swapping books, and I do my best to read her body language. Does someone's posture change when they're manipulated by an older man? Did mine?

I approach her carefully. "Flo, we need to talk."

For the briefest of moments she looks happy to see me back at school. Then she notices the worry in my posture. "What's wrong?"

"Girls' bathroom." I tip my head.

She fidgets with her skirt, an uneasy step in the opposite direction. "I have ceramics."

"You can be late."

Florence eyes me like she's wondering what I know. "Is everything okay?"

"I just want to talk."

"Have you been drinking again? Should I go find Jo?"

Her suggestion hits me sideways. As if Florence understands my relationship with Jo. As if Jo would care about my drama after everything I've done. I keep my voice low, but I stop holding back. "I found the text, Florence. I know you took my phone. Responded to Vaughn."

She starts walking. "I'm late to class."

I stay on her heels. "Laurie said he picked you up in Boston that night. Said you'd been crying."

She flinches but keeps moving. "This isn't the right place to talk about—"

"Did Vaughn come on to you or something?"

Florence stops in her tracks, and for a second I think she's going to slap me, but she grabs my arm and yanks me into the girls' bathroom. "You don't know what you're talking about," she says as she ducks to check each stall.

"I'm sorry, but Laurie said you denied going to Boston. You lied to the police, Flo. Why would you hide that?"

She wipes her eyes, her yellow hair dull under the bathroom light. "Let me explain."

So there's something to explain.

A lump forms in my throat, a terrible mixture of jealousy and empathy. Vaughn tried to kiss *me* at his studio. He was texting *me* on New Year's Eve. It could've been *me* running from his apartment in tears.

Florence comes close, lowers her voice. "I'm sorry I took your phone, but Fred doesn't text me the way he texts you, and I needed a chance to talk to him."

"About what?"

She turns the tap, splashes water on her face, and uses a rough paper towel to wipe it off. "Look. I never told my parents about Europe."

The bathroom's quieter than it should be. So quiet, I can hear my own heart beating. "You told me they'd agreed."

Florence sounds exhausted. "Come on, Amy. You and I both know they were never going to say yes to a program like that."

"You've been acting like we're about to hop on a plane."

"We are," she says. "I worked it out."

"What are you talking about?"

Florence rests against the sink for a moment, but as soon as she starts talking, she paces. "I couldn't give up on our dream. Maybe it wasn't a big deal to you, but to me?" Her neck muscles flare. "Europe was everything."

"It was everything to me, too."

"You say that, but you have your sisters. I have nothing. No one."

"You've always had me."

She scoffs as if I've never given her all of myself, and I guess she's right. There are parts of me that belong only to my sisters.

She leans against a bathroom stall, arms tight across her chest. "I've read articles about Kitty Bryant. She's from the East End, which is, like, the poorest area of London. Her dad was a garbage collector, and yet *she* went to Fred's summer program. There's no way she had twenty grand."

"So?"

"So, I asked Fred to pick me up on New Year's Eve. I thought we could talk at his party."

I shake my head slowly, a strange nervousness building in my gut.

"We went to his apartment," she says, "and there wasn't a party, but it's okay. It was better that way. We were alone, so we could really talk."

"Flo—"

"I asked him about scholarships, and he wasn't opposed, said he'd done it before."

I replay every interaction I've ever had with Fred Vaughn. His hands on my shoulders, his voice in my ear. *You're special, Amy. You just don't know it yet.*

"What did he want?" I ask.

Florence bites her lip so hard, it swells. "He didn't want anything."

"He just gave you a free pass, no questions asked?"

"He asked a lot of questions. About me, my work. We got to talking, and we . . ." She trails off, makes an obvious effort to smile. "We kissed."

My heart cracks. "You didn't."

"It's fine. It was nice."

"Oh, Florence."

"How many times have we scrolled through pictures? Called him the hottest guy in the world? So what if I kissed him? So what if we did more?"

"He's like thirty-five," I say.

"It's fine. It's not a big deal. I just went with it."

"Flo, I'm so sorry." I reach for her hands, but she snaps them away.

"Don't act like that. Vaughn didn't do anything wrong. It happened so fast. We got caught up in the moment. Both of us."

My stomach sinks deeper.

"I wanted to keep going. I wanted to be with him." She pauses, her expression suddenly blank. "I never said no."

For a moment we stand still, and a thousand unspoken things pass between us. Florence has never kissed anyone, much less gone further, but she's been dreaming about the moment since kindergarten. I know she didn't go to Vaughn's apartment expecting to hook up with him. I know she's scared, and I'm scared too.

I ease her into my arms, and when her forehead meets my shoulder, her tears begin to fall. We stay this way until we're both wrung out, and I want nothing more than to take her hand and leave this bathroom.

But just then she says something that brings time to a drawn-out pause.

"I should've listened to Beth."

"What?" My heart stills in my chest.

Florence wipes her nose. "She tried to stop me from leaving with Vaughn that night, but I didn't listen. I thought she was drunk, pissed off because of your fight. She called Fred a creep, and I couldn't believe she would do that. I apologized, rushed him into the car."

My breath comes in quick, shallow gulps. "She called Fred a creep?"

Florence doesn't seem to understand my concern. "Yeah, but he laughed it off. It wasn't a big deal."

I picture Beth outside Vaughn's gallery warning me to be careful. The way he eyed her like she was too smart for her own good. "Florence, we need to talk to the police."

She shakes her head. "No. No way. You know what happens to girls who report stuff like this. It'll be my word against his, and my parents—my parents can't know."

I glance over my shoulder to make sure the bathroom door's still shut. "Fred tried to kiss me once. At his studio. Beth walked in on it."

Florence stiffens.

"She knew what he was doing," I say.

Florence blinks away tears. "No. No, he wouldn't hurt her."

"What if you aren't the only one?" I ask.

Florence looks confused.

"What if we go to the police together?"

"It won't be enough," she says.

She's not wrong. Our stories alone may not be enough to make the detectives look twice at Fred Vaughn, but I think I know where I can get more.

I'm not a big reader, ask Jo, but for hours I read articles about Kitty Bryant, everything I can find. Florence was right about Kitty's story. She was born to a garbage collector in the East End, all talent and no resources, then along came Fred Vaughn. In old posts Kitty credits him for recognizing her abilities, giving her a future. She calls him her mentor, her hero. But in recent posts, he disappears from her feed.

This isn't the first time I've stalked Kitty, but it's the first time I've done it without wishing I could have her life.

In those old posts, Vaughn's all over her. His arm draped around her shoulder, his gaze dripping down her body.

I tap into her DMs, but I have no idea where to start.

I type something out, tempted to gush about her work, call myself her biggest fan, but Jo's taught me how to self-edit. "Think of Hemingway," she always says. Fewer words, more meaning.

@AmyMarch: My cousin and I are doing Fred Vaughn's summer program. Any advice?

My heart races as I send the message, but I force myself to calm down. Kitty's a famous artist with a serious social media following. She won't respond right away.

I shut my eyes and beg for sleep, but a few seconds later, my phone buzzes.

@KittyBryantArt: Please tell me you haven't paid the deposit.

CHAPTER FORTY-FOUR

(THEN)

A couple of days after I told Henry I was going to Plumfield, his grandpa turns eighty-seven. The three of us sit around Mr. Hummel's kitchen table huddled over a double chocolate cake with trick candles.

"Watch this," Henry whispers in my ear as his grandpa makes a wish.

The candles flicker out, and a few seconds later, they whiz back to life. Mr. Hummel does a double take, and when he realizes what's happening, he breaks into a belly laugh that makes his eyes water.

Henry laughs too, then carries the cake to the counter, where he serves it on paper plates. For such a brooding tough guy, he's so gentle with each perfect slice, the frosting neat and glistening.

"It's delicious," says Mr. Hummel after his first heaping bite.

I confirm with a nod, mouth full of chocolate. The cake's rich and flavorful, but the story behind it is even sweeter.

BETH IS DEAD

Henry asked his supervisor at Lotty's if she had a good recipe, followed her handwritten instructions, and after mistaking salt for sugar the first time, made it again.

While we eat, Henry asks his grandpa about the past, and Mr. Hummel's eyes sparkle. Though he can't remember breakfast, he remembers every sun-drenched detail of the sixties. "Your grandma and I never missed a weekend at Walden Pond. . . ."

His story's long and winding, and though I'm listening, I can't stop thinking about Henry. His handwriting clings to sticky notes that he's posted around the house.

"Take pills with breakfast: two blue, one pink."

"Eat lunch at noon."

"Getting the mail? Put on pants."

He cares for his grandpa without complaining, a habit I'm certain he formed while he cared for his mom.

I hold his hand under the table, and when his grandpa retires to the lounge chair in front of the TV, I tip my head toward his room. "Video games?"

He smirks like he has something else in mind.

I do too.

We set up the game console, pretending like we're going to play, but as our garden loads, my heart races. Henry and I haven't been fully alone for a while. He's been busy helping his grandpa, and my sisters are always around. But the day Mr. Hummel had a heart attack, Henry and I were interrupted in the back of his truck, and I haven't stopped dreaming about what might've happened if we'd never gotten that phone call. I edge toward him, and when our arms brush, we share a glance.

"Hey," I say.

"Hey," he says back.

And just like that, we're kissing, controllers tossed aside. We're upright for a few breaths, but soon enough we're halfway under Henry's covers, my head on his pillow. Without much thinking, we do what we've done before. Shirts over heads, my bra undone, but when Henry's fingers find the button of my jeans, we both stop.

"What're you thinking?" he breathes.

I swallow a nervous lump in my throat and wonder what my sisters would do. Amy would reach for Henry's buttons, Jo would slap him in the face, and Meg would probably say something like, "I'm thinking I want to be with you," which is exactly what comes out of my mouth.

Henry kisses me deeper than he ever has before. "I want to be with you, too."

He unbuttons my jeans and slides them down. Cool air kisses my legs, and Meg's voice leaps to mind again.

"Condom," I whisper.

Henry nods, fumbles in his bedside table.

My heart pounds in my throat, and just when I think I'm going to change my mind, he sits on his heels in his patterned boxers. "I'm not gonna lie. I'm a little nervous."

"Really?" The question comes out with a laugh, a rush of relief. Henry seemed so experienced in his grandpa's truck, but now he tucks his chin, bare chest rising and falling.

"It's okay," I say. "I'm nervous too."

"You think we should wait?"

I stare into his blue-gray eyes, and my heart swells for his messy hair, his humble shoulders. My pulse has never fluttered so fast, but for once in my life, I don't have to channel Meg or any of my sisters to shake my head and say, "I don't want to wait another minute."

CHAPTER FORTY-FIVE

(NOW)

Kitty Bryant calls at midnight a few days later, and we talk for two hours straight. It's early morning in London, and there's a bird squawking outside her flat.

"Bloody asshole," she keeps saying as she struggles to shoo the bird away, but I don't mind the noise. It reminds me that life's still happening somewhere far away from this nightmare.

Kitty tells her story like someone who's gone through a lot of therapy, like she's not afraid of it anymore. "We met when I was thirteen."

She explains the way she craved Fred's attention, and my stomach turns over. "I get it."

She sighs. "The first time he held my hand, I thought I'd made it."

I picture the art gallery, the first time I ever met Fred Vaughn. When he slung his arm around my shoulder, I felt like I mattered in a way that I'd never mattered before.

"The summer program isn't real." Kitty puts me on speaker,

makes breakfast while we talk, eggs on toast and strong black tea. "It's real enough that you'll hop a plane and show up at a villa in Italy or Portugal, but once you're there, you won't leave, not for the whole six weeks."

"What about the art critics? The mentors? The gallery owners?"

Kitty lets out a wry laugh.

By the time we hang up, I have six names, six girls with the same story as Florence, all willing to tell Detective Davis what they know.

My teeth chatter, rage coursing through my veins. I trusted Fred Vaughn. Idolized him. Fantasized about soaking up his wisdom in the European sunshine. He's the reason I tried to pry Aunt March's money from Beth's fingertips. The reason I fought with Beth on the night she died.

I throw on my coat and take a deep breath, preparing myself to ask Meg for a ride to the police station. Boots in hand, I creep down the hall and whisper into the next room. "Meg?"

My eyes adjust to the darkness, and Meg's empty bed comes into view.

Jo answers instead. "Why are you up?"

"Where's Meg?" I ask.

Jo turns on her light, a long, aching yawn. "She went to stay with John. What's the matter?"

Jo and I haven't really spoken since she called me disgusting for my arrangement with Aunt March. There's a cavern between us, but I need to tell someone what I know. "Jo, I . . ." My voice thickens. "I don't know what to do."

"Can't sleep?"

I feel like I'm going to be sick, but I force out the truth. "I think Fred Vaughn might've killed Beth."

I expect her to throw off her covers and charge toward me, intensely curious, full of questions, but instead she waves me off. "Go to sleep, Amy."

"I'm serious."

"It's two a.m."

"His summer program is a hoax."

"I could've told you that."

Her lack of concern feels like a blow to the stomach. "Fred's not a good person, and Beth knew about his dark side. She warned me about him a long time ago."

Jo rolls her eyes, but she's listening now. "What dark side?"

"I talked to his protégé. The artist in London."

"Kat?" asks Jo.

"Kitty," I correct. "She called him a con artist. Said he lives off the money from these summer programs, and"—I pause, gather my strength—"he only invites girls. Girls that he likes."

Jo straightens up. "What do you mean?"

I pull up social media, show Jo the way Vaughn keeps young girls tucked under his arm.

She leans toward the phone. "Holy shit."

"What?"

"That's Vaughn?"

"Yeah."

Jo's face loses color. "That guy was at the vigil just ... watching."

Chills spread from my neck down my arms.

"I remember his glasses," says Jo. "He was idling up the road. Staring at us."

Tears prick my vision. My voice comes out tight and shaky. "He tried to kiss me once, and he did more with Florence."

"Our cousin, Florence?"

I nod, and in one rambling breath, I share the details. The way Florence texted Vaughn from my phone, begged him for money, the way he took advantage. "Beth knew what Vaughn was doing. She called him a creep the night she died."

Jo doesn't say another word. Instead, she shoots out of bed, grabs her phone, and rushes to the hallway.

"Where are you going?" I ask.

"I'm calling Detective Davis."

I stay on her heels. "I should be the one to call him."

"I've got it," she spits.

"You don't know the whole story."

Jo pins me with a look of disgust. "I know enough."

"What's that supposed to mean?"

She ties her hair in a bun like she needs it off her neck. "Nothing."

"No, tell me. I need to know. Because it seems like you're mad at me for what Vaughn did."

She hesitates, but her voice comes out harsh and raspy. "This is just like you, Amy. You thought a famous artist invited you to his summer workshop because what? Because you're special?"

"He liked my work," I mutter.

"You're reckless, and you were always jealous of Beth's talent. You wanted to prove yourself, to trot off on some grand

European adventure, and you wanted it so badly that you couldn't see the red flags."

"Are you seriously blaming the victim?"

"You're not a victim. Florence is a victim. Beth's a victim. And you're the one who put them in danger."

With that, Jo strides down the stairs.

I stand in her wake, unable to breathe, hot tears rolling silently down my cheeks. I've been blaming myself day after day, minute after minute, for everything that happened to Beth, but Jo's blame cuts deeper.

She's supposed to be my sister. My confidant. And yet she's so quick to point fingers, to put me down, to make me feel smaller than I ever thought possible.

I hate her.

I hate her, and I want to hurt her.

The urge starts in my fingertips, rushes to my chest, my temples. I want to destroy Jo the way she always destroys me.

In a furious stupor, I go back to her room and search for a way to ruin her. I think of ripping the sheets from her bed, tearing her books from the shelves—and then I see it.

Jo's precious notebook.

Resting in the trash can.

I swear, she throws the damn thing away every few days, but she always pulls it back out. Not this time.

I glance over my shoulder, and when I'm sure she's gone, I sneak it into my hands. She's a fool for leaving it out in the open. All her tender thoughts. Her carefully crafted essays.

I don't type anything up, she once told me. *Not until it's perfect.*

It would be so easy to wound Jo, to stab through her armor. This notebook is her weakness. Destroying her words would destroy her soul.

I take the notebook and run to my room, imagining the ways. I could rip out the pages and shred them to bits. Or better yet, I could throw the whole notebook in a fire. Wouldn't it be thrilling to watch it burn?

I crack open the cover and flip through the pages, picturing them all as a pile of ash. But then something stops me.

Jo's handwriting.

It's slanted, frantic, like she couldn't keep up with her own thoughts. I read, and I feel like I'm creeping into a dark cave, afraid of what's ahead.

Jo's been writing about Beth's murder, turning it into a book. A horrible title stains the first page—*Beth Is Dead*.

For a moment I feel like nothing's real, like I'm suspended in time. I read about the morning we found Beth, and like an out-of-body experience, I get the gory details from Jo's perspective. The way I climbed the hill, fell to my knees, touched Beth's neck, and let out a scream.

This is private.

Worse than *Little Women*.

The depths of my heart shoveled out on a page.

I can't believe Jo would do this, but then again—she needed a story. One that would stun her editor and fly off the shelves. A chill slithers from my head to my tailbone.

Jo staged a break-in for the sake of her fame.

What else was she willing to do?

CHAPTER FORTY-SIX

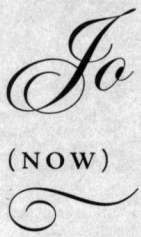

(NOW)

In the late morning the detectives invite me down to the station for more information on Fred Vaughn.

I storm out of the house without a single word to Amy. I know I shouldn't blame her, but her ignorance made Beth a target, and for that, I can't forgive her.

The interrogation room is small but energizing: gray carpet and two chairs, a fluorescent light buzzing overhead. Detective Davis sits down beside me, and for the first time ever, I feel a sense of camaraderie with him.

On the phone last night, he thanked me for being vigilant and forthright. "This is a good lead," he agreed, and I'm still riding the adrenaline rush. After all the drama, all the wrong turns—Sallie Gardiner, John Brooke—we may finally bring justice to Beth.

"All right." I set my elbows wide on the table, ready and eager to bring this case home. "What do you need to catch this guy?"

Detective Davis takes a swig from a coffee mug, but the liquid's vibrant.

"Orange juice?" I ask. "Really?"

He nods. "Can't do caffeine on days like this."

"Like what?"

"Days when big cases crack open."

I sit back, enjoying the spine-tingling thrill of closing in on a killer. It's so exhilarating that I almost forget my personal connection to the case.

Then Davis brings me back to reality. "Walk me through what happened on the night of the incident."

"I told you on the phone—"

"Tell me again. From the very beginning. For the record."

I exhale my excitement and take my time, eager not to leave anything out. "Here's what I know. Amy and Beth left for the Gardiners' party around nine. After that, Fred Vaughn was texting Amy."

"And during this time, you were home?"

"Yes, but I know what happened. Amy told me everything. So Florence, our cousin, used Amy's phone to communicate with Vaughn, and—"

"What time did your mother come home from her shift at the hospital?"

I squint to think. "The sun was coming up when I heard the door. Maybe six a.m.? But Florence went to Vaughn's apartment earlier than that. One a.m., if I had to guess."

Detective Davis sips his orange juice, smacks his lips. "So, is it fair to say that you were home alone from about nine p.m. to six a.m.?"

My mind skips, my heart along with it. Something's not

right about this conversation. I thought we were working together, but Detective Davis seems to be hiking a different trail. "That's not important."

"I think it's very important," he says.

I sit back, slip my hands into my lap. "Fred Vaughn assaulted my cousin, and Beth knew what he was doing."

Davis shifts into a power pose, his elbows on his knees. "Jo, I'll be honest. I'm not concerned about Fred Vaughn right now. I'm concerned about your alibi."

I look around the room like I'm being pranked. Like someone's about to pop out and yell, *Gotcha*. "I was home—"

"Alone," says Davis. "For nine hours. During the time of your sister's murder."

I shrink into my chair but force out a laugh. "This is ridiculous. I'm doing your job for you. Fred Vaughn—"

"Is it true that you've been offered a book deal?"

My limbs feel heavy, my pulse erratic. Detective Davis doesn't play fair. He tricked me into coming to the station, and now he's asking questions that don't have anything to do with the case. "How is that relevant?"

Detective Davis reaches for a manila folder. I didn't notice it until now, lurking on the far end of the table. He peels back the cover, pulls out a fresh sheet of paper. "I have an email from your editor."

A lump forms in my throat.

"It's a nice email," says Davis. "Very complimentary of your writing. But there's a story here."

"Did you hack into my—"

"Correct me if I'm wrong, but it seems like you turned in an early draft of your manuscript, and your editor deemed it uninteresting."

"She didn't call it un—"

"'We need a hook,'" he quotes from the email. "'Something that will grab the reader and refuse to let go.'"

My heart races, my senses heightening. Detective Davis carries dark circles under his eyes, and his tie's crooked, haphazard, like he got dressed in a hurry. Was he working all night on this angle?

I dig for a retort, but I can't help sounding nervous. "I've had a book deal since mid-August. This isn't anything new."

Detective Davis returns to the folder. "I have a few more emails, but they're far less interesting. An idea from you. A polite but stringent rejection from your editor. It's back and forth like that until your editor says, 'Maybe this isn't your time. Maybe we should wait until you have something more exciting to write about.'"

My throat tightens. I can't speak.

"Jo, I'm on your side here. That must've hurt. A life-changing offer snatched from your grasp."

My voice comes out dry. "That's not official. I still have a chance."

"You must've been upset. Desperate. You needed something real to write about." Davis sets the envelope aside and reaches under the table for a notebook.

When he places it between us, my chest constricts. It's a college-ruled notebook with a black cover, water stains from the time I dropped it at Walden Pond, and just last night it was resting in my trash can. "How did you get—"

"You've been writing quite a bit lately." Detective Davis takes his time, savoring this moment like he savored his orange juice. One by one, he flips through the pages of my personal notebook.

"How did you get that?" I demand.

Davis doesn't answer my question. Instead, he turns the pages toward me as if I haven't read them, as if I didn't choose every word on every line. "Jo, these details are"—he chews on his thoughts—"incredibly vivid."

I cross my arms, refuse to look down.

Davis jabs a finger at my writing, quotes phrases that sound particularly dark in this setting. "'A frozen stone.' 'A fast gash.' 'Blood seeping into the snow.'"

This looks bad. It looks really bad. I search for my voice. "I was just . . ."

"How many followers do you have on social media?"

"Why does that matter?"

"Answer the question."

"A couple hundred thousand."

Davis nods slowly. "How many did you have before you faked a break-in at your own home?"

"I don't—"

"Twenty-five thousand," he says. "You had twenty-five thousand, but your following skyrocketed after you fabricated a crime."

I swallow hard, furious and afraid. "Beth was my sister. I would never—"

Detective Davis leans toward me like I'm in a hole and

he's about to bury me. "Jo, I can't help but see a pattern in your behavior. You got a book deal after staging the break-in."

"That's not—"

"I think you needed something to write about, something that would bring your publishing contract back from the edge."

"I didn't—"

"I think you killed your sister for the story." Detective Davis lands his theory, his voice clinging to the air like humidity.

I try to breathe but only choke.

He ducks to meet my eyeline. "Guilt doesn't feel good. The truth will take this pain away."

Tears escape from my eyes, roll down my cheeks. "I loved her. I loved her more than anything. You have no idea what you're talking about."

Detective Davis does his best to look kind, but it only screws up his face. "Tell me where I got it wrong. Did you have an accomplice? Maybe you couldn't bear to do it yourself?"

Anger sparks inside my chest, but it doesn't catch, doesn't turn to flame. I'm heartbroken, unable to fight back. "Am I under arrest?"

He looks smug, like he's finally worn me down. "You will be soon."

I don't care what he thinks of me. I don't care if I go to jail. But I had my notebook last night. It was stuffed in my trash can, which can only mean one thing. Amy handed it over. Amy believes that I could've taken a rock to Beth's head or shoved her down the side of a hill—and that shatters me.

I stand up and open the door. "I want a lawyer."

CHAPTER FORTY-SEVEN

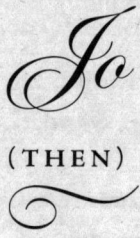

(THEN)

New Year's Eve. I've been counting down the days. It's not that I love confetti or champagne or the ridiculous pressure to kiss someone at midnight. I love an empty house. And for the first time in a long time, the house will be empty for hours.

I've set up my room with the perfect working conditions: a warm blanket, a crackling candle, and a stack of books written by my greatest inspirations. I'll need them tonight.

I don't have writer's block—I don't—but my editor has presented me with a problem that I've yet to solve.

I open my notebook to a blank page and feel the weight of the task at hand. After a few unsuccessful attempts, I have one last chance to ramp up my writing. If I don't, my book deal will die before it's even born, but I can't worry about that now. A new year is a new beginning. And mark my words, I'm going to begin this one with an idea.

"Jo?" Beth's voice carries down the hallway.

I crack my door. "I'm writing."

"Is this outfit ridiculous?" she asks.

"Come show me."

"No, you come here." She pauses. "Please?"

I groan, slide off my chair. Beth never goes to parties, but Amy talked her into this one—her last hoorah before she heads off to Plumfield.

In the doorframe of the bunk room, I tip my head at the outfit. "It's not ridiculous, but it's not exactly . . . you."

"Oh, come on," says Amy, who's buried in the closet. "She looks hot, and we're late."

Beth looks more uncomfortable than anything else, encased in one of Amy's bodycon dresses. She stands before the mirror, adjusting the skintight fabric. "Maybe we could find something more breathable?" she asks.

Amy emerges from the closet with an armful of options. "I'm calling Meg. She would love you in that dress. I think red's your color."

I flop down on the bed and sort through Amy's hangers. "We don't need Meg's help."

In seconds Meg's face appears on Amy's phone. She's in her cramped apartment bathroom applying a sophisticated mauve lipstick. "What's up?"

"Doesn't Beth look amazing?" Amy turns the phone for Meg to see.

I snatch a yellow dress off the pile and fly into the frame. "No, no, no, the red's all wrong. She should try this."

Beth shrugs. "I'm too pale to wear yellow."

"She's right," says Meg.

"Rude," I offer.

"It would only be rude to let Beth leave the house in yellow." Meg smacks her lipstick as if her answer is gospel. "Jo, what are you wearing?"

I check the clock. Every second I spend in this room is a second I'm not spending on my work, but I can't seem to pry myself away. I love these moments when we're not doing anything but talking over one another, existing together. "I'm not going to the party," I say.

"Why not?" Meg sounds shocked and dismayed.

"She has to write." Amy answers for me, her nose in the air.

Meg lets out a loud raspberry. "Boring."

Beth whirls around. "I think it's amazing. Jo's determined."

"I'm on a deadline," I say flatly, "and I need the whole night, because I've never been so stuck in my entire life."

"You'll figure it out," says Beth. "You always do."

I'm sure it's a compliment, but it cuts deep. I'm Jo March, I'm expected to succeed, but I'm afraid I don't have it in me this time. I slump. "What if I can't figure it out?"

Meg's done with her makeup, and she's moved on to her hair, a curling wand jabbing into the frame. "You're talented. If this book doesn't work out, there will be others."

Again, a compliment that slices through me. "Are you saying I should give up?"

"You could," says Amy.

Beth tries on another dress, one of Meg's hand-me-downs, frilled and cutesy. She swoops toward the bed, and the ruffles settle. "You won't give up. I know you better than that."

I nod.

"But you have to stop trying so hard."

"What do you mean?"

Beth sits beside me. "You're trying too hard to live up to the Jo March in Dad's book, but you've said it yourself a hundred times—Meg's not a romance novel, I'm not a perfect angel, and Amy's not a villain. Maybe you don't have to be a hero."

I turn the idea over and over again. It sounds freeing, but I can't quite agree. "I like being a hero."

Beth hops up. "Take it from me. It's nice to be someone else for a while. To be flawed and rebellious, and oh my god, I know what I want to wear!"

Part of me wants to stop Beth in her tracks, ask her when and where she's been rebellious. "Every detail," I want to say—but she looks so inspired, so suddenly excited, that all three of us ask, "What is it?"

"Jo." She runs off. "I'm going to borrow something." For a minute she's gone, rummaging loudly through my closet, and when she returns, she's clutching a dress that I'd never, not in a million years, expect her to wear.

"That?" I ask.

Meg giggles, "Oh, Beth."

Amy reserves her judgment. "Put it on. Let's see."

Beth rushes into the dress, and when it's on, I'm surprised by how well it suits her. It's snug but not too snug, a boatneck with long sleeves that falls just above her knees. And best of all, it's made entirely of sequins. She spins on the rug, catching light.

"It's . . ." I trail off, caught up in the complexity of Beth. She's reserved, no doubt, and she's always preferred to let others stand in the spotlight, but tonight she looks thrilled to be wearing a dress that can't possibly be ignored.

"It's like a disco ball," says Meg in a satisfied tone.

Amy starts a slow clap. "Abso-freaking-lutely."

"You like it?" Beth rounds her shoulders, an uncertain posture, but there's a light in her eyes. She knows she looks good.

"That's the one," I say, dusting my hands.

"You'll be the talk of the party," Meg agrees.

Amy rolls her eyes hard like she can't stand letting someone else steal all the attention. "Can we just go?"

"Be safe!" calls Meg.

"Yeah, yeah." Amy smirks.

Meg's leaving her apartment now, a purse slung over her shoulder. She's hardly in view, her phone jostling while she locks her door. "Love you like crazy," she says.

And my sisters chime in.

"Love you," says Beth.

"Love ya, loser," says Amy.

I don't answer. I'm thinking too hard about the idea of being a hero. It's an honor, but it's exhausting, and if I'm honest, it's not true. I'm chaotic and complicated and often confused, and it's a crime that other girls might think I'm not.

"Beth, you're a genius," I say.

"I am?" she asks.

An idea swells inside me. I could, perhaps, write about myself. I scramble to my feet and down the hall, but halfway, I realize my mistake. I rush back to the bunk room, slide to a stop. "Ames, Beth, have fun at the party. And, Meg? You still there?"

"Here," she chuckles from Amy's phone.

"You know I love you too."

CHAPTER FORTY-EIGHT

(NOW)

When I get home from the station, the snow flurries that have been falling all day turn to sleet. Ice pelts the roof, frigid and gray, and my only consolation is that no one in Concord will be leaving home tonight. I'm not the only one whose life has been halted.

I crawl into bed, unable to get warm. I need to cry, to force out the deep ache in my chest, but I'm so far past tears. All my theories have come up dry. Fred Vaughn's doorman confirmed that on New Year's Eve, he returned to his apartment before Beth's supposed time of death, and his case has been handed to the Special Victims Unit. And Sallie Gardiner? Turns out she tried fleeing to Paris because she witnessed Vaughn picking Florence up from her party and told the cops everything. When he showed up at the vigil, she took it as a warning to stay quiet.

Now I look guilty. My own sister believes that I am.

Some time passes, maybe minutes, maybe hours, before

Mom comes in. She's wearing her scrubs, and I imagine her leaving the hospital midshift, stunned by the news of what her daughter might've done. I'm afraid to look her in the eye, afraid I'll see judgment, afraid she'll be weighing—if only a little—whether or not I could've snapped and done something awful.

I bury my face under my pillow unprepared for whatever Mom's going to say, but she doesn't utter a word. She lifts my comforter just enough to slide in beside me and wraps me in her arms. I rest my head against her chest and shut my eyes as sleet hisses against the windows.

We stay like this for a while, an embrace so tight that I almost forget the world outside of Mom.

"I know you, Jo," she says at last.

Her words warm me through. It's been so long since she and I have done anything but clash, and it's never felt so good to be loved, to be believed. I look up, tears blurring my vision. "Did the detectives call you?"

She shakes her head. "Amy did."

I jolt back, comforter falling. "Amy—"

"She feels awful."

I sit up fast, fire in my lungs. "She gave them my notebook. She turned me in."

Mom purses her lips like she's heard the whole story. "It was a mistake, and she knows that now. She regretted it the moment she left the station."

I'm so disgusted with Amy. She stole my Jeep—*my Jeep*—and drove without a real license to put my personal notebook in the hands of a detective we both despise.

I get off the bed, desperate to move. My feelings are shifting too quickly, ricocheting around my body. "The detectives think I'm a monster."

"They're wrong."

"Amy thinks—"

"Amy knows you didn't hurt Beth."

"I didn't." I heave in a breath. "I promise I didn't."

Just then Amy appears in the doorframe, tearstained cheeks and tired eyes. "Jo, I'm so, so—"

I don't let her apologize. "How could you?"

"I'm sorry," she whines.

"Do you realize what you did? You made me a suspect."

"I didn't think."

"You're such an idiot!"

Amy hardens, mutters, "You deserved it."

"Excuse me?"

"You deserved it!" she yells.

My vision tunnels, Amy's pale, twisted face in the center. "You'd like to see me in jail, wouldn't you?"

"Maybe." She practically growls.

"Then you and Laurie could use Aunt March's money to run off behind my back."

Amy's neck flushes, and I realize that Mom doesn't know what happened between Amy and Laurie. I'm opening her secrets like soul-baring letters, and the satisfaction travels all the way to my fingertips. "You kissed him once, and you think you're in love, but he loves me. He always will, and you hate me for it."

Amy curls her hands into fists. "You don't care about Laurie. You only care about being famous."

"That's not—"

"*Beth Is Dead?* How could you even dream up that title without shivering?"

A cold sweat breaks out on my neck. I think of the pages I filled in my notebook, the salacious details of Beth's case, written for a world that loves true-crime podcasts and documentaries about teen girls gone missing. "I don't . . ." My voice trembles. "I don't know."

Amy squirms like she needs to shed her skin. "You wrote about the worst day of our lives, the most terrible thing that's ever happened to us. You exploited me. Exploited Beth."

My throat tightens like a tap, my voice struggling to get through. "I was never going to share it."

"That's exactly what Dad said."

I tremble, teeth on the verge of chattering. "I don't know why I wrote those things. I couldn't stop myself. The story just poured out of me."

"You were processing," says Mom. It's the first time she's spoken since we started fighting, as if she knew we needed to have it out. "Your dad's the same way. He can't understand his life unless he puts it on a page."

My mind brightens, clinging to the possibility that I'm not broken and strange—but simply my father's daughter. "Is that true?"

Mom eases off the bed, takes my hands. "You didn't write those chapters to hurt anyone; you wrote them to stop hurting."

A weight lifts off my chest, my breath filling my lungs for the first time in weeks. Mom tucks my hair behind my ear. "Everyone wants to know why your father ended *Little Women* the way he did. I've never condoned it, but I've always known the answer. That car accident stunned him to his core. We thought we could lose Beth that day, and he couldn't get past the terror until he wrote it out of his head."

"I'm worried about him." Meg's voice drifts in.

I didn't know she was listening, but Mom and I move to the doorframe to find that she's standing just outside. "I've been too hard on Dad," she says. "I thought he wrote his book for selfish reasons, but I think I was wrong. I think he was putting us first in his own strange way."

"Maybe," says Amy.

"Maybe," Mom echoes.

"He loves us," Meg continues. "I think he wanted the rest of the world to love us too."

This explanation sinks into my heart, buries itself, and begins to grow.

He wanted the world to love us.

He wanted the world to love us.

"Meg!" My own voice sends a chill down my spine. "You're onto something."

My thoughts race, tangling, connecting. I've been so quick to dismiss my sister's theory that *Little Women* made Beth a target. It didn't seem possible that any reader would hate Dad or his characters enough to hurt our family.

But what if the killer wasn't motivated by hate?

"You've been blaming the protesters," I say to Meg. "But what if the killer was a fan?"

She shakes her head. "I don't want to play detective anymore."

I can't stop. Fresh blood fills my veins, and my theory gets clearer with every heartbeat. "What if someone loved the story so much that they wanted to make it come true?"

"Oh my god," says Amy.

"I'm going to dig into Dad's book reviews, all the forums, the responses to Beth's interview. I'll find the biggest fans of *Little Women* and track them down."

"Please don't," Meg groans.

"What if she's right?" asks Amy.

The three of us face one another, poised and ready to argue again, but Mom breaks it up, grips my arm. "Jo, you can't. You're in real trouble. We can handle it, but you need to calm down for a while, focus on clearing your name."

My voice comes out hot, exasperated. "I'll clear my name by finding the real killer."

"You're only going to make things worse," says Mom.

I fight to control my anger—I'm so tired of yelling—but the energy inside me whistles like steam. "I don't care. I don't care if I make things worse. If I ruin everything. I'm too angry to give up now."

Mom lays a hand on my cheek, and I wish I could swat it away, but I can't. I need her. I need her to calm me down. "None of this fighting will bring her back."

Tears fall from my cheeks to my shirt. My knees falter.

"How can you accept that? How come you're not sick with rage?"

"I am," says Mom, and for the first time her voice matches mine. "I'm angry every second of every day. I've never been so angry in all my life. But I won't let it get the best of me." She looks from me to my sisters, a warning to each of us. "If we can't control our anger, we won't survive."

At first I think she means this literally, because I feel like I could die from the pain of missing Beth. But Mom's never so dramatic. She's not talking about death, she's talking about the death of our family.

If we can't stop warring, we'll lose one another.

CHAPTER FORTY-NINE

Beth

(THEN)

On Christmas Eve the whole family bustles around the kitchen. None of us is a fabulous cook, least of all Jo, who burns everything she touches, but we do our best to help Mom. Henry and I stand in the corner of the crowded room plucking herbs from stems, the sweet aromas of rosemary, sage, and thyme.

"This is really nice." Henry rests his head against the wall, more at home than I've ever seen him.

Christmas Eve has always been one of my favorite holidays: the feast, the carols, the cozy fire, and when we were little, we always put on a performance. Jo would write a play, teach us all the lines, and we'd stumble through it for Mom and Dad while they smiled and clapped at every mistake.

Dad. I miss him like a pit in my stomach, an ache in my bones. If he were here, he'd be baking his signature chocolate tart. It always surprised me that a man so creative and scattered, a man who never wore two socks that matched, had a knack for baking, could measure out the precise ingredients and mix them to perfection.

"I just wish . . ."

Henry interrupts, a smile from ear to ear. "I've never had a Christmas like this. It was always just mom and me, Grandpa every now and then."

I kiss him on the cheek, thrilled that he'll be joining us for dinner. His grandfather's coming too, and the seven of us will almost fill the whole table.

"I just wish you could meet my dad," I say.

Henry nods curtly but keeps his focus on his herbs.

"Maybe he'll show up tomorrow," I say.

"What do you mean?" Henry stops what he's doing, a rosemary stem dropped on the counter.

I shrug like I'm being silly, but deep down, I'm serious. "I know we haven't heard from him in a while, but he always turns up eventually, and it's Christmas. I keep thinking he's going to walk through the door."

Henry moves closer. "Don't do that to yourself."

"What?" I ask.

"Don't hope for something that's not going to happen."

He's serious, eyes shadowed by his brow, but I laugh it off. "You never know. We could have a Christmas miracle."

"Don't be naive," says Henry. "Your dad's not coming home."

I draw a quick breath. "Oh, come on. He can't stay out in the woods forever. He always comes home eventually. Why not tonight?"

Henry shakes his head like I'm being ridiculous. "I can't believe you want to see him after what he did."

"What? The book?"

"He killed you off."

I glance over my shoulder as our voices rise. Thankfully, Jo's mixing something that requires three bowls, two whisks, and an unreasonable amount of clanging. "He's still my dad," I whisper.

Henry strains. "You hate that book. It ruined your life. If I were you, I'd never want to see him again."

This is my fault. I've only told Henry bad things about my dad, none of the good, the great. "You're right. I don't like the book, especially not the way it ended, but I still love my dad."

"Why?" asks Henry.

I gape, searching for the right words to explain unconditional love. "Henry, where is this coming from?"

He breathes through his nose like he needs to calm down. "Look, I'm sorry, but you're better off without your dad. He's not coming back, and I think it's about time you accepted it."

I take a step back. "You don't know what you're talking about."

Henry peels a carrot, a sharp, steady motion. "I'm sorry." He averts his gaze. "I just don't want to see you disappointed."

An explanation comes to me slowly, like pinpricks of light through darkness. Henry will never see his mom again. It's probably heartbreaking for him to imagine a parent coming home. "Oh, Henry."

He looks up.

"This is about your mom, isn't it?"

He keeps working at the carrot long after the skin's gone.

"I know you wanted her to get better. I know you're devastated."

"Yeah." He sets his jaw like it's all he can say.

"You're trying to protect me, aren't you?"

The carrot breaks, and he drops it on a cutting board. I ease the peeler out of his grip and steady his hands between mine. "I'm so glad you're looking out for me, but my dad only left for a while. He's coming home."

Henry chews his lip so hard that blood beads up. "Promise me you won't get your hopes up."

I understand that he's coming from a place of grief, but I'd rather keep dreaming that Dad will walk through the door like he always does, his duffel bag dropped, his beard too long. "I'm not afraid of getting hurt," I say.

Henry drops my hands, shakes his head. "Don't tell me I didn't warn you."

Henry stays tense and broody through dinner, but I refuse to let him ruin what's always been my favorite night of the year. We linger for hours around a crowded table, candles low, the remnants of honey-roasted ham and mashed potatoes on every plate.

Seconds ago I swore I'd never eat another bite, but I can't resist asking for a third slice of Meg's cinnamon apple pie.

"You're going to be sick," she laughs.

"Worth it." I grin as I measure out a hunk.

Mom raises her glass at the head of the table, a glimmer in her gaze. "I'd like to make a toast." She waits until we all settle. "My husband usually does this at the beginning of the meal—"

"Poor Dad," Jo laughs. "We always rush him through it."

I smile at the memory of Dad with a full glass of wine and a fuller heart. We've never, not once, let him finish his toast before we've dug into the rolls, but he's always managed to get out enough compliments for us to know that he's proud.

"To our new friends," says Mom. "Max and Henry Hummel."

I reach under the table for Henry's hand, but he pulls it away, and I wonder, with a pang, if he's still upset about his mom or upset with me. Either one seems unfair.

"To Meg, for Harvard. To Jo, for the incredible opportunity to publish a book. To Beth, for enrolling at Plumfield. And to Amy—"

Without warning, Henry stands up from the table. All of us jump, but he doesn't apologize. He drops his napkin, stretches to his full height, and huffs. "Excuse me. I'm not feeling very well."

As Henry walks out the door, his grandfather looks confused, like a toddler being left behind. "Is it time to go home?"

I hurry to my feet. "No, Mr. Hummel. We'll be right back." I give Mom a quick glance. "I'll check on him."

I follow Henry through the kitchen and into the backyard, where he walks to the edge of the patio and looks up at the frosted treetops. "I'm sorry, but I can't take it."

"Take what?" I ask.

His breath clings to the air, his fists resting at his sides. "I can't believe you're really going."

"To Plumfield? We've been through this."

"I know we're pretending it's okay, but it's killing me."

Wind whips through the backyard, bone-chillingly cold. "Henry, please come back inside."

He turns to face me, bomber jacket pulled tight like a defense against the world. "And do what? Eat apple pie while your mom toasts to a future you're chasing without me?"

"It's Christmas," I say, begging him to drop it.

"I care about you, Beth."

"I care about you, too."

He shakes his head, rubs the back of his neck. "I thought you wanted to change your life, but you're no different than you were the day I met you."

I look through the window at my family around the table. Jo is midstory, making a face while the others laugh. "I really want to go inside."

"Why? So you can hang out with your family?" He rolls his eyes. "They don't appreciate you."

His words grab me, yank me into the argument. "How dare you?"

Henry looks satisfied that I'm finally joining the fight. "I know you, Beth. I know you better than anyone. Your family thinks you're timid and small, and you're so desperate to prove them wrong. You're waiting for your dad to come home so you can tell him you have this big dream."

My heart thuds, pressure building in my throat. "That's not true."

He charges toward me. "Wake up. You're not going to Plumfield for yourself. You're doing it for them. For him. For a man who thought it was okay to kill you at the end of his book."

My head spins, the past six months rushing back to me. The shock of Dad's book launch, the horrible embarrassment of being presumed dead, the *Teen Vogue* interview where I sat up tall and said, "Wait and see what I do next."

Henry closes the gap between us and grabs my hands, his palms clammy. "You want to prove that you're alive? Don't go to some stuffy boarding school. Stay here with me."

I think of the time I've spent with Henry, laughing all night, playing video games, our bodies pressed together in his cozy twin bed. Then I think of the way he reacted when I decided to chase my dreams, so selfish, so cold. The way he's talking about my dad, my family. "Henry, I can't—"

"If you can't stay here, then let's run away."

"I can't be with you." It comes out like the first note of a freshly tuned piano, clear and true.

He takes my wrists. "Don't say that. You don't mean it."

I'm caught in his grip, but a weight lifts off my shoulders, clarity rushing in. I have no doubt that Henry holds me deep in his heart, but this isn't how you fight for the people you love. "I think you should leave."

His face turns red, a mixture of embarrassment and anger. "I'm not leaving. It's Christmas."

"Exactly. It's Christmas, and you're ruining it. Tell my family your grandpa's tired."

"No. No way. I'm not leaving unless you take it back. Say we're still together."

"I don't know."

"I'm in love with you."

"I love you too, but—"

Henry backs me against the house. "Don't tell me this is over."

My heels nip the brick, my hair catching. "What are you doing?"

He swallows hard like he's holding back tears. "I can't lose you."

"Stop this."

At once he breaks away. I stay against the house while he paces.

"I'm sorry," he says. "I don't know what happened. I'm just—"

"You need to go," I half whisper.

He shakes his head. "Not until you tell me it's okay. Tell me we can work this out."

I'm stunned, confused, but I nod. "We can talk later."

He wipes his eyes.

"But only if you go."

"Okay," he sniffles. "I'll go."

I'm shivering now, teeth clacking, but I wait outside until Henry excuses himself, and I can hear Mom saying, "Oh, that's too bad. Beth's about to play Christmas carols."

I imagine telling my family what happened, Meg rushing in to comfort me, Jo saying, "I knew he was trouble." I can't bear it tonight. I don't want to be seen as a child again.

I may need to lose Henry, but I refuse to lose the girl I became while we were together.

CHAPTER FIFTY

Jo

(NOW)

I promised Mom I would lie low for a while, but I spend all night searching the underbelly of Dad's book reviews. I've avoided them until now, but by midnight I'm knee-deep in the ugly world of other people's opinions, and I understand why my sisters have never liked *Little Women*.

Most people see Beth as a sweet little goody-two-shoes who was "literally destined to die." Every weirdo from here to California wants to get freaky with Meg. And everyone—I mean, everyone—hates Amy.

I, on the other hand, am the subject of infatuation. Everyone wants to be Jo March, and after reading a couple thousand comments, I wish I could tell them that being Jo March isn't all it's chalked up to be, and that, by the way, the very best part about my life is that I was magically, miraculously born with sisters—the very sisters that you assholes are so fond of harassing.

At some point Meg gets annoyed by the light from my

laptop, shoves off her sheets, and plods to the bunk room to sleep there instead.

It only spurs me on.

When I'm finished enduring book reviews, I comb through social media and chat forums, and by the end of the night I've collected an organized list of standout responses. While most people brush Beth off as an insignificant character or fail to mention her at all, I've found three people who seem particularly enamored with her.

After sunrise I find my sisters. "Can you look at these usernames?"

"I'm busy," says Amy as she scrolls through her phone in the top bunk.

Meg's curled up in Beth's bed, pretending to sleep, but her eyelids flutter.

"Please," I beg. "It'll only take a minute."

Amy rolls to face the wall, keeps scrolling. "Do you have any videos of Beth playing the piano?"

"Amy, focus." I climb the ladder to the top bunk and hang over the edge to get her attention.

She's lost in her phone. "I can't find a single one."

She sounds so mournful that I give in and consider her question. "I guess I can check, but I don't think I have one either. She never let us film that stuff."

Amy locks her phone, drops it on the bed. "We should've done it anyway. Gotten right in her face."

"She would've loved that," says Meg from below, groggy and sarcastic.

Amy digs her hands into her forehead. "I just want to hear her play."

I haven't thought of this, but now that Amy's mentioned it, I crave the sound of Beth's piano. Every note like a fleck of her soul.

"You know what?" An idea comes to me slowly. "Plumfield might have one."

Amy sits up. "Plumfield?"

"They filmed the auditions. Maybe they kept them."

Amy swings her legs over the side of the bunk and jumps.

"Jeez!" Meg shouts as Amy hits the ground.

I wheel around. "What are you—"

"I'm going to Plumfield." Amy shoves her feet into a pair of sneakers.

I laugh. "We have school."

"So what?"

I don't argue, because I genuinely can't imagine going to school either. In fact, I think I won't. But Amy can't Uber to New Hampshire. "What're you gonna do? Steal my car again?"

"Laurie will take me."

I puff out a breath as she leaves the room. I don't blame her for moving quickly. Taking action is the only thing that's felt right and good lately. But wow. She threw out Laurie's name like it was no big deal.

Meg sits up, plants her feet on the floor like she needs to steady herself in Amy's wake. "Did she just—"

"Yeah," I sigh. "Yeah, she did."

It's hard, near impossible, to hear Amy claim Laurie so

casually. I remember all the times he swung by to pick me up, the two of us getting ice cream and laughing through the brain freeze. As much as I hate the two of them together, I know it's what he wants. What he needs.

And so, through the pain, I focus on what I can control.

"Will you look at this?" I get down to Meg's level and, without waiting for an answer, shove my laptop in her face.

She blinks at the screen. "What is it?"

"They're usernames. Three people who seem obsessed with Beth—which is rare, believe it or not. There's one who defends her on every site by replying to every negative comment."

Meg reads, winces.

"See?" I ask. "It's creepy. This person says they'd kill to meet Beth in real life."

"I'm sure it's just a figure of speech."

"This one says, 'Beth March, be mine or die.' What if someone acted on one of these comments?"

"You heard Mom. You need to stay out of it."

"Detective Davis dragged me into the station and blamed me for murder. If you were me, would you stay out of it?"

Meg shuts her eyes. "I know it's hard, but we should let the police—"

"You don't get it."

She opens her mouth to protest, but I don't let her.

"I'm going to Henry's," I say.

"Henry?"

"He can trace the IP addresses."

Meg clutches a pillow, exhausted, unmoving. "I wish you'd

let it go, but I know you won't, so do me a favor. If you try something dangerous, bring Henry with you, and at the very least—turn on your location tracker."

I set my jaw, open my phone, and make a show of doing just that.

* * *

The Hummels' house squats between two colonials, just a lopsided gray box with a bike leaned against a broken fence. Henry answers the door in boxers and a ratty band tee, hair mussed from sleeping—or perhaps from wearing a video game headset for too long.

"Jo?" He steps outside despite the cold, his bare feet on a snowy stoop.

I squint into the house, but Henry nudges the door shut. "My grandpa's asleep. He's been really tired since he came home from the hospital."

"Meg told me about that. I'm so sorry."

Henry looks exhausted, ragged, with tension in his neck, his shoulders. "Thanks. At least it wasn't a heart attack this time."

"Are you okay?" I ask.

He shrugs like he's getting by, but the film in his eyes says otherwise.

I find his hand. "I'm sorry I haven't come around more. I've been so caught up in my own grief that I haven't been checking on anyone else."

Henry nods, and a fresh energy rises through him. "Thank you for saying that. No one has said a word to me. It's like the whole world forgot that I loved Beth, that I lost her too."

"I know you did."

He's not done. He drops my hand, pacing now, back and forth on the little stoop. "When we went back to school, I thought everyone would say something, check in, but it's been crickets."

I watch Henry pace, and I can't help but worry. He's clearly not doing well. "You must be cold. We should get inside."

"My grandpa doesn't talk anymore, and he's all I have."

"Come on." I edge the door open, usher him into the warmth.

He's shivering, goose bumps covering every inch of his skin. I hate that I'm here to ask him for help. Yet another selfish endeavor. But I can't ignore the pressing at the back of my mind—the three usernames that need to be investigated.

"Henry," I offer. "You know what's made me feel better?"

He looks at me, and we lock eyes.

"I've found a little solace in seeking out the truth."

His jaw tightens ever so slightly, and I recognize my own anger, my own desire to hunt down whoever's responsible for the cavern in my heart.

"You can help me," I say.

He backs away, eyes cast down. "I don't know."

"I understand your hesitation. I made a mistake with Sallie Gardiner, and I'm sorry for dragging you into that, but this time I'm really onto something."

Henry wrings his hands. "I'm busy taking care of my grandpa."

But the old man's sleeping comfortably in an armchair.

"Henry, please."

"I don't know." He hedges for a moment, then he kicks the carpet like he can't think of another excuse. "Yeah, okay."

"Thank you."

"Just give me a second to—" He gestures to his boxers, and I plant myself politely in the hallway. I'm in a hurry, but I can allow him the decency of some real clothes.

When he's done changing, he lets me into his room. It's messier than it was the last time I came over, put away in a hurry, and it smells like Henry's been skipping showers, neglecting to change his sheets. I make a mental note to check on him at least once a week. This room has depression written all over it.

"So, here's the deal." I slide my phone onto Henry's desk. "I did a deep dive into the *Little Women* fandom, and I found three people who talk about Beth basically nonstop."

Henry lowers himself into his gaming chair, a stiff nod.

"These are the usernames. I'm hoping you can trace the IP addresses or something. Figure out who they really are."

He looks at the names, sets his fingers on his keyboard.

"So, you know how to do it?" I ask.

His screen remains blank. "I'm thinking."

"Right. Yep. Take your time." I sit on the edge of his bed, wary of the discolored sheets, my hands tucked neatly in my lap.

Henry stares at the blank screen like he's not sure what to do, and I worry that I've asked too much of a boy who's clearly sinking into himself. I draw a breath to get him started. "You might have to pull up the chat forum. It's called—"

"Jo, I don't want to do this."

"I know it's exhausting, but I need your help. It'll only take—"

"I have work." Henry stands up, shoves his chair under his desk with surprising force.

I glance at the clock, scrunch up my nose. Beth always hated Henry's morning shift. It meant he'd be unreachable from sunrise to noon. "Aren't you a little late?"

"Exactly," he says as he grabs his wallet and house keys.

But it's hours past sunrise. There's no way Henry's headed to work now.

"When do you get off?" I ask.

"I don't know."

"Will you be here this afternoon?"

"I don't know."

"Can I call you?"

"Jo, I really don't know." Henry shoves his arms into an old plaid coat and storms into the hallway.

I follow him into the living room, but he's so frustrated, so done talking, that he leaves the house, screen door banging, and I'm suddenly alone with a snoring Mr. Hummel.

I watch in disbelief as Henry starts his truck and takes off in the opposite direction of the diner. "Where is he going?" I mutter under my breath.

Mr. Hummel coughs himself awake. "Beth? Is that you?"

Beth was always more beautiful than me, strawberry-blond hair and the softest hazel eyes, but to a man who's not wearing his glasses, I probably look like her. "Sorry, Mr. Hummel. I'm on my way out."

He gets to his feet, hands trembling. "Honey, I've been meaning to talk to you."

I glance at the front door, eager to bail, but my phone's still in Henry's room. "Mr. Hummel, I'm not actually—"

"I haven't seen you in so long."

"I'm not Beth."

He plods toward me, determined to air whatever's been on his mind. "I know what happened between you kids, and I gotta say—I think you should stay together."

I stop, breath caught in my chest.

Mr. Hummel offers a gentle smile, and though his version of reality is never quite right, he seems sharp and focused in this moment. "People argue. It happens. But you two are a good match. I've never seen Henry so happy."

I'm not sure how much I can believe what Mr. Hummel's saying, but I'm desperate to know more. "What did we argue about? I mean, what did Henry tell you?"

The old man waves me off like it was kid stuff. "We left Christmas Eve in a hurry, and Henry didn't want to talk about it, but I got the story out of him. New Hampshire's not that far away. You don't have to break up just because you're going to a new school."

"Break up?"

Mr. Hummel lays a hand on my shoulder, an imploring grip. "I'm glad to see that you're coming around again. Henry's not himself without you."

My heart thuds slow and hard. Mr. Hummel's often confused, but if he's got his story straight, Beth and Henry might've broken up on Christmas Eve. I remember that night, the way Henry stood up to leave the dinner table, the Hummels rushing out before carols, Henry making an excuse about his grandpa being tired.

My phone rings in the next room.

Mr. Hummel returns to his armchair, and a hollow feeling grips my stomach.

I drift down the hallway, deep in thought, the house closing in around me. My phone rings again, face up on Henry's desk. It's Meg, but as I go to answer—something catches my eye.

A plastic storage bin lurks beneath Henry's bed, the edge sticking out like it was hidden in a hurry. It's nothing special, the kind of thing everyone has stashed in a closet, but it's crammed full of books, dozens pressed up against the clear sides. I'd recognize the covers from a mile away.

I get to my knees, pry open the lid, and unload every book Dad's ever written. Most notably—a bookmarked, dog-eared, well-loved copy of *Little Women*.

CHAPTER FIFTY-ONE

Meg

(NOW)

The detectives ring the doorbell, and of course, I'm home alone.

My sisters should both be at school, but Amy's probably halfway to Plumfield, Jo's tracking IP addresses with Henry, and Mom's getting coffee with Aunt Mary, who insisted on taking Mom's mind off the investigation for a few hours.

I call Jo, whispering, "Come on, come on, come on," but she doesn't answer, and the doorbell rings again.

I haven't seen the detectives since my screaming match with Kirke on the night of John's arrest, and my stomach knots at the prospect of speaking to them alone, but they're here together. It must be important.

I find the courage to answer the door, and the two of them stand with their shoulders back like they're satisfied. Like they know something.

"Meg—" Detective Kirke tries to get going, but her boss interrupts.

"Is your mother home?" The rough old man invades my space, peers over my shoulder into the house.

I stretch taller. "She's out getting—"

"When do you expect her—"

"What's going on?" I ask, ruffled.

Detective Davis is breathing too deeply, thrumming with energy like a hunter who's just shot an animal through the heart.

"We need to speak with your mom," says Kirke.

"She just left, but—"

"We'll come back." As briskly as he arrived, Detective Davis pivots and stalks off toward his squad car.

Kirke offers an apologetic smile, but when she turns to follow, I catch her by the arm.

"Wait!" I shout, and too late, I realize that I shouldn't be grabbing a detective. With an awkward grin, I release my grip, but Kirke's jacket holds a wrinkle.

She stares at the fabric. "Meg . . ." She takes her time, and I fear that I'm in for a lecture, or perhaps an arrest, but at last she softens. "Can I ask you a question?"

I steel myself. "Is it about John?"

"Have you . . . have you ever been afraid of your father?"

I laugh, relieved that it's something so silly. "Why do you ask?"

Kirke glances at the squad car, lowers her voice. "We've talked to every border crossing from here to Seattle, and, Meg"—she pauses—"your dad never left the country."

My heart stills inside my chest, a flash of Dad driving away in his old white Cherokee.

Vancouver, he told us.

Vancouver, he told the press.

"Are you sure?"

By the curb, Detective Davis rises from the car, his voice deep and booming. "Kirke! Let's go!"

The detective winces like she's said too much, but before she goes, she chances one last question. "Do you have any idea where your father could be?"

I think of his usual route from here to his hometown, overnight stays in New York, Chicago, Minneapolis, Billings, and Spokane. In theory, he could be anywhere, but why would he stray from his plans?

"I'm not . . ." Before I can answer, a memory rises. Dad hugging us on the driveway the day he packed his car, unable to let go.

He believed he had to flee for our safety, his reputation, but he didn't want to leave us.

What if he didn't?

An image strikes me. Our cabin in Mount Washington. A creaky little home under a sky full of stars. It would be hard to live there for six months, no electricity, no running water, but it's two hours outside of Concord if you're obeying the speed limit. Just far enough to get away while staying close.

Detective Kirke huddles with me, like we're on the same team. "Meg? Anything?"

I can hardly focus, conviction pumping through my blood. Dad's at the cabin. He's been there all along. I'm sure of it the way Jo's been sure of all her theories. I could tell the detectives, but what if I'm wrong? Worse, what if I'm right?

If I share this information, the detectives won't deliver Dad to the people he loves. They think he killed Beth. And just like John, they'll march him to the station. Lock him in a cell.

"I have no idea." I speak slowly, as if I'm flabbergasted. "No idea where he could be."

Minutes later, the detectives gone, I rummage through Mom's filing cabinet to find a sheet on which she's detailed all my parents' passwords. She showed me once, saying, "You're the oldest. You should know where they are if something happens."

Heart racing, I log into Dad's credit card account and scan the charges. Back in June, he bought gas, racked up a decent grocery bill, then withdrew a large sum from an ATM.

I click on the grocery charge, and my heart careens.

Last time Dad shopped, he shopped in Mount Washington.

Now I understand what Jo loves so much about theorizing. It's a thrill to be right.

I find my phone with shaking hands, but just as I start to call Jo, she bursts through the front door.

She's winded, red-faced, clutching a plastic bin full of books. "Meg—"

"Jo—"

We talk over each other, both of us giddy and fearful and high.

She raises the bin. "There's something I need to—"

"The detectives came by—"

"Henry was acting weird, and—"

"I know where to find Dad."

At this, she falls silent, the bin suddenly weighing her down. Like a child, she lifts her chin, a tender, rose-colored question. "You know where to find—"

"He never left the country. The detectives checked. And the last time he bought groceries, he bought them in Mount Washington."

She drops the bin, her face brightening like it all makes sense. Like we should've known from the very beginning.

"He never left, Jo. He couldn't leave us."

She laughs like she's satisfied, heartened. For a moment I think she's going to cry, but she firms up. "Goddammit. I knew he was camping."

For the first time in days, a warmth flickers beneath my ribs. It burns and burns, and I clutch my chest. I forgot how it feels to hope.

"We have to go find him," I say.

Jo leaves the house. "You drive. I need to read."

I grab my keys, and Jo hauls the plastic bin down the driveway.

"What is that?" I ask.

In the car, she pulls out a copy of *Little Women* that looks like it's been read a hundred times. "This," she says, "is evidence."

CHAPTER FIFTY-TWO

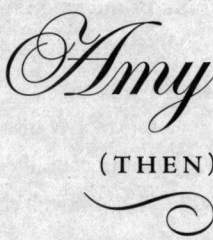

Amy

(THEN)

Beth and I stand in the driveway of the Gardiners' mansion arm in arm. Music pours from the house, people spilling onto the porch, a jam-packed dance floor visible through the windows.

Usually, a party this crowded would hit me like a caffeine drip, but tonight I can't imagine having a good time. Before we left home, I made the mistake of reminding Beth that this would be our last hurrah before she leaves for Plumfield. Now she can't stop talking about her new adventure, and I can't stop picturing myself in quicksand, sinking, going nowhere.

Beth adjusts the dress she borrowed from Jo, sequined and sparkling. "Come on," she squeals, "let's dance."

I look at her sideways. "Dance? Really? Who the hell are you and what did you do with my sister?"

She lets out a giddy laugh, hips swaying before we reach the front door. "I've always loved dancing."

I snort. "Okay, sure."

"I'm just glad to be leaving. I don't care what these people think of me anymore."

For half a second, I'm happy for Beth. I've never seen her like this, so breezy and excited, but her gain is my loss.

I follow her into the party, and she throws her hands in the air, lets out a totally uncharacteristic shout. I pull her close, eyes wide. "I know you're leaving, but I'm stuck here, so maybe you could try not to embarrass me."

She raises a mischievous eyebrow. "Let's get a drink."

I've never seen Beth drink more than a sip of Mom's wine, her lips puckered like she couldn't stand the taste, but when we reach the kitchen, she pours two Solo cups full of pink champagne and drains one while she hands me the other.

"Whoa," I say.

She chokes on the bubbles, eyes watering. "Hurry up. We're celebrating."

I'll never miss an opportunity to drink champagne, and I sure as hell won't pass up a chance to see Beth get tipsy, but as I knock back my drink, I can't ignore the bitter aftertaste. Beth's celebrating, but tonight I'm drowning my sorrows.

She refills my cup, takes a sip from the bottle, and tosses it empty in the trash. As we head for the dance floor, a girl from Beth's grade throws an arm around her shoulders. "Beth!" She stumbles, already drunk. "I can't believe you're going to boarding school. We're really going to miss you."

I've never seen this girl in my life. She must be an acquaintance at best, but Beth acts like they're besties. "I know, right?"

I laugh into my champagne. Beth has never made a real

friend at Concord High. "I don't need them," she always says. "I have my sisters."

The girl waves to her clique and they shuffle up to Beth like she's a shiny object.

"Your new school sounds amazing," one of them says.

"You're going to be famous," says another.

I gulp down my second cup of champagne and disappear onto the dance floor. While I sway to the beat, my phone vibrates in my back pocket. It's Fred Vaughn, and his messages send a knife through my heart. He talks to me like we're friends now, and he believes so deeply that my life will change in Europe. Thanks to Beth, I'll never have a chance to find out.

Florence stumbles over, vodka on her breath. "I can't find my phone. Can I borrow—"

I shove mine in her hand, and for one glorious song, I'm alone, lost in the music, sweetly dizzy from all the champagne.

Soon enough, though, Beth finds me. "Sorry about those girls. It's hilarious, isn't it? They've been ignoring me since kindergarten, and now that I'm leaving—"

"I need another drink." I wrestle my phone back from Florence and shove my way to the kitchen, where I pop another bottle. Beth nips at my heels, holds out her cup.

"I think you've had enough," I say, but it's me who's had enough. I feel loose, wobbly, and gloriously uncaring.

Beth yanks the bottle from my grip, and while she fills her cup, she eyes a boy across the room. "Do you know that guy?"

I shrug without looking.

"He's cute, don't you think?"

I raise an eyebrow. "What about Henry?"

"What about him?" asks Beth, and my stomach turns.

This isn't normal, and after two and a half cups of champagne, I can't stop myself from saying so. "You're acting like a freak."

"What?" She's smiling at the guy, flirting with her gaze.

"You're not acting like yourself."

She sips her champagne. "You mean, because I'm not boring anymore?"

"I mean, because you're being a jerk."

Beth looks taken aback. "I'm not—"

"You have a boyfriend, remember?" I drop my cup in a trash can and head for the front door, but the dance floor's so crowded, I can barely move.

Beth catches up quickly. "I'm just having fun."

"Yeah, well, your version of fun is making everyone feel like shit."

She stills in the center of the dance floor, people gyrating around her, and for just a moment I see my sister underneath the façade. "I didn't mean to . . ."

She trails off, and it's harder to yell when she's looking at me like this. Like she's hurt. "It's fine. It's whatever. You're just . . . you're rubbing Plumfield in my face."

Realization softens her gaze. "Oh, Ames. I'm so sorry."

"Really? Because you haven't shut up about it."

"I wasn't thinking."

"No, you weren't."

She melts toward me, as kind and self-deprecating as ever.

"I've been so focused on myself. I know how badly you want to go to Plumfield."

I don't want her pity. I wave her off. "You don't get it."

"Aunt March should've given you a chance to apply."

"This isn't about Plumfield." My heart thuds, the room spinning. I promised Aunt March I would never tell Beth about our agreement, but I can't hold it in. "I had an opportunity that was better than Plumfield, better than anything you can imagine, and now it's gone."

"What're you talking about?" Beth moves closer, genuinely curious, and her interest makes me sick.

My stomach roils, the taste of champagne coming up my throat. For a second I think I can fight it, but my mouth waters. I push through the crowd, run for the upstairs bathroom, and fall to my knees in front of the toilet. I heave, and old bubbles burn my nose, leaving me coughing, gagging.

Beth holds my hair off my neck. "Are you okay?"

"I'm fine." I shove her away, rinse my mouth at the sink.

"Too much champagne." She winces.

I'm so embarrassed, flushing red. Beth never drinks, and yet I'm the one who's getting sloppy. "I said I'm fine."

Beth watches me until I settle. "What were you talking about? Your opportunity?"

I flatten my gaze. "I'm not supposed to tell you."

"You can tell me anything."

She's so caring, so thoughtful, so angelic. I can't stand another second of it. "Can you stop being so fucking nice?"

"Amy."

"Do you really want to go to Plumfield? I mean, really, truly?"

She gapes like she doesn't know how to answer.

"I had a chance to study art in Europe. Fred Vaughn has a summer program that would've changed my life, but the deposit's due in January, and I don't have the money."

"Fred Vaughn?"

I look at her sideways. "I know you don't like him, but you're a prude, and he's the best artist making work right now."

Beth looks disgusted. "How much does he charge?"

"Too much. Way too much. And I asked Aunt March for money, but she'd already promised it all to you."

Beth leans against the sink, loses color as she processes. "When did you ask Aunt March for money?"

"You don't even want to be a musician. You always say that you only like to play for us."

"I know I've said that, but—"

"I'm desperate to be an artist. It's all I want. It's everything to me."

"Don't you care what I want?" Beth's voice comes out quiet.

I harden. "You can't possibly want it as much as I do."

She breathes through her nose like she's trying not to be angry, but I want her to be angry. I want her to explode the way I'm exploding.

"Let me ask you this," she says. "If Aunt March couldn't give you the money, then why didn't you find it elsewhere?"

"I don't want to talk about this."

"You're telling me you care about this program more than anything in the world, but you didn't try to borrow the money from anyone else, didn't try to raise it—"

"I thought you'd never use it." The truth comes out harsh and loud.

Beth's voice reduces to a whisper. "What?"

"Aunt March said that I could have her money if you didn't end up going to Plumfield, and I never, ever, imagined you would."

Beth sinks to the edge of the tub, tears welling on her lashes. "You never believed in me."

I wish she wouldn't cry. I hate her for crying. She's making me look aggressive, when really, she's just so fragile. "Oh, come on," I sneer. "Don't act like that."

To my surprise, she stands up, wipes her eyes, and charges toward me. "How do you want me to act? You want me to fight?"

"I want you to tell me like it is."

"Really?"

"Do it."

"You're a selfish bitch!" Beth hardly gets the words out before she gasps and claps a hand over her mouth. "Oh my god. Oh my god, Amy, I'm so sorry."

I smirk, both stung and impressed at the same time.

She rushes over, forces me into a hug. "I didn't mean it. I promise. I can't believe I said that."

I laugh while I hug her back. "I didn't think you had it in you."

"Forgive me. Please."

"It's fine. It's cool."

She presses her forehead against mine, and we breathe for a beat, eye to eye. I don't deserve this break, this momentary truce, but I savor it. Then Beth takes a step back and returns to the fight. "All this time. You were waiting for me to fail."

My voice cracks. "You don't know what you want, Beth. You've been so wishy-washy. Plumfield or not? Plumfield or not? I know exactly what I want, and you're the only thing standing in my way."

Beth's tears come fast and freely this time. "I guess you wish it were true then, huh?"

Rage courses through me, the nausea that comes with hurting someone you love. I nearly say yes, but I can't go that far. I can't wish that Dad's book got it right. "Just give up, Beth."

She struggles to speak through her tears, utterly devastated. "I thought . . . I hoped . . ."

The door flies open, and Laurie rushes in. I didn't know he was at the party. Maybe he just arrived. "What's going on?"

He takes stock of the room, and when he sees Beth sobbing, he looks at me like I've done something terrible. Heat throbs in my temples, a sudden urge to shed my skin. I'm so sick of being destructive, but it's impossible to be anything else when everyone expects me to be a villain.

Sallie Gardiner shoves her way inside, and in seconds she's holding Beth. "What happened? Are you okay?"

"It's not fair!" I yell.

"Come on." Laurie grips my shoulders.

"It's not fair!"

Laurie wrestles me out of the bathroom, where Florence and a whole hallway full of people are gaping at me, but before I have a chance to feel embarrassed, I shout, "You know what, Beth? Maybe I do wish you were dead!"

CHAPTER FIFTY-THREE

Amy

(NOW)

Laurie drives toward Plumfield in a comfortable silence, and I love him for it. After days filled with arguments and theories, I don't want to hear anything but the sound of the road.

I'm done with the investigation.

Yesterday I believed in my bones that Jo killed our sister, until I handed her notebook to Detective Davis and realized what I'd done. Hours before, I would've thrown myself off a building to prove that it was Fred Vaughn. And earlier still, I blamed myself without question.

After doling out enough accusations for a lifetime, I've come to this conclusion: I don't care who killed Beth. She's gone either way, and I can't do anything to bring her back.

Arriving at Plumfield feels like stabbing myself between the ribs and twisting. If Beth were still alive, we'd be here for a very different reason. We'd show up with a car full of clothes and sheets that would go on her new bunk in her new dorm. I'd be seething with jealousy, moping no doubt, but when I hugged her goodbye, it would be hard to let go.

"How do you feel?" asks Laurie.

I shake my head.

Outside the car, it should be freezing, but the buildings block the wind, creating a snow globe of stillness. There's a library, a faculty residence, a performing arts center that towers above the rest. Student dorms, a gallery, and a gray little office labeled PLUMFIELD ADMINISTRATION. That's where we start.

A plump, cheerful woman sits behind the desk. She's wearing a massive wool scarf inside the building, and as the door shuts behind us, I can see why. The force of it sends a gust through her hair. She rubs her nose, which is drippy and pink. "How can I help you?"

I don't have to explain much. Everyone at Plumfield has heard about Beth March, the pianist who was supposed to show up for the spring semester.

"I heard she was absolutely brilliant," says the woman.

I can't bear to agree in the past tense, so I just nod. "Do you think we can get a copy of that audition video?"

The woman stands up. "I'll have to ask around, but I don't think it'll be a problem. Just get comfortable, and I'll see what I can do."

She gestures to a row of scratchy-looking chairs, but when she departs, I'm drawn to the window. Plumfield Administration may be the smallest building on campus, but the view would be hard to beat. From here, I can see the web of sidewalks that tangle from building to building, students changing classes.

When I've imagined Plumfield, I've pictured Concord High without all the troublesome academics, a fantasyland where you can hang out in the art studios all day long. But these kids don't seem to know the meaning of the phrase "hang out." They walk with purpose, musicians lugging instruments, dancers wearing buns and pink tights that poke out of their coats.

"Jo was right," I say.

Laurie leans closer, his breath fogging on the window. "It's annoying when that happens."

I flash him a smile, but it fades quickly. "She said I'd never make it here. Said I wouldn't even get in."

"That's not true—"

"I think it is," I say. "I never really thought about what it would mean to go here, the responsibility of it. I just wanted to do something special."

Laurie slides his hands into his pockets. "I understand the feeling."

"I thought Beth was too boring, too shy, too cautious, but she took life seriously. I've never taken anything seriously."

"Ms. March?" The woman behind the desk returns, her wool scarf unwound as if she heated up during her hunt for the video.

"Did you find it?" I ask.

"You're in luck. What's your email address?"

A few minutes later, Laurie and I warm our hands in his car, and I download the video so we can watch it without waiting for it to buffer.

"You ready?" I ask.

Laurie takes the phone from my trembling hands, a finger hovering over the play button. "Ready when you are."

I nod, and he taps the screen.

It's been nineteen days since I last saw Beth. Nineteen days since I've heard her voice, her laugh. She walks onstage wearing a jacket that belongs to Jo, sleeves rolled up so they won't get in her way.

"Name?" asks one of the judges.

"Elizabeth March."

I close my eyes, overwhelmed by the way she floods back to me. All the little things I've forgotten. The sheen of her hair, the slope of her shoulders, the way she folds her hands.

"Ames?" Laurie sounds worried, and I'm about to tell him I'm okay when he taps my shoulder. "Look at this."

I wipe hot tears from the corners of my eyes. "What is it?"

He points to the audience, the back of someone's head. "Did you know she was at Beth's audition?"

"Who is it?" I squint, but as soon as I ask, the answer hits the pit of my stomach. Straight, long, yellow hair. "You've got to be kidding me."

Laurie turns the phone for a better look. "Did Beth invite her?"

"Yeah, right. Beth didn't even invite me."

I grab for the phone, call Florence on speaker, and keep watching. On video, Beth answers a couple more questions— seventeen years old, from Concord, Massachusetts—and then, like the first long-awaited snow of the season, she begins to play.

BETH IS DEAD

Her music drifts through the car, wraps me in a memory of the way our house should sound. Full. Resonant.

"Uh? Hello?"

I forgot that I called Florence. Her voice comes through the speaker, huffy and frustrated. "Amy, what's going on?"

I should pause the video, but I let it play over our conversation, a dizzying melody.

"Amy? Are you there?" Florence asks again.

Her nagging lights a fire inside me, and I load up a question, ready to shoot, when someone else enters the frame.

"Florence?" My voice goes cold.

"Amy, where are you? What're you doing?"

I watch the screen as Henry Hummel storms down the center aisle. For a second it looks like he's not going to stop, like he's going to jump onstage and rip Beth from the piano, but to my surprise, Florence chases after him. I pause the video, switch to the call. "I need to know what happened at Beth's audition."

Laurie's car chugs out a cloud of hot air while Florence tells us everything. "I didn't even talk to Beth, I swear. I just wanted to see how she did, so I could—"

"So you could see if she was going to fail."

Florence sounds guilty. "Well . . . yeah, okay? I wanted to know if you'd be getting your money or not, and I know that's awful, but I didn't interfere, and honestly, it was a good thing I was there, because Henry wanted to stop her audition."

I'm frozen for a moment, lost in thought, wondering why Henry never mentioned any of this.

Laurie takes the phone. "Flo, what did he say that day?"

Florence lets out a long sigh. "He was really upset. He didn't want Beth to leave him. I thought it was sweet that he loved her so much."

Laurie and I exchange a glance over the phone. In the moment I might've interpreted Henry's actions as love just as Florence did, but after everything that's happened, he sounds possessive. "Why didn't you tell me about this?" I ask.

"Are you serious?" asks Florence. "You would've jumped down my throat if you knew I'd gone to Beth's audition, and honestly? I didn't think it was important. It took a while and a handful of tissues, but I convinced Henry to go home. Beth never even knew he was there."

Laurie puts us on mute, talks in a hushed tone. "You don't think Henry could've—"

"I don't know." My heart pounds. I haven't considered Henry a suspect, not even for a second, but he's been pretty quiet since Beth's murder.

Laurie goes cold. "What if he couldn't let her go?"

"You think he killed her to stop her from leaving?" It's counterintuitive, but somehow it feels true. Henry and Beth had a whirlwind love, hands held on the way home from school, phone calls that lasted well into the night.

Florence's voice comes out of the speaker. "Amy? You still there?"

I take us off mute. "Flo, we have to go."

"Okay, but—"

"I have to talk to my sisters."

I hang up and race to dial Jo, but when I find her number in my favorites, a notification stops me.

Jo March has started sharing her location.

"That's weird." I tap into the app where my family members are all listed as unavailable. Though we seem like the kind of family that would follow one another's whereabouts regularly, Meg made it pretty clear that she thought tracking was an invasion of privacy (ahem, sleepovers with John?), and since she's the oldest, we all agreed.

"Jo's sharing her location," I say. "And she's not in Concord."

Laurie leans in, our foreheads nearly touching. "Looks like she's an hour outside of town, maybe two."

I zoom into the map, and it hits me like a shock of cold water. "She's on her way to Mount Washington."

CHAPTER FIFTY-FOUR

(THEN)

I rest against the window of John's car, head spinning, champagne bubbles hot in the back of my throat. Did I puke? I can't remember.

"Yeah," says John, "but it's okay. You got the door open first."

Oh my god. I must've asked that question out loud. My cheeks fill with heat. I've never been so embarrassed in my entire life, and yet I feel like I could laugh, like I'm floating. I giggle into my hands, and suddenly, they're slippery and black. I've been crying. Amy told me this mascara was waterproof. Such a liar.

"I love her," I say.

John's car rumbles gently, stopped at the end of the block. Laurie's house sits in front of us, big and beautiful against the night sky. I can taste the vomit now, stale and sweet in the back of my mouth. The past few minutes return to me like a wave of heat.

I remember waiting for John behind the Gardiners' massive

hedges, an empty bottle of champagne at my feet. I remember fighting with Florence. About what? I'm not sure. Then I remember the warmth of John's car, the advice that I didn't want to hear: "You can't back out of Plumfield." I remember crying, panicking, gagging, John's hands going up, "Are you going to be—" Tires screeching, the car swerving, hitting a tree, my stomach lurching.

"Your car," I say now, sick with guilt.

John looks worn out, exhausted, actually. "It's not that bad, but I think we should get you home."

"I need to talk to Amy."

"Will you be okay if I start driving?"

"Is she still at the party?"

"I don't think we should go back to the party."

I look at him sideways. He doesn't understand how broken I feel. Fighting with Amy smashed me into a million pieces, and I know she must feel the same. I can't move forward, can't do anything, until I know that someday, maybe not tonight but someday, we'll be glued back together.

"I just need a minute," I say.

"Beth—"

Before John can stop me, I open my door and rush toward the park. Wind whips, biting through my dress, but the Gardiners' house isn't far. I climb the steep bridge, legs burning, desperate to make this right.

John follows me. "Beth, wait. This isn't a good idea. You need to go home."

I walk faster, shouting. "I love Amy no matter what she says."

"I'm sure she knows."

I stop at the top of the hill, whirl around. "She's right, though. I've been so selfish. Ever since that stupid article came out, I've been thinking about me, me, me. What am *I* going to do? How can *I* prove that *I* matter?"

"It's okay to follow your own dream." John climbs toward me, teeth gritted against the effort. He's so patient and steadfast, it's no wonder Meg can't seem to stay away from him.

My teeth chatter, voice trembling. "That's the thing. I don't even know if Plumfield's my dream. I'm not sure I really want to go, and Amy's so certain. She's so certain that Europe will change her life."

John comes closer. "That doesn't mean she deserves the opportunity more than you do."

"Yes, it does."

My head spins, but about this, I'm certain. Amy knows what she wants, and wanting something with all your might should give you a better chance at having it. If it doesn't, then what's the point of hoping? Of praying?

John slips out of his coat, offers it to me.

"I'm fine." I step away, shivering.

He sighs. "Even if Plumfield doesn't work out, you deserve a chance to try it."

"I've never wanted anything as much as Amy wants to go to Europe with that creep."

John stays close. "That can't be true. If it were, she would've found the money some other way. She could've worked, pitched a lemonade stand, but instead she just waited."

Darkness surrounds us, playground equipment like a ghost in the distance. To our left, the craggy hill.

John talks with his hands, imploring me to listen. "Amy doesn't see the world the way you do. She doesn't think about what could go wrong, she only imagines that everything will go right."

"I'm going to fail," I say.

"Maybe. But can you imagine, just for a second, that you might succeed?"

My thoughts run away without me, and I picture myself at Plumfield in a group of friends, all of them artists. We're backstage, about to walk on for a performance, an audience waiting. I'm tingling, nervous but excited, and I can almost see it.

I can almost see myself happy.

Then I picture the night I met Henry, the thrill of imagining our love story, and Christmas Eve, the way we fell apart. "Nothing works out for me. I'm better off at home."

John rubs his forehead. "We shouldn't talk about this now. You've been drinking. Please, take my coat."

I'm so cold, but I hate being babied, and I hate feeling out of control. I want to be home, safe, warm, nothing out of place, nothing uncertain. And I have to see Amy. I can't go to sleep without settling our fight.

I turn for the Gardiners' house, but I'm too close to the hill.

I stumble, my ankle twisting. The horizon slants, and I grope for something to catch, but I'm falling.

John shouts, yanks my arm. My shoulder screams.

I grip him tight, and my nails find purchase in his skin. He pulls me to safety, where I breathe into his chest. My eyes sting from the cold, but I can't blink. I'm stunned.

John's jacket is torn, beads of blood surfacing on his arm.

"I'm so sorry," I whisper.

He's breathing hard too, still gripping my shoulder like I might go down again. "Please. Let me. Get you. Home."

I don't argue after that. My heart's charging too hard to say anything else.

John stays quiet until we've driven the rest of the way down the block and we're sitting in front of my house.

"Listen." He can hardly look at me, like he's afraid that if he does, he'll scare me off. "I know you'd do anything for your sisters, but you don't have to live for someone else in order to love them."

I drag my hands over my face before I look at John. "I'm sorry about your arm."

He covers the scratch with his sleeve. "It's nothing."

"I owe you."

"You don't." He pauses. "But if you did—I'd ask you to sleep on this. Don't make a decision about Plumfield tonight."

I swallow, nod.

"If you don't want to go, I'll understand. But I want you to make that decision for yourself, not for Amy. Not for anyone else."

I feel like I should say something, but if I do, I'll cry, so I nod again and open my door. John doesn't drive away until I'm safe inside, then I hear his engine, his old Ford chugging off into the night.

I'm quiet in the entryway, back against the front door. There's a light on upstairs. Jo must be awake, still writing. I imagine passing her room, the way she'll lean out and ask me about the party.

I can't talk to her. Not now. If she knows about the fight, she'll be on my side. She'll trash-talk Amy and fire me up, tell me I can't let go of Plumfield, not for anything, and I don't want to hear it. I don't want to hear that Amy's wrong, because she's right.

I've never wanted anything the way she wants everything.

I told John I'd sleep on Plumfield, but sleeping won't help. I need the park. I need to lie on my back and look at the stars and find the answer in the sky.

When I'm sure John's gone, I slip out the door, back into the cold, and charge up the street, wiping my tears. I climb the hill beside Laurie's house, and the park comes into view, the swing set we loved as kids, my sisters always swinging higher than me.

I'm searching for a clearing, a view of the sky, when I'm interrupted.

"Beth?"

Henry faces me at the top of the hill.

CHAPTER FIFTY-FIVE

Jo

(NOW)

"You're killing me."

I grip the edge of my seat while Meg gingerly navigates the traffic out of town.

She keeps her hands at ten and two, lips pursed. "Don't judge my driving. I shadowed a trauma surgeon last summer, and you know what I learned? Traffic laws exist for a reason."

I resist the urge to climb over the console, sit on top of her, and floor it. Yes, I know how it feels to stand in the center lane of the interstate after an accident, your sister in the back of an ambulance, and still, I'd do anything to move faster. Our family cabin's only a two-hour drive outside of Concord, and if Dad's really there, we can't arrive fast enough.

While we drive, I flip through Henry's personal copy of *Little Women*. The pages hold so many notes, I can't even begin to decipher them all. "He must've read this a hundred times."

"It's weird," says Meg. "When I went to sit with him at the hospital, he acted like he hated the book. Said that Dad deserved to be canceled."

"Oh, he definitely hates it." I rotate the pages so I can read what's been scrawled into the margins. Henry criticizes every mention of Beth, lamenting the way she's portrayed as meek and gentle.

Beth deserves a voice!

A dear and nothing more? Nothing more?

His handwriting turns my stomach. "He hates the book, but he loves Beth."

Most beautiful girl in the world.

Made for me.

Perfect.

I delve deeper into the book, work my way to the car accident, the chapter where Beth takes her very last breath. "Holy shit."

"What?" asks Meg.

"It's gone." I flip back and forth just to be sure, but there's no denying the ragged edges of a chapter ripped from its spine. "He tore out the ending."

"He what?"

"The whole thing."

Goose bumps appear on Meg's arms. She cranks up the heater. "Why would he tear out the ending?"

I swallow, nervous. "Maybe he didn't want her to die."

Meg gives me a twisted look, and I feel the same sickening confusion. Something's off about Henry—the way he obsessed over Beth, the way he bolted when I asked for help with the IP addresses. But if he loved Beth—character or not—then why would he hurt her?

As the scenery changes from city to sky, stark buildings to snowy pine trees, I fill Meg in on my conversation with Mr. Hummel.

"He has dementia," she says.

And she's not wrong. Everyone in Concord has a story about Mr. Hummel getting confused, buying milk three times in one day because he forgot he'd already done it. When he spoke to me earlier, he was mixed up enough to believe that I was Beth, but his story sounded crystal clear. "He thought they broke up on Christmas Eve, and come to think of it, I didn't see much of Henry after that."

Meg considers. "Beth would've told us."

"Maybe," I sigh, but I'm not so sure. A few weeks ago I thought I knew everything about my sisters, but Amy hid her desperation to jet off to Europe, and Meg concealed years of academic fraud. I didn't tell my sisters that I planted the recording device under Beth's piano all those months ago.

We all have our secrets—surely Beth had some too.

Our family cabin is nestled in the deepest woods of Massachusetts, a tiny shelter amid stark-white snow.

Dad's car marks the landscape, but I stifle my excitement. The old white Cherokee's been buried by a storm.

If Dad's here, he's not doing well. When we stay at the cabin as a family, the lack of electricity calls for candles, a woodburning fire, but today the chimney's cold, the windows dark.

I picture him unshaven and freezing in a creative frenzy, wearing fingerless gloves to expel his latest novel. Or worse—drowning himself in the sorrows of the past year, accepting the lies of his villainy as truth.

Meg's worried expression tells me she's thinking the very same thing. She hesitates, but with a deep breath she steps out into the snow.

We ease our way up the path, listening for any sound, but the woods are quiet for miles. When we reach the porch, I knock, and as soon as my knuckles meet wood, the door edges open.

Meg and I exchange a look, but our fear seems ridiculous. This is the place where we come for vacation, to hike through the flowers in spring and roll through the leaves in fall.

"Dad?" I call into the cabin.

My voice echoes back, the acrid scent of old food carried with it.

I push the door open and peer into the living room. Someone's definitely been here, but the place has been empty long enough for the remnants of breakfast to rot on the table.

Meg coughs, her breath clouding the air. "That smell."

Dad's laptop sits beside the putrid breakfast, plugged into a portable charger but open and cold as ice. I tap the keys, and it doesn't even think about coming to life. "It's like he left in the middle of working."

Meg circles the room, lifts a coat off a hook. Dad's favorite. Left behind.

"Jo, I'm scared."

"Don't be." I set my shoulders, determined to stay calm. "There has to be an explanation. Dad must've gone somewhere."

Meg ventures into the largest bedroom, and the sound of heavy drawers echoes through the cabin. "All his clothes are here," she says.

It doesn't make sense that Dad would leave in such a hurry. Even if the protesters found this address and scared him off, he would've come back. He wouldn't go months without his car, his laptop, his clothes.

I ease through the house, my boots heavy on the creaky wooden floors. "Meg?" I continue down the hallway, but my heart's in my throat. "The back door's wide open."

She joins me outside the bedrooms, where a frigid breeze rustles the curtains. Shoulder to shoulder, we step outside, and we're met by a wide expanse of stillness.

"You don't think he went out there." It should be a question, but Meg says it like a fact, and I want to believe it. There's no reason Dad would hike into the woods. He doesn't hunt. And it's freezing. He wouldn't survive.

"Where is he?" I ask under my breath, more of the universe than of Meg.

To our left, a pile of firewood sits half chopped, a log split and abandoned, an axe leaning against the house.

Meg steps off the back porch, her boots leaving prints in the blanket of white. "He left in the middle of . . . everything."

I stare at the axe, and a sick thought rises through me. It's too clean, reflecting the sky. "Meg."

She turns.

"Come back."

"What's wrong?"

"I have a bad feeling . . ." I can't get the theory out of my mouth.

Behind me, footsteps.

CHAPTER FIFTY-SIX

(THEN)

Henry stands before me with tears in his eyes.

We haven't spoken since Christmas Eve, and though I don't want to see him, I miss him. He smells like he came from a shift at the diner, like bacon and coffee.

"Can we talk?" he asks.

I wish I'd grabbed a coat before I left the house. Jo's dress barely reaches my knees, the fabric thin and sheer. "It's late. I need to get home."

"You said we could talk. You promised."

It's dark, not a streetlamp in sight, but I can make out the shape of Henry's face, his blue-gray eyes. Our last conversation still clings to my bones, but he's calm now, and he deserves to have closure. "We can. We will. But it's freezing."

Henry unzips his bomber jacket. "Take it."

I'm too cold to decline, so I slip the jacket over my arms. It's warm from his body heat, a reminder of being close, not a breath between us. "Walk me home?"

"I don't want to break up," he says.

I start walking toward the bridge, but Henry stays put, his shoulders heavy. "I really miss you."

I stop, sigh. "I miss you too, but—"

"You're my best friend. My only friend."

I can't help reaching out. A hand on his shoulder. "I think we need some time apart."

He tenses. "I don't understand. I said I was sorry. We can do long-distance. I'll visit you in New Hampshire."

I can't stand the idea of rehashing our fight. Not tonight. Not while I'm drunk. "Henry, I need to get home."

"I can't lose you. I love you."

I almost admit that I love him too, but the feeling's harder to access now. Henry looks strange in the dark, his eyes rubbed red. "Consider it a break," I say.

He shakes his head, growls. "I gave up everything for you."

Those words strike the air like a tuning fork at the wrong pitch. I take a few steps, but he grabs my wrist. "You don't even know. I've been telling you that I left Rhode Island after my mom died, but I didn't. I left her behind just to be with you."

I think he's confused, tangled up in his emotions, but my heart beats in my throat. "Henry, what are you talking about?"

"You needed me." He drops my wrist to throw his arms out wide. "I came here to protect you, and this is how you repay me?"

I draw inward, backward. "You came here to live with your grandpa, because your mom—"

Henry sounds frustrated, disgusted, like I should've

figured this out by now. "I left my mom in Rhode Island. I left her because you needed my help."

I keep edging backward, slow, small steps. Henry must be losing his grip on reality. "Your mom is gone," I say.

"It's not my fault."

"Of course it's not."

He jabs a finger through the air. "It's your fault. I came here for you. I didn't know how much my mom would miss me. I didn't know she'd get worse without me."

Pressure builds behind my eyes, fear coursing through my veins. "I don't understand."

"I fell in love with you, Beth. When everyone else thought you were small and insignificant, I saw you."

"You didn't know me," I shout, and then it hits me like a gust of wind. In a flash, I picture us in the booth at the pizzeria, Henry promising he'd never read *Little Women*. "You lied." A chill runs down my spine. "You read the book."

Henry keeps his voice low, but it feels like he's yelling. "You're lucky I did, because I defended you. People said horrible things. Called you flat, naive, but I knew better. I knew you had a spark."

I back away quickly. "You're a stalker."

Henry flinches. "Don't say that. Don't hurt my feelings."

"Get away from me!" My joints ache from the cold, tears blurring my vision. I run, but I'm slow.

"Stop!" Henry shouts. "You'll be nothing without me. You'll go right back to being the sister nobody loves, the one who dies at the end of the book."

A fire lights inside me. I think of the girl I was before I met Henry. I may have been timid and sensitive, I may have lacked ambition, but I always—*always*—knew I was loved.

Henry catches up to me, grabbing. "Wait! I need you!"

I turn to face him if only for a second. "I don't need you!"

It happens so fast that I can't stop it, can't even think to step out of the way. Henry lunges and shoves my chest with so much force that my breath leaves my lungs. I plunge backward, and my stomach drops—

I catch air, then I land with a thwack against the hard-packed snow.

I'm rolling, falling, grasping.

Roots. Rocks. The ground so cold, it almost feels warm.

And then a deafening crack. I bash into something impossibly hard.

Instant ringing. Hot and sharp.

My vision goes black, and when it fuzzes back in, I'm lying next to a boulder. A boulder that I must've hit as I plummeted down the hill.

My head hurts. It hurts more than anything's ever hurt before.

I roll to my back, but my neck feels crackly, stiff.

I can't see, everything's bright.

For a moment I don't remember where I am or why or what's happened to me.

Someone scrambles down the hill, boots scraping, slipping. "Beth?" The voice comes quietly, muffled through the nonstop, high-pitched ringing. "Oh my god, Beth?"

BETH IS DEAD

Henry's face comes into focus, and white-hot panic rips through my chest. The past few minutes come back to me. The fight. The shove. The fall.

Henry reaches for my head, color draining from his face. "Oh my god. What should I do? You're bleeding, Beth. You're bleeding a lot."

Am I bleeding? Is that what this is? Is that why I feel so impossibly warm?

Henry paces. "God. Fuck. This can't happen. This can't happen again."

I try to move, but I'm so heavy, and my head throbs so hard that my vision goes in and out.

"What should I do?" Henry asks himself. "What should I do?"

I think of Jo, her face so clear in my mind's eye. She always knows what to do. And Meg. She'd hold my hand through whatever's happening.

I try to speak but my throat's too dry, too stiff. I blink, unable to make out anything beyond Henry.

He panics in my tunnel vision.

"What should I do? What should I do?"

"Get help," I whisper, but I don't know if he can hear me. He's still pacing, hands in his hair.

He kneels beside me, his face blocking the whole sky. "Fuck," he says again, but this time he's not angry, he's crying, whining. He brushes my cheek. "I love you so much."

Tears seep from my eyes. I try again to move, but I'm slipping, losing consciousness.

Henry scoops up my torso, and a great sense of relief washes over me. He's going to lift me. We're going to move. We're going to get help.

But no.

Henry clutches me for a moment, his tears landing on me like rain. Then he raises my arms one by one, slides his bomber cleanly off, and lays me back in the cold, cold snow.

"I'm so sorry," he says, his bloody jacket balled in a fist.

My mind scratches, an animal fear. *Don't leave me*, I want to scream.

"I'm sorry," Henry repeats through sobs as he backs away. "They can't find out. They won't understand."

My breath comes fast, tight, short. I can't get air. Can't get enough.

The sky turns dark, absent of stars. Henry runs, and I'm desperate to follow, but I can't move. Can't even remember how.

I need to find Jo and Meg and Amy. I have to find Amy. To tell Amy that I love her. God, I love her.

But I'm slipping, slipping.

Then, laughter.

Amy's laughter.

Is that her?

"Is that you?" I try to yell.

Her voice comes through the trees, brash as ever. "I fucked up, Laurie. I really fucked up."

"It's okay," he says.

Laurie? Is Laurie there too? Can he hear me?

BETH IS DEAD

Amy groans. "I didn't mean it. I didn't mean any of that awful shit. I have to tell Beth I'm sorry."

Laurie shuffles. "Whoa, whoa, whoa. Hold on. You're drunk. Maybe you should tell her tomorrow."

Their footsteps sound so close. I picture them ambling up to Laurie's porch, and I know I should yell, but I don't have it in me. I'm so achingly, painfully tired.

"I need her to know," says Amy. "I need her to know that I love her."

"She knows," says Laurie.

I do.

I know it no matter what she said.

I know it always and forever.

Their footsteps fade. A front door opens and shuts. I'm alone. I'm alone, and I'm scared, I'm so scared—and then, Jo.

I can almost hear her voice.

And there's Meg, a gentle hand on my cheek.

And Amy? She's coming back.

It's okay. We're okay.

The light in my eyes gets brighter, safer, all-consuming. I'm forgetting to breathe. I'm going, going, out like the tide, and I think I might be ready.

Then I gasp for breath.

Another. Another.

Something occurs to me.

A truth so sharp, it wakes me up.

I open my eyes to look at the stars, and I know what I want.

I want it so much, I could cry from the ache.

I want to live.
Not for Plumfield.
Not for a love story.
Not to prove that I'm worthy of living—but to live.
"You have," Jo whispers in my ear.
"Not enough," I want to say.
She grips my hands. "We love you."
There.
That's it.
That's how those words are supposed to sound.

I can't leave. I can't leave my sisters. I swear, I'll be homesick even in heaven. But I don't have a choice, I feel my breath slipping, so I hold their love deep in my heart, and slowly . . . gently . . . I go.

CHAPTER FIFTY-SEVEN

(NOW)

Henry Hummel stands in the hallway of the cabin, and the truth hits the bottom of my stomach like an anchor.

He killed Beth.

The weight helps me focus, heavy but grounding, all my other theories washed away. He must've followed me. I picture him driving away from his house, idling at the end of his street, panicking while I carried his books to my Jeep. He must know that I've read his inner thoughts, read the way he fantasized about Beth.

I glance at Meg but only briefly, only long enough to show her that we're in danger.

She knows. I can tell because she eases toward him, uses her damsel voice. "Henry, thank god you're here."

He stays in the hallway, hands buried in the pockets of his coat.

Meg pretends to need Henry. She never gets credit for being brave, but look at her now. "Our dad's missing. We thought he went to Vancouver, but he never left the country, and it looks like he was here. Maybe you can help us find him."

Henry doesn't say a word.

My thoughts move from one fact to the next. This boy didn't love Beth—he had an obsession, the proof in the margins of his well-worn book. If we'd traced the IP addresses of the usernames I flagged, I think one of them would've led right back to his fingertips. That's why he ran.

My phone vibrates in my back pocket, mercifully on silent. I ignore it, but it vibrates again, so I talk to hide the buzzing, add to Meg's story with a Disney princess kind of urgency. "There's a laptop on the kitchen table. It's practically ice, but you're a wizard with computers. Maybe you can get it running again. Maybe that'll help us track him down."

"Where are they?" asks Henry.

Meg fumbles the question. "That's just it. We have no idea where he could be."

"The books!" Henry shouts. "Where are my books?"

I step in front of Meg, because this is my fault. I didn't think before I snatched his prized possessions. I didn't have a plan. I open my palms to Henry. "I'm sorry. I shouldn't have taken them."

"Where are they?" he shouts.

My mind races, my heart along with it. I can't tell him the truth, can't let him reclaim the best evidence we have against him. I think hard, spin a story that might earn his favor. "Henry. Please. You have every right to be mad, but I couldn't help it. I thought I was my dad's biggest fan, but you—"

"What did you do with them?" He finally comes out to the porch, eyes rimmed with red like he's been crying, rubbing them too hard.

"I was so amazed. All your thoughts in the margins."

"You can't turn them in."

"I would never—"

"I can't let you turn them in!" A bird flaps off in the distance, frightened by Henry's volume, his voice rough and raw.

I swallow my fear and move closer. "I would never give away your books."

"The cops won't get it. They'll think I didn't love her."

"Who, Beth? Of course you loved her. Why else would you rip out the ending?"

Henry eyes me like I'm a snare and he's a beast, skittish but nearly trusting. "She needed me," he says.

A chill travels down my spine, the woods beckoning from afar. Meg and I could turn and run, risk Henry catching up, but I sense a story at the back of his throat, and I want it. I want it more than my safety.

"She was happier," I admit. "After you moved to Concord."

"Everyone thought she was dead. She believed it herself. I had to remind her that she was alive."

"You did," I say, but it's almost impossible to hide the disgust in my voice.

Henry grips his forehead like his thoughts are moving too fast. "I didn't mean for this to happen. She wasn't supposed to die."

Beside me, Meg squeezes her eyes shut, fighting tears.

I can't cry. I can't panic. I have to make Henry feel like I'm on his side. My voice comes out on a shaky breath. "It was an accident, wasn't it?"

He stamps his boot, and Meg shudders. "I defended her,

protected her, gave up my whole entire life for her. You have no idea how hard it's been. My mom died when I left home. She died alone. And I've spent every day looking over my shoulder. All for Beth."

He's not making sense. I grab at the pieces, but I can't put them together. "Did you see her that night? Did you meet her at the park?"

Henry's neck turns red. "I'm not the only one who thought it was sick. Sick that she died at the end of that book. But I'm the only one who did anything about it."

"Did you push her? Did she fall?"

Meg's sobbing now, unable to stop.

Henry walks right up, so close, I can smell his breath. "I wasn't going to hurt him. I just wanted to talk. I needed him to know that he broke his own daughter, but he didn't want to listen."

My whole body goes stiff and cold. I strain to look at Meg without moving my head.

We're not talking about Beth. Not anymore.

Henry drags his hands over his face like he's forcing out the story. "It wasn't hard to track your dad. I came here to talk, but he thought I was the problem. Thought I would hurt Beth. I was never planning to hurt Beth. I loved her."

I think of the breakfast abandoned on the table. Dad's laptop open like he was interrupted midsentence. The axe against the house, too clean.

My voice comes out clotted, thick with tears. "You didn't."

"You're judging me." Henry jabs a finger into my sternum.

Meg whimpers.

"You can't judge me for what happened. It's not my fault. I tried to send a message at first, but your dad wouldn't answer my calls, and he thought one of the protesters vandalized the garage, so I waited. I waited until he left home, and I followed him here."

"You're evil," says Meg.

I don't know what to do, how to regain control. I think about fighting, running. My gaze darts around the snow.

Then Henry's hands land hard on my shoulders. "Don't even try."

I falter, my knees weak.

Meg lunges. "Let go of her!"

We grab, rip, scratch, but all at once Henry emerges from the tangle, arms extended before him.

"No," says Meg.

My voice breaks. "Henry, you don't have to do this."

He grips a pistol between his hands, a finger on the trigger. "Get in the house."

I raise my arms. "Henry, please. We can work this out."

Henry shakes his head like he's lost all hope. "Your dad was going to turn me in. Keep me away from her. I didn't have a choice. I killed him. And I still couldn't save her." His arms shake, tears rolling down his cheeks. "I couldn't save her, because everyone would find out what I did."

I fight to stay standing, his words like a fist.

Dad's rich brown eyes. The scent of new pencils. His finger striking air whenever he had an idea.

He can't be dead. It can't be true.

And yet I feel his absence. A part of me stolen, a gaping wound.

I double over, retch on the porch.

"Into the house!" Henry yells.

My mind lags, desperate for a plan. We're the only cabin for miles around. Screaming will do nothing but waste my energy. I wipe my mouth on the back of my hand. "Okay. Okay, we're going."

Meg and I shuffle into the house, both of us crouching like we can hide from the gun that's pointed at our backs.

"Into the living room." Henry circles us, shuts and locks both the doors.

Meg's phone buzzes. It's on silent like mine, but the cabin's so quiet, we can hear the vibration.

"Phones out!" Henry yells.

At his instruction, we take them out. I have fourteen missed calls from Amy, but I can't risk calling her back, calling for help.

"Shut them off," says Henry.

We obey and stand in the middle of the living room, a place where we laughed as kids, roasting marshmallows over the fire, performing plays that poured from my mind, Dad alive and beaming like he could watch us do anything for any number of hours.

I need Henry to believe that we can work this out, so I tell him again and again and again that we will, but deep down, I don't know how we're going to leave this place.

He killed our dad. He killed Beth. And he's going to kill us, too.

CHAPTER FIFTY-EIGHT

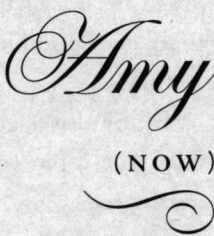

Amy

(NOW)

Laurie drives as fast as he can while I navigate from the passenger seat. "Left."

He jerks the wheel, and we skid on a patch of ice. At once he draws a sharp breath, eases up, and regains control of the car, so we can speed into the backwoods. "Sorry." His breath comes hot and fast.

We've been driving for nearly two hours, back from New Hampshire and down to the cabin in Mount Washington, but now we're close, and we can't get there fast enough.

I've called Jo and Meg a thousand times, and neither of them has answered. But the cops are on their way. I tipped them off at the start of our drive, and though I'm sure we'll beat them there, they shouldn't be far behind.

Laurie sounds panicked. "Try Jo again."

This time her phone goes straight to voicemail.

"Something's seriously wrong," I say.

Laurie revs the engine, and the scenery blurs, faster, faster.

At the last turn, I tell him to slow down. I don't know why Jo and Meg have gone to the cabin, but they would never ignore my calls unless they were in trouble. We have to move carefully.

Laurie drives gently, rocks crunching under his tires. Up ahead, the cabin comes into view, rich wood against a pale landscape.

"There." He points to Meg's car.

I draw a hand to my mouth. My sisters are here. And they're not alone. An old truck idles near Meg's car, doors wide open, as if someone leaped out and ran. Adrenaline courses through my veins, strong and metallic. "Oh god."

Laurie stops the car, fear in his eyes. "What is it?"

My heart pounds deep in my chest. "That's Mr. Hummel's truck. We were right. We were right about Henry."

Laurie throws open his door and rushes from the car.

"Laurie, wait!" I strain to keep my voice down, follow him into the snow.

"Jo's in danger." He charges ahead.

I grab his arm and yank him back. "We should wait for the cops."

Laurie's eyes widen. "They don't know the back roads like you do. They'll never get here fast enough."

Detective Davis promised he'd be fast and that he'd contact a closer precinct for help, but Laurie's right. Henry stopped his truck quick and hard, the body splattered with ice and mud. He's angry, and we don't have time to wait.

I nod agreement to Laurie, and we edge toward the house

with gentle, snow-padded footsteps. We cling to the trees, slivered behind one and then another.

The cabin's dark, but three figures move inside.

Henry, Jo, and—

"Meg's here too." I recognize her silhouette immediately, my stomach dropping.

Laurie stays close, his voice pressed to my ear. "We'll make a run for it. Break the door down."

My muscles twitch, desperate to act, but something holds me behind the trees. Inside the cabin, Jo and Meg huddle together. I can only see Henry's back, a plaid coat, but there's something about the way they're standing.

Laurie moves, but I yank him back. "Wait."

"Come on."

"He has a gun."

Laurie falls still. "Are you sure?"

I nod, teeth chattering.

"Okay." Laurie's eyes go wide. "Okay, it's okay. We just have to be smart. We could break through the window, surprise him from behind."

My heart pounds, every beat like a fist to the chest.

Laurie clutches my shoulders, turns me to face him. "I'm going for the window."

"No. You can't."

"I have to do something."

I shake my head, grip his coat, his shirt. I can't let Laurie go alone, but I'm not smart like Meg or brave like Jo or selfless like Beth. What am I supposed to do?

Tears fill my eyes, then a memory trickles through my fear. My sisters and I are at the cabin rehearsing one of Jo's plays, tucked in a hideaway, laughing until we cry.

The attic.

Climbing up will be risky. If Henry hears us, we'll be his new target, but I can't let anything happen to Jo and Meg. I may not be brave, but I've always been reckless.

I take Laurie's hand and pull. "Come on. I know what to do."

CHAPTER FIFTY-NINE

Jo

(NOW)

"How?" Henry yells, the pistol still gripped between his hands.

I don't know. If I'm honest, I don't see a way out of this. But I'm not going to tell Henry that. "Put the gun down, and we'll figure it out. We can make a deal. Meg and I don't have to tell anyone. Ever."

Henry shakes his head, a slick of snot under his nose. "I don't believe you."

"If you put the gun down, we'll come up with a plan, but I need to think, and I can't think with that thing pointed at my—"

"Shut up!" Henry's on the verge of crying again, eyes red and swollen. His arms must be getting tired, but he holds them up, keeps us cowering by the fireplace.

My thoughts are like a burrowing animal, digging hole after hole after hole.

Dad's dead. Henry killed him in this cabin. He might've died by this very gun, or worse, by the axe that's resting against the house. I want to scream, to will Dad back and burrow into his arms, but I need to think, I need a plan, or else Meg and I will suffer the same fate, our bodies dragged into the woods and buried.

I shut my eyes and dig for a story, something—anything—that would make Henry trust me, and while my eyes are shut, my senses heightened, I hear the smallest sound.

If I didn't know better, I might think it was the wind, sleet or leaves brushing the side of the house, a squirrel scratching, but the sound brings me right back to our childhood, the four of us climbing the footholds on the back of the house, sneaking up to the attic to rehearse our secret plays.

Breath fills my lungs, and when I open my eyes, the cabin returns to full color.

It's Amy. It has to be.

I talk to cover the sound, improvising. "Henry." My voice comes slowly at first, an idea forming along with it. "I know what you're thinking. We're witnesses, Meg and me. We know too much, and you can't let us go—"

"Jo, stop." Meg shudders behind me.

But she doesn't understand. I know what I'm doing. Like Dad, I'm a very good storyteller.

"There's something you haven't thought about," I continue. "You've lost sight of Beth in all of this."

Henry wipes his nose on his shoulder. "You're trying to confuse me."

I clasp my hands in supplication. "Listen to me, Henry. If you kill us in cold blood, we'll become the focus, the talk of the entire country. We'll be on every channel and in every social media feed, and everyone will forget about Beth."

"That's not true."

Meg laughs, the light returning to her eyes. "She's right."

What started as a lie feels more real with every word, my voice growing certain and fiery. "No one will talk about the introvert, the observer, the beautiful daydreamer who didn't want to think about growing up. They'll talk about us, the girls with ambition, plans cut short. The soon-to-be Harvard grad who left her high school sweetheart behind. The author in the making. We'll overshadow her, and that would be a terrible shame."

Henry whines, the gun trembling in his grip. "I'll never forget Beth. I'll make them remember—"

A thud from the hallway.

I wince before I can catch myself.

Henry's muscles tighten. "What was that?"

I picture the hatch to the attic, Amy lowering down and landing. "Probably the wind," I say.

"That was inside." Henry's voice rises. "That was inside the house! Who's there?"

My heart pounds in my temples, but I listen hard for any sign that Amy's coming.

It happens in a blur.

She vaults out of the kitchen and crashes into Henry, both of them smacking to the ground.

The gun fires. Meg screams. Both of us hit the floor.

Amy wrestles Henry to his back and pries one hand off the gun with her jaw clenched, a low groan forced out of her throat.

Henry fires again, and a bullet whistles through the room.

A window shatters. My ears ring.

Amy pins Henry to the ground and traps his arm, the gun against the floor. I run to kick it from his grip, but to my surprise, another figure emerges from the kitchen.

Laurie bounds from his hiding place and lands a heavy boot on Henry's hand. The bones crunch, and Henry cries out, the gun clattering away.

"Grab it!" Laurie yells.

I take hold of the gun, the metal warm from firing, and back against the wall while the others keep Henry down. In the distance, a siren wails.

Clever, clever, Amy. Must've called them before she came to our rescue.

My head swims, and for a moment I see the room as if I'm hovering outside myself. Three sisters, a boy who's loved not one but two of them, and a murderer caught, weeping on the ground.

This would make a jaw-dropping story, a story so hot that the whole world would read it.

Beth's murder.

The investigation.

The wrongly accused sister solving the case at the end.

Sirens fill my ears, blue and red light flooding the cabin.

I come back to myself, sinking to my knees. Cops fill the room, boots landing hard, and they wrestle Henry into handcuffs. I drop the gun and cry into my hands, the thrill of the chase draining from my body.

This story is everything I wanted, everything I needed—and I'd give anything not to have it.

CHAPTER SIXTY

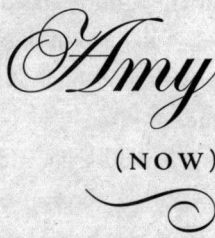

(NOW)

Two months have come and gone since we tackled Henry at the cabin, but mentally I'm still there. Knees aching against the wood floor, palms slick with sweat as we hold him down until the cops haul him away.

On a Thursday in a pin-drop-quiet courtroom, Henry pled guilty to one count of second-degree manslaughter and one count of second-degree murder.

He'll be in prison for life.

Most days I'm relieved. I'll never have to fear that Henry's lurking behind me in a dark hallway. But sometimes I wonder what Beth would think. She was so forgiving, so skilled at seeing the fleck of good beneath all of someone's bad. Would she feel for him? Would she visit him behind bars?

Jo tells me no. "He's not redeemable," she says, but I'm not convinced. I think Beth would have an infuriating talent for remembering that Henry was alone in the world, that his mother's death left him broken, and that in the sickest of ways, he thought he was defending Beth by killing Dad.

I like to think of her that way, because if she could find a bright spot in all of Henry's terrible darkness, she'd find one in me.

She'd forgive me for failing to believe in her.

She'd forgive me for what I said that night in Sallie Gardiner's bathroom.

She'd forgive me for all the times I wished she didn't exist, as if only one of us could stand in the sun.

"You ready?" Laurie reaches for my hand. He's sitting beside me in the back of Jo's Jeep, dressed in a suit, a handsome tie.

We're not dating, not officially, but we can't seem to be apart. We're so much calmer together that even Jo has acknowledged our happiness, accepted that she and Laurie will only ever just be friends.

"Sure," I say, but I'll never be ready to get out of this car, no matter how beautiful the day, the glimmer on Walden Pond.

Mom and Jo have already found a place on the dock, two boxes of ashes in their hands.

Laurie helps me out of the car, and I loop an arm through his to keep from falling.

"Ames!" A raspy voice comes from behind.

Aunt March steps out of a cab, looking like her usual just-off-the-plane self.

She's not the wreck I expected after the loss of her brother, but I think she's a lot like Mom. She deals with her pain by focusing on what she can fix.

"I just got off the phone with my lawyer." She strides up, heels pricking the gravel. "I have good news. God knows we could use it."

I can hardly look her in the eye after everything that's happened. She knows better than anyone how much I wanted to steal what Beth had.

"Can we talk after?" I ask.

"We found it," she says. "And it's a lot."

"Found what?" Meg comes up from the road, arm in arm with John.

I raise an eyebrow at Aunt March. It doesn't seem right to discuss this now, but she nudges me to deliver the news. "We've been looking for Dad's royalties," I say.

"Amy," Meg scolds.

"I know how it sounds, but *Little Women*'s been selling so many copies, more with all the attention from the trial. I figured Dad's backlist must be selling too, and just imagine what we could do with the money. We could help with your apartment. Pay for Jo's college if there's enough."

Aunt March lifts her chin. "We can do a lot more than that."

The news rushes through me, cool relief laced with giddy excitement. "We could do something for Beth, set up a Plumfield scholarship in her name."

Meg chuckles, but she's not mocking me. There's a lightness in her voice, a weight that's slowly lifting. "That would be nice," she says.

Mom gestures from the dock, waving us over.

We have to go, we have to press onward and say our

goodbyes, but before we do, Aunt March leans over to whisper, "I think we have enough to set aside for Europe."

I pull back, look at her sideways. "Europe's a bust. Fred Vaughn—"

"I'm not talking about that creep. I'm talking about you and me. We could go for a couple of weeks, hit all the best museums. I think your dad would approve."

"Really?" I ask, my chest lifting.

Aunt March shrugs like it's up to me, but something shines in her eyes. I always thought she preferred being a lone wolf, but she's really hoping I'll say yes. "I think it could be fun," she adds.

"Yeah," I say. "I think so too."

It's hard for me to imagine having fun in a world without Beth, but I think I'll have to try.

She hardly ever raised her voice, but she stood her ground when it came to her sisters, and if she thought for one second that I was going to waste my life being miserable, she'd shout the way she did in Sallie Gardiner's bathroom.

As I walk out onto the dock, I picture the two of us fighting that night. Beth calling me a selfish bitch, our foreheads pressed together in a momentary truce.

When I need her most, I'll remember her like that. Fuming and full of life and staring right at me when anyone else would look away.

CHAPTER SIXTY-ONE

(NOW)

Mom hands me a box of ashes, and it doesn't seem possible that Dad's inside.

The detectives found him buried in the woods, unearthed him, and moved him to the morgue.

He died in Massachusetts, but I never saw his body, so in my mind he's in the Canadian Rockies, writing under a large expanse of stars, and someday he'll come home.

Mom still mourns her last words to him, "Don't ever come back." But I've promised her, and I believe, that wherever he is, he understands. In his book he wrote that the little women would grow up to "conquer themselves so beautifully," as if life is a struggle against oneself.

Dad struggled against himself.

I don't think he'd blame us for struggling against him every now and then too.

We open his box first, maybe because we've had more time to process his absence, or maybe because parents are meant to go first.

When we lift the lid, my knees buckle.

John stays at my back, strong and comforting. "I've got you," he says.

I lean into him, relieved that our relationship's no longer a secret and that he forgave me for hiding the way I felt about him.

"I love you." I've told him so often lately, making up for all the time we lost while I couldn't admit it.

I'm on academic probation at Harvard, but by some small miracle, I'm still a student. Sallie, on the other hand, chose to withdraw before they could expel her and is taking a gap year in Paris. Now that I won't be doing her coursework, my classes will be manageable. I might even tack on a minor in English literature, partly for the joy, and partly for Dad.

I don't need a man. If things go to plan, I'll graduate with honors, go to med school, and become a doctor. I'll make a better life for myself without the help of any relationship—but I want to be with John.

I want to ditch campus on the weekends and order takeout in his cozy apartment. Someday we'll move his piano into a place we call our own and I'll be his audience every morning. I want to start a family with John—after residency, of course—and kiss him every day until we die.

Mom says a few words about Dad, tells the story of how they met. A coffee shop, their orders mixed up, his peppermint tea, her double-shot espresso.

When tears muddle her words, Jo takes over.

She thanks him for being her greatest inspiration, and it

strikes me how differently we saw him. I never cared about his writing. I cared about the moments when he taught us to ride bikes, pushed us on the swings at the park, laughed so hard, his glasses slid down his nose.

That image stays with me. His glasses. His rich brown eyes. In all the *Little Women* controversy, I had forgotten the way he looked at me, wide-eyed and spellbound.

Mom reaches over, and we steady our hands before spilling the ashes.

Over the pond, I let go, and as the wind carries Dad away, I wish I could take him back, if only for a moment. If only to tell him that I get it now.

I hated him for turning us into spectacles, but I think all parents see their children as the most interesting people who ever lived. He wrote us as he saw us. Like we were the best story ever told.

CHAPTER SIXTY-TWO

Jo

(NOW)

If I were to write a story about the end of Beth's life, this would be the perfect setting. Walden Pond reflects the sky, creating a boundless image that gives me hope for where she's gone.

It's the blue of dreams, dappled with sunlight, and still, it's little comfort. I need Beth now more than ever. She's the only person I've ever known whose optimism never felt forced. If she were here, she'd tell me that life is precious because it's fleeting, and I'd believe her.

I hold the box of ashes to my chest, and for a moment I can't let go. I won't let go. I'll never let go.

But some things simply refuse to be stopped.

I tip the box, and the fine silt slips out. "Throw them with me," I say, voice rising. "All at once!"

My sisters take hold of the box, hands on top of hands, working together through their tears.

"All at once," Amy echoes.

"All at once," says Meg.

Mom nods, approval in her eye.

With a whooping cry, we toss the ashes to the wind. Tears blur my vision, but I blink them away. I don't want to miss this. I don't want to miss the way Beth flies through the air, carried off until she's only a memory, only in our hearts.

We say our goodbyes and share our favorite moments—not big ones exactly, but little glimpses of time, like her bedhead in the morning, the week she attempted ballet lessons and promptly quit, the constant gift of her smile, and how she always hung up the phone by saying, "Love you, love you."

We take turns saying it now.

Then, aching, body and soul, we walk up the dock, all of us close until my phone rings.

I move to ignore it, but the name on the screen catches my attention. "Just a second." I separate myself from the group, my voice low.

"Hello?"

"Yes, Jo, this is Nan Dashwood."

The call doesn't last long, but when it's over, I'm a different person, a person who's lassoed the moon and pulled it close.

"What was it?" asks Amy.

"You're grinning," says Meg.

When my voice comes out, I sound like Dad, words bunched together like I'm too excited to give them space. "That was my editor. She likes the book. They're going to publish it."

"No way!" cries Amy.

Meg throws her arms around me, whispers, "Dad would be so proud of you."

I close my eyes and imagine the way Beth would react.

She'd take a moment, take in the news, and then she'd say with hands on my shoulders, a genuine smile, "I knew you could do it."

And that was her magic, wasn't it? She knew I could do it when I didn't know myself.

As we find our cars, Meg loops an arm through mine. "You don't have to tell us, but I'm curious. What did you end up writing about?"

Amy lets out a disapproving hum. "Oh, you definitely have to tell us. But if we're going to be pissed, you should wait until we're not crammed in the car."

"I think you're going to like it," I say, and I draw a breath to tell them.

I could've written about the murder, all the heart-wrenching, adrenaline-pumping things that happened to us. The whole world would've gawped at the details of the investigation, how the remaining March sisters narrowly escaped the same fate as Beth.

But when I took to a blank page, something else poured out.

I scribbled down stories about Beth. All of Beth. The real, messy, imperfect Beth.

In a matter of days I sent a whole book's worth to my editor along with a message—take it or leave it—because I don't want people to remember our sister for the way she died.

I want them to remember that Beth lived.

ACKNOWLEDGMENTS

First, I owe so much gratitude to Louisa May Alcott for writing a story that has lived in so many hearts for so many years. Spending time with her characters has been a privilege. I sincerely hope she approves from above.

A heartfelt thank-you to everyone at Sarah Barley Books and Simon & Schuster for giving this project infinite love and energy. I couldn't have asked for a better publishing home.

Sarah Barley, I will always treasure sharing this "first" with you—my first book and one of your firsts with your eponymous imprint. Thank you for instantly understanding my vision and bringing it into focus.

Major shout-out to Lizzy Bromley for this drop-dead gorgeous cover (pink has become my new favorite color!). To Amanda Brenner, Hilary Zarycky, Lynn Kavanaugh, Katharine Wiencke, Chava Wolin, and Alma Gomez Martinez for your incredible care and attention. To Alex Kelleher-Nagorski, Maryam Ahmad, and Cassandra Fernandez for spreading the word. And to Justin Chanda for championing this story from the very beginning.

To my whip-smart agent, Sara Crowe, thank you for plucking me out of the slush pile and believing through all the hurdles that this was possible. Also to Ginger Clark and Nicole Eisenbraun for giving this book a passport.

I can't give enough thanks to everyone at the DFW Writers' Workshop. Without you, this book would not exist.

Thank you especially to my early readers: Jenny Martin

ACKNOWLEDGMENTS

for offering to swap manuscripts at a time when I was ready to give up. You didn't know, but you kept me from quitting. Brooke Fossey for your unparalleled eye and footsteps in which to follow. Leslie Lutz, Lauren Danhof, Lauren Lanza Osias, Rebecca Seifert, and Karoline Chapman for your invaluable feedback and even better friendship. A. Lee Martinez for a decade's worth of honest advice. And Dana Swift for reading every word of every version of this book. Meeting you in line at the DFW Writers Conference will always be one of the most important before-and-after moments of my life.

Thank you to my friends Kelsey Tolleson and Amanda Jackson for caring about this journey and being there every step of the way.

To David Morring for being the most inspiring and supportive "day job" boss a person could imagine.

And mostly to my family, who are the greatest people in the world. Like Jo says in the book, the very best part about being me is that I was magically, miraculously born into a life with sisters.

Sarah Bernet Griffin, thank you for being my favorite reader of all time. Your stamp of approval is all I really need. And Emily Bernet Welch, the most creative person I know, thank you for saying yes every single time I've ever asked, *Can you help me figure this out?* There's never been a problem we couldn't solve.

Finally, the biggest, deepest thank-you goes to my parents, Nancy and Blake Bernet, for raising me to believe that I'm capable of anything. I am because of you.